"Faithful Fugitive is a work of fiction taken from events that have happened, or are believed to happen in the future. In this book Ellison masterfully combines his creative mind and depth of knowledge to bring forth some wonderful reading."

– Deborah Werther, Orthodox Jewish Chaplain

" I really enjoyed the intrigue and the topic of 'end time events.' The experiences of this family, their personal responses, their inter-personal challenges, and their real flight from various kinds of dangers became very real to me... the manner of writing put me right into the story with them emotionally... especially when the grizzly bear might still be lurking nearby! This story is very realistic and compelling, taking the reader right along with them as they run into problems in their escape from many dangers."

– Carolynn Lord, Elder Lansdale SDA Church Pennsylvania

"When my wife and I read 'Faithful Fugitives' it captured our imaginations about one possible way the world could end. When we finished, we immediately began studying Bible prophecy with enthusiasm. What a great way to encourage Bible study afresh!"

– Eric J. C. Ellison, SDA Doctoral Student in Theology

FAITHFUL FUGITIVES

James Ellison

TEACH Services, Inc.
P U B L I S H I N G
www.TEACHServices.com • (800) 367-1844

Copyright © 2018 James Ellison

Copyright © 2018 TEACH Services, Inc.

ISBN-13: 978-1-4796-0870-6 (Paperback)

ISBN-13: 978-1-4796-0871-3 (ePub)

ISBN-13: 978-1-4796-0872-0 (Mobi)

Library of Congress Control Number: 2018934096

TEACH Services, Inc.
P U B L I S H I N G
www.TEACHServices.com ● (800) 367-1844

DEDICATION

This book is dedicated to my family and friends. They have read this book and have given me sound advice and counsel as to the timing of the events, theology, grammar, and the telling of the story. I specifically name; Jami Ellison, Eric Ellison, Autumn Mincinoiu, Bonnie Beres, Brian Rice, and Bob Maxwell.

"The fact that a movement to establish error is connected to a work which is in itself good is not an argument in favor of the error."

~ Ellen G. White, *Great Controversy*, page 587.

Table of Contents

PREFACE

A WORD OF INTRODUCTION FROM THE AUTHOR. As a youth I was filled with curiosity about the end of time. I didn't know the word eschatology then like I do now, but that was what I was studying—last day events. I monopolized every pastoral visit to our home. I would scooch under the end table, place my elbows on the floor, prop up my head, and endlessly ask the same question: "What's going to happen next, and next, and next?" When I was older, in seminary, and then in my own pastorate, I studied the prophecies of the Bible, the Book of Revelation, and the Spirit of Prophecy. I'm not an expert on everything that's going to happen. The more I study, the more I am humbled by the seriousness and the complexity of the forces of evil arrayed against us and the watch care and love of a rescuing Godhead. I try to imagine what it will be like. My mind likes to create stories and scenarios in which the people of God endure and eventually rejoice. I enjoy composing story ideas into presentations of truth. Some may ask the question, "Why use the story format to showcase the last-day events?" My answer is many books have been written about what is to happen, but few have made it into story form. Jesus taught using the narrative style, because stories are easier to remember. Parables paint pictures. They help us to see the truths and at the same time intellectually digest their implications. As the reader follows this tale, it is hoped that they will automatically identify with one or even several of the characters, making applications that will fortify their own faith and helping them to determine from within to study and be stalwart in the midst of indescribable pressure to surrender to Satan's sophistries.

LET THE READER UNDERSTAND! This is a work of fiction. To be more exact, this is a work of fiction about a future **real** event of powerful proportions impacting every man, woman, and child on the face of the earth. No one will have the luxury of being uninvolved. The author's intent is to paint a word picture of the emotions and turmoil of that coming upheaval caused by religious bigotry in a way that seems logical, yet moving. No one knows, and certainly this author does not know, **exactly** how the final conflict will begin or progress. It is the author's conviction that the mark of the beast could very well be an innocent, perhaps noble, urge to achieve a common humanitarian goal (as depicted in this novel) for the good of the world. What the author firmly believes is that Jesus *will* come, Satan *will* be vanquished, and this world *will* end. There is no equivocating about the final result. If this creative story, made from make-believe characters, can stir the convictions of the reader to step closer to the side of Jesus, walk a walk of better conviction, and dig deeper into the Bible and Spirit of Prophecy, then it will have achieved its purpose.

BELIEVER BEWARE. Life doesn't just go on. There is a culmination. Whether that culmination is achieved on a deathbed or on a hillside witnessing the grand arrival of a rescuing Savior, everyone will have a closing moment. The preparation is the same. All worldly needs, attractions, concerns, and wants will have to be subjugated in preference to a consuming faith in a loving, restorative Jesus. What the believer must understand is that no diluted faith will suffice; no noble compromise to keep peace with non-believing friends and relatives will work. Sensate youth will have to stand alone on their own faith and not ride on their parent's convictions. Membership in church does not constitute a free pass or a discount ticket to fly to heaven. The believer must stand alone on the ascension rock of Jesus Christ their Lord. There is no other way.

Enjoy the story. Be moved by the subject.
Search the scriptures.

CHARACTERS

Larsson Family

Mike: Father, head elder of the local SDA (Seventh-day Adventist) church and teaches adult Sabbath school lesson.

Rachael: Mother, children's Sabbath school teacher.

Janelle: Teenage daughter (twin) attends SDA academy. Is attracted to Darin at school. Loves her independence.

Jason: Teenage son (twin) attends SDA academy. Enjoys surprises and soccer.

Church Members

Jerry Taylor: Pastor of the SDA Church. Wife's name is Judy.

Heidi McKessy: Eighty years old and close friend of Veronica.

Veronica Jones: Also eighty and close friend of Heidi.

Academy People

Philippe Chennault: Principal.

April: Janelle's best friend.

Darin: Janelle's love interest.

Cox brothers: Students at school who are Jason's nemeses.

Steve Rojas: Jason's soccer buddy.

Coach Weldon: Spiritually active teacher concerned about coming issues.

Jonathan: Student.

Kathy: Student.

Madeline: Student.

Charlene: Student mother.

Work Associates and friends of Mike

Marshall: Roman Catholic who believes in a post-millennial concept of Jesus' return after humankind changes the world in preparation for His return.

Zack: Christian Supremacist.

George: Married to an atheist.

Glenda: Gold-digging secretary, believes in a pre-millennial rapture.

Leo: Believes the rapture comes halfway through the seven years of tribulation (Mid-trib.) before millennium.

Shelly: Christian, full-blooded Arapaho. Not in favor of church dominate. Favors the post-seven-year tribulation rapture before the millennium.

Alejandro: Atheistic friend whom Mike has witnessed to over the years.

Rachael's Friends and Witnessing Contacts

Megan: Rachael's sister and non-attending church member.

Walt: Megan's husband and non-attending church member.

Kristine: Next door neighbor.

Rochelle: Friend from church who stopped attending upon her divorce.

Chris: Rochelle's ex and no longer living locally.

Loren: Chris and Rochelle's daughter, caught in the middle of a custody battle.

Molly: Rachael's college roommate at Newbold, England.

Jenny Rutherford: A Newbold friend living and working at Grantham Press.

Arvid and Ragnar: Leaders at the press from Norway.

Jeremy: Darin's friend from former school. Witness discussion at donut shop.

Sandra: Darin's friend from former school. Witness discussion at donut shop.

Bert: Darin's friend from former school. Witness discussion at donut shop.

Other Important Characters

Warwick: England's Archbishop of Canterbury.

Very Right Reverend Robert Grayble: Executive vice-president for world religious affairs.

Reverend Ophelia Marcbright: President of the National Spiritualists Association of Churches.

Froelichs: Neighbors living around the corner from the Larssons.

President O'Donnell: Former military officer.

Guadalupe: Lady with power over snakes, assistant to Dr. Moreno.

Doctor Angel Moreno: Minister of the International Spiritualist Association of Churches. Healer and mentor to Snake Lady, Guadalupe.

CHAPTER 1

Snowflakes landed on the plaque like dew on Gideon's fleece. It was covered with moisture, but all three knew what it was and what it said. It was titled, "Footprints." Jason showed it to his mom and dad. They nodded in silent agreement. Jesus would carry them from this moment on. All three, as if on cue, looked at their foot impressions in the wet grass behind them. Their hearts wanted to see the reality of the conviction that compelled them. Jesus would indeed carry them. They walked slowly down the street past neighbors who were shut inside dark silent houses. A thief had boldly seized their house and SUV with strong-arm tactics emphasized with a shotgun. They were on foot attempting to flee to the mountains just like Jesus told them to do when He said, "When you see the desolating sacrilege standing in the holy place, flee…" Around the corner they could see a glow that illuminated the trees and houses in the immediate area. A fire had started. They were drawn to the conflagration even though they knew it must be the artwork of evil. The fire was coming from where the Froelich's house was located. They peeked around the corner, afraid of what might be happening to their new friends and fellow believers. No car was in the driveway. Men were standing across the street, admiring their work from behind parked cars. The Larssons hoped the Froelich's were not at home. Several evenings had been spent in their home and always the family car was in the driveway, not the garage. Hope surged in their hearts as they came to believe that the occupants had fled before these unholy thugs had unleashed their hate.

A burning maple tree acted as a torch illuminating the front lawn. Flames in the house licked at the gables over the front porch and the second-floor bedrooms. Noisy conversations cluttered the night. As the three took in the scene from a distance they were startled by an explosion that blew the structure apart. Heat so hot blasted the area that it turned the snow into rain. Chunks of wood flew outward, peppering the surrounding buildings with splintered shards. They ducked, covering their heads and turning their backs. They could hear the shouts and cheers. Dust and smoke clouded the near vicinity of the crater, pink insulation like cotton candy drifted through the air mingled with raindrops.

"Yeah! Look at that!"

"Finally! I thought she'd never blow. Where'd you place those explosives? In the basement? It took forever."

"It's gone now. That'll teach 'em. Dumb Saturday keepers!"

The air was saturated with malevolence which brooked no diversity. This mob would turn on anyone they thought might have a hint of divergence from the accepted norm. The trio hustled away trying to keep out of sight, a task made difficult by the crowd of observers coming out of every house and looking from every window. An onlooking neighbor spotted them and yelled out to the mob.

"Hey, look it's the Larssons. They're one of them, too!"

Mike, Rachael, and Jason moved as quickly as they could around the corner. Jason took the lead, "Mom, Dad, I know what we can do." He ducked through some shrubbery and behind a garden wall. A backyard gate opened to a yard loaded with toys, bikes, tricycles, and a trampoline next to a playhouse. He dropped to his knees and crawled under the trampoline and then turned to help his mother with her bundle. He led them to the other side and into the playhouse. They scrunched into it and closed the door. Jason had to explain, "Billy's sister likes to hide in here. She asked me and Billy to pull the tramp over in front of her house to make it secret. Some secret," he said.

"Let's hope it is secret enough to hide us from those vigilantes," Rachael answered.

"Think of it this way, Mom—we traded houses and got a tramp in the bargain," Jason tried to sound upbeat with his lame humor. The trio remained silent, hoping no one could hear them or would think to look in this yard so close to where they had been spotted. Shots rang out in the distance. Men yelled instructions and commands were given to get into cars and chase down the fugitives. Whimpering noises could barely be heard, but when they all cuddled together the composite warmth soothed their troubled souls.

"I was just thinking about what we were doing a couple of months ago," Mike whispered softly.

"What were you thinking, honey?" Rachael asked her husband in an equally quiet whisper.

"I was thinking about how we were all sitting around the table eating supper and listening to the President's State of the Union Address. Life was so predictable back then."

"And Janelle was with us," she added sadly.

CHAPTER 2

Mike's head was swimming with strange words. He couldn't pronounce most of them because they were all new and the doctor rattled them off so quickly. Two names were marginally clear—glioblastoma and astrocytoma— and the rest were blurred in a thick alphabet soup. He didn't know what they meant but he knew what they were: different tumors of the brain. The doctor urged surgery to relieve the pressure on the brain and to remove the presenting symptoms—it was the only way to know for sure what they were. He was quick to assure Mike that some tumors are benign, but just like anyone else receiving the bad news his mind wandered into "c-word" territory. The recommendation was for immediate surgery. He didn't want to believe it. Absent-mindedly he drove back to work as if everything was as before, demonstrating the characteristic of denial when bad news hits an individual. Realizing where he was going he continued, his professionalism driving him to return to work and to be the present and available supervisor he had become.

Walking onto his floor he ran into Marshall and Zack, who were excitedly talking about possibilities. When they saw their boss they sought to include him in the news. "Mike, did you hear about what The President's going to do tonight?"

"No, what's he going to do?" Mike didn't want to brush them off.

"President O'Donnell's going to call America back to Christianity. The news people are saying that it will be a part of his State of The Union address tonight. Finally, we're not going to be a hodge-podge collection of rag-head terrorists, Jews, and atheists. Everyone is going to be citizens of a righteous nation. That's what I heard on the news this morning," Marshall explained.

Over the years working with Marshall and Zack he knew they had a latent prejudice against minorities. When terrorist attacks occurred, they were the most vocal in spewing out invectives against radicals and their peace-minded kin folk—in short, all Muslims. They were against immigration for anyone with different cultural, ideological, or heredity common to radicals. Today, Marshall added his distaste for Jewish Americans and atheists. Mike didn't want to get caught up in their discussion. "That's interesting. I need to check my email to see if there are any fires I need to put out. Excuse me." He went to his office where he could be alone. He left the door open to catch the conversation that continued without him. He wondered if the President's speech would be as life-changing as Marshall hoped. Trying to concentrate from a distance pushed some of his negative thoughts aside. The subject was compelling. The President's determination to return America back to a Christian nation could be a precursor to forced false faith, a characteristic of religious oppression mentioned in Revelation 14.

* * * * * *

Jerry was not a yellow-page preacher, meaning he never repeated a sermon that he had preached before, but today he was tempted to resurrect one from his files. He felt strongly about being open to the Holy Spirit as he prepared. But, today he felt empty. He had never had so many funerals in a row. Tomorrow he had to say something encouraging. The truth of the moment was that pastor Jerry Taylor suffered from compound grief. After so many funerals given for beloved elderly members, his emotions were pulled downward.

The pastor did not realize how important this sermon would be for many as they would face the coming tribulation just months in the future.

Memories of their nice Christian characters served to remind him that they were no longer there to encourage him and to pat him on the back for his sermons.

Focusing on that loss caused Jerry to realize what he needed to say. He needed to point out how important God's people are to each other and their role in sustaining each other in the faith. An appeal to the mourners to make-up the loss of this saint's positive attitude would speak to his own spirit as well as others. The pastor did not realize how important this sermon would be for many as they would face the coming tribulation just months in the future. He always believed that Jesus' coming could be soon, but many Adventists were tired of the continual admonition for them to be ready. He had to temper his words on the subject. Yet now as he worked in his study preparing his funeral remarks, he had no clue as to how soon the second advent was and how much his faith would be tested.

* * * * * *

Rachael swung by Twin Feather Lakes Academy on her way home from shopping at a nearby mall and meeting with her book club friends. The conversation had turned to the many catastrophes and terrorist attacks that had recently occurred. Because her book club friends were committed Christians their choice of reading and their ensuing conversations were often spiritual. They mutually concluded that Jesus' predictions were coming true in spades. When the discussion got around to Jesus coming they diverged on the point of what that event would do to the world. Rachael expressed her feelings that the earth would be changed into a wasteland during the millennium. Her friends countered that after the rapture Jews would accept Jesus as the Messiah. One felt that Jesus would set the world aright and bring in the golden age. As good friends they agreed to disagree. Later, when she looked back on that conversation, she would wish she had pursued her perspective a little more by citing Biblical texts to support her point. She felt she had time on her side.

In the car she spoke to Jason and Janelle about her book club conversation. Neither of the twins seemed to get into her recounting of the experience. Janelle was answering texts from her friends and Jason was reading the latest news about world soccer player changes and projections. Jason didn't say or mumble a word. Janelle, on the other hand, was able to say, "I see," "Yes," and "Uh huh," at the appropriate times, indicating that she had understood her mother. How much she really did get could be debated.

Rachael thought of her children's faith. She wondered if they would grow into committed Christian adults. She decided to engage them in more directive conversations—that is, whenever or if ever they were off their electronic devices.

* * * * * *

Mike struggled to do his work. The bad checkup news and the discussion with Marshall and Zack crowded out his ability to focus on the sales reports stacked on his desk. He did and also did not want to think about his tumors. He wanted to deny that it had happened, but every time he experienced an electrical shock to the left side of his face, the reality of it snapped back into his primary thinking. He wondered why the Lord had allowed this to happen. His doctor was urging him to take the referral and schedule with the recommended neurosurgeon. Mike's vision was slightly impaired. He leaned forward to see the screen when trying to read smallish letters. When Mike added it all up he felt that neurosurgery was an extreme solution to a minor annoyance. Even though the doctor had urged immediate action, Mike wanted to slide it to the back of his mind.

Listening to the prognosticators on the news predict the impact of the President's speech caused Mike to plan his evening around evaluating the State of The Union Address himself rather than accept the words of a media which needs to sell stories to viewers for higher ratings. By the time he closed the office door he was of the mind to go home and not tell his family about the tumors until later. He wanted to tell Rachael first and the teens later. If he said something right away he would probably never get to watch the State of The Union. Besides, the symptoms were manageable. He would wait and pray over the issue in his private time with the Lord.

He called Rachael on the phone to tell her about the President's speech. They decided to watch the broadcast while eating dinner.

CHAPTER 3

"Why are we watching TV? We never watch TV at supper!" Janelle exclaimed.

"Tonight is different becau—"

"But, Dad, you said yourself, 'family dinner shouldn't be cluttered up with other stuff.'" Jason entered the discussion.

"Jason, give your dad a chance to explain. He and I talked about this earlier. There's something important happening and we all need to see this," mother explained.

"You're right, Jason, family dinner should not be cluttered with outside stuff. It is a time for the family to be a family and share each other's experiences of the day. Tonight, however, there is a special message from the President. And, from the sound of it, we, as a family, will want to discuss his speech afterward during family devotions. It's the State of the Union Address and usually I would not make a big deal about it, but the guys at work are hearing pieces of information on what his comments might be and the thoughts are disturbing for us as Christian believers," Mr. Larsson said. He turned the small portable halo-projection television toward the dinner table but kept the sound muted. Scenes from the capitol were playing with different senators and congressmen and women materializing from the changing images. Their names and states were written below wrapped around the bottom of the picture.

"It looks like your mother has prepared a very nice dinner this evening. Would someone like to pray for our food?"

"I will," Janelle answered. "Dear heavenly Father, thanks for our food and for the all the things You give us. Bless the missionaries and all the pastors and our teachers at school. In Jesus' name, amen." Janelle seemed to be in a hurry.

The family started to unfold napkins and began to pass the food around. The casserole was hot so Mrs. Rachael Larsson performed the honors of scooping out the main entrée.

"Honey, I can see that the President has not entered the congressional chamber and there might be a delay; perhaps you could explain to the children your concerns about the President's speech tonight."

"Ah, well…yes, that might help. I have been concerned for a while now that our President is very interested in uniting all the Christians of the nation into one happy corporation of believers. Rumors have it that he would like to have one body of Christian leaders represent all denominations and set the example for the rest of the world that the United States is a Christian nation. He supposedly wants to create a department of spiritual development. It's a stated dream of his to bring about the reverse of the Reformation. He is sympathetic about the differences of the various denominations, but thinks that, as a whole, we should all be able to get along, agreeing on the beliefs we have in common."

"Is that really possible?" Rachael asked.

"Well according to President O'Donnell, he thinks it *is* possible. When he was a general officer in the army he saw the chaplains work together as a team for a common good. They were of all denominations and helped each other serve soldiers in many circumstances. He sees the possibility of the churches of the world coming together in the same way in common causes to serve mankind."

"That's not a bad thing, is it?" Jason asked.

"Yes and no. It is very good for Christians to come together to help people in need. But when we organize into one super church, the side effects might not be so good. For instance, would there be a requirement for individual distinctive beliefs to be abandoned in the name of unity? To come together under one common organization could spell problems for some faith groups who are not in the majority."

"Dad, look! The President is getting ready to talk," Jason remarked.

The camera focused in on President O'Donnell as Mike Larsson un-muted the sound. The family turned to watch the three-dimensional holographic image as it moved in front of them. Each of the family members had their own feelings surface as the President stood at the podium, waiting for the applause to subside.

For Jason, watching TV during dinner was a novelty. His friends at school had all the latest on what was happening on all the popular channels and programs. He always felt that he was an outsider when it came to the discussions on TV entertainment. He wasn't allowed to watch until all his homework was done and then his parents would control the type of programs he could watch, which turned out to be very few in number. Tomorrow at school he would at least be able to talk intelligently about what the President had said. And he could use what he saw tonight to write his paper on current events.

Janelle couldn't care less about the President's speech. She had a "big" issue in the making. "Colossal" is the word she had used at school with her friend. Darin had made known his attraction for her during lunch by asking her to sit with him alone. She wanted… no, needed a video talk with her best friend and confidant, April. Dinner, dishes, devotions, and this dismally long dialogue were keeping her from intense deliberations over "what he said, what she said" at lunch. April could share in her feelings better than anyone, because they had talked for ages on the subject of "Who does Darin really like anyway?"

Rachael Larsson was worried. Her family was her responsibility. Her first regard was to have each of her children safely in a relationship with their Savior. The teen years are so difficult. Both her children were testing the concepts she and Mike had taught them from the beginning. On top of her concern was this scary prospect of the final stages of the conflict between Christ and Satan. *Would she be up to the task and would her children follow her lead*? These questions dominated her thoughts as she fought to focus on what the President might say in the next few moments. She chewed her lower lip, which was an indication to her husband of her nervous state. He gave her confidence. She knew they were in agreement on these important priorities. It was a blessing to be married to him. She didn't know what she would do if her husband didn't share her faith. Her sister struggled in her relationship and, in comparison, she praised God for Mike and his spiritual leadership.

Mike was determined. He felt the leadership mantle of his family upon his shoulders, both spiritual and practical. He needed facts so he could act or wait. His discussions at work compelled him to try to calculate the next moves and all the necessary ramifications. If he reacted too soon, he could throw the family into disarray. He knew the last events would move swiftly, but whether one event over another signaled the time to flee needed to be deciphered. He had a small Onyx 4000-B, a virtual note-book, on the table next to his plate. He was ready to take notes.

A snap jolted his left cheek like a miniature lightning bolt. He jumped. It was right at the moment when the President began.

~ ~ ~ ~ ~ ~

Mr. Speaker, Mr. Vice President, members of Congress, my fellow Americans:

Tonight, I come to you with grave concern. I would like to report to you that our country is doing great and headed for higher plateaus of excellence. Unfortunately, I can tell you that only with the concerted effort of this great nation can we indeed be headed for higher plateaus. Presently, this nation is struggling. Moments before coming to this podium, I was delayed by the news of yet another attack on the citizens of this country. The news media, no doubt, will be broadcasting full details after this address. Suicide bombers have attacked the United States Embassy in Bern, Switzerland. At this moment, specifics about the assault are minimal and we are awaiting more information on casualties. This follows numerous other attacks on our embassies across the globe. It is a coordinated attack and an affront upon sensibilities universally held by principled citizens. The organization taking responsibility for all previous attacks has called this nation of ours the "Great Satan."

Normally a president would not let a single event of news dominate the broader picture of the State of the Union address, but I must point out that this recent atrocity serves as an apropos introduction to the general tenor of my speech tonight.

Our nation has been beset by a multitude of natural and manmade disasters. I don't need to remind you of the devastating earthquake that California sustained just hours ago. FEMA and its resources will be tasked with the mammoth job of restoring a degree of normalcy to the region ravaged by the 9.0 phenomenon. This congress has been swift and compassionate in the past to enact timely federal assistance for reconstruction. I applaud this great congress for its action.

[The president stops to applaud and is joined by the members of the chamber applauding itself.]

A moment ago, I said FEMA has been tasked; they are also strained to provide help. This is true because of the two hurricanes that struck our east coast and gulf coast. Our National Guard has been mobilized to cover and assist FEMA in these two events. Our resources have been strained to the limit. Fires ravaged the west because of the sustained drought that has parched large areas of grassland and forest. One prairie fire consumed crops, farm houses, ranches, and thousands of head of cattle. Food prices are on the rise because of the destruction of our resources. Recreational businesses are suffering. This government is assisting these multiple concerns by rushing fiscal and physical aid to the localities affected.

Again, I do not have to remind you of the bombing attack on Wall Street last June. Our enemy has tried to affect our banking and commerce. We are the wealthiest nation on earth. Our country is great and strong and we are recovering from these setbacks. We will not go down in defeat. [applause] *We are not the Great Satan. We are a nation built on Christian principles, strong and true.* [applause] *We have been hammered by these disasters and these attacks on our home soil and abroad. But, it has been my experience that, when a hammer is being used, it signifies something is being built, built strong and sturdy. I see the United States of America responding to these calamities with backbone and resolve. The hammering we are receiving now is going to make us greater, stronger, better in the future.* [sustained applause]

I would like to report to this congress and to the American people that we have had victories in the wars on crime and drugs. I would like to do that, but when I was elected I promised the citizens of this nation I would tell the truth. Anybody is willing to tell the truth if the truth is good news. When the truth is not comfortable, many will avoid speaking about it or try to spin what is bad into what looks good. I will not do that. [Minimal applause] *Crime has gone up in all areas, especially in the area of theft. On top of these inappropriate levels of crime, small, petty larcenies have jumped. Grocery stores are reporting the shoplifting of bread, milk, and other necessities. It doesn't take a scientist to see that this economy is affecting people terribly and we need to help them. When I mention these disasters, I am aware of the problem of appearing to trivialize the other calamities that have occurred by not mentioning them specifically. I, of course, do not want to minimize the victims of the tornados in Oklahoma and Arkansas. My address this evening cannot name every tragedy, every pain, every momentous problem we face. Time does not allow. I must speak to the bigger picture and focus on the overall solution.* [polite applause]

Our country was created on sterling principles, noble Godly ideals, and virtuous standards. Our Founding Fathers wanted our nation to be an example to the world, a city set on a hill. To set the pace in humanitarian enterprise, world peace, compassionate government, and spiritual nurture. We have endeavored in this adventure, only to fall short of those goals. Many times we have surged upward, only to slide back from totally achieving. In the early twentieth century a fair majority of citizens wanted spiritual change. National party conventions, the Democratic, Republican, and Progressive parties, all sang rousing hymns to inspire the delegates to a higher divine calling for national spiritual fervor. They knew where they must be and wanted to achieve that plateau. Global war overshadowed that zeal then—made them look to the loss of life and the atrocities of war. If they only knew that the enemy of all mankind was thwarting their efforts, holding them back, clouding their vision.

That same enemy fights us today. The evil one of this world seeks to cast our focus downward. He would have us believe that there is no God, that disasters happen, and people suffer. Well, I don't want us to be cast down. I want us to be lifted up. I want to say with confidence, "God Bless America!" I have a vision: A vision of a nation that leads other nations in claiming God's blessings. [Spontaneous applause erupts] *I am calling for citizens to unite and bring back God's benevolence. We can achieve His favor once again. We can recapture the spirit that made us great in the beginning.* [More applause]

We are a great nation on the cusp of greater achievements. Our birthright is to soar to grander highs and bring in the spiritual millennium of global faith in one God, one people, one purpose. [Sustained applause]

I do not wish for this night to be forgotten. I do not want my words to float on the air and dissipate into history. America, I call upon you to remember and to commit. Come together in solidarity. We need to pray, plan, and promote. It starts now and continues until God once again listens to a righteous nation.

Two weeks from today is the National Day of Prayer. This day of prayer has been on our calendar year after year for decades. This year it should be observed by all. Here is where we start. Here is where it will begin. I have had many meetings with religious leaders of many denominations. We have come up with a plan to initiate at the multitude of prayer breakfasts, prayer vigils, and prayer conferences across the land. The one over-encompassing theme is that we should pray for unity: [Applause] *unity of purpose, unity of brotherhood, unity of common doctrine. With God answering our prayers, combined with our determined efforts, we can put aside our dividing differences. We can come together and feel once again the showers of blessings originally designed for this nation.*

At these prayer events there will be a way we can demonstrate our solidarity. As we gather here tonight in this chamber and near our video monitors, there are trucks traveling to the furthest points of our nation bringing tokens of our desire to be one people. At my request, these little bracelets—I am wearing one right now [The President rolls back his sleeve to reveal a small, red, soft rubber bracelet on his wrist]—*these adaptable little devices are being shipped to every state and every community. They can be purchased for a mere five dollars. The proceeds will go to aid the victims of all these disasters I spoke of earlier. I have given instructions to have them available at the prayer meetings, breakfast, and vigils I spoke of earlier. If some cannot afford the five dollars, they are to be given away free of charge. Everyone can wear them to show his or her support for this nation, for the people suffering from calamity, and, most of all, their willingness to change this country back to the principles it was founded upon in the beginning: "One nation, under God, indivisible."*

~ ~ ~ ~ ~ ~

The Larssons stared at each other across the table. Rachael stopped chewing her lip to start a sentence, "Do you think that could be the mark of the beast in the—"

"Ma, I don't think so. You're jumping to conclusions. Kids are always wearing different colored armbands to show their support for victims and, ya' know, whatever. The Prez is just capitalizing on a fad that's been going on for like … ever," Jason answered.

"Honey, what do you think?" Rachael looked at her husband.

"For now, it seems innocent enough. It's a fund raiser for disaster relief with the attached ideology of agreeing with the concept of national unity," Mike answered, wanting to say more, but not wanting to put down Jason's comment and also wanting to listen to the address.

"He sounds like a preacher preaching a sermon…ah, a political sermon," Janelle observed without taking her eyes off of her Onyx. The family agreed with their daughter's assessment, but had to return to the monitor to hear what the President was saying. The President was explaining the meaning of the solidarity bracelet.

~ ~ ~ ~ ~ ~

…red symbolizes the right spirit. I feel it symbolizes the spirit of the American people—the "can do" spirit, the spirit of compassion, the spirit of harmony. We will wear red to evoke the presence of the Spirit of God. The circle represents the unbroken link we all have in common with one another. Now, I do understand that a bracelet like mine may not appeal to everyone. Our female partners might prefer other, more stylish, options. There are designer styles available at a slightly higher cost and the bracelet does not have to be

worn. Embedded in the bracelet is a computer chip that will allow the wearer to donate more to the cause of helping disaster relief. The owner can make contributions from his or her bank account by simply moving the band in front of a special scanner, automatically donating fifty dollars. Each armband bracelet will have its own registered code unique to the wearer of the band. It reads the owner's DNA and will not function unless the device is touching skin. This could end up being the only item you will need to carry on your person, for it is capable of many functions. It can be your bank, purse, wallet, locator for your children when they're on a date, entre for medical treatment. It detaches and can become a keychain without a key. It can be programmed to start your car remotely … I could go on and on. It has universal applications. You don't have to wear it on your wrist; it detaches and can go into your pocket or purse. If you're wearing gloves on a cold day, you can hold it against any exposed skin, like your head, to activate it. It just needs to be near your skin. For now, I would prefer that as many as possible would wear the red bracelet to demonstrate their solidarity with the nation. Later, the chip can be removed and put almost anywhere the owner wants. The chip is smaller than a grain of rice. Inside the chip is a small motivator that powers the chip to function. The motivator has a thousand-year life span and receives a charge every time it is used. Later, I plan to have the chip removed from the bracelet and put into a key chain or into my watchband. For me, it represents compassion for the victims of disaster. It represents unity of a nation. And it represents coming together into one faith. We will be a righteous nation once again.

~ ~ ~ ~ ~ ~

"Now that makes me somewhat nervous!" Mike said. "I wonder when or if it will become mandatory to have one and to have to worship on Sunday because of it. This might be bringing us closer to an equivalent of the mark of the beast. I thought the mark of the beast would be ideological rather than physical, but maybe this could develop into a physical mark." For Mike, this could signal the beginning of the end. His mind went into hyper-drive planning his contingency moves. He tuned out the president and tried to think of what the Bible and prophecy said about what would come together at the end of time to cause the final conflict. He also jumped way ahead to what Jesus said in the book of Matthew about the "Desolating Sacrilege," asking himself the delicate question of what they needed to do. As a man, he was always trying to make a comfortable life for his family. Now, circumstances were telling him to re-examine his approach to life, to re-look at his values. What should they do? His dark eyebrows furrowed in concern. His normally smooth forehead appeared to have developed wrinkles in seconds. The clear blue eyes remained bright and alert.

Rachael observed the transformation. The years she had spent with him, as his bride, made it possible to read his silent thoughts. He was like a fourth-grade chapter book to her warm, caramel eyes. Like her husband, Rachael exercised regularly and was trim and fit. However, she was concerned about whether she was up to the demands of what this turn of events would mean to her abilities. She, too, wondered when it would be time to act. Would this fervor on the part of the president be a flash in the pan? Would or could her family maintain the status quo a little longer? She wanted so much to have more time to convince her sister and her friends that the Lord's coming was near and that they should get ready. Her gaze shifted to her children and her thoughts and concerns radiated out to them as they sat at the table.

Jason was into the president's speech like it was another homework assignment. He appeared to be avidly watching, catching details for a paper he might have to write for school. She wondered if he was getting the spiritual implications. He looked so much like Mike, only thinner, with less bulk to his frame. He loved soccer, which made him fleet of foot and lean as a cheetah.

Janelle had her head down, long curls hiding her face, looking at her electronic school companion, the Onyx 4000-S. Never seen without the device, it sometimes made her look studious and at other times aloof and distracted. Was she disinterested now? It was hard to tell. Good at multitasking, she could hold a serious conversation on a school subject, check electronic messages, and expertly primp her hair when a good-looking teen boy entered the classroom, all in the same instant. Rachael worried about her commitment to Jesus only because she could never tell where her focus was at any given moment. Her prayer for supper seemed superficial—perhaps because she was focused on some guy at school and wanted to read her messages to get the latest on his possible attraction or attractions. Janelle was at the top of her class when it came to good looks: a dazzling smile that added accent to her cherubic face with high cheek bones and diminutive dimples. She wasn't the athletic type, but could outsmart anyone at the ancient game of tetherball.

The family processed the news from the State of the Union Address each in their own way. Mike couldn't wait to turn off the projection and get down to the needs of the moment, yet he knew some other details might pop up that would help him clarify a future time frame for action. He kept his attention on the unfolding presentation, listening for key words and subjects. The president had segued to the topic of the national budget, the need for better management, and a focus on the need to recover from the multitude of disasters. Mike's mind started computing the list of necessities and arranging them in order from the needed now and the needed later. The easy solution was to plan to go to the cabin when the time came. That meant that it had to be stocked with food and necessities, but then, maybe not. God would provide. Or maybe He would provide after a certain point and they had to survive until then. He seesawed for a moment. Then his thoughts came to a screeching halt. The most important responsibility as a father and husband was sitting at the table. He was making the mistake of transposing his responsibility for them into action and planning, but what he needed to do was to lead them spiritually. He relaxed back into his chair and began to plan his discussion which would follow the president's speech. His first move would be to get Janelle's attention away from that Onyx. He looked up at his wife and saw her worried smile. She was waiting for his lead. It warmed his heart to know she would trust his judgment. She had all the tools and talents to lead this family, better than he, yet she deferred to him. He was humbled by her team spirit. He would need her wisdom to get through this ordeal. Nothing of his personal dilemma entered his thoughts. He was totally preoccupied.

The State of the Union Address went another fifteen minutes, with the president exploring the national debt, tax reform, and the total phasing out of archaic fossil fuel usage.

Mike's thoughts centered on his family and his worry over his children. Then another thought hit him, like a prize fighter's punch to the stomach.

CHAPTER 4

His worry over his children produced twin flash memories which came to his mind at the same instant. Mike was remembering the day that his kids were standing next to their shiny new bikes with their helmets on; both were eager to learn how to ride two-wheelers. They were on the cusp of greater freedom. Jason demonstrated bravery over trepidation; Janelle was the reverse. He took Jason first because he knew if he took Janelle first, Jason would try to surprise everyone by learning without help. Jason liked surprises; everything had to be a surprise to him and from him. He feared that Jason's competitive nature would end in a crash with scraped knees and possible broken bones. The first of his twin memories was him running next to the bike, holding the seat, as Jason got the feel for balance and control. Then he yelled, "Let me go Dad!" A moment later, he said, "Surprise! See? I already know how." With one hand off of the handlebar Jason lost his balance, turned too abruptly, and folded into a clump of metal, rubber, arms, and legs. His crash did little to encourage Janelle as she watched.

The other memory was Janelle's attempt. She was nervous and timid. She over-steered, wobbling from side to side. The only thing going for her was her determination to be independent. Her words were a mantra of hope, "Not yet, Daddy, not yet. Don't let go please, not yet, not yet, Daddy." Multiple trips up and down the street came to a moment when Mike had to surreptitiously let go. Uncertainty traveled with her for several hundred yards and then she wanted to ride over to her best friend. It was over a mile away; her accomplishment translated into independence.

These twins were different in so many ways. And here, this evening, at the conclusion of the President's address, he faced a fear neither of his two offspring had faced—a fear that hit him in the solar plexus. He feared for their spiritual lives. He was about to let go. He had to let go. He feared they would not take the importance of his words to heart. He paused and looked at Janelle for a moment.

Under his gaze, Janelle realized her father was waiting to say something important. She reluctantly laid aside her device and folded her hands in her lap. Any observer could tell she had more important social tea to brew.

> *He had to let go. He feared they would not take the importance of his words to heart.*

"I am worried about what I am going to say next. Janelle … Jason … what I have to say to you is disturbing. No parent would want to throw their children out into a world unprepared."

"What did you mean, Honey?" Rachael asked with concern.

"I want to talk about spiritual responsibility."

"Okay."

"As parents, we are responsible for spiritual development in our children. We want to bring them along slowly, helping them to learn and apply the principles as they are ready to accept them. Then, in the teen years, the years you two are in right now, we see a challenging and testing of what we taught. The hope is that, in time, you will see the truth of what we trained in you. Unfortunately, based on what I heard tonight, both of you may not have that luxury.

"When you are young, the burden of spiritual leadership rests on us, the parents. If the Lord were to come when you were babies, your salvation would be in the hands of a loving God. When older, there comes a degree of accountability. Your salvation depends a great deal on the nurture we provide. Your love for Jesus hangs on your association and familiarity with Him in church services, Sabbath school, and devotions. Your faith is genuine and real and at the same time somewhat contingent upon our helping you find and feel His love on a regular basis. When that dependency ends I do not know. I don't have an answer for that. I'm guessing it happens close to now."

"Why are you telling us this? Don't we want to talk about the President and then go do our homework or something?" Janelle asked, wanting to speed things up.

"Tonight, as I listened to the president, I got the very scary thought for the near future that 'what's done is done!'"

"Honey, what do you mean?" Rachael was reading concern in the tone of Mike's voice.

"What I mean is … we have come to a point of decision. If the President is ushering in the final conflict with this ID band and spiritual unity, if he plans to unite all the churches under one common doctrine, and if he intends to enforce solidarity with Sunday worship, then our children have to stand on their own two spiritual feet. Their individual convictions have to be their own and they have to be firm enough to withstand the temptations. They can't ride into the kingdom while we hold on to them. They must become their own spiritual fortresses. We, as parents, have to let go just like I had to let go when they were learning how to ride bicycles."

Rachael started to chew on her lip again. Silence hung over the dinner table like the Israelites' pillar of cloud by day. Jason was the first to respond. "Okay, wha'da we do next?" Nobody answered his question. Janelle shifted forward a little, laid her folded hands on the table and looked at her mother. "Does this mean I get to choose for myself?"

Rachael hesitated; Mike answered, "It means you *have* to choose for yourself."

"Good! I like that."

Rachael's mind spun webs of concern around what her daughter's words could mean. She wanted to ask, yet didn't want to hear a negative answer if she did probe for the meaning. Their eyes met across the table, each surmising what the other was thinking. For Janelle, her mother's lip chewing was a dead giveaway.

"We have to watch events carefully from here forward," Mike started the family response to the president. "We need to see where all these prayer breakfasts are going. How much unity is going to be pushed upon us and how far they are willing to go. I, for one, will not accept a bracelet. It just seems so … How can I describe it? … well, it's too much is what I have to say. Jason, you're right in observing that it is an old fad that's been around for a long time. Back in 2004 or 5, I remember church members, especially youth groups, were wearing bands of commitment. They would make vows to remain virgins until marriage. Or they would tie a white cloth around their arm symbolizing they belonged to Jesus. Some denominations would do that more than others. Some of our academies did that during Week of Prayer. But these bands which can be worn around the wrist or pressed against the skin of your forehead have too much in the way of personal accountability attached. I mean accountability when it comes to knowing who and where you are. You heard him. You can locate your kids with them if you are wondering where they might be. Tell me, family, what do you think?"

"Well, I personally don't want a bell tied to my tail! Where I go should be my own business," Janelle responded.

"It makes me nervous. It could be what is predicted for the end of time and…then again, it could be another attempt to try to achieve what he said happened in the early twentieth century or, or … it could be a test from the Lord to see if we're ready. It may be a call for us to study more and get our hearts ready for something bigger later," Rachael added.

"I don't think crazy little bracelets or key chains or wallet strap hangers, or whatevers, amount to the mark of the beast. The president is just trying to make money for disasters that will soften the effect on the national debt, which has always been with us. When the national debt has been at its lowest or almost nonexistent, we have had financial disaster and recession. He's appealing to the people to unite behind a cause to help ease the effect on the budget so he can get re-elected. He's a crusader for a cause. And, just like all politicians, he is stirring up support for the vote. In this case, people voting with money." Janelle's comment surprised her parents on many levels, for it spoke of an understanding of the political world at the same time as it minimized the disturbing capabilities of the bracelet. Rachael wanted to unpack her daughter's words to find her attitude of spiritual commitment underneath.

"So, you're saying that all this was a political move and probably won't go anywhere significant. Is that what I'm hearing?"

"Yes … and no. It depends on who and how many jump on his agenda."

"Janelle, you surprise me. You seem to have an understanding of politics beyond your years," Mike complimented.

"It's no big deal. We've been studying political history in class the last couple of weeks," she replied.

"You're only paying attention in class because You-Know-Who is interested in that stuff," Jason interjected.

"I like the class and the teacher, Miss Randal. So there! Mind your own business, you scrawny Swede."

"It's true! She likes Darin. Did you two talk about politics while you were holding hands at lunch?"

"We weren't holding hands!"

"Yes, you were. I could see them beneath the table. By the way, if I'm a scrawny Swede, you would have to be a desperate dim-wit giggling at his every word."

"Why you—"

"Okay, that's enough. Janelle, I agree with you about the not wanting a bell on my tail, but are there any spiritual reasons for why this might bother you?"

"Ah, if they can track us when we have one of those, that means it could be known to everyone what church we go to. And, if our church didn't comply with the common norm then we would be immediately labeled. That's, of course, if this whole thing morphs into something bigger."

"Alright, that's a good point," Mike answered.

"Not really, because they already know who and what church we go to. They don't need those devices to follow us." Jason looked around the table. "They have filters on messaging programs that tell them what our preferences are, duh! Like preferences for Darin over Brad."

"Mom, make him stop, please!"

"I think we should focus on the devotional applications of what we heard tonight," Rachael reacted, with an unmistakable focus on her son.

"And another thing, to be fair to the Prez, these bands are no different than the all-seeing eyes of cyber-world," Jason added.

"So, what we have seen this evening is an event that could go nowhere and then it could go marching into the final conflict between good and evil. No matter what happens we still need to have a personal response. What should we do?" Mike asked.

"No matter what happens, I'm going to double my efforts to explain to my friends what the issues are and that they need to get their hearts ready for Jesus' second coming. I'm going to start tonight after devotions and give my sister Megan a call and ask her if she heard the President's speech. Do you two have any friends you want to see have a closer walk with Jesus?" Rachael's steady look at Jason persuaded him to leave the Darin subject out of the dialogue.

"Everyone I know at school already believes. They'd think I was crazy trying to convince them to believe when they already believe," he answered.

"Are you sure they all believe? Maybe you'll find some that are just going along with the crowd," Rachael asked.

"What about the Cox brothers? They don't seem to have a religious bone in their bodies," Janelle added.

"Maybe … We're not that close. They kinda, well, ya'know." Jason shrugged his shoulders. Janelle knew what that meant. The Cox brothers had not been the nicest of individuals. They had physically bullied Jason in previous school years. He had found a way, somehow, to avoid them and stay out of their path. She had a perfect opportunity to get back at her brother, but somehow it didn't seem right. Revenge was not an option in her world, even though he deserved it for telling mom and dad about Darin. Besides, they were talking about witnessing and it wouldn't be appropriate to get into another squabble.

"I think the President's speech is a perfect way to bring up several different subjects related to faith and Jesus' coming. Asking them about what they thought would be a good lead in. Don't you think?" Rachael ventured.

"Yes, I agree. Today at work, the office was already buzzing with guesses as to what the President might say. They should be animated tomorrow for sure," Mike added.

"The thing about this is the innocence of a little bracelet to help victims of disaster. I would think nothing of it if it was only just that, but the President has made this into a great campaign to get us all together religiously. Then the technology applications of this device bring to mind possible abuses. They could be used in a multitude of ways. It could be like *1984*."

"Mom, what happened in 1984 that was so bad?" Jason asked.

"It's not what happened; it's what was written," Mike started to clarify. "*1984* was a book written a long time before that year depicting a futuristic society. Cameras could see what you were doing all the time. It's where the phrase, 'Big brother is watching you' comes from."

"That's what I meant, Jason and Janelle. It is possible, with this device and with its apps, that it can watch our activities and whereabouts," Rachael added.

"But that's illegal!" Janelle responded.

"Yes, it is. From what I read in the Spirit of Prophecy, though, rules like that will disappear like pixels on a screen when the electricity is turned off."

"We don't have pixels anymore, Dad. That's so yesterday," Jason reminded.

"You know what I mean. Laws are obeyed only when they are enforced and are thought to be reasonable by the general public. At the end of time, the majority are going to want to keep tabs on the minority, especially if it is to their advantage. The general public will agree that the people who are going against the system must be stopped or, at least, captured and put away. Later, they're going to want to execute them. What's illegal now will become accepted and required later."

"Put to death? You mean murdered?" Janelle reacted.

"Martyred is a better word. Janelle, you've heard this before. Why do you seem so surprised?"

"I guess … well … because … tonight makes this seem closer. It could be us, not someone years from now." Mike and Rachael didn't feel it was necessary to add comment to Janelle's words. They remained silent. After a while Mike suggested they read Revelation chapters thirteen and fourteen. It was sobering to read the words that spoke of a time they might be facing. They took turns reading, passing the Bible from one to another around the table. Mike explained some of the words and symbols using his knowledge of the book, *The Great Controversy*. Knowing that the second beast was the United States clarified the evening's words spoken from the Chamber of Congress. Jason asked about the mark of the beast.

"Dad, it says 'mark.' Wouldn't it be more like a tattoo instead of a bracelet?"

"There are symbolic and literal interpretations of the mark of the beast. One favors the symbolic interpretation of the mark rather than a literal application. A great portion of the book of Revelation is portrayed in symbols, so that's why bracelets, or tattoos for that matter, may not be the actual mark of the beast. It could be a popular view or belief that everyone has to agree to or go along with. People agreeing with their heads could mean a mark on the forehead, or just going along with it because it is mandatory or popular could be symbolized by the right hand. It could be an actual mark. If it is a real mark, then I think a lot of vain people would reject it because it would clash with clothes or make them look ugly. We'll see," he shrugged.

"I am wondering about the words 'free and slave.' There are no slaves now, are there?" Janelle asked.

"In some third world countries slavery is permitted and accepted. There's illegal slavery, of course, human trafficking below the legal radar. Perhaps that's what prophecy is speaking of. The inspiration of Scripture is always correct. It's man's interpretation of scripture that is many times incorrect."

"What about the word slave being symbolic, too?" Jason interjected.

"Good point. What would it represent if it was symbolic? I think what the scriptures are trying to say here is that the whole world is being affected by this requirement to worship the beast and his image, "small and great, rich and poor, free and slave." The symbolism would have to be taken in context and the context points to a vast majority of worshippers giving homage to the beast—the extremes of every existence."

"To kind of add these things together, if we symbolically take these references to the mark and the majority, I would say it represents people from all cultures and economic levels agreeing to band together in one whole to follow the ideology, er thinking, of popular opinion. Am I right, Honey?" Rachael summed up.

"Spot on."

"Why would any thinking person want to follow the crowd when the Bible warns against this very thing?"

It represents people from all cultures and economic levels agreeing to band together in one whole to follow the ideology.

"I know it seems so simple, doesn't it? However, when the food on your table and the roof over your head is threatened, most will opt for self-preservation. And … then there is that fact that people don't read the Bible anymore. They let their preachers explain it—"

"Which they don't, because preachers today don't really use the Bible. I've watched preachers preach from their web sites and it doesn't seem to be biblically based." Janelle saw her folks looking at her with curiosity. "Don't worry, Mom and Dad, I had an assignment in school to evaluate different denominational worship styles. Rather than attend, I just watched several on my Onyx 4000-S. I got an A, okay?"

"We weren't worried, just surprised." Rachael explained. The family continued reading through Revelation 13 and to the last verse of chapter 14. At the end, they decided to pray. Janelle volunteered without hesitation.

"Dear Father in heaven, tonight we see things happening in the world that may or may not be the final events we read about in the Bible. But, it makes us think. We want to be ready. We want not, I mean, to not disappoint You in a way that, or, I don't know, my words are all mixed up. I guess what I'm trying to say is that I'm afraid and I want You to take away my fear. I don't think I'm strong enough for everything that might happen. I need Your help, er … I guess I should be praying for all of us and not just me. We need Your help. Please take care of us. In Jesus' name, amen."

"Amen. I couldn't have said it any better myself. Thank you, Janelle, for that prayer. 'We need Your help. Please take care of us.' That's one prayer I am going to pray every day," Mike praised his daughter. He was wondering if his talk about standing on their own two feet had sobered them to the situation.

Rachael couldn't have been more pleased with her daughter. The prayer demonstrated a depth of concern that was more personal than her prayer over the food earlier. She was paying attention and had felt the impact of the moment. She rested her concerns that had arisen earlier. Then she turned and winked at Mike.

The kids had a different view on the situation. Jason was into the moment and responding to the stimuli around him. Standing on his own was not a significant issue. It never occurred to him that he was dependent on anyone for his attitude or salvation. He reacted as he saw things, adapted to what was before him. Because of the Cox brothers' depredations, he redefined his role of the moment away from the attitudes others thrust upon him. This made him somewhat introverted and independent. He preferred doing, discovering, and data-gathering over friendship.

Janelle was more sensitive about pending expectations. She didn't like being pushed into a pre-programmed way of thinking, but she valued others' views. She wanted freedom to choose, even if it meant being different. Unlike her twin brother, she wanted loads of friends. She felt more truly herself when she was in the midst of a circle of companions, sharing insights and feelings to sift and assimilate into her own core of belief. Her sensitive nature jumped on the words her father had spoken about being her own person when it came to the crunch of personal faith. She desired autonomy, but not without associates.

Mike concluded family worship. "We have a lot of things to think about and do. For now, I think the best course of action is to keep doing the things we normally do and watch and pray. Watch for any signs that we know are going to happen at the end, not just the mark of the beast. For instance, all these disasters are indicators."

"I am going to talk to my sister and then, if there's time, my friends Kristina and Michelle." Rachael scooted her chair back and went to the den.

Mike watched as his family separated to their various places. It was time for him to think through the list of things he had to do to get mentally and physically ready for the unknown. His mind worked on needs and actions. He put stylus to tablet and made two lists: one for before confirmation that this was the end and the other list was what he needed to do once he knew this was it. He labeled the top of each list with, "PREPARATIONS," and the other with, "NO TURNING BACK." One item for his

first list caused him to pause: "Dr.'s appointment." Pondering that sobering truth ended when he put a question mark after the listed item.

* * * * * *

The image wavered into view on the video phone's holographic application of Rachael's Onyx 4000-L. "I know, you're calling about the President's broadcast, okay Sis?"

"Yes, I am. What did you think about it?" Rachael asked.

"Just a minute. I need to close the door." Megan's image disappeared
for a minute and then she materialized back into view. Her voice was quieter. "Walt and I had a disagreement about it. Ach! I don't know. He
says all my comments are just superstitious hubbub. When the President
started talking about God's blessing, he left and went into the kitchen
to make a sandwich. I know deep down he believes in God, but he is so
mad he doesn't want to admit that anything Christian can be true. I wish
we had gone to a different church. Those deacons really hurt him and he
won't listen to anything spiritual. I agree with him…" her sentence ended
in a sigh.

"I'm sorry. Do you think this could be it—the end-time events?"

"You and I think differently about that stuff. It could just be what
President O'Donnell said it is, just a call for help and a joining together to
stand behind other Americans needing our help."

Rachael was used to Megan's mixed up theology. At times Megan was
quoting the truths she had learned as a child growing up in an Adventist family. At other times she was espousing her newer adult concepts.
Rachael wanted to keep her talking about the issue before them that,
from an Adventist viewpoint, was disturbing. "Don't you think the armbands are a little too intrusive for a fund raiser?"

"I guess, maybe." Her voice dropped even lower. "Even though he
isn't into the religious stuff, Walt still wanted to get one right away, for me
also. It's like a cool, new piece of technology to him, you know? He has all
the latest gadgets. I wasn't enthusiastic enough for him. He says the price
will go up later and he likes the angle on the banking options it provides.
He heard about them before on the 'What's New' program he watches all
the time."

"I hadn't thought about this until you mentioned that Walt said the
price might go up, but it does seem odd that they sell them cheaply and
give them away to the poor. It looks like they have a bigger agenda than

just promoting disaster relief. So, if he gets one for you, are you going to wear it?"

Megan hesitated before answering. "I suppose I will. Just to keep him happy. What's the harm, right?"

Rachael knew that Megan's mixed beliefs were a compromise in a religiously divided home. "I don't know for sure if there is harm, but Mike and I aren't going to get them and I'm assuming the twins agree with us."

"Why are you saying that you assume? Don't they agree with you already? They're only kids."

"We talked about that tonight after dinner. Mike told them that they have to be able to stand on their own spiritual feet, make up their own minds how they believe."

"Interesting."

"Why do you say that?"

"Because I thought they did and believed pretty much what you tell them. They're like religious clones of you and Mike." These words struck Rachael deeply. She didn't want to seem dictatorial in her childrearing; it had been an issue Megan had with her parents when they were young. Megan had always been the independent one, ready to buck the system. When she got engaged to Walt, the issue of being unequally yoked came to a peak. Megan let it be known she was going to make up her own mind and let the folks know that she didn't appreciate their cramming their form of religion down her throat. It really wasn't that way, but it was felt to be that way by Megan's headstrong attitude. Tension existed between her and her parents for years, with them rarely talking. When Megan struggled with infertility, Rachael was the only one she could confide in. Things eased a little when Walt joined the church. Her antagonistic views moderated and she rejoined with him. The war with the folks ended and an easy armistice lasted until the folks died in a car wreck on the interstate. Megan became pregnant after in vitro fertilization and regretted not having mended fences earlier. Rachael decided she would not enter into Megan's old debate about free choice on faith and her liberal viewpoint. She was treading on controversial ground already.

"We raised them to try to think these things through, but we also wanted them to understand thoroughly what we believe. It isn't easy to let them find their own way, especially now when all this is happening and they're so young. I'm worried," she confided.

"I wouldn't be. Your views on what's going to happen are way too conservative. I know about the mark of the beast and the testing truth of the Sabbath, but for me, I think it will take an entirely different environment than what we have now. This President seems very honest and wants to bring back a moral climate—"

"So why did you and Walt have a disagreement?"

"Because, I started to explain what I was taught, as a child, what the folks believed, and what you believe. I ended up defending you and the folks. I don't know why I did that, but it started a discussion that brought up old issues. You know Walt—he is so gentle; it is difficult to see if he is really angry," Megan answered.

"He's still hurting from those comments from the deacons and feels strongly that it meant they rejected him. If I talked to some of them and convinced them to apologize, would it help?" Rachael asked.

"I doubt it. He won't come to the phone when they call and if he answers the call, he hits the cancel button."

"I'm sorry. I'll keep praying for him and you. It must be difficult for you."

"Thank you."

"Megan, please promise me you'll keep watching these events and, remember, the last moves will come swiftly. I wouldn't want you to be caught by surprise."

"I doubt I'll be caught by surprise. I know you'll call me at every nuance you see in the news, good or bad."

Rachael felt the slight irritation in Megan's voice. "I will call you, because I love you."

* * * * * *

"Come here, my sweetheart. I can tell you can't sleep either," Mike said. He folded her in his arms and she laid her head on his chest. "I need you," he added.

"Yes, okay," She cooed, not knowing exactly what he meant.

"I need my best friend. I need to talk to my best friend. I'm worried."

"Me, too. I'm worried. Afraid worried."

"Yes, you said it. I'm afraid. I didn't think I would be afraid when this time would come. I thought it would be exciting and glorious to be alive when Jesus comes, but now it's, it's overwhelming to think of the difficulties we will face. And—" He intended to bring up the tumor issue, but stopped to address himself to her response.

"Are you sure this is it?" she asked.

"To be honest, I don't know for sure. But, I don't want to be caught off-guard if it is. So, I'm assuming it is, within reason of course. I've tried to list the things I can do now without going beyond a point of no return in our everyday lives."

"What would you say would have to happen for you to think that we are at the point of no return?"

> *What would you say would have to happen for you to think that we are at the point of no return?*

"That's not easy to answer. Waiting to the point of hearing the death penalty for not worshipping the beast I think would be too late. We would want to be out of the way by that point. When we bought this house, we wondered if we would ever pay it off. Thirty years seemed such a long time. Now, if things develop into the final conflict, paying off the house is not an issue and the money we put into it is no longer important."

"I have an idea. We could sell the house and use what was left over to spread the word about the spiritual issues at stake and warn people that His coming is near," Rachael suggested.

"That presents a problem. When? When would we sell the house and what would we live in until we have to drop everything and flee as Jesus tells us in the Bible?" Mike countered.

"I see what you mean."

"If we wait until too late, we won't be able to sell it because, 'no one will be able to buy or sell.' We would be prevented from selling. It would have to be before that, but not too soon or we could end up having to rent and the move might take up time and effort we wouldn't want to deal with at that juncture. Perhaps when the issue of Sunday worship comes to a serious head in discussions, then it might be the right time. Or, when the false messiah appears and claims to be the Christ; or when the plagues start to happen. What do you think?"

"You're right, it's not easy. Right now, the prophecies of wars and disasters are happening with rapidity, just like the Bible predicts. For the conditions to happen as they are portrayed in Revelation, some of our freedoms should start disappearing or be violated, you know, civil liberties. I have always thought that His coming has to be still in the slightly distant future because religious freedom is still practiced. Tonight we saw what might become a violation of civil liberty for non-Christians, but we don't know for sure this unity the President is calling for will become more than just words."

"I see two types of violations to religious free exercise happening in the future. One, as you say, is non-Christians, but the other is when certain Christians are not tolerated, namely those who don't worship on Sunday. If either or both of those start happening, as you say, 'more than just words,' should we make final preparations, like selling the house? I need your wisdom."

"I'm not wise. I'm just stumbling along in this. If the words become acts, then we have a strong indication that things are escalating. Then again, there are so many predictions of events and circumstances that will happen that we might be overlooking something."

"Yes, we'll have to keep our eyes open all the time. Ah, I need to bring up another problem."

"The kids?" she asked.

"That is another problem, but I'm thinking about something else."

"Okay."

"I went to the doctor this morning."

"You did? You didn't tell me. What's happening? Was it an eye doctor? 'Cause you seem to be having trouble reading," Rachael asked.

"No, it's not my eyes I don't think. I've been concerned about a problem with electrical jolts and twitches I've been having in my face. I went to my doctor several days ago. He ordered an MRI and today he gave me the results."

"What were they?" Rachael's voice tone registered concern. Her faced registered her characteristic worry.

"I have a couple of tumors close to the brain stem. They are causing these shocks to my face."

"Oh, Honey! Oh no! How bad is it? What does the doctor say about treatment?" Her hands clasped his hands and held on like she was going to slip and fall waiting for his answer.

"The only way we can get rid of them is surgery. The tumors are too close to the brain stem to do anything else."

"Surgery? Brain surgery? That's serious."

"Yes, I'm afraid so."

"When? Right away?"

"I don't know. I have a referral to a neurosurgeon. I would have to meet with him first to see what he recommends. Right now, I'm not sure I want to go through that. If this trend in politics keeps going the way it seems to be going, I want to skip surgery and be able to deal with the issues at hand. I don't want to be helpless in a hospital bed when my family needs me. Remember Maria Behr? She was in the hospital and rehab for two months after her brain surgery."

"I do. I remember how discouraged she was at how slow things proceeded. But, Honey, what if you don't get surgery and you become incapacitated? It would be the same thing."

"I suppose I should at least see what the surgeon has to say."

"And this time I'll be going with you. No Lone Ranger, okay? I think it would be good if we prayed together," she suggested.

"Let's pray. So far it's just been me praying about this, wondering why God has let this happen. I like praying with my wife."

CHAPTER 5

"What about atheists? Don't they have a right to the free exercise of their … non-faith? This is supposed to be a free country, isn't it?" George was interjecting his concerns into the conversation with some energy. The morning coffee break was animated in its discussion over last night's State of the Union address. Several had made their convictions known. Most were in agreement that the country needed a change like the President had said. When Marshall and Zack had come down strongly on a need for better, more Christian, principles to run the country, George had decided to ask his question. The reaction on the part of the listeners was chilly.

"You've got to be kidding! They're the reason our country is not being blessed. The hand of God is against them and because they are among us that means God's hand is against us too!" Zack explained.

"You can't say that completely. Some of our nation's problems are because we are a Christian nation. The radical Islamic Jihadis are attacking us because we *are* Christian," Floyd answered.

"Maybe God would protect us from these idiots if we were more aligned religiously, like the President wants. And, if you sympathize with the atheists, then you are supporting them. George, are you an atheist?"

"No, but my wife is; I worry about how people will treat her. In our relationship we have always respected—"

"She better get with the majority if she knows what's good for her," Marshall interrupted.

"A person can't just give up their opinions at the drop of a hat," Shelly countered.

"If you want to enjoy prosperity, then you and these outsiders are going to have to make a decision or the decision will be made for you," Marshall answered.

Mike listened and knew this discussion was getting darker in the veiled threats that stood behind the words. He was the section manager and had to keep peace. "It might be best if we returned to our desks and got a little work done. I see the President has stirred up some strong feelings and we have to remember that we can agree to disagree. We're all friends here." The ad hoc group of conversationalists undraped themselves from the perches they had occupied and took their coffee cups back to their work stations. His mind was weighing the tenor of the interchange that had just happened. He was seeing some attitudes surface where he had not seen them before. The President's speech had emboldened the silent majority and galvanized some of them to speak their minds.

He had plenty of work to do, but this conversation in the break room disturbed him. He closed the door to his office and turned on his monitor to watch the national news programs. He chose the flat screen option to watch, turning it away from view to the doorway and ear receptors to keep the rest of the office from hearing him listen into the reports. He wanted to know the political pundits take on the address.

The reports were a mixture of comment about the country's reaction to the President and the on-the-scene pictures of destruction at the embassy bombing in Switzerland and the earthquake. It seemed that the three events were top billing and the media was milking the audiences' desire to see and hear these three stories. What surprised Mike was the media comment that the White House was strangely quiet about public reactions on the speech. Usually the President would follow-up the State of the Union with a round of public visits and speeches to clarify and promote the words from the night before. Nothing was reported. White House correspondents were hard pressed to explain the quietude. The pundits spun their opinion on the silence, saying that the President and his team were waiting to see if the public were for or against his proposals. One comment was made by the anchors: "Polls show that the majority of voters classify themselves as Christian." That comment was said almost in an aside manner and would be overlooked by most listeners. Other than that little sentence, the normally liberal press made no mention of the suggestions by President O'Donnell to move the country into a more conservative religious posture. For once, the media was like Mike, waiting to see what would happen. It didn't matter if the media was liberal or conservative; they still made their money on the whims and interests of the majority of viewers.

For the rest of the morning and into the lunch hour Mike followed the news and performed rote tasks of electro-signing proposals and purchase agreements. Later than his usual time for lunch he came out of his office to see an almost empty floor. People who regularly ate at their desks had opted for something away from their work associates, or so it seemed.

He grabbed his coat and gloves and was headed for the door when he saw George sequestered in his corner cubical. He decided to see what was up. When Mike approached, George quickly said good-bye to his wife, whose upper torso and face was seen hovering for a moment above his desk. She was obviously at work and sitting behind her control console.

"Where's everyone? We're the only two left on the floor," Mike opened the conversation.

"They all went down to the grill. It's Glenda's birthday."

"Oh, I forgot. With all the buzz about the President, I guess I put it in the back of my mind. I should be there. How about you? Why didn't you go?"

"I wanted to talk to my wife without anyone listening in."

"Then I came along and spoiled that. I'm sorry."

"No, no. We were done."

"I saw what happened this morning; rather, I felt what happened to you this morning. I want you to know that, in my opinion, this country's concept of the freedom of religion must include freedom of conviction on both sides of the coin. You know me, I'm a Christian. I would like nothing better than to see everyone have a relationship with God. However, faith must come from an honest search and a personal conviction. For some, that experience hasn't happened as yet. Each individual must find God in their own way. The right to personal belief should be protected. I saw that right being overlooked this morning."

"Thank you. I appreciate your candor. I felt alone this morning and fearful for my wife. If she doesn't get one of those ID bracelets she will look like she doesn't care about the disaster victims. She does, but wearing the bracelet is tantamount to being a Christian. She doesn't want that."

"I sympathize with her. She shouldn't be forced against her will," Mike said.

"We were talking about that just now. I'm glad I'm not the only one in the office. Thanks, Mike, for understanding."

"Anytime you feel like it, don't hesitate to come to me; we can talk."

"I will."

"I guess we should go down to Glenda's celebration."

* * * * * *

Rachael balanced a warm loaf of bread in one hand and rang the doorbell with the other. Kristine, her neighbor, was a long-time friend; their friendship had developed over the years through shared joys and sorrows. They had prayed together and praised God for answered prayers. They were of different denominations and both had attempted to win the other to their point of view. Kristine came to the door with her hands wet from rinsing dishes.

"Let me guess; you baked that bread specifically for me so we could talk about last night, am I right?"

"You know me all too well," Rachael said with a smile almost breaking into a giggle.

"Come on in. You don't have to bribe a best friend just to talk about religion."

"What do you think about what was said?"

"I think it's wonderful. Finally, we have a President who is setting the example in religious leadership. Our nation is going to be Christian once again. We can praise Him together." Kristine paused when she saw Rachael's face; it did not mirror her own exuberance. "You seem not to be as happy as I am. What's wrong?"

"I'm worried about some specific things that don't seem right."

"What kind of specific things … uh, specifically? What's not right?" Kristine was sitting down on one end of the couch watching Rachael as she was settling herself on the other end.

"I'm worried about a couple of things, side effects really, one of which is that when religion becomes popular it usually becomes shallow."

"Okay, but don't you think that shallow faith is better than no faith and then a little faith can lead to a greater faith? God can work with someone who prays a little. When their prayers are answered, then they want more of God's blessing and then they grow stronger in the Lord and pray more. Revival means faith is becoming popular. I pray for revival all the time."

"I don't disagree. What I am concerned about is that popular faith that doesn't have a strong foundation in the Bible can lead to abuse if it is made a requirement for others to follow."

"I didn't see that last night. What I saw was a President concerned about his country and the suffering people who need to be helped. We need to be a Christian nation who performs Christian acts of kindness. The President is a Christian leading the way. Bless him! I'm glad I voted for him."

Rachael prayed silently that she would know the right words to say. She didn't want to make this into a confrontation. "In many ways, I am happy that people are talking about being Christians and doing the right thing for the victims. It is needed now more than ever with all these bombings and natural disasters. The gospels of Matthew, Mark, and Luke all mention earthquakes and famines and terrible events. We have read those passages together. This is the end of time, these things are happening, and Jesus' coming is near. We both know that. What I am concerned about is false religion, as it is mentioned in the book of Revelation. It talks of—"

"Oh, please, let's not bring that book into the discussion. It's full of crazy symbols, bugs, and dragons. Everyone knows that dragons are mythical. I don't know why that book is even in the Bible!"

Rachael paused. Normally she would not progress in the discussion and turn a friend into an enemy, but now things were different. She had to move on. "I know you believe that all scripture is inspired. I do too. There has to be a reason why Revelation was included in the Bible. Kristine, Revelation is a prophecy. Please promise me you will read chapters 13 and 14 and tell me if it doesn't bother you what is predicted."

"My pastor told me to leave Revelation alone—to leave it to the professional theologians to figure out its meaning. He's a good pastor and I trust him."

"Kristine, you love Jesus. We have prayed so many times together. I know you love Him with all your heart. Your pastor loves Jesus. You have told me so much about your pastor that I am convinced he loves Jesus too. Just listen to me on this one last thing about the book of Revelation. The first words in the book are, 'The revelation of Jesus Christ.' That means the book is coming directly from Him. I wouldn't want to miss even one word of Jesus. And I know you would not want to either." There was a pause as the two let Rachael's words echo in their hearts. Then Rachael tactfully changed the subject. "This bread is still warm. I'll have to confess to a little selfishness. I really wanted to have a taste of your homemade jam on a slice of this warm bread."

* * * * * *

Current events suddenly became the subject of American History class at the Twin Feather Lake Academy. In fact, most classes had discussions about the President's State of the Union Address. The American History teacher assigned a paper to the class as a substitute for a mid-term test. They had until next Monday to turn it in. They were supposed to compare the now with the historical references that the President alluded to in his speech and add their own understanding of what is supposed to happen in the last day events. It was slightly out of the purview of the class subject, maybe more in line with Bible class, but completely in keeping with the teachings of the church-sponsored school.

Jason worked on his Onyx 4000-TS. Both he and Janelle had them, along with practically every student in the school. The Onyx 4000-S was specially equipped for students, hence the "S" designation. Mike had the "B" model for his business applications and Rachael had the "L" model for her literary aspirations. Jason longed for the "TS" model because of its design for technology and science. These devices carried most every-thing people needed for the modern world. All of them included commu-nication programs and could be configured in a moment to project three dimensional images of conversations when the situation was right. Having phones as well was unnecessary except for the need to carry a smaller device in one's pocket or purse.

Jason worked on his Onyx studiously. He had his outline already con-structed. With his fingertips, he transferred whole quotes from the EE (Electronic Encyclopedia) and with a touch inserted them into his out-line. He would cut what he wanted out of the quote and then with a tap relegate the whole source to a footnote that the teacher could touch, see the expanded quote blossom in front of him, and then check if he had taken the smaller quote out of context. Every essay had multiple layers that ensured accuracy. Jason just needed to write his comments and con-clusions and he would be done. When it came time for Jason to turn in his work, he needed only to tap the corner of his work pad and the teacher would have it in a split second, because Jason had started his essay by indi-cating what the work was for, which class, and for which teacher.

Janelle had the same class and assignment. She wondered why the teacher gave everybody so much time to complete the essay. It could have been done in a single class period if the teacher had decided not to have a big dialogue on "why this State of the Union was different than previous Presidents' State of the Union addresses." She planned to work on her essay at home. It was lunch and Darin was sitting beside her again. This was a continuation of yesterday's dream. She was surprised in her revelry of the moment by the last part of his question.

"… So, are you going?"

"Yes, of course, as long as you're there." She wasn't sure what she had just agreed to, but because he was starting to stand and her lunch was almost eaten, she surmised it was now. They walked out of the cafeteria past Jason, who always sat next to the main door. It was one of his many defense mechanisms against the Cox brothers; teachers usually stood by the door to monitor lunch so the Coxes stayed away from him. Down the hallway, the couple stepped into the music room to find about two dozen kids facing the gym teacher, who was politely waiting for everyone to settle. He had the chairs in a large circle. They were greeted with a big smile and a nod. The teacher looked out the door, checked the hallway for any more attendees, and then closed it and began.

"It looks like everyone who's coming is already here. Let's begin. We are here to pray about the current status in the world. The President spoke last night about the tragedies and then wanted everyone to get on the same playing field, so to speak, about Christian unity. As Adventists, we see this as a possible turn toward the conditions spoken about in the Bible and the Spirit of Prophecy. It occurred to a couple of us this morning that we should have a prayer session about it. It never hurts to pray. I see the word has gotten out to some of the other classes and I'm glad you have chosen to come. We have about twenty-five minutes, so let's begin. I think an open prayer where each prays spontaneously would be the best. I will close with the final "'amen" when everyone has had a chance to pray that wants to. Let's bow our heads." Coach Weldon leaned forward in his chair with his eyes closed and his elbows resting on his knees.

"Dear God, our minds are focused on You because we want You to be with us at this time…" one female student opened.

"There are so many people who are hurting out there because of the disasters and bombings that are happening. Please be with them, Lord Jesus…" another added.

"Yeah, God, people are hurting…"

"Please, Jesus, help my aunt and uncle who are in California. Their house was kinda ruined…" A silence followed that was long enough for some to think this was all that was going to be said. Then a senior girl spoke. "Father in Heaven, I'm worried sick because of everything the President said last night. He said that everyone needs to be a Christian and wear an identity bracelet and pray so that the nation will get Your blessing again. That sounds okay, but my mother says that this could turn ugly and become the beginning of the end, ya'know, I don't know if that is what's gonna happen, but I'm afraid if it is, that I might not be ready. Please be with me and get me ready…"

"I want to be ready too…"

"We need Your help. Please take care of us…" Janelle spoke her prayer from the night before.

"Yes, we need your help…" Darin echoed.

"Our lives are in Your hands. We ask for Your divine protection. Please send Your Holy Spirit to us…"

"Jesus we need You. We know You are coming, but not until Satan comes first pretending to be You. I know I don't want to worship him by mistake. I want to worship You…" The gap in prayers momentarily made the whole world seem quiet. The teens were thinking.

"I don't think I'm completely ready. I keep thinking and doing the wrong things. Please Lord, forgive me. I don't have any strength to do the right things. I need the Holy Spirit. I can speak for the rest of us in the room; I know they need the Holy Spirit too…"

"Yes, I do too…"

"Me too…"

"And me…"

"Lord, we're together asking, begging, for Your Holy Spirit." Sounds were heard as the teens started to slide to their knees. Soon all were kneeling, beseeching Jesus for the Holy Spirit. Breathing patterns started to change; a few tears trickled down cheeks.

"Father, I need to ask my friend Janelle to forgive me for a bad thing I said a couple of weeks ago…" Kathy admitted.

"I forgive you," Janelle quickly stated.

"Father, I'm supposed to leave my gift at the altar and go make it right before I come to You. Now I ask You, dear Heavenly Father, forgive me. I leave my heart as a gift at the altar for You," Kathy offered with a tremor in her voice. Janelle wanted to soothe her, but was aware the group was in prayer, so she continued to talk to God.

"Father, we come to You for forgiveness. Kathy has asked for my and Your forgiveness and I have said that I do forgive her and I know, You, dear Lord, forgive her. But I want to add that I stand between her and You as a forgiving friend. She is in need of comfort, as I am in need of comfort. I, too, have not been perfect. I sin and say things that can be misunderstood. Forgive me of my unknown sins, sins that others can see but I don't see, but most importantly, that You see." Janelle squeezed Darin's hand in support.

"God, I know I have to say I'm sorry to Beth and she's not here. I promise to go straight to her and ask for her to forgive me after we're done here. In the meantime, can You let me off the hook of sin? I am really sorry," Madeline stated.

"Father in Heaven, this school needs a revival and I see it starting here with forgiveness. I, too, need to be forgiven and I need to make sure my relationships with fellow teachers and our precious students are empty of any sins of misunderstanding. I give myself to You anew and ask for You to point me to those with whom I need to make things right," Coach Weldon added.

"You know me, Lord. You know I need to be forgiven. If this school is going to get ready for the end times, I can't be the one person that keeps us from being united in Spirit. Please forgive me. I'll be more specific in my prayers tonight, but You already know the ones I mean." Jonathan uttered.

"O God, it isn't just us who need to be forgiven. It is the whole school. This whole school needs to be ready and it needs to be a witness to the community. Please, O God, forgive this whole school of their sins. They are good people and they will ask You themselves when we tell them how important it is. The end is near; they will listen. I know they will. Don't blame them for their sins; blame us, blame me," Kathy interceded.

"Please send the Holy Spirit and clean all of us."

"Yes, please come Lord Jesus."

"Make us ready with Your presence. Make this whole school ready."

"Give us the right words to say."

"Yes, we need the right words."

"We are confident that we can do it if You help. We know what's gonna happen; we can tell them."

"God, we are so weak, we can't do what You want us to do without your help. We have friends outside of this school, in the church, and in our neighborhoods who need to be better Christians. We need to tell them..." Janelle spoke from her heart and felt a hand searching for her hand. It was a student on her other side. She took a peek and found others in the circle reaching out to hold each other's hands.

Darin began to pray. "Lord, bring us—" the bell rang, interrupting his prayer. The lunch hour was finished. The group looked at each other, eyes passing from one face to another.

"Do you feel that?"

"You mean the Holy Spirit? Yes, I do. He's here."

"This is wonderful! I can feel His presence. We should keep praying."

"I agree. Keep praying and I'll get permission for us to stay here." Mr. Weldon slipped quietly from his knees and exited to the hallway. It was the thing he absolutely did not want to do. He was torn between facilitating the prayer session by keeping it going and staying in the circle feeling the Spirit wash over him. The teens began again.

> *He was torn between facilitating the prayer session by keeping it going and staying in the circle feeling the Spirit wash over him.*

"Thank you for sending Your Holy Spirit. We feel so close to You now…"

"Yes, Jesus, thank You for listening to us…"

"Forgive me, Jesus, forgive me. I know You are listening. Please forgive me and take my sins away and put them in a trash can…"

"Dear Father, and Jesus, and Holy Spirit, I learned last night that I have to stand on my own two spiritual feet. I didn't think I had to be ready this soon. It's scary, Lord Jesus, and if the devil tries to kill us, I'm not sure I can be brave. Jesus, Your Holy Spirit has to be with me or I am afraid I will fail. What can I do without You? I don't want to be alone…" Janelle prayed.

"In the past, sometimes I feel like I prayed to the ceiling. Right now, I feel as though Your hands are on my shoulders. I feel unworthy and yet so comfortable. It's good to be with You," Darin began and then continued, "Lord, bring us to where we need to be spiritually to face all the bad things that are going to happen. Teach us to be leaders in these bad times. Help us to lead many to You and have them ready to face the last things that are going to happen." Janelle leaned on his shoulder in approval. Her heart was warmed by her understanding of their mutual commitment to Jesus. This was more than she had dreamed of in a guy.

The group continued praying for help and guidance and for the people suffering from all the disasters. They knew individuals in their families that needed help, both physically and spiritually. Prayer ascended for all the families in area churches that were grieving over the many deaths of elderly grandparents and senior members of congregations. They made covenants with the Lord, planning to call and visit the ones they knew to be in need of spiritual nurture. They became aware that more students were slipping quietly into the room. Coach Weldon held the door and kept it from shutting loudly. He had an ear to the praying students and an eye on the hallway as word spread about the presence of the Holy Spirit. His desire was to pray and forget everything else and soak in the experience. It was a prayer answered after years of teaching. His inward motto was to teach spiritual heath as a higher priority than physical health. Many of the students knew of his priorities and looked to him for advice and direction. Today he was thrilled over the answer to his daily prayer for his students; it was a dream come true. Several teachers slipped into the music room. As was their custom, they stood next to the door like it was lunch hour or study hall. They were taken by the intensity of word and thought in the prayers. They couldn't remain detached. They slipped to their knees next to the petitioners and wrapped arms around shoulders and clasped hands with others. Soon the boundaries between student or teacher or leader dissolved, and they found themselves equally taking hold of the Holy Spirit's promise of where there are two or three gathered together.

After a while it became apparent that keeping one's eyes closed was unnecessary. They talked to God respectfully while sharing their thoughts on what needed to be done. Eyes glistened with joyful thanksgiving as the conversation included Jesus whose Spirit was in attendance. The prayers were not artificial or formulaic. If someone had accidentally entered the room they would have thought it to be a close-knit group planning a massive campaign to inform the world of danger. If the entrants took time to listen, they would be overwhelmed with the words directed to an unseen but very real and present Savior, ethereal vibrations would penetrate their souls with awesome splendor. These kids were in connection with the King of the universe. They were about to turn their world upside down with compassion for one another. Before they knew it, another and then another bell sounded. The school day was coming to an end.

Their prayer conversation with God then took a turn toward asking for His help that evening. They wanted His direction in telling their families and their neighborhood friends about the spiritual dangers ahead. The entreaties were just as fervent, just as bold. Then someone quietly, barely audibly, started to sing. The words were from an old song: "There's a sweet, sweet Spirit in this place, and I know that it's the Spirit of the Lord…"

* * * * * *

Mike called home to tell Rachael he had made the appointment with the neurologist. He added an extra thought. "Sweetheart, I've been thinking about the twins and the current situation. I really want them to focus on what's happening with the President's program—"

"Me, too."

"Well, maybe it would be wise not to tell the kids about me until we know more. This would allow them to process the moment more. I have to admit, the thought of tumors competes with my concentration on the transpiring spiritual events. My disappointment over these brain tumors makes me have to fight harder to think about fulfilling prophecy. I'm in a battle to stay on top. I wouldn't want the twins to forget the moment by getting their attention diverted like me."

"Perhaps you're right; I've been praying for you every spare moment," she explained.

"Thank you, Sweetheart. We'll tell them after the appointment. I've got to go."

"Same here, I'm praying for you. Love you."

"Love you, too."

Rachael left an hour earlier than usual to pick up the twins from the academy; she wanted to stop by a friend's. For years, she and Rochelle had been friends at church. Before Rochelle's breakup with her husband, their families had shared Sabbath dinners together, gone on afternoon hikes, and camped together during summer breaks. Now it was awkward. Anytime she was with Rochelle, the conversation was always on the divorce and the next sequel in the saga of the fight. It seemed to Rachael that the fight was one-sided. Her ex was not as antagonistic as Rochelle. He was always reacting to the newest court action that Rochelle could manufacture. Rachael had to force herself to continue being her friend. She and Mike had liked her ex when they were family friends. Chris had always been the opposite of a deadbeat dad. He set up an automatic payment for child support through his work and attempted to visit his daughter as regularly as possible from out of state. As Rachael listened to Rochelle's complaints she could see the exaggerations and the intensity of her hatred for Chris. She was convinced that Rochelle secretly regretted her divorce and was still in love with him, even though she was remarried to a non-believing husband.

Today Rachael visited Rochelle with great hopes. The turn of national events must have had an impact on her friend. This was a missionary visit in which she hoped that the conversation would be about spiritual issues. She drove into the driveway and saw her friend waving from the door. Rachael had called ahead. They met on the sidewalk, exchanged greetings, hugged, and strode arm-in-arm into the house. This was a good start for the final product she was aiming to achieve.

"We haven't talked since … How long has it been … a month? Two months?" Rochelle began. "Please, have a seat."

"I'm sorry to say it's been at least two months, maybe a little longer. I came b…"

"That means I've got plenty to tell you. So much has happened. Sweet little Loren is beginning to see Chris for what he really is—a creep! I've been trying to break it to her a little at a time so it won't overwhelm her. Now, she doesn't want to see him. And it's driving him wild. Ha! He drives all the way here and she rejects him at the door. It's a waste of his time and gas. And then his support check was two days late, so I asked my lawyer to file a petition for him to be in contempt of court…"

Rachael had to quell her thoughts in order not to react to what Rochelle was doing to Loren's father. She would have liked to make a few carefully phrased statements about how it was Chris's right to have quality time with his eight-year-old daughter. However, she was here on a

She was here on a much greater mission. She wanted her friend to see the dimensions of a world in cosmic conflict.

much greater mission. She wanted her friend to see the dimensions of a world in cosmic conflict. Three souls were at the cusp of a decision that had to be made. She knew Rochelle understood the truth and could respond to her entreaties. Loren was an innocent child tied to her mother's lack of spiritual commitment. Her husband, Gary, would need to be instructed in what was at stake—introduced to a loving Savior. He would be the hardest to reach in the shortened time frame. Rachael's thoughts raced over these dismal details while Rochelle babbled on. She missed the question,

"… don't you think so too?"

Normally, Rachael might have pretended to agree not knowing the question. But the topic was always her divorce and supercharged with negativity. She apologized. "I'm sorry again. My mind drifted to my worries as you were talking about yours. What did you say?"

"I was wondering if you agree with me about how much Chris needs to be taught a lesson."

"Roch, maybe Chris has been hurt enough. He doesn't get to visit his daughter like he wants to and he probably is still hurting from the divorce. You know, he came to us to apologize for the divorce and explain that our time together would never be the same. At that time, we could tell he really loved you and Loren. So, maybe it's time to let things go. He's starting all over again. You have to too."

"I can't start all over again. He keeps coming around bothering Loren and me. I want him out of my...and Loren's life permanently!" The emphasis Rochelle put into her words made the moment afterward seem inordinately quiet. Rachael sought to fill the unsupported silence.

"I'm worried. Not just worried, really worried."

Rochelle should not ignore the statement the second time it was brought up; it would be out of taste. However, she linked it to her own addiction of thought. "You're not worried about Chris, are you? Because if you are..."

"My worries are about a completely different problem." And without hesitating she plowed a deep furrow into her field of concern. She needed to plant desperate seeds of alarm in her distracted friend. "Our lives, as we know them, are going to abruptly end! I'm not sure I am up for the things we are going to face."

"What are you talking about?" Rochelle asked.

"All the things we believe in for future events before the end, are almost in the present. We are facing the final conflict. I'm here in your living room because I'm worried for me, my family, my kids, my husband, and for my good friend Rochelle."

"What things? Tell me, please."

"Did you see the President's speech last night? The State of the Union?"

"Are you kidding? All that political drivel? I never watch that stuff."

"I don't watch it either, but last night was different. There is a call for national unity in religion. The government is selling and giving out bracelets that we're all supposed to wear to show we are on the national bandwagon. The President is trying to achieve one nation under God. The bracelets have identifiers embedded within them that can track everyone, control bank accounts, and perform every function people need to live. The bad thing is that to not wear one of these devices is to show that you are not concerned about this country or the people in need, or the commonality of faith. This is what our pastors and evangelists have been talking about. It is what the Spirit of Prophecy is warning us about. The Bible prophecies indicate this kind of movement at the end of time, where governments will dictate belief. Soon the other events will unfold. Rochelle, we have to get ready."

"I'm taking a little vacation from church right now. I want to get all this mess with Chris resolved. I don't have time for secret sisters and women's ministries retreats. I've got a daughter to protect; besides, whatever the government gets interested in takes years to enact and countless discussions, pro and con. I think you're overly worried. Anyway, I've got this idea that you can help me with. If you could come to court with me and testify to the truth about Chris' behavior with Loren, it might really help."

"You know it might be months before that even gets to court. In the meantime we have to think about our salvation. What if this is it? We have been told the final events will move swiftly. What if things move so fast that everything is too far progressed when your vacation from church is done? You could be lost."

"I'm not going to get lost. God helps those who help themselves. Right now, I'm helping my daughter. God respects a mother's work. He'll understand."

"Rochelle, I want you to see what's going on. Could you promise me that you'll watch the things that are happening? Those bracelets the President wants everyone to wear have little tiny chips that read your DNA. If it becomes mandatory for everyone to have some form of identification on their person, please sit up and take notice. The President said that eventually he will take the chip that is in the solidarity bracelet and have it put in his watch band or key chain to be with him always. I suppose that is so it can never be lost. Do you know what that means? It means everyone that does that will be marked. It already is being shopped as the most humane thing to do in the light of all these disasters. If Gary comes home with these devices for you and Loren, don't use them—"

"Don't get me started on Gary. It's like he's in his own world and I don't exist. We had an argument the other day and he went on about Chris as if I was having an affair or something."

Rachael couldn't help but think that Gary's suspicions were the same as hers. She had to stay on track and not get pulled into a discussion about her husband. "Roch, I'm going to need to go pick up the kids, but I would like to have prayer for you."

"Maybe next time. I'm not in the mood. I'm angry. When I get to talking about the idiot Chris, I tend to get angry. I don't feel like praying."

"I pray for you every day."

"I know, thank you. You're a doll. Think about helping to testify in court."

* * * * *

Rochelle's mood permeated Rachael's resolve. As she drove to the school she felt powerless to help her friends, her sister, and her husband. They each had their problems and their own arenas of concern. Mike's needs were different than the others. She didn't worry about his connection with the Savoir, but his situation weighed on her mind burdening her with trepidation. Then with the others they just didn't seem to be aware, as in one case, or not concerned about the events unfolding about them, in the other cases. It made her doubt the convictions she had about the speech. She had to ask herself if she was overreacting. Could bracelets just be an innocent method of raising money for charity? It would be embarrassing to get all mobilized to march into the kingdom, tell your friends that they could be missing out because the second coming was weeks, maybe days, away from happing, and then find out that the world was continuing on in its blithe manner and no mark of the beast was being imposed on anyone. As she contemplated the alternatives, she couldn't bring herself to believe that assuming the status quo was best. Being ready at all times could not be a bad thing, even if it meant that friends thought her excessive. She didn't think that she had played the alarmist to the level of a fanatic. Still, she felt defeated and defeat can drag one down. She prayed, wondering with God if she was reacting too soon. Her prayer caused her to feel even more defeated because she explained to Him how she had hopes for her sister, neighbor, and church friend. She questioned herself and the words she used. She asked Him if it was possible that her hopes for them were tied to her own possibly defective interpretations of the President's speech. Perhaps she was making too much of it and applying it to her constant desire to see spiritual transformation in those to whom she felt called to witness.

She pulled into the parking lot and waited inside the car, alone with her thoughts. She didn't always pick up the twins. They drove the family car when she didn't have plans. Today, her thwarted plans weighed on her and she didn't get out of the car to talk, like the other parents; she thought and prayed. It startled her when there was a rap on the window. She rolled down the window to greet Charlene.

"Look, something's different," Charlene began without preamble. Her finger pointed toward the soccer field. Rachael's eyes followed the direction of the index finger on Charlene's right hand. A thin layer of snow dusted the grass on the playing field. Scattered across the field were students in clusters of threes and fours, with arms linking the small groups together. They stood on the cold turf heads down and unmoving. Other students were exiting the school, some to cars, others to stand and watch. "Is this Week of Prayer? I haven't heard that it was."

"No, I think this is a response to what happened last night." Rachael got out of the car to step a little closer and get a better look. Her concentration was interrupted.

"Mom, can I drive? Is that why you got out of the car?" Jason was approaching from the opposite direction. He was completely unaware of the scene near the gym.

"What happened last night?" Charlene questioned. Rachael was split on whom she wanted to answer first.

"Jason, can you explain to Mrs. Philips what happened last night?" She sought to involve Jason in the conversation between her and Charlene. Then she thought of a better question, "No, better yet, can you tell us what's happening on the field?" She pointed.

He looked, took in the scene, and shrugged his shoulders. "I don't know."

"Charlene, they're praying and I'm wondering if it has something to do with the President's speech last night," she explained.

"I didn't watch anything last night. Little Bonnie was sick with the flu and I had my hands full with the family. What did the President say?"

Jason decided to answer. "The President is all excited about bringing this nation under one God and one faith to help all the victims of the disasters. He's wanting everyone to wear special bands to show they're … well, ah, in agreement. It seems like that's all the teachers could talk about today." His gaze shifted over to the soccer pitch where the groups were reluctantly parting, hesitant to let go of hands. Janelle could be seen arm-in-arm with Darin, walking and smiling broadly as they came toward the cars.

"How can that be related to what just happened?" Charlene asked.

"I don't know for sure, but it might be a response like I had. I can't stop praying and asking God for His help. I've been trying to reach friends with the message all day today, on the phone and in person," Rachael emphasized.

"This sounds serious. What else did the President say?" Charlene's eyes darted back and forth between the two standing before her. Rachael didn't wait for Jason's explanation.

"What the President is asking from the nation sounds like it could be the beginning of the end. The band Jason spoke of is a mini tracking device that can read DNA and can control bank accounts and other things. He is pushing for everyone to get them to demonstrate their solidarity by wearing—"

"What I said!" Jason kicked in.

"—arm band bracelets. And it appears he wants denominations to come together into one church. What he really wants is to get God's blessing back for this country by calling everyone back to God. And—"

"Mom! You'll never believe what happened today!" Janelle sounded out of breath as she was running up to the car with Darin in tow behind her. They were holding hands. Rachael shifted her attention because it meant answering her and Charlene's original question. "The Holy Spirit came to school today!"

"What?"

"We were praying and then we could feel the presence of the Holy Spirit. It was beautiful, so awesomely beautiful! He's with us now, right now, Mom!" Janelle's radiant face, coupled with Darin's equally happy countenance, along with his enthusiastic nodding in agreement, sent ripples of confirmation down Rachael's spine. The effect burst outward into goose-bumps all over her body. She had to hug her daughter in celebration. With Janelle still holding on to Darin's hand, it was somewhat awkward so Rachael wrapped her left arm around Darin, whom she had never met before.

"This is wonderful! You have to tell me everything."

"Can it wait until tonight? Darin and I have made plans to visit some of his old high school friends and witness to them. Can I go with him now and we'll catch up later? We have to hurry if we're going to catch them at school."

Rachael had to fight back her natural curiosity about what happened to allow her child to do what any Christian parent would love to see— their offspring involved in mission work. "Yes, yes that would be great. I'll get the news from your brother. Let's have a short prayer for your success." The four bowed in prayer: Rachael, Janelle, Darin, and a surprised Charlene. Jason was already in the driver's seat behind closed windows. "Father in Heaven, we ask you for the victory in the lives of the young people that Darin and Janelle will talk to today. Give them the words to say; let the Holy Spirit work is my prayer. In Jesus' name."

"Yes, Father, give us the words. Thank you for the gift of the Holy Spirit. We feel strong and bold because He is with us now. Amen," Janelle added.

"Mrs. Larsson, I'll have your daughter home as soon as possible. It's a school night. We'll message ahead," Darin assured her.

"Thank you." The two adults watched as the teens hurried to the car. Charlene was still in shock.

"Am I dreaming? I need to talk to my kids to see what happened to them. I hope it's the same. I'll talk to you tomorrow." Charlene dismissed herself and headed for her car where her children would be waiting.

The news, as sketchy as it was, bathed Rachel in a feeling which reversed her negative thoughts of before. If this was the end, there would also be signs of the Holy Spirit working in a powerful manner. Also, the prediction of the youth being involved and finishing the work echoed in her mind. She again felt that the last-day events were upon the world…at least in her little part of it. She entered the passenger side of the car and Jason started immediately to back out of the parking spot.

"Jason, what do you know about what happened at school today?"

"Well, some kids were having a prayer session today and my fifth hour class was empty 'cause the students and teachers were at the music room. I used

> *If this was the end, there would also be signs of the Holy Spirit working in a powerful manner.*

the time to get my current events paper finished. I'm way ahead of schedule on that one. I'll have plenty of time to practice my soccer moves."

"You didn't go to the prayer session?"

"No…It wasn't a required thing so I stayed. Why?"

"Janelle said the Holy Spirit was poured out and they could feel His presence. You didn't hear about it?"

"No."

"You didn't feel anything?"

"No, Ma. I was working on my paper."

Rachael's turbulent ride from friend to friend and then to school with Janelle's great news to Jason's naiveté about the great moment gave her the feeling of being in a rowboat near a windswept shore. She wanted Jason to have experienced the Spirit, and was guarded in her asking him questions because she didn't want to send him on a guilt trip. She quietly asked God for help to know what to say to Jason that would nudge him into investigating the spiritual revival that some of the kids at the academy were experiencing. She could relax into her prayer with her best friend Jesus because Jason was driving. However, she still needed to keep watch while she prayed because it was her son who was driving. Jason was savvy enough not to speed, as he knew it might curtail his precious time behind the wheel, but he did act over-confident. She prayed, remained vigilant, and said little out loud.

CHAPTER 6

Mike was stuck in traffic. He was the last out of the office because he wanted to have another reaffirming talk with George and because he had to catch up on work which had accumulated because of his personal distraction and the news broadcasts. As he sat at the tail end of a long, double left turn lane, he had to admit that he always came home about this time of the evening, later than necessary. Nearly always there was that red sports car making the same turn. Then the silver sedan with the "support our troops" ribbons on the back idled next to his in the other lane. An auto parts pickup truck was sometimes there, but he couldn't see him this evening. Every day he drove home with the same crowd of unknown commuters around him. Without the cars separating them, standing this close together meant someone might strike up a conversation. Under different circumstances these people could be his friends. They would know he was a Christian, perhaps they might even ask him about the President's speech and he could witness to them. It made him think about all the people who might not know what was happening…the hundreds of millions of people that didn't know the issues at stake.

A feeling of dread swept through his heart, *How are these people going to know? When will it become apparent that Jesus' coming is near and they have to avoid the great deception?* These thoughts circulated in his head. He prayed, "Lord, please give us time to get the message out. So many have to hear about the truth. Give me the strength to endure during this time. I am Your servant. In Jesus' name, amen." He was startled into admitting that he wanted to delay God's coming. He found himself in dissonant thought, wishing for God to slow everything down and longing to see the Savior beckon him to soar up to Him in the air. He had to add a postscript to his prayer, "And, Lord, I recognize that in everything Your will must be done." His amen was drowned out in beeps from behind him. The light had changed and he hadn't moved.

* * * * * *

The positives outweighed the negatives. Rachael made herself focus on the great news from school and committed herself to trust the Lord for the rest of her concerns to be met with His grace. She hummed around the kitchen getting dinner ready. She had a lot to share with Mike. Jason gave her a certain amount of disquiet. She questioned if he was uninterested in the prayer session, or if he was totally oblivious to what had happened at the school. She could tell that other students were not in the circle of students affected by the Spirit because of the sideline interest of many observing from the parking lot. Janelle was a highlight in her mind. At this moment, she was witnessing and enjoying companionship with the Holy Spirit. And, Rachael, on the other hand, was humming around the kitchen performing routine tasks as if the world was not on the brink of chaos. She stopped. Again, her mind confronted her with the overwhelming conviction that life seemed the same. Her familiar kitchen, home, and family had not changed. Her basic schedule was the same. She was doing and acting very much like nothing was different. No police officers were at the door demanding identification and running her family off to jail for nonconformity. She wasn't in danger. She wasn't afraid. She was humming *Marvelous Infinite Matchless Grace*…In two more days the Sabbath would begin and they would have family vespers and then get ready for church the next morning. The life she was leading was unchanged. *How long will this way of life continue?* She had to ask herself. Did she need to keep their lives as normal as possible or should she act differently? How should she act if she did change to something different? When should she make the change and what would the change be? She had already gone out of her way to tell her friends and try to get them to see things differently. She wondered if she had "jumped the queue," as a British acquaintance had said so many times when she befriended her in the one year she spent at Newbold College. The new thought catapulted her into determination to call her friend in England and find out what she thought about the turn of events here in the States. She started making calculations to figure out the time difference and the best time to call.

Meanwhile, Jason was in the backyard practicing his shots on goal. The grass was still wet from the afternoon's warmth and the melted dusting of snow from the night before. He wore his cleats to keep from slipping on the grass. The extra time from the canceled class enabled him to get the practice he needed. He was a little put out when his mom called him in for dinner.

"Don't forget to wash your hands before you set the table. Your father will be here any minute."

"If Dad's not here yet, why did you call me in so soon? I was just getting the hang of my left foot shot-on-goal."

"Your father just called to tell me he's about five minutes away. He should be here any minute." As if on cue, the side door opened and Mike walked in. He kissed Rachael and greeted Jason.

"Where's Janelle?" he asked.

"She's out with Darin witnessing." Rachael couldn't help watching his reaction with anticipation and delight. She had planned to drop this bomb on him as soon as he walked in the door.

"Witnessing?" His eyebrows shot upward.

"Yes, isn't it wonderful? I've got lots to tell you about what happened today. I know this sounds corny, but you'll need to sit down for this, and supper too."

"Okay, just let me hang up my coat and … Darin? Who's Darin? Is he a nice guy?"

"That's Janelle's new boyfriend. She's really into him," Jason answered. Mike momentarily looked at Jason and then with concern at his wife.

"I met him today. He seems nice and assured me he would have her back early because it's a school night."

Dinner started with prayer and then Mike had trouble eating because he forgot to chew as he listened. His day was clouded with worry over the overbearing attitudes that some at the office exhibited towards those who didn't seem enthusiastic about national solidarity on the subject of religion. The news that the school had a season of prayer attended by the Holy Spirit lifted his spirits in exponential proportions. He needed this boon of encouragement. He thrilled at his daughter's sudden urge to witness and looked with concern at his son's lack of involvement in the discussion. Jason was gulping his food down like water to a thirsty camel. He was about to ask his son how the revival at school had touched him when Jason hastily put his dish in the sink.

"Dad, Mom, can I practice a little more out back until you're ready for family devotions?" It surprised them that Jason could sit through the conversation and not be excited about the subject. They nodded their approval and Jason crashed out the door to practice, using the light from the back porch. The time together would allow them to speak to each other more distinctly about their emotional impressions of the day. Rachael's attempts at witnessing were first on the docket. Mike commiserated with his wife's attempts with minimal results. He encouraged her with thoughts that her words may have had an effect she didn't see. He then made an observation.

"Honey, things are starting to add up. The disasters by land and sea, earthquakes, wars between nations, and the war the Islamic terrorists are waging against us. The President's call for national religious unity is only a small part of the total picture. Then the fact that our academy is in the midst of a spiritual revival with kids running out to witness. We have been told that the Spirit will be poured out in the last days and the youth will finish the work. Things are starting to add up."

"Yes, I thought of that too. It thrilled me when I heard about it. It still gives me goose bumps. But is this just a local phenomenon? Is the Spirit being poured out elsewhere? I haven't heard," she wondered.

"I guess we can find out. All we have to do is call some of our school friends who live in other cities," Mike answered.

"I'm planning on calling my friend, Molly, in England. We spent so much time talking together about the differences in our culture. I really wanted to catch up on things with her anyway. The best time to catch her is late tonight when it's morning over there."

"That could get you a perspective on what's happening overseas. I think I'll call Rick; he's in Montana teaching in one of our schools up there. Maybe we'll find that this is bigger than just us."

"I wish it was happening in Jason's life like it is in Janelle's. He seems to be missing what it is. It's like he doesn't know or care."

"I noticed," Mike said introspectively, then added, "We'll pray that he does." The two concerned parents clasped hands and prayed for their children. Then they cleaned off the table, washed the dishes, which they usually left until after devotions, and then called Jason in for spiritual time together. After their family prayer, Mike excused himself to go into the study to call Rick. A few moments later, Rachael slipped in to watch the conversation. Rick was excited. He explained that the faculty had an early morning prayer together before school. And the classes seemed to all gravitate towards the subject of religious freedom in light of the State of the Union Address. A couple of the classes ended in genuine intercessory prayer where students were trying to make amends for sins they committed. It looked like two mini-revivals. Other classrooms were animated in their discussions, but didn't gravitate towards prayer like the previous two. He said the teachers met afterward to compare notes and had a season of prayer for themselves. The prayer circle of teachers felt the Spirit working with them and they grew overpoweringly confident that their prayers would be answered. He couldn't keep from thinking and praying about the experience.

Mike and Rachael shared with him the news from Twin Feather Lake Academy. They rejoiced in the news and had prayer together over the vid-link. They were in the midst of saying their goodbyes when they heard Janelle coming in the front door. They hurried to greet her and thank Darin for his help. They wondered if he would come in or just drive away in the car after dropping her off. They needn't worry because they were standing in the living room facing each other and holding both hands.

"Hello, I'm Mike."

"Ah, Dad, this is Darin. Darin this is my dad. You've already met my mom."

"Nice to see you again. How did it go?" Rachael asked.

"Well, it wasn't easy, but we...Can we sit down? We've been standing a lot."

"Okay, lets." They moved to the sofa and chairs. Janelle and Darin didn't hesitate to sit close and hold hands.

"We went to Darin's old school—the high school where he went last year. We met some of his old friends and started to talk to them. That part was easy but, except when his old girlfriend showed up, then it was, you know, ah, awkward."

"Janelle handled that like a pro and introduced herself to her and they became friends," Darin complimented.

"I wouldn't say friends, friends. It was more like an uneasy truce friends." Janelle could see the polite stares on her folks' faces as they listened to her preamble, so she decided to get down to answering her mother's question. "They were like surprised to see us and at first it was Darin catching up with his friends. Then we went to the Dunkin' Donuts® shop down the street and talked there. The place was packed and we had to stand at these tall tables. The witnessing came as easy as anything. Right, Darin? It was easy getting into the subject?"

"Yes, sorta. After talking about a bunch of, you know, regular stuff, Jeremy asked me how it was at my new school. So I told them about how when we prayed today the Holy Spirit came and joined us. They all got kinda quiet, but they listened. Some of my friends aren't Christians and some are. But they listened. We told them how it felt and how wonderful it was. Then my friend Jeremy, who's a Christian, said, 'Do you always pray at your school?' I told him that we do before every class and sometimes at the end of class, but today was different because we prayed for several hours…"

"They couldn't believe that we would pray for several hours, but our answer was that once you feel the Holy Spirit, you don't want to stop," Janelle explained.

"What happened after that was amazing! You tell them, Janie," Darin said. The fact that he had called her by a nickname barely registered with Mike and Rachael. They wanted to know what happened next because the two teens were animated with enthusiasm.

"Several wanted to know how it felt. And we said 'wonderful, of course,' but Darin added, 'He's here with us now.' And that really blew them away. They were looking at us with surprise and doubt and belief and…well, they were confused. And then Jeremy said something really surprising to us. He said, 'I can see it. You look different, like you're sunburnt.' He said exactly that, 'sunburnt.' I looked at Darin and it dawned on me that he did look different, well, like he had been at the beach all day."

"Janie did too. It was the first time we noticed it," Darin added. Mike and Rachael were sitting on the front edge of their chairs leaning forward. The teens were definitely radiant with energy which they thought was related to success and infatuation with each other and the story. They could be excused from not seeing it as it was winter and the two had just come in from the cool night air.

"Several of the kids wanted to know more and some made excuses that they had to go. It was a smaller group after they left," Janelle said.

"I know some of the ones who stayed weren't Christians," Darin explained.

"Jeremy was the one that asked most of the questions. He asked why we were praying so much. And Darin said because of what's happening in the world with all the disasters and earthquakes. He explained to them about the prophecies in the Bible where Jesus said there would be earthquakes and famines and wars. They agreed with him. He said we were praying because we are near to when Jesus is coming back to earth."

"That's when they started to talk about all kinds of things like the rapture and the bottomless pit and how the Jews are going to have a second chance, and…One kid was saying that Russia or some evil power to the north was going to attack on horses and the blood would flow from all the dead as high as the horse's bridle. We didn't know what to say to all that. Other teens we didn't know heard them and gathered around us. It was awkward, because they too were adding some crazy things about dispensations and Armageddon with tanks and airplanes and stuff. We let them talk and then we said what we believed would happen. They got quiet again because it was so different. Some shook their heads at us. We explained about the mark of the beast, how it would come in the name of Christian unity. That the real battle of Armageddon was a battle of faith between good and evil—a battle in the heart."

"Did they believe you?" Mike asked.

"It was hard to tell. Jeremy and Sandra were very interested. They asked most of the questions. Most were kinda quiet listening like. Then one kid with sports glasses, I don't remember his name…"

"Bert."

"Yeah, Bert said something scary. He said, 'You guys seem to be going against the system. The President wants us to get together to bring back God's blessing. If you think that's the wrong way to go, then you are going to spoil it for everyone else. My father says that anyone that doesn't join us is against us, like the enemy.' I was so surprised," Janelle said.

"It threw a blanket over the discussion. The only ones that talked after that were Janie and me. It was like the others were afraid."

"What did you say?" Rachael asked.

"We told them they have to watch what is happening. If this unity thing starts taking away our freedom of religion then it can't be from God. God wants us to choose Him freely, not be forced to have faith in Him. Then we talked about the false coming of Jesus. That Satan will try to make it look real but it won't be real, and everyone, almost, will be deceived. Then Sandra asked how Jesus is supposed to come and we said from above, in the air, with a loud trumpet blast and lots of angels. It will happen after there will be a death penalty for anyone that doesn't agree with the false Jesus who came already. We didn't mention about the Sunday/Sabbath issue because we thought that might be too much for them to grasp right away. Then Jeremy asked 'Why would anyone want to disagree with the false Jesus if he's pretending to be Jesus? Wouldn't he try to do nice things?' We agreed that he would try to do nice things like miracles and such, but he would also set up false worship and require everyone to worship him without exception. We told him that that doesn't sound like Jesus," Janelle explained.

"Bert told everyone that they should not listen to us. Pretty much most of the kids left after that. Jeremy and Sandra stayed. We ordered some pastries and talked some more. We talked until a little while ago and then had prayer. We think they might be coming to church this Sabbath."

"That's wonderful! You two did a fantastic job!" Rachael reacted.

"I agree we should have prayer and thank the Lord and His Holy Spirit for helping you guys today," Mike directed. They then bowed in prayer. They each took turns praising God for His working through them. After prayer, Rachael said they must be hungry for some good food and then they went into the kitchen to eat. Mike explained about his call to Rick and it reconfirmed to all that the Spirit was working in other places besides their home town. It was late when Darin left.

* * * * * *

Janelle and her mother talked for what seemed like hours. Rachael was going to stay up so she could get Molly in England at a decent hour. Janelle had a lot to share with her mom. They sat side by side on her bed, discussing the events of the day. Janelle shared the fact that she didn't want to go to sleep because that would mean that this wonderful day would be over.

"I wouldn't want to go to sleep either, what with the experience you had of praying and having the Spirit be there in such a mighty way."

"I'm afraid I might lose the Spirit, you know what I mean?"

"Why would you lose Him?"

"Because when we prayed He came after we confessed our sins. If I sin and He leaves me, I won't know if I am genuinely sorry."

"Every time you ask, He answers. Jesus promised to be with you always."

"But..."

"But what?"

"Well, it's really funny somehow. Is it possible for a person to want Jesus to come and not to come at the same time? Is it a sin to want Him to wait?"

"Why would you not want Him to come?"

"I ... well, it's strange. You know how you try to figure out how your life is going to be? You try to guess about what your husband will look like and how he will act; will he be an Adventist Christian? What will my children look like? Where would we live?"

"Yes, I do. I did the same thing when I was your age."

"I always thought it would take until I was in college before I might find the right guy. But, today was really special. Darin and I worked perfectly together. He's so dedicated. If it wasn't for him I would not have known about the prayer group in the music room. At his old school we were a team—like missionaries going to a foreign land…ah, school. Oh, Mom, we both want Jesus to come and we want others to be ready. But, secretly in my heart I want to know what it would be like to marry him and work for Jesus together. If Jesus comes soon will that happen? Is it possible, you know, to be married in heaven?"

Rachael couldn't answer that question with a simple yes or no. She remembered the text in Luke where Jesus said there would be no marrying and giving in marriage after the resurrection. It bothered her to think that she wouldn't be Mike's wife in heaven. She knew that marriage was created by God in the Garden. If God created marriage before the fall would He then stop it after the earth was made new? There were arguments on either side of the issue. She didn't know which position she should take with Janelle. In the moment she took to think of these two conflicting thoughts, she decided to give her daughter the palliative answer. "Honey, anything God has ready for us in heaven will be far better than we can imagine here on earth. When your father and I talked about this one time, he said something very sweet. He said, 'If I can't be married to you in heaven, then at least I'll hang around you all the time.' We'll have to trust Him to make our lives complete and beautiful."

"I hear you, Mom. We'll have to trust Him."

"You need your sleep. You better get some rest for tomorrow."

"I'll try, but I think I'll have trouble falling asleep with this great big smile on my face."

* * * * * *

Rachael left her daughter and went to the office to make the call to England. While the connections clicked faintly in the background, she thought of how much she would like to reconnect with her friends from Newbold College. Molly's face and upper torso materialized before her on the desk. It almost seemed real, the connection was so good.

"Hello, my friend. What reason brings you to call me at this hour of the morning? It must be really late for you."

"I was thinking about you today and with all that's going on, I decided not to put it off. I miss my friends from Newbold. How are you doing?"

"Just ducky, I suppose."

"John and the kids doing fine?"

"Yes, we're all right. Can't say that for the country in general, but we're alright. I had to stand in queue for a loaf of bread yesterday. Took most of an hour."

"Is the drought still going on? Is it that bad?"

"'Tis been going on for over three years now, with no let up. Our rivers are mostly dried up without ta' rain."

"It's getting that bad?"

"Yes, it tis. One of the MPs made a statement last week that working families should have priority and be able to jump the queue for bread ahead of those who are not working. He received rounds of criticism for saying that. Enough about our problems; how are Mike and the twins?"

"They're great. Janelle experienced a revival today, I mean yesterday, in the school and went out witnessing. Mike talked to a friend in one of our academies in Montana and there's a revival going on up there as well. I'm wondering if you have heard of the Spirit moving in your country."

"Yes, I have, a little one up in Grantham, at the press. Jenny's up there now."

"Jenny Cummings?"

"Jenny Rutherford—she's married now."

"What's happening there? I'd like to know."

"You can call her. Do you have her number? I rang her up a fortnight ago, so I know the number is current. Here it is now." Molly typed in the number and it showed on a small screen at the bottom of the image. Rachael hit a button and the number was stored in memory. "What do you think is going on? Revivals in different places at the same time; do you think they're related?"

"I think so."

"Why?"

"Well, the timing is interesting. The President calls for national unity on religion and wants everyone to wear a tracking computer device on their arms in the form of a bracelet, sort of like it could be the mark of the beast. You know, the Spirit of Prophecy predicts the United States will lead other nations to worship the beast and the false prophet. Anyway, this happens and then there are revivals the very next day in our schools. I think it could be the beginning of the end, don't you?"

"Rachael, darling, I don't know. I don't want to rain on your parade, but neither do I want you to be running around Robinson's barn with me unnecessarily. We talked about this when we were roomies, remember? Some of us here don't look at Mrs. White's writings in the same way you do in the States. Many believe the way you do, but I, for one, can't see it that way."

"You've read *The Great Controversy*, I know you have," Rachael pointed out.

"Yes, I have…Can I be honest with you?" Molly asked.

"Always."

"It seems to me that Mrs. White writes like the whole world revolves around the United States. Jesus' predictions for the last days are for the world, not just for the United States, you see. She's a good spiritual writer, I'll give her that. She appeals to the heart and the mind. You can tell she's inspired when she writes in *Steps to Christ* and in the *Desire of Ages*, but when it comes to the prediction of America being the center of…well, I can't go along with it. I hope that doesn't spoil it for you."

"Molly, I too believe that the predictions of Jesus are for the whole world. I also believe Mrs. White wrote for the whole world. She said there would be disasters and famines and droughts and she said that Jesus' return would be after Satan attempts to mimic His return. His players will work great signs and wonders in the heavens and on the earth. They, or he, will even make fire come down from heaven to copy the work of Elijah. If something like that happens, you'll have to take notice even if it happens in America."

"I guess I would have to, because I have an open mind, but there has to be a global element to it."

"I agree with that and everything else that happens. It must be universal in scope to include all of humanity."

"That's my point exactly."

"I called you because I wanted to know if there is an outpouring of the Holy Spirit in other places. What you say about Grantham kind of confirms that. Have you heard of anything else happening?"

"A friend at church last Sabbath mentioned that something was happening in Tyrifjord, our school in Norway. The kids took an unscheduled holiday to witness in the major cities there. They claim the Spirit moved them and the teachers are in agreement. Jenny might know a little more. There are some Norwegians on the staff there. Ask her when you ring her up."

"I will. But before we sign off, I would like for us to have prayer together." The two friends prayed together with hands extended toward each other. It was virtual reality. Rachael ended the link and entered the number for Jenny. The picture wavered a brief second and then corrected to a clear focus.

"Rachael, what a pleasant surprise!" She was obviously standing behind a kitchen counter with a large bowl of flour and a bottle of milk partially visible in the picture. Flour covered her arms up to her elbows. "You're just in time to help me make scones. You're up early this morning for your time zone."

"I haven't been to bed yet. I'm kind of on a mission for information. Are you making sweet scones or cheese scones? The sweet scones at Newbold were heavenly."

"You'll have to taste mine, they're better. Today I'm making cheese scones because bread is short. What information are you after?"

"My daughter experienced a revival at her academy yesterday and another academy in Montana had a similar experience. I heard that Grantham Press had one, too. Is that true?"

"Yes, it was truly wonderful. It happened during morning worship for the workers. My husband came home that day all excited and filled with the Spirit. They didn't get a lot of work done that day because there was a lot of repentance and restoration going on about the place. My husband is a manager there and the people are some of the nicest you'll e'er meet. It seemed strange for them to be asking for forgiveness when they are great Christians in the first place. As they prayed, they felt something. None of the shouting, jumping around, speaking in tongues, mind you, just a gentle feeling of…Harold said it was a feeling of comfortable acceptance. We prayed and I felt it too as it filled me. It made me want to look around to see if He was there."

"That sounds absolutely wonderful."

"It is. There are plans for the workers to go around to the area churches to spread the word. The press is paying for their travel expenses. We're hopeful the revival can spread."

"Jenny, are there any churches in the area experiencing special manifestations of the Holy Spirit?"

"No, not churches, not yet anyway. Wait until next Sabbath; we're hopeful. Last week word came in from Norway that the students at Tyrifjord were out witnessing. The word came with a large order for literature to be used. They were running out of message sheets and e-cards for our books. They weren't selling them like they normally would. They were giving them out higgledee piggledee. They wanted to get the word out with no cost to the readers. There's a good portion of the Spirit being used there. Arvid and Ragnar, who work here, are from Norway. They've been singing the news and purposely attending and praying at every opportunity. Some say they might have been the spark that got the press workers started here. I'm sorry. I'm going on and on, aren't I?"

"You should! It's exciting. This is what we want as a world church. I think the end is coming."

"It most certainly is, deary."

> *This is what we want as a world church. I think the end is coming.*

CHAPTER 7

Like Janelle, Rachael laid in bed with a large smile, unable and unwilling to go to sleep. She felt a little guilty for being happy because of what she heard from England while her husband's health was in question. Sleepy tired, she made herself get up to get the family breakfast. Despite the lack of rest, she had buoyancy to her every move. She communed with God in her heart as she set the table and filled tall tumblers with orange juice.

Janelle came down the stairs like she was on a tilted trampoline. They embraced like they would never see each other again. Her enthusiasm had not diminished and possibly had accelerated. She wanted to tell Rachael about the personal study she had that morning. Rachel listened with joy in abundance and then gave her short synopsis of her late-night/early-morning talks with her friends in England … the same talk she had with Mike before he stepped into the shower. Janelle was thrilled that the Spirit was moving in different parts of the world.

Jason was next down the stairs with a question, "Mom, are you going to need the car today or are you driving us again?"

"I think you'll drive today because I've got some catching up to do. You two be careful."

"I've got claim for the drive to school. You can drive home, unless Darin's going to take you somewhere to do some smoochy, smoochy," Jason spoke quickly.

"I don't think that is first on our list, although I wouldn't mind if he did. Our absolute priority is keeping the Spirit with us and spreading the good news about Jesus' soon return," she answered without a hint of resentment. This surprised Jason and it almost registered on his face. His jibe hadn't worked. It bounced off Janelle like bullets off Superman.

"Hey, everyone, real quick. Listen to this. The President is in a news conference and he's making more statements. I back recorded it." Mike rushed into the kitchen with his Onyx at full volume.

~ ~ ~ ~ ~ ~

…The island countries need our help. Global warming is accelerating melting icecaps three times faster than anticipated. The result is the oceans are rising and submerging these tiny nations. I have directed our navy to rescue them before it's too late. Most of their arable land is underwater and the inhabitants are living in their fishing boats or on the sides of small mountains and extinct volcanoes. I've instructed Immigration and Naturalization to allow these climate refugees into our country without the normal protocols. They will starve or drown otherwise.

I call upon our citizens to pray that God will restore these peoples' homelands. God the Creator can reverse these trends in the environment and can restore these countries to their original states. Pray and He will answer. In the meantime, please give donations to help with the cost of temporary housing until we can absorb them into our economy or get them back to their countries when God answers our prayers. It is our duty as Christians to help them and introduce them to the Christian faith. They're mostly Islamic. Our action in this will be an example to the world and to the radical factions that think we are the Great Satan. We shall teach the radical elements in Islam a lesson in humane treatment of the unfortunate, something they don't provide for their very own brothers and sisters.

I have called world religious leaders to a summit to discuss a coalition of churches. From Gallup surveys recently conducted, the vast majority of this nation's citizenry agree with me that we need to drop the barriers that divide our faith groups. We need to show the un-Christian people of this world that first, we are one faith, one Lord, one baptism, and second, nations thrive when they worship the true Christian God.

My next comments are directed to the non-Christian communities: the Islamic, Buddhist, and Jewish communities. I have asked your leaders to this summit as well. All faith groups should come under one umbrella of God's protection. We all worship the same God. It is important for you to under-stand that our nation's survival is dependent upon the majority of believers. I urge you to get on board now, join the prayer groups, and put on the solidarity bracelet. Let it be seen so everyone knows you support the cause of a righteous nation under one God. Your lives, your prosperity, your continued American dream, depend on it.

To the Christian majority, I entreat you to accept these branches of faith. Let them be grafted into the tree of life along with us. The fruit will be, once again, the blessings of a benevolent God.

Now I'll entertain questions. Yes…

~ ~ ~ ~ ~ ~

Mike paused the recording. "I think we need to get to school and to work. But I have one observation of what we just heard. It sounded almost like a threat to the Muslims, Buddhists, and Jews. This makes me even more nervous." The family silently agreed, each in their own thought world, nodding heads in agreement. "We go to work and school with a new determination to be ready for His soon coming. Let's pray for His contin-ued presence in our lives today." Mike led the family in prayer, gathered his satchel, and went to the car. The new day had begun. The twins left moments later, leaving Rachael in her kitchen.

The living room beckoned with its more comfortable seats. Morning sunlight heated the room like a downy comforter in winter. It illuminated the cheery paintings and décor of the room. The room was a refuge, a sanctuary, a green valley by still waters. She settled into a living room chair adjacent to the sofa and coffee table to think, pray, and plan. Nor-mally, she would exercise after everyone was gone, but today she wanted to count things up, savor the positives, commune with her Lord. She thanked her Savior over and over. Prayer for her was an ongoing conver-sation without preamble or prologue. In one of her praises of thanksgiv-ing for the spreading revival she thought of her pastor and how much he would appreciate the news. She wanted to call him. His office hours at the church were from ten to two. Every member knew he was in personal study before ten and then did his visits after two. She didn't want to dis-turb him. She knew he would rejoice with her about the news of Montana, England, and Norway. She had to believe that he already knew about the revival at the academy. She would wait until ten to call. The quiet house, the soft chairs, and pillows performed their duties and lulled her to sleep.

The dream was different than any she had before. An angel walked beside her, pointing to various scenes to the left and right, and in front. Her strides were effortless. It was like she was gliding and not walking. The scenes were of clusters of people going about daily, routine activities. There were families eating together at a table. There were women shopping with friends. Children were playing in backyards. Students seated in classrooms were listening to teachers. Office workers gathered around a conference table. Many individual groups seemed to be gathered closely into frameless videos. She was above most of the scenes, which made her think she was walking on a bluff. When she looked down, she discovered she was flying. Immediately her gaze went to the angel with her. He smiled and pointed again to the scenes. This time she saw more individuals, angels of two kinds, dim and bright, standing by each person in all of the groups. She sensed immediately they were agents of evil and virtue. She looked intently at one scene—the classroom; each student had two angels nearby. In some cases, one angel of light would have his arms out preventing the other angel from getting to the student. In other cases, an angel would be standing back with a worried look, waiting as the other dark angel was kneeling next to or bending down beside the person of interest, suggesting things into their ears. In other places, evil angels were gesticulating to good angels, pointing and threatening, warning the other to stay away from their property. The same was true with the other scenes. In every scene, Rachael was in the picture. She saw herself talking with the people in the groups. Some listened, some were distracted. Each individual was a great controversy in miniature. Her attending angel touched her arm again, directing her vision upward and she saw the dark heavens part and beams of bright light pour forth. It was awesome in its brilliant glory. It was all light with no visible figures, a prelude to when Jesus would appear. She wanted others to see it, not to miss the big moment. She looked down again to alert them and she saw where the angels in light were leading their charges upward. The individuals left behind were bodies, corpses wrapped in soot and ashes. She wanted to see who was lifted upward and recognize any she could, however her gaze was inexorably pulled upward to get a glimpse of her Savior. She thought she saw angels peeking around the edges of clouds, like children hiding behind curtains playing hide and seek. Before she could see Jesus, she was back in her living room. Her angel lingered for a moment and said, "Everyone must decide for themselves. The time is very near, days not years. Persevere in your efforts to tell them. Some will listen." And then he was gone.

The bright brilliant morning sunlight streaming between the curtains appeared to be a 15-watt bulb in comparison to what she had seen a minute before. Her well-appointed and carefully decorated house seemed like a dismal attempt to tidy up a cave.

Rachael called Mike first. When he answered she blurted out, "I fell asleep and I had a dream."

"You were tired; you were up most of the night," he soothed.

"No, I had a dream with an angel by my side. It was one of those dreams, so real, so chilling, so, so…inspiring. I was transported through the sky, watching battles between evil and good angels. The dream was like an answer to my worries and failures of yesterday. Jesus sent my angel to encourage me. I feel so privileged, so honored. Mike, I can't describe it in all its beauty. I almost saw Jesus coming. It was all light and He was almost there, I mean here." Rachael started to cry.

"When did this happen?"

"Minutes ago. My angel was just here in our living room talking to me. He said I shouldn't give up. That some will listen."

"'Your sons and daughters will prophesy.' It's happening as predicted. In the latter days the Spirit will be poured out and people will start to prophesy. It's wonderful to think it is happening in my own family. I'm proud of you. God picked you because you are special. I knew it all along," Mike emphasized.

"Honey, it wasn't a prophecy—it was an encouraging dream. He was telling me to keep witnessing, not to get discouraged."

"Can you tell me what he said exactly?"

"Every word, I'll never forget this. He said, 'Everyone must decide for themselves. The time is very near, days not years. Persevere in your efforts to tell them. Some will listen.' Those are his exact words."

Preparations need to be made. I can't help thinking we're on our way home!

"That was a prophecy. He said, 'days not years.' That means the year for a day principle is reversed. He's coming soon! Not years from now, but days from now. He's almost here! We have little time left. We have to get ready!" Mike's mind was shooting forward, totally oblivious to his medical diagnosis, to analyze what needed to be done. His list of PREPARATIONS needed to be executed and also some of the NO TURNING BACK. "Honey, I need some time off. I'm going to ask for vacation time to start as soon as they will let me. Preparations need to be made. I can't help thinking we're on our way home!"

"Yes, we're on our way home."

* * * * * *

Rachael was able to reach her pastor later in the day. He had had another funeral and wasn't in his office. He called her back when he had the time. Rachael wanted him to know what she had learned about the academy in Montana and the stories she had heard from Grantham Press and Tyrifjord. He had already told her he had heard of the revival at their academy. They rejoiced at the news of the four locations, two abroad, one in Montana, and the one close to home, where their children attended and where the pastor's wife worked. He too wanted to share what he had heard from other locations. An Adventist church in North Dakota was also enjoying an outpouring of the Spirit. It seems that a men's prayer breakfast had been planned hastily for the men to gather and to pray before they went off to work. They were concerned about news events and wanted to ask God for help. The Holy Spirit answered. One of Pastor Taylor's friends called to tell him the news.

The pastor then turned the conversation to personal interest in the Larssons. Rachael shared with him her delight in Janelle's participation and then shared her lack of success with her sister, neighbor, and friends. His advice was to not give up, to which Rachel replied, "That's what the angel said." The pastor was startled with intrigue. She had to tell him about the dream. Again, he was thrilled for her and for himself. This was a wonderful validation of God working in the people of his church. He asked permission to tell the church. Rachael didn't know if he should. "I don't know, Pastor, if we should. It was a message for me personally not to give up telling my friends because some will listen. It wasn't a message for the whole church, I don't believe. Besides, I wouldn't want to set myself up as a messenger of the Lord. After all, it was just one dream."

"I understand. We do have to be careful at times. Some can make false applications about the use of prophecy. However, if God chooses you to speak to us in this difficult time, it must be an important message that we need to hear. Don't hesitate to tell us and I will support you."

"Thank you, pastor, I'll remember that. For now, I think God was trying to build up my confidence and remind us that the time is near. I wouldn't hesitate to speak to others if He directs me to."

CHAPTER 8

The Sabbath morning sun shone brightly in the car windshield as the Larsson's car nudged into a parking slot. They were early but the lot looked like it would if services had already started. The church would be crowded today. Janelle met many of her friends from school and they hurried to the youth class. The pastor was waiting for them, along with the teacher. Jason was a little less anxious to get to class. He spent time at the water fountain then cruised around the church with a couple of buddies like he always did. Sometimes he made it to class, sometimes he didn't. Mike taught the adult class in the front left of the sanctuary near the piano. Rachael taught the juniors downstairs. Classes were already full and the chatter from various conversational groups was animated.

After prayer, Mike opened his class with the question, "Is everybody ready to leave?" The question caught many off guard. Some looked around as if it meant they had to move the class to another location. Others waited for Mike to explain. He repeated the sentence again and stood there expectantly. Some caught on. Eighty-year-old Mrs. McKessy said, "I've been ready for eighty long years. It's about time!"

Mike smiled and then repeated, "Is everybody ready to leave … and go home … home to heaven? We are at the threshold of history. Have you been seeing the news? Have you been aware of what's happening? Tell me what you've been seeing and hearing?"

The class answered, tumbling over each other in their enthusiasm. Each had a perspective. Mike watched as the discussion multiplied. People were anxious to speak; some raised their hands not wanting to interrupt others, but wanted to have their chance to tell the good news. The lesson was on Romans chapter 5. It was almost forgotten. Mike knew there was a text that needed to be brought up. He waited for the chance to explain it and quote it to them. The verses illustrated perfectly the emotional application of Rachael's dream. He wasn't teaching the lesson. He stood and listened to the member's talk of their conversations with friends and relatives in other states and countries. One member indicated that a revival was happening in Ottawa. Another said she heard of a church in downtown Austin, Texas, that felt the Spirit's power during midweek prayer meeting. One simply said, "It's happening!"

Mrs. McKessy raised her hand and Mike called on her. She paused for effect. "I hate *dirt*! ... I don't want to be put *under* it! ... I don't want to walk on *top* of it! ... But … I do want to fly *away* from it! I'm going *home*!"

"Amen, sister! When you throws down yo' cane be careful not to hit me wit' it, 'cause I'll be right behind ya!" Veronica Jones added.

"No you won't! You won't be behind me, because you and I will be holding hands!" Heidi McKessy retorted.

The class continued to add perspective and observations. It was a feast of mutual experiences and knowledge of His soon coming. Mike concluded class by bringing them back to the lesson. "Recently a woman had a dream that caused me to look at Romans 5 and the first two verses in a fresh, new way. It reads, *Therefore, since we are justified by faith we have peace with God through our Lord Jesus Christ. In Him we have access to the grace in which we stand, and we rejoice in the hope of sharing His glory.* "It is apparent today that God's grace is giving us peace of heart in a troublesome time. His grace reassures us, calms us when we witness, and even when we don't see the results of our efforts. And then, we are very close to sharing the glory of Jesus' second coming. Comparing His glory with our nice things down here is no contest. His glory will make everything down here on earth look dark and dreary. His coming will bring peace in the place of conflict, glorious victory in the place of defeat."

* * * * * *

The platform was minus the pulpit. An expanse of carpet stretched from organ to piano. Several microphones were evenly scattered about on

the floor. Pastor Taylor stood in the middle of the dais waiting for parish-
ioners to settle in their seats. He prayed, invoking the Lord's presence.
Then he began to explain.

"This week has been a revelation of gigantic proportions for me personally. I can't begin to tell you how I feel. The Lord has spoken to me in
so many ways that my head is spinning with the good news. Let me begin
by saying that Monday began as another round of funerals like the weeks
before. It seems like every Sabbath I have been announcing another
death, another funeral service, and asking you, my dear members, to pray
for these grieving families. In my over twenty years of ministry, I have
never had this many funerals in a single year. It has had a strong effect on
me. I grieve for each of these dear saints. It's possible for a minister to get
compounded grief in performing these services. Some counseling profes-
sionals call it compassion fatigue; I call it cumulative grief. I have become
discouraged. Last week at this time, perhaps you noticed that my sermon
was less than enthusiastic. I have been struggling and praying for His help.
He answered my plea … but, the encouraging answer He gave me was also
the same answer He gave to the world. 'Lo, I am coming soon.' This week
I have seen a multitude of evidence that His coming is very near; as the
facts roll in, my spirits rise. Joy supersedes discouragement. I would like to
shout to the heavens; I would like to dance like David did in front of the
Ark of the Covenant. The Lord's presence is near, just like David believed
as he led the symbol of God's presence into Jerusalem. I am humbled. I
have longed for this day and have wondered if I would see it. Now I am
convinced it is here.

"In some of my sermons, I have listed the signs of His second coming:
natural disasters as well as manmade ones, wars and rumors of wars. I have
talked about the involvement of governments, especially our government,
in forcing a weak, superficial faith upon the general population. Prophecy
is supposed to return when our sons and daughters prophesy and our old
men dream dreams. And lastly, I have spoken about the outpouring of
the Holy Spirit and the youth finishing the work. This week I totaled all
of these signs in my head: the President's behavior, the disasters, etc. I listened to a dear friend tell of her dream where an angel gave her a message
of comfort. And then at our academy something extraordinary happened.
The Holy Spirit came among our students and caused a revival. I want you
to be thrilled like I was when I spoke to these dedicated teenagers.

"Once I had a sermon on revival, maybe you remember, and I will tell
you briefly what I said then. When God's Spirit attends in a mighty way,
several things happen. There is an asking for the Spirit to come and the

asking is accompanied with true repentance and forgiveness among fellow believers. Unity in the group of praying believers is important. And then there is a tremendous urge to witness. True revival has those ingredients.

"Today in Sabbath school I met with some of our students who were a part of that experience. I asked their permission to do what we are going to do today. I have asked them to come up here on the platform, use these microphones, and describe what happened. When I heard them talk about their experience, I was moved by the Holy Spirit that was with them. I had a sermon ready to preach today, but I would rather have you feel the same way I felt when I talked to them yesterday and again this morning. It may end up being the best worship service you'll ever have on earth.

"Now, I am asking for the teens to please join me here on the platform. Thank you, here they come now."

The teens gathered and stood around, unsure of what they were supposed to do. The pastor picked up one of the microphones and handed it to the nearest teen. Darin and Janelle were standing to one side holding hands. They looked at their new friends, Jeremy and Sandra, who remained where Darin and Janelle had been sitting. It was apparent to the pastor that the teens were unsure of who should take the lead. He attempted to get them started,

"So when did all this start?" Addressing the group still did not help. Darin decided to get the ball rolling. He picked up one of the other microphones and began.

"Coach Weldon, I guess, suggested a prayer session during lunch last Wednesday. The word spread and then during lunch we went to the music room to pray."

"And then what happened?"

"We prayed." The other teen holding a mike answered. Then Janelle used Darin's mic.

"It was all unexpected. I didn't know of the prayer meeting until Darin suggested it. We went in and started to pray." Janelle continued to tell her own story and the other teens got more animated by nodding approval. "The reason we were praying is because we didn't feel strong enough to face what might be coming. We asked for His help and then started to ask for forgiveness." At that point, others started to add their agreement to what she said and included more detail about the desire to forgive. When they explained how they had started to kneel in the music room to ask for the Holy Spirit to help, the group started to kneel on the church's platform. One student started to explain her prayer and actually began the prayer. Others prayed spontaneously. Their prayers were more seasoned because they were used to praying frequently in the last few days. They focused their prayers on Christian believers in general asking for them to understand what was happening. They asked for the Spirit to help, to move the people to ask and understand the points of importance in the final days.

Then one teen named Josh turned his concern upon the congregation, which was listening to their prayers. He wanted them to understand that, for the Holy Spirit to work, they needed to be of one mind like the disciples on the day of Pentecost. He didn't stop there, but continued to ask for God to forgive the members for their small arguments and to have them forgive each other. Then he got even more personal and spoke directly to his parents, "Dad, Mom, the Spirit is telling me now that I should ask you for your forgiveness. I haven't thought of it before, because families are always supposed to forgive each other, but the Spirit has asked me to say this now just in case you might be thinking that I'm not sincere. I am truly sorry for the heartache I have caused you and the bad words I have used. I'm different now because I want to do God's will. Thank you, God, for giving me the strength to apologize to my parents. Maybe You wanted me to be an example for everyone here today. If that is true, then I am Your servant. Tell me what I must do and I will do it for You."

The church was moved by his sincerity. "Amens" could be heard as well as some movement. Josh's folks had left their seats to kneel with their son. Tears were coursing down their cheeks. Other teens prayed. Darin prayed for his father, who was divorced from his mother and living in another state. He wanted the words to say to him when they talked. He prayed for his grandparents. He wanted them not to have too much difficulty when Satan's angels would be persecuting God's people. "Lord, if it is Your will, allow me to be there with them to carry them out of harm's way." Others prayed, asking for guidance on what He wanted them to do. In the background whispers could be heard throughout the sanctuary. Despite the fact that prayer was ongoing, people were moving quietly about and murmuring in each other's ears. They were asking for forgiveness just like Josh. Handclasps and hugs followed confessions and requests for pardons; then people made their way to the front to kneel in an ever-widening circle.

Prayers turned into entreaties asking for more of the Holy Spirit. Mature voices were mingled with teen voices in prayer. Some of the prayers were captured by the microphones and many were not. Electronics were abandoned in the fervor of request.

The Spirit washed over them.

Tears of thanksgiving caused some words to quiver in their utterance. Hearts beat faster. Minds searched for any sin that may not have been forgiven. Some spoke them aloud, others asked silently for the Savior to take them away. Two strangers, new to this congregation, added their pleas to the Redeemer. They knelt next to their new friends from the donut shop, Janelle and Darin, caught up in the Spirit and power of reconciliation that was permeating the congregation of renewed believers. Their churches were Christian, but they hadn't felt the power of the Holy Spirit in their church as they felt it at this moment. Jeremy and Sandra prayed aloud next to their new friends, tokens of the reaping that was to come.

Mike and Rachael were kneeling and praying on the opposite side of the crowd from their daughter. They were thrilled on many levels. Their chosen local church was now fully engaged in the enterprise of the Spirit. Their daughter was leading with the other teens. Their pastor was thrilled and had done just the right thing inviting the teens to tell their story. They couldn't see Jason and where he might be in the crowd, but were assured that he couldn't miss what had happened in this medium-to-large size church. They prayed both silently and aloud with the congregation. The congregation worked out their plans for witnessing in close communication with the Divine presence. The church was mobilizing before their eyes, more accurately, their ears, as they listened to the prayers for help and guidance. They could see the work of the Spirit within the minds of those who were praying.

Some of the work projects of the church seemed so unproductive compared to the monstrous task of getting the message out to as many as possible in the shortest time. Those projects had planted so many seeds of good will with the homeless, the needy, and the destitute.

The church was mobilizing before their eyes, more accurately, their ears, as they listened to the prayers for help and guidance.

Now the Spirit was redirecting these faithful believers to go out and call them in. Planting had to take a back seat to the harvest. Planting would have to accompany the harvest virtually at the same time. There was no time for slow maturation. Jesus was at the gates.

Singing praises came naturally. "My God, is an awesome God…" were words sung into one of the many microphones when there was a short pause. Someone had been moved to sing and the moment was perfect.

As one anthem followed another, people stood. Bright, moist eyes shone as familiar words were more meaningful in the breathtaking context. One short song, sometimes uttered after the main prayer and sung many Sabbath mornings of the past, had a strong impact as they sung it today, "Spirit of the living God, fall afresh on me."

* * * * * *

It was much later than usual when the worship service came to an end. Fellowship potluck was served afterward. Having prayer to bless the food was no problem—getting people to line up was. Clustered about everywhere in the fellowship hall and out in the hallway individuals were talking and sharing. They were into spiritual food more than physical food, like Jesus at the Samaritan well.

Jason and a couple of his friends were first in line to fill their plates. Their teen tummies were never able to achieve the ultimate full-tank status. As they balanced overloaded plates with cups of juice and plastic ware, they talked soccer. One concerned member couldn't believe they would be on that subject when everyone else was reveling in the Spirit. The gentleman asked them, "Wasn't that wonderful how the Holy Spirit could be felt among us?"

For a moment Jason soaked in the comment, not knowing what the man was talking about. Then he nonchalantly answered, "Pretty awesome, I guess." He then moved to a table with his buddies to scarf down their food, leaving the man wondering if they knew what he was talking about.

Janelle, Sandra, Darin, and Jeremy sat at another table where there were two adults. The discussion was, of course, primarily on the worship service and then it included the other signs of Jesus' soon coming. The prejudice against various denominations and non-Christians came into the conversation. Jeremy told of the news he listened to this morning. Terrorists had bombed two synagogues: an orthodox service on Friday night in San Francisco and a reformed synagogue this morning in Miami. He explained that the newscasters were citing radical Islamic factions as the primary suspects because it was a way to attack their sworn enemy, Israel. The news confirmed what Janelle and Darin were trying to explain about the end of time where strong religious prejudice would be a part of the attitudes of various elements and the eventual dominance of superficial Christianity forcing others to worship in one unified form. That fact of Muslim against Jew had to be explained. Darin made the distinction that it could cause government leaders to step in, in an attempt to control the violence, possibly forcing Jew and Muslim to obey Christian tenets whether they wanted to or not. Jeremy and Sandra were attentively interested.

Mike put his hand on Jason's shoulder as he was scooping up the last morsel of a casserole he liked. "So what did you think?"

"'Bout what Dad?"

"The worship service?"

"It was okay."

"Just okay, not great or awesome as you say?"

"I don't know. I'll say yes."

Mike could see that the reason he didn't see Jason in the crowd at the front of the church was because Jason had not been there. He determined they would talk about this at a time when his friends were not nearby, most probably on the way home this afternoon. He was disappointed in his son and troubled about how he would approach the problem. He had made a speech about how his children were old enough to stand on their own to face the final conflict. He regretted his comments. He wanted to maintain the parental prerogative to guide his son and to arrange the environment to the best advantage for his spiritual commitment. It diminished the afterglow of the worship service. He prayed inwardly that the Spirit would be with him to say the right words to get his son on track. For this task he needed Rachael's help. He wished he didn't have to tell her and have her feel the same sorrow for Jason's shallow connection to Jesus. He waited until it was almost time to leave. It was late afternoon when the congregation was able to pull away from the environment that fired their souls. They kept validating the presence of the Spirit with ad hoc prayers and ongoing celebration for the uplifting worship. They felt they had received more from the Holy Spirit than what they had contributed. Telling others was a way of saying "thank you" to the Divine Guest. They departed with plans to contact friends and relatives with the good news and ominous signs of His nearness.

Janelle asked her folks if they minded her spending the evening with Darin and her friends. Mike saw it as an opportunity to have a talk with Jason in the car on the way home.

* * * * * *

"I feel like I could run a marathon without any effort at all," Mike said in the car as they drove home.

"I know how you feel. It seems like I am ten years old and doing endless cartwheels on the front lawn. It has been exhilarating," Rachael added.

"Jason, how would you describe what happened today?" Mike looked through the rearview mirror to watch his son's reaction.

"It was okay, I guess."

"Okay! Just okay?" Rachael asked in surprise. "That had to be the closest thing to worship in heaven I have ever experienced. Were you even there?"

"Yes, I agree. Worship today was like … well, like what the pastor said it would be, 'the best worship service you'll ever have on earth.' You remember the pastor saying that, don't you?" Mike asked. There was mostly silence in the back seat. Rachael turned around and stared at her son as he debated his answer.

"I wasn't there."

Rachael wanted to exercise firm parental direction. She was so disappointed. Mike laid his hand on her leg, consoling in an unseen manner. It caused her to pause before speaking. She thought of how disappointed she was in the reactions of her friends to her witnessing. This moment ranked higher on the discouragement scale. Her son's apathetic behavior of not being in church at a time when the world was moving toward chaos was one facet to her distress. The other feature was that he missed the outpouring of the Spirit. The day's experience taught her to pray rather than say. She turned her head forward and then bowed in intercessory prayer. She asked God to place in her the best possible spirit of compassion towards her son. While praying she recalled the text in Galatians about the fruits of the Spirit as patience, kindness, goodness, faithfulness, gentleness, self-control. While she prayed she heard Mike talk.

"You probably had a good reason to not be there. You were with your friends and at this time, friendships are important. It is through friendship that we are able to persuade people to see the truth of what's happening in the world on a spiritual level. You were probably discussing the events of the last few days."

Rachael listened and could sense the fruit of the Spirit's presence in her husband as he demonstrated gentleness and kindness. Then the Spirit led her mind to recall the exchange between Janelle and Jason the other morning when he was needling her with the "smoochy, smoochy" comment. Janelle had exhibited self-control in her response to her brother. It humbled her to realize the Spirit had entered her family members and was guiding their reactions. She vowed she would do the same.

"Jason, I love you. One of the hardest things for me as a Christian is that I want everyone to have the exact same experience that I have, at the same time. This past week has taught me something different. The school had an outpouring of the Spirit and I wasn't there. The Lord waited for me to feel His divine presence on another day and in a different manner. God speaks and works with each individual in different ways and at different times. I have to remember that. God has a great plan for you, so don't be disappointed that you missed the church service today. He will come to You in His own way and in a way that will thrill your heart," she explained.

"Does God like soccer?" Jason asked.

The question from the back seat surprised the parents in the front. They didn't know how to answer. "Why do you ask?" Mike ventured.

"'Cause I like soccer. Why can't we wait a little while on this stuff? I'd like to win the soccer tourney this year. All the guys are talking about how we have the best chance to win it all."

"By 'stuff,' do you mean getting ready for His soon coming?" Mike asked.

"Yeah. God understands, doesn't He?"

"I'm not sure Jesus is going to plan His coming around your soccer schedule. I know you love soccer. It's good exercise and it's nice to have purpose. That's why we let you play with them during the week, but a lot of the games are on Sabbath. When is the tournament?"

"May."

"That's three months from now," Rachael was surprised.

"I'm guessing that the tournament will be scheduled on a weekend just like last year," Mike added,

"But all the guys say I'm their best forward. They need me. God will understand, won't He? It's kinda like witnessing. They like me and want me on their team. They listen to me when I teach them my techniques. They'll listen when I talk to them about faith in God."

"They probably would, but what about the Sabbath? We know that that's going to be a test of loyalty. Will they listen to you when you talk about keeping the Sabbath after you have ignored the Sabbath?"

"Dad, how can the Sabbath be all that important? It can't be more important than believing in Jesus. That's more important, right?"

"You're right. Believing in Jesus is most important. The Sabbath is the *testing* truth, Jesus is the *saving* truth. Satan will try to pull Christians away from Jesus by having it be popular to worship Him on the false Sabbath, Sunday. Believing in Jesus means trusting in Him under all circumstances; one of those circumstances is avoiding the counterfeit worship Satan will set up. He will pretend to come as Jesus, ask people to worship him and that worship will be on Sunday. It will seem like a small thing to most people, but the biblical Sabbath becomes important as an identifier of who is who, Jesus or Satan. Satan won't trick you on a saving truth; it will be on a point of loyalty, very subtle."

Jason was quiet for a minute. Rachael felt Mike's explanation had been a clear presentation of the issues involved. She knew Jason must be seeing it clearly. Her hopes were up.

"But, that's not happening now. I don't see any false Jesus in the news asking to be worshipped. We've got time. I can still play with the guys. God will forgive me for wanting to help the team on the Sabbath. Besides, it's my decision, right?"

The parents were in a quandary. To continue the discussion meant it might end in an argument. Mike wished he hadn't told his son that he had to stand on his own two feet. It would be easier to control a child. Now he was facing a youth feeling his power of choice. He looked at his wife and both their eyes communicated apprehension. The remainder of the trip home was silent.

CHAPTER 9

Monday's national news was disturbing, but not all together unexpected. The Larsson household had heard about the bombings during activities on Sunday. Three churches, in Chicago, St. Louis, and Omaha, were bombed by suicide bombers. Almost one hundred were killed, hundreds more were injured. Radical Islamic extremists claimed victory in the name of Allah. By mid-morning Monday, the media was abuzz about the White House's news conference. The President was going to make a speech. Everyone expected that he would deplore the acts of senseless violence, promise Americans that the perpetrators who sponsored these suicide bombings would be caught and punished, and call for prayer for the grieving families. What they didn't expect was President O'Donnell's swift action. He called for all mosques to be shut down and searched. He said they have become "hotbeds of planning and deceit for heinous crimes of terror." Then he added that they would be "immediately searched and if evidence of illegal activity was found, the property and contents would be subject to seizure." He did not allude to any proof of evidence beyond a shadow of doubt to support his claim.

True to form, the American Civil Liberties Union reacted strongly, hurling out epithets against the government and threatening to sue in behalf of the citizens of the Islamic faith. The President's press secretary answered the threats within the hour by stating that the ACLU would be held complicit with the enemy at a time of war. All assets, including bank accounts, would be confiscated; personnel would be arrested, held for treason, and tried in a military tribunal if they proceeded with their threat.

Local reporters were sent to area mosques to collect reactions and record closures. Scenes of police cars with flashing emergency lights could be seen. Various views of imams and support workers for the buildings were seen being forcibly hustled away to avoid contamination or the destruction of possible evidence. Individuals who were interviewed evinced the range of emotion, from intense outrage to controlled anger in the form of carefully crafted criticisms of America's freedom of religion. Crowds began to gather on the streets and grassy verges of the mosques with signs scrawled on poster-boards. The signs were not complimentary. They blamed Islam for innocent deaths. They demanded restitution. Some commanded the Islamic believers to go home to the deserts of the Middle-East, not recognizing that many adherents were native-born Americans. Several signs repeated the theme, "We will always remember St Louis, Omaha, and Chicago!" In some places, rocks and an assortment of debris were hurled against windows and doors.

Commentators and experts were seen talking on panels, analyzing the story from every angle. In different ways, the same comments were uttered to explain the behavior of the President and of the angry mobs.

"For years now, the Islamic community has been strangely quiet about their radical brothers who are performing these acts of terror."

"Pent-up emotions for all these crimes against innocent people have driven the American citizens to act out against Islamic worship."

"The American people want it to stop. They are demonstrating at the only visible expressions of these radical extremists, the local mosques."

"Polls, conducted since the President's news conference, are strongly in favor of the President's action."

One panelist made an observation that caused others to pause and think: "In these scenes we are watching and in the interviews we hear, I haven't heard any mention of San Francisco and Miami. It's as if the bombings at the synagogues didn't happen."

Mike listened to the news reports at the office. Rachael had the television on while she worked in the house. Late in the morning, Mike called Rachael for a brief conversation.

"My vacation was approved starting the end of this month. Because it was for so long a time, they needed to work out coverage in my absence."

"It will be good to have you at home with me. There's so much we can do together," she answered.

"Have you been watching the news?"

"A little. I've had it on while I've been doing the laundry and straightening the house. So what do you think of what's happening?"

"I think it's an indication of what will happen to us."

"In what way? Bombing?"

"No, I'm thinking of how they will close our churches and seize the property for themselves. We'll have nowhere to worship," Mike explained.

"By that time we'll be fleeing anyway, I'm guessing. In the past, it would be difficult for the government to make bold moves like they did today with the mosques. Now I can see that the government is getting away with it in the name of war defense. Remember how Japanese Americans were put in containment camps during World War II? Those people were U. S. citizens and then suddenly they were treated like POWs."

"Yes, the barriers protecting our freedoms are starting to come down. Ah, one of the reasons I called is because I invited some people home for dinner. I just talked to George and Sheila. She works the night shift at the hospital and she goes back on shift tomorrow. Tonight is the only time they can come this week. I said it wasn't a problem. I'm hoping you don't mind. He's not a practicing Christian and she's an atheist."

"I … guess I'm glad I was straightening up. My plans were to make some calls and visits this afternoon; I can make a few calls and have a nice dinner ready."

The barriers protecting our freedoms are starting to come down.

"I'm sorry to drop this on you. Thanks for helping. George seems to be on the wrong side of the prevailing opinions. And once the office staff sees I'm not one of them, they'll turn on me also. George is open to me, but guarded with everyone else."

The husband and wife team said their goodbyes and Rachael went immediately to the kitchen to plan dinner. She selected dinner off of a menu screen on the wall and ordered what she needed from the read out that said she was lacking some of the items in her pantry and refrigerator. She tapped the list and sent it to the other side of the board where it automatically purchased the items from the grocery store and had the items delivered to her house. The cost was automatically deducted from their bank account. She resumed her house cleaning with the intention of getting ready early so she could make those calls she had planned earlier. She wondered what it would be like for her to talk to an atheist at this time of earth's history. Before, when she had talked with them, she always felt it was her duty to lay the ground work and make them into friends, slowly breaking down prejudices they had built up. Her prayers were for her to say the right things at the right time.

* * * * * *

Pastor Taylor met with other area pastors and the academy administrative staff. Although most of the teachers were in class with students, some of them were able to attend the meeting. They began with round-robin prayer and then the principal opened with his concerns. He wanted everyone to know why he had called this meeting. In his communication with other Adventist educators, he found that two of the colleges had suspended classes in favor of street witnessing and neighborhood canvassing with literature and dialogue. Colleges were free of legal requirements for mandatory class time. Elementary, middle, and high schools had state requirements they had to abide by. He had only one item on his agenda: when should they close down school and let the students be with their families and get ready for the end? It was sobering to think of the reality of the times. Usually, the school board meeting was in the evening and they discussed the bottom line—finances. Money to keep the doors open was not a priority. Setting students and families free to navigate the heavy issues of life and death was a priority. When, not if, was the center of the focus.

It was a surreal meeting. Academic merit didn't matter. Individuals dedicated to Christian educational excellence had to rethink their ultimate purpose. It was like telling a plumber to forget the leak. It was all about timing. If they closed too soon, it would bring social services down upon their heads for officially sanctioned truancy. The local government would be alerted to their anti-ideological position from the majority. Non-attending students and their parents would be rounded up and questioned. The meeting centered upon what events or signs would be the best indicators of when to stop. They prayed to end the meeting, fearful and happy at the same time. The general feeling was that the time was not yet, but they would communicate by either closed meeting or secure conference calls to decide if the time was ripe.

* * * * * *

Mike had lunch away from the office. He wanted to call some friends and former work associates and talk over the issues. He settled on a park bench in a small grassy island too tiny to be called a park. He called an old friend who he knew was an atheist. He wanted to get his feel for what was happening and perhaps plant a few seeds, or at least water the ones he had planted before.

"Mike! What's up? No wait, let me guess. You're wondering about my response to the President. You want to convince me to get one of those wrist bands. No way, Mano!"

"No, Alejandro, exactly the opposite. I'm not getting one of those solidarity bracelets."

"What, you're not a Christian anymore?"

"I'm still a Christian, but I see this as an oppressive behavior that forces people to be Christians on the surface and not deep down in the heart."

"You're not calling me to become a Christian for real are you, amigo?"

"Nothing would make me happier than to have you become a Christian like me, but I was primarily calling to see how you feel about all this stuff the government is doing. A friend at work has a wife that is atheist and my friend is being treated as an outsider because he's married to her. It made me think of you and what you may or may not be going through. Are you okay?"

"I'm okay. I'm hiding my opinions right now, but my family's aware of my stance. You've heard me talk of my dislike for the church and how they treated my sister when she got divorced. I know that was a long time ago and the church has changed their position, but it hurt then and I'll never forget. If the church rules were rules back then, supposedly by God and the Pope, then why suddenly did they change the rules? I think they were losing a lot of people and made a business decision. The church doesn't represent God; they're just looking out for their own pocketbook."

"Alejandro, I hear what you're saying and I'm sympathetic. How is your family treating you?"

"They're worried, of course."

"Worried how?"

"They, ah, want me to not buck the system. They want me to at least try to look like I'm in agreement. You know, get an arm band and show it when necessary. They think this is going to be the big thing and the Christians are going to be the leaders in this world. My sister said I should take communion. Now that's a change. She's the one they treated like...well you know, nothing. She says it's important to go along with the majority."

"Are you going to go along with the majority?"

"I don't know. If I have to, I will. You're not going to go along with them?" Alejandro asked.

"No."

"Why?"

"Because I would be doing it for selfish reasons and not for the right reasons—selfish because I would be getting what I want for the time being and it would be turning my back on God for the wrong reason."

"How could accepting their arm trinket be turning your back on God? You're already honest in your heart. I know you are."

"Because this system that is developing is the wrong way to go about converting the world to Christianity. It borders on coercion, well maybe not now, but it will."

"You sound like you can see the future. How do you know this will be coercive?"

"The Bible predicts this in the book of Revelation. Religions and governments are going to come together in false worship. They will make people worship in a prescribed way. It won't be very spiritual. There will be some sort of identifier that will label everyone as worshippers of this false system. The Bible calls it the mark of the beast."

"Yeah, I've heard dat. Do you think this arm band is the mark of this beast?"

"It could be a precursor, a starting point, depending how it is used. It has some of the elements of what the Bible is talking about. It is an identifier with its tracking capabilities and its other applications. Getting people to agree to wear this to show their unity is tantamount to having a permanent mark or something. Who knows what the devil has up his sleeve? God wants free will; Satan prefers coercion."

"What do I care if people want to worship in the wrong way? I'm an atheist."

"Well, those who don't have the mark of the beast won't be able to buy or sell. You'll have to agree with them and take the mark if you want to eat. On top of that, later they will issue a death decree upon those who don't have the mark."

"That's a little much to swallow. Not in America—it can't happen, right?"

"Look what happened to the Muslims; suddenly they can't worship in their own mosques. One swift move and they're without places of worship."

"I'm going to have to think about dis. I didn't like that they were making me show Christian unity; now I have different reasons to think about what's going on. I'm almost done with my lunch break. I have to go. I'll talk to you again, amigo."

Besides witnessing to Alejandro, Mike wanted to get some feeling for what might be a good approach talking to Sheila and George. The conversation seemed to have a positive bent to it and Alejandro had said he would think about it. He tried to extract from the conversation what might be useful as he walked back to work.

* * * * * *

As they moved from the dining room to the living room, Sheila spoke to Rachael.

"George has told me how your husband has been supportive when many of those in the office are less than concerned. George appreciates it very much. I can see the same form of kindness in you. Thank you for inviting us over. It has been a lovely evening. You have a lovely house and this living room is so bright and cheery."

"Thank you."

They settled into chairs with the visitors together on the couch. George jumped into a topic that he was burning to bring up.

"All these so-called Christians are becoming snobbish towards me and indirectly towards my wife. But you aren't. Why not?"

"For us, faith is by choice, not by popularity or by government directives. I think I'm right when I speak for Rachael and me, when I say we are not in agreement with what is happening. I was very uncomfortable when I heard the conversation last week."

"Religion should be by choice. I have to make a minor correction to what George said. He said, 'indirectly towards his wife.' It is because of me that they are acting snobbish. They know I'm an atheist and they think I should just fall in line with them. As if!" Sheila clarified.

Mike's prayer for guidance was answered with a thought about his talk with Alejandro. "Tell me, I'm interested, why are you an atheist? I promise not to judge."

Sheila felt safe talking with this kind couple. She didn't worry about what they might think. For a moment she hesitated, composing how she could tell the story. George tried to help her, opening the difficult subject by saying what she might feel uncomfortable saying. "My family was a big problem. They have been less than kind. Go ahead, sweetheart. They'll understand."

"Actually, that is the middle of the story. It started when I was little. My family didn't believe in a God. Mom, Dad, and Grandma, I called her 'Maama,' didn't believe in anything. I loved my Maama. We spent a lot of time together. She was the reason I became a nurse, because I wanted to be just like her. She always maintained that this was all there was in life. In death, there was nothing else. 'Death is death,' she said. 'Nothing happens after that!' Mom and Dad agreed and I grew up thinking that way too. Then Maama died. I was a teen and it hit me hard. She was the one who met me every day after school. When Mom and Dad had to travel for business, and they traveled a lot, I stayed with Maama. When she was dying, she asked everyone in the room the question, 'Who here is not going to die?' It was her way of saying that death was the end and we all have to accept it. When she died the next day, I was torn apart. She had been everything to me. Part of me deep down inside wanted there to be something else, some continuing of life. She was so precious to me. But, she died with that conviction and I wanted to be brave like her.

I met George and then I met his family. It was Maama that caused me to be proud of my atheism. But it ran up against their belief. They couldn't stand to hear me say there wasn't a God and there wasn't an afterlife. It was a challenge to them. They told me all sorts of things. At first it was stuff like I would miss out on heaven, then I was denying the Holy Spirit, and then I would go to hell. Later, it became more descriptive and cruel about how I would burn forever and ever. I was becoming more and more disenchanted with his family. Then they told me Maama was writhing in hell in excruciating pain because she didn't believe in Jesus." Sheila paused.

"At that point I, too, was embittered with my family. I knew how much Maama meant to Sheila. I was embarrassed by how they tried to scare her into believing. I stopped attending church completely after that. Now, I am questioning the whole concept of God and the afterlife. I'm sorry, honey, I interrupted your story. Please continue."

"It became a nightmare to visit his family or to have them visit us in our home. They would do all kinds of crazy things. Like bless the salt shaker. Then they would tell me that every time I used the salt I would be using God's blessing and I would be blessing my food like when they pray. Then they prayed over our bed. They explained that every time we had sex it would be a religious rite, thanking God for procreation. They said it would honor God and He would give us children. They wouldn't greet me like they greeted George; instead they would bless me in the name of Jesus and ask for my mind to be healed of the disease of atheism, before they even said 'hello.'"

Rachael moved from her chair to the space on the couch next to Sheila. "I am so sorry. That was awful. God doesn't seem very real when Christians act like that. I would have a difficult time believing in God if that is all I saw."

"Thank you for your understanding. I have one more thing to get off my chest."

"Please, go ahead, tell us."

"I avoid seeing George's family as much as possible without being unkind or antisocial, but now it seems that Christians at work and those who know me are starting to treat me as the reason for all these disasters. It's like George's family is everywhere. I'm sorry, honey, for saying that."

"No, no, don't be sorry. I feel the same way," George quickly answered.

"I want you to know, you will never be treated like that by us," Mike said. Rachael added her concurrence by hugging Sheila and holding her hand.

"You're Christians. I can see the Bibles and the pictures on the wall. I read the *Foot Prints* plaque you have hanging over there by the front door. You quietly prayed over your meal, without uncomfortably including me. Thank you for that, by the way. However, don't you believe in hell where people who displease God burn forever?"

"No, we don't believe in an everlasting burning hell and we, like Maama, believe that death is death."

"I don't understand. Don't all Christians believe in an afterlife and hell?"

"We believe that death is death and when we die we go to the grave, not knowing anything because thoughts perish too. Then Jesus comes and raises us to a new life and we go with Him to heaven. Then we enjoy the afterlife. We don't believe that there will be a hell in existence somewhere in the universe where people will be in agony for millions of years. It wouldn't be a very loving God who would allow that kind of a place to exist. Also, it wouldn't seem fair for Him to consign people to a punishment forever for a mere, seventy, eighty years of life where they didn't believe in Him. I believe in a God who loves us completely and would do everything for our happiness," Mike explained.

"That sounds completely different than what I've heard," Sheila observed. "You have a different belief than most people. Did you make that up yourselves?"

"No, we got it from the Bible and there are millions of believers in the world who believe as we do. We are Seventh-day Adventists," Rachael answered.

"Other Christians say they get their beliefs from the Bible. How can one be sure they are right?"

"There are many interpretations of the Bible. It is important to take the whole Bible front to back to make an accurate interpretation. For instance, the subject we were just talking about has many texts about death and the afterlife. One must consider them all together and then add in other texts that help it all make sense. Like when I said God is a loving God. One cannot take away from God's love by interpreting a hell of torment. Responsible use of the Bible means taking it as a whole, without trying to put or read into it your own preconceived ideas," Mike described.

"It sounds good the way you spell it out. But it all has to come down to belief. There are no facts."

"You're right, there are no facts. Experience grounds my faith."

"What kind of experience?"

"I spend time with God every day. I read and pray and then I find that what I have read and what I have prayed about becomes a part of my day. I can see His working in my life and answering some of my prayers. After doing this on a regular basis, I can see that He has been leading me and my life for years. It's a sense of His presence that gives me the experience I am talking about."

"Does God talk to you?" Sheila asked.

Rachael immediately thought of her dream. She didn't want to appeal to Sheila on a level that would not, or might not, happen for her. She didn't want to be sensational or appear as a crackpot in her eyes by relating her dream. Neither did she want to lie about the most recent message from the angel. "Indirectly. He speaks to me in many ways, mostly through the Bible."

"It all sounds wonderful for you, but that's just it. It's for you and your way of life. I have never sensed a presence of anything in that way, and probably never will."

"I guess I would have to say the same for me. When I grew up attending church, I didn't sense anything either. Admittedly, I didn't get into it very much. I horsed around with my friends more than paid attention to the preacher," George added.

"I don't want you to think we are trying to push religion on you against your will. We are Christians and it is difficult for us not to talk about our belief. I hope you don't feel uncomfortable in this conversation." Mike tried to take off any pressure that they might be feeling.

"Oh, no, no, no. I'm not uncomfortable. I've been asking the questions. I have to admit, though, it would be nice to experience what you're talking about. Kind of like proof that there is something there."

"That's simple. Ask Him. Ask Him to help you understand and then keep your eyes open for anything. You'll be surprised at how, or in what manner, He will answer you," Mike promised.

"That would be a prayer and I don't know how to pray."

"God doesn't stand on formality when an honest prayer is sent His way. I have prayed many a one-word prayer. Usually the word is 'Help!'"

Mike added overemphasis to his last word. Janelle answered from the kitchen, "Dad, what's wrong?"

"See! Answered prayer. Nothing, Janelle, I was just demonstrating my helplessness." The foursome smiled. Janelle came to the living room.

"Mom, Dad, can I borrow the car to go over to April's house? We planned to work on a school paper together, but I think she wants to talk about what's happening at school. Maybe we'll get some school work done."

"Sure, see you later."

The conversation changed in the direction of the Larsson's kids. The evening became a foundation for developing a long relationship that might not have enough time to mature.

* * * * * *

The news late in the week and into the weekend was about the searching and seizing of mosques. In some cases, extremist literature was found, but in most cases copies of the Qur'an were the excuse the government was looking for to shut down the mosques. It was as if the police and the National Guard were attempting to make excuses for terminating Islamic worship. The FBI was stretched thin in covering all the sites, however they were the lead organization on all investigations.

Demonstrations continued against the people of Islamic faith; marches and gatherings erupted at area mosques where shouting and signs were used to blame them for the bombings of the Christian churches. There were counter-demonstrations by Muslims and Muslim sympathizers. Sometimes there were clashes of the two groups. Rocks were thrown, fists flailed, and arrests were made. By far, the majority of those arrested were believers in Allah.

The White House blamed the riots on radical extremists and promised they would be prosecuted to the full extent of the law.

The media/press was abnormally quiet about the government's heavy hand in dealing with the disturbances and with the closing of so many mosques. They didn't even talk about the delay in the reopening of the ones not found to have provocative jihadist literature. There were no man-on-the-street interviews asking for Islamic opinion. No counterpoint discussions were seen on C-SPAN. The ACLU was also quiet. It might have been because the media didn't seek them out for their reaction, although the ACLU never had a problem with getting to the media in the past when they saw blatant violation of civil liberties. For most viewers and readers, listening to what was not said and reading between the lines was not a forte of their abilities. The diet of news and reactions to the news was slanted in favor of the government. The liberal press seemed, on the surface, to favor the Christian conservative government.

CHAPTER 10

A snow storm curtailed a number of activities for the Larsson household. Jason was unable to practice his soccer. The schools were closed and travel on the icy roads kept Rachael from visiting and witnessing to her friends and relatives. She limited herself to video calls which were not as effective in personal witness. Mike still had to go into work for the few remaining days before his vacation started. He had a 4x4 and used it to pick up some of the other employees from his office. The office remained open because the storm wasn't covering all of the fifty states and Canada. Several workers took vacation time and stayed home. Mike could not because he was using all of his accrued time later.

A foot of snow lay on the ground by 8 a.m. By noon, there was another foot and then by mid-afternoon the wind picked up and the storm turned into a full-scale blizzard. Weather forecasters explained that climate change was coupled with the melting polar ice caps and an increase in oceanic temperatures. They said that it was difficult to predict storms because all the computer models were based on former weather patterns when the oceans were cooler and the poles were more stable. They even spoke of magnetic shifts occurring where solar radiation from sunbursts could now enter the atmosphere at different angles, in new locations, and in greater intensity causing even more hikes in global temperatures.

Jason spent time in his room watching reruns of World Cup matches featuring Manchester United, his favorite team for all time. Janelle was on the phone planning with Darin. Rachael was in the office talking to Rochelle, getting an eyeful and an earful of the latest tactic she was using against Chris. Rachael kept looking for an opportunity to turn the topic to spiritual things. It wasn't happening. Her transmission had a window appear indicating a call from Molly. She excused herself to answer Molly.

"Hey, girl, I'm so pleased you called. I was thinking about you this morning when I woke up and saw all the snow. I wish I could send you some of this moisture."

"We don't need it. That's why I called you. I've had this bee in my bonnet for several days now because I wanted to talk to you, but then I waited to see if it was just a temporary phenomenon."

"What are you talking about? Did you get some rain?"

"Yes! But, I have to tell you the whole saga."

"Go ahead."

"Well, if I told you this story a week ago you would think I was barmy, but this really happened. The Archbishop of Canterbury made a big show of it and went to Windsor Park west of London and had a platform made. Then he called the BBC and had them cover the event. He said he was going to pray for rain. He dressed in his fancy robes and then he took the biscuit…"

"The biscuit?"

"Oh, I forget sometimes you're American. Taking the biscuit means he made a big show of it."

"Like, we say 'taking the cake,' sorta. I guess."

"Yes, well he slowly walks to the top of this stage, stands there all solemn like, and then raises his hands. After another pause, he shouts, 'Let there be rain!' He keeps his hands in the air and waits. Some of the cameras turn to the perfectly blue sky and then back down at him and they wait too. And then … Bob's your uncle, it starts to rain! With a cloudless sky, mind you. Everybody was in sixes and sevens, they didn't know what to do or think. The clouds came later and it's been raining for four straight days. We have flooded fields. Our rivers are full to over flowing."

"That is some story. Did it really happen or are you, as you say … barmy?"

"I know you're playing with me. Yes, it happened just like that. I've watched it several times on YouTube.

"That's amazing. What do you think about it?"

"That's why I called you. When we talked before you mentioned the Elijah deception. This is part of that. Elijah prayed for rain after he prayed for fire. This is half of the Elijah story on Mount Carmel."

"It is."

"However, the manner in which he did it was…How do I explain it? … Presumptive. The Archbishop presumed upon God. I don't think Elijah demanded. I think he asked, and politely at that."

"I agree. The way you described it sounds like God at creation. Speaking the world into existence saying, 'let there be…' Only the Archbishop is not God. How do you think he did it?"

"He had to have help, no two ways about it."

"Help from who is the question."

"It says Satan will appear as an angel of light and his servants will also disguise themselves as servants of righteousness. This could be some of their, or his, work of trying to woo people away from the true God."

"My thoughts exactly. I forgot to tell you one detail."

"What's that?"

"Our drought here has been three and a half years, just like it was in the time of Elijah."

"All this adds up. We are seeing a multitude of indicators."

"That's another thing I wanted to tell you. America is taking the lead. Our parliament is following, cracking the whip on mosques and Islamic people. We've had several close downs and people arrested. Religious freedoms are disappearing."

"The last movements are supposed to be swift. I guess we'll have to fasten our seat belts, so to speak. Molly, are you ready spiritually and everything?"

"I am, deary. All these signs are telling the tale. Church has been wonderful the last two Sabbaths. You can tell there's a revival going on. Grantham has demonstrated some real spirit. They are not charging for any of the literature they are printing.

> *The last movements are supposed to be swift. I guess we'll have to fasten our seat belts.*

Orders are doubled and donations have come in unsolicited. Jenifer told me when I called her three days ago. They are proud to be assisting in the last great push."

"Molly, I'm thinking that the next time we meet won't be too long from now, and it won't be here on earth."

"I can't wait."

"Neither can I. We just have to watch out for the deceptions and not be pulled into them. Let's have prayer together."

"I'd like that."

* * * * * *

The blizzard blew with gale force winds. Newscasters cautioned people to stay indoors. Some intrepid reporters attempted to stand in the wind at various street corners to give the viewing public a sense of how dangerous the storm was. The pictures were distorted by the thick swirls of snow streaming by the camera lenses. Each 3D video looked like a shaken snow-globe sitting on a coffee table. Concern occupied Rachael's thoughts. She called Mike to see if he knew how bad the storm was. He answered from the parking garage.

"They're letting us go home early, but the ramps are snowed in and we are shoveling the drifts so we can get out. We only have a few shovels and the snow is coming in faster than we can clear it out."

"Be careful. The news says that visibility is near zero. If you get out, will you be able to see where you are going?" she asked.

"I didn't know that. I'll talk with the others. Maybe we'll have to stay the night in the office. I'll call you back. I love you."

"I love you too."

A little later he called to let her know they would be in the office for the night. They were getting organized for the evening and he didn't stay on the line long enough for Rachael to tell him about the news from England.

* * * * * *

Mike started to organize the office for staying the night. George pitched in. The break room became the center of focus with some soft seats, a couch, and a table with four chairs. The vending machines provided as much sustenance as possible. Corn chips, candy bars, and soda pop comprised the majority of their dining options. Three bags of popcorn were highly prized. The coffee pot was set to brewing. Most called home to explain where they were to their families and then they watched the news channels. With work a low priority, the small group gathered to talk and watch the news in the break room. Someone brought out a deck of cards

and started a game of hearts. Attentions were divided between conversations, the game, and the old flat screen TV mounted on the wall. Mike and
George centered their focus on the news along with a few others. One of
the bags of popcorn was separated into paper bowls and passed around.
Mike asked George about Sheila. "Is your wife at home?"

"She's at work. Her shift starts at three, but she went in early to make
sure she would be able to get there."

"In her line of work, there's no such thing as a day off for a blizzard,
am I right?" Mike guessed.

"You are. If you can't get there, someone will come for you in an SUV
or a snowmobile."

"We needed a snowmobile to get home today. Hey, what was that? I
missed it," Mike asked suddenly.

"They stopped talking about the weather and now they're on religious
reform," Shelly answered.

"What did they say?"

"Listen, they just switched to a New York reporter at the old UN
building." Mike focused on the words; George introspectively turned his
focus on the screen.

~ ~ ~ ~ ~ ~

*"… at it for several hours, all day basically. No one knows if an agreement
has been reached. At this point, we can only speculate as to why theses Protestant leaders are meeting and not including any Catholic representation. The
President made this request. Perhaps this is the first step. We will have to …
wait a minute … here they come now. They're stepping up to the podium and
they look like they're going to make a statement.* [The camera swiftly pans
to the main platform. Various networks are scrambling to get a seat in the
front of the auditorium.]

*"Our purpose for meeting here today is historic and it was the product of
arduous prior groundwork that, we think, is a creative opportunity. It has taken
five hundred years for the rift between Christian faith groups to be addressed.
I think it apropos that we are meeting in a historic building such as this. It
was established to ensure peace among the nations and now it is achieving
reconciliation amongst the religious ideologies of faith. Today, the leaders of
the majority of Protestant denominations have come together to resolve the
issues that divide us. I have been asked by the President of the United States
to head this august synod of forward thinking reformers during these deliberations. We all agree, the needs of this world are so horrendous that we cannot*

continue to lead spiritually without mending fences and presenting a unified whole to the world and to God. We have resolved to band together into one religious organization. This is a wonderful accomplishment. Let me hasten to state, no one denomination was asked to violate their individual expressions of faith. Denominational integrity has been maintained.

"Our resolution is to focus on what we hold in common, not what makes us distinctively different. We present to all of Protestant Christendom the five fundamental tenets of belief. They are: Faith in God, Jesus as Our Savior, the Bible as our basis for faith, Sunday divine worship, and benevolence toward the poor. Every fundamentally sound Christian faith group holds these truths dear to their hearts.

"Once we agreed to coalesce into one unified whole, we then sought for a structure for governance. We organized a representative council that would coordinate activities, finance, ordination, missions, and all liturgical needs, including ministry to the downcast. We purposely left open the chair of leadership.

"Next on our agenda this evening was a resolution to bring together the two great halves of Christianity. A video conference with the Pope has been most productive. We invited him to chair our council and we pledged to blend our efforts with his for world reform with the substantial resources at his disposal. I was pleased that we asked him and even more pleased that he consented. I can confidently state and with deep pleasure announce the rift is now gone. We are one church, under one God, in a vineyard ripe for reform! Amen."

~ ~ ~ ~ ~ ~

Mike sat momentarily stunned by the announcement. It was expected because prophecy said it would happen, yet surprising because it was so sudden. Others, like Marshall and Zack rejoiced. George watched Mike's reaction, knowing he was not in agreement. It took a few moments before their eyes met. There was a quiet nod between them. George understood Mike's attitude about freedom of faith and the worship on Sunday. He did not know the impact this news was having on his friend's emotions. Mike dropped deep into thought about the differences that had to be overcome for this coalition to happen. Protestantism was reaching its hands across the gulf to form an alliance with the Catholic Church. There was a significant theological stance that had to change or be forgotten in the rush to join. Notes from his basic theology class from Union College came to mind. The Catholic Church and Protestants, in general, disagreed on the fundamental point of salvation. It was faith in the work of rites in opposition to faith alone, using the symbolism of rites. Communion saves vs. saving faith in the Savior that communion represents. He said, *wow* inwardly. An electrical snap in his jaw added to the moment of surprise. His hand automatically went to his cheek as if he was reacting to the news. He wanted to phone Rachael immediately, but was distracted by the conversation between Marshall and Zack.

"The President is right—we have to get together to win back God's blessing. The churches are agreeing with him and the Muslims are getting whipped into compliance," Zack emphasized.

"I think we're in for a soaring economy, with prices stabilizing and sales increasing. I'm getting into some Proctor and Gamble stock," Marshall predicted.

"That means I'll have to stop playing the commodities market; food prices should level off and there won't be as much escalation due to these disasters. I've made a killing so far, but common stock will be the place to be here forward," Zack planned.

"I wouldn't plan on too rosy of a picture for the future," Mike cut in.

"Why?" Zack asked.

"Because … The Bible predicts disasters and famines and more wars."

"But, if we come together as a nation, then God will bless us. Look! I heard there was a drought in England that was stopped by the Archbishop. It was a miracle. My minister spoke about it in his sermon last Sunday. He commanded the rain to come and it came. See what God can do if we come together?"

"Oh, I believe that God blesses in marvelous and miraculous ways. But we have to understand that at the end of time the world is going to be torn apart with earthquakes and afflicted with all kinds of problems."

"Where does the Bible say that?" Marshall asked with incredulity.

"Matthew twenty-four. I think I remember the words correctly. It says, 'For nation will rise against nation, and kingdom against kingdom, and there will be famines and earthquakes in various places. All these are but the beginning.' Jesus says it will be like giving birth. It's what has to happen before we are taken to heaven and the earth will eventually be made new."

Marshall thought for a moment and then answered, "It looks like that has already happened. We've had everything in the way of disasters, wars have been everywhere. The radical rag-heads have attacked us on our own land, in our own cities and churches. With the President leading us, we are going to have a new earth under Christian leadership worldwide. The President's Catholic. He'll do what the Pope tells him to do."

"Yeah, that's it. This world is changing for the better. The only thing that will slow things up is people who can't see the truth. Like atheists," Zack pronounced. He was looking at George.

"Diversity is an American fundamental. As Americans, we believe that everyone is supposed to be free to worship or not worship as they see fit. Is the United States going to forget what made it great in the first place? America is a melting pot, racially, culturally, and religiously," Shelly cut in.

"What's your play in all this? You sound like a bleeding heart for all the poor non-Christians who need a break. Give *me* a break! Give *America* a break! This country needs to be blessed once again. It started out Christian. It was Christian people who established this nation. It will return to its greatness with Christians," Zack answered.

"You forget the Native Americans—they were here first and they knew how to conserve our natural resources, unlike the pioneers who wasted the land. You ask what my play in all this is? It is that I am a full-blood Arapaho. That's my play in all this!" she emphasized.

"So you worship the sky god. He hasn't helped your people very much," Zack sneered.

"I'm a born-again Christian and I worship God on Sunday, just like you do. However, there is a problem when church dominates politics. Don't you remember your world history and American history classes? In the Middle Ages, the church dominated and people were tortured and killed, and then in our own colonies the church leaders, who were the civic leaders also, tortured people for adultery or condemned them as witches. They were also in the new land because of the lack of religious freedom in the old world. I worship God voluntarily because of what He did for me on the cross. I don't, and wouldn't, worship Him if I was coerced to do so by the government. The old way, the church dominant, has raised its ugly head again. You're acting like bullies if you think you can make people be Christians against their will!"

"Folks, I need to interject here. Our conversation is becoming a little heated. Remember a while back I said we needed to agree to disagree? That's important. It's important now because we are stuck here tonight and need to get along. It probably would be good if we all took a little break," Mike soothed. Since Mike was the manager, they had to follow his direction. Mike wanted to get more information about the rain in England so he could tell Rachael. When the group got engaged in other things, he went to Zack to ask more specifics.

"Zack, I want to ask you something." Zack's face looked questioningly, but with wariness thinking the boss might get after him for his remarks. "My wife spent some time during college in England. She has friends over there. What's this about the Archbishop praying for rain? I'd like to tell Rachael about it." Zack visibly relaxed.

"The Archbishop took the bull by the horns and asked God for rain. It started to rain even though there weren't any clouds."

"Really?"

"It's on YouTube. Let's go to my desk. I'll show you." The two settled around Zack's desk to watch. When he accessed the menu, which included the Windsor story. there were a number of other stories on miracles. Zack was surprised. "These weren't here last time I looked," he reacted. First they watched the Archbishop call for the rain, and then they pulled up some of the other stories. One was about a five-car crash on the Autobahn in Germany. A man extinguished the flames, ripped cars apart with bare hands to free the trapped passengers, and then laid his hands on the burns, which disappeared. The stranger could not be found. The next video, like the first, came from a phone camera. It showed an earthquake with walls collapsing and a street full of frantic people running. One woman was running with a child in her arms. The child had a compound fracture of the leg. The bone was protruding through the pants and bleeding. Another woman stopped her, took the child, and set him on his feet. Suddenly, there was no streaming blood, no broken leg, only a clean hole in the pants where the bone had been. The camera moved toward the victim and then sought to capture the woman who had performed the miracle. She could not be found as the view rapidly shifted from left to right and then back again to the lady and the boy, who was testing the leg by stomping on the ground.

The next videotape was from a professional news crew in Costa Rica. A reporter was explaining, in Spanish, with subtitles, the huge snake infestation that had swept through town. He gave details that the snakes were the poisonous Fer-de-lance and how people and children were bitten and suffering, some were at the point of death, and then something miraculous happened. A lady appeared. He said he would let the video tell the story. The scene shifted to a street near a school with people running to and from the school yard. Men were using shovels to bash snakes, which could be seen squirming across the roads, sidewalks, and over the playground walls. A woman appeared in the middle of the street and picked up a writing serpent and held it over her head. The Fer-de-Lance did not harm her, even though it is a breed known for its lightening quick strikes. She commanded in a loud voice, "Look!" Many stopped what they were doing to watch. She laid the snake on her shoulders and bent down to a suffering, bitten mother protecting her child. She touched the mother and took her hand bidding her to stand. The effects of the poisonous bite were gone. She then directed everyone in a loud voice to look at her and be healed. There was a moment of confused hope, then a murmur of surprise, and finally a rejoicing, which included some careful dancing away from the still plentiful vipers. The woman with the serpent on her neck walked away from the camera down the street motioning with her hands to follow. At first the people thought she meant them, but then it was apparent she meant the snakes. The ground moved as if by command. The surface became covered with sliding, wiggling bodies acting like puppies chasing a succulent bone. The slithering parade moved down the street to the small river and when the leader of the procession stepped into the water, the vipers entered and were washed downstream by the current. The reporter sought an interview with the lady still holding the one snake around her neck. At first she ignored him. Then, by repeated address, he was able to bring her out of a trance. Translation was written across the bottom of the screen.

~ ~ ~ ~ ~ ~

"Senora, may I have your name?"

"My name is Guadalupe."

"That was truly amazing. How did you do that?"

"I was told by the spirits; they are my masters. The Great Spirit of the sun and the moon and the stars commands the essence of every living thing. The Great One told the lesser ones to direct me. I obeyed."

"Is the Great Spirit you speak of a demon?"

"Oh, no, no, no. Demon is a bad name for a strong force. The force obeys the Great Spirit. The Great Spirit controls him and he, in turn, tells me to save the people by controlling the snakes."

At that point in the conversation the snake around her neck uncoiled, stretched out attempting to examine the microphone in the reporter's hand. The reporter withdrew his hand to a safer distance and curtailed the interview before other questions could be asked.

~ ~ ~ ~ ~ ~

They watched that video several times and then watched the Archbishop story again several times. It was truly amazing. Miracles of majestic proportions were coming into full examination, as prophecy said they would. What would follow had Mike leery and transfixed at the same time. He questioned what other actions of supernatural power could be next. Mike's mind was fitting together more pieces of the puzzle. The picture was forming in clarity with a few blank areas yet open. He understood what needed to be in the missing areas, but not exactly the detail and the shape. Satan was probably hiding the last pieces in his hip pocket—the one large piece where he enters the picture. "Mike, you seem deep in thought. Aren't you impressed with these manifestations of God's power?" Zack asked.

"I am impressed. What has me thinking is what might be around the corner."

"Like what?"

"Well, when I read the Bible, I see Christ and Satan in warfare. They're in competition, so to speak. They both want converts. God's Holy Spirit will be poured out on His people and they are going to perform mighty works, healing the sick, bringing sight to the blind, just like Jesus and the disciples did at the beginning…"

"That's what I'm talking about! Bring it on."

"Like you, I look forward to His Holy Spirit's blessing. But, and it's a big but, Satan is also going to pretend to be Jesus and do mighty works. We have to be careful and watch."

"Are you thinking that the Archbishop is really Satan and this rain is the work of the devil and the miracle shouldn't have happened?"

"Archbishop Satan? No. Do I think the people of England should suffer more? Of course not. My wife has friends there who have been standing in bread lines to get a single loaf

The signs of the last days are telling us the time is near.

of bread. I don't wish that drought on anyone. What I'm saying is that the signs of the last days are telling us the time is near. With the time for Jesus' return close it means many of these things will be happening all over the world; some will be from God's hand and others will be from Satan's hand. It causes me to cheer and worry at the same time."

"Instead of worrying, I plan on helping the President get this country on track, clean this place up spiritually, and then Jesus will honor us with His coming. Am I right?"

"Noble aspirations. But I think there is a fatal flaw in the plan."

"What fatal flaw?"

"Jesus is going to come when this world is in the worst possible chaos. When He comes, the Bible says the wicked will be destroyed by the brightness of His coming. Before He comes, Satan will come and pretend to be Jesus. It's as simple as that. Jesus warns us to not be deceived."

"I don't know. This is new to me. I'll have to talk to my minister about this. Ah, I need to telephone my wife. I promised to call her, so she wouldn't worry."

"I need to talk to Rachael, too. Same deal as you. They worry about us, don't they?"

"They do."

* * * * * *

The wind howled through the buildings and houses, rattled windows, and caused bare branches to scrape on the sides of the walls. The effects compelled humans to snuggle into comforters and pillows, attempting to be warmer than what they would have felt normally. Rachael and the twins gathered around the Onyx view-screen to talk with their marooned husband and father. He spoke to them from the privacy of his office. They compared notes on the weather from their two locations and then spoke of the events witnessed by Mike on YouTube. Rachael hastened to tell Mike of her conversation with Molly. Mike added his perspectives on that phenomenon and told her briefly about the other items. Of particular concern was the conference of the Protestant leaders in New York. Janelle's excitement over the fulfilled prophesy of Protestantism and Catholicism was visibly apparent. She understood. She immediately wanted to tell her new non-believing friends about the prophesy, the friends she had made at Darin's former school.

"Just wait until they hear about this," she said.

"It depends on their degree of spiritual sensitivity as to whether they will understand its import, sweetheart," Mike cautioned his daughter.

"Why would they not understand this? It was predicted in the Spirit of Prophecy."

"Well, for several reasons; one of which is that the writings of our church are not authoritative in *their* minds. The best you might get out of them is a, 'That's interesting.' Remember, we have a special gift given to our church to prepare us for the future. Another reason it might not be effective is because the fulfillment of prophecy is for the believer. 'I tell you these things because when you see them come to pass you will believe.' Jesus spoke that to the disciples who were already believers. Prophecy is a validation and an encouragement to get ready. What I would do instead is point them to Jesus, then explain how He wants us to be ready for His coming. Tell them there will be some great deceptions beforehand. I just had a talk with a fellow believing Christian here in the office, but I had to be careful because he knows so little."

"I'll keep that mind. Thanks, Dad," Janelle answered.

"Jason, what do you think about all this? It looks like the time is short."

"If you say so, Dad. I haven't heard much about this Protestant/Catholic thing before you said it. How's Satan s'posed to take over this whole thing?"

"I don't know. I just know he's going to take the expected place of Jesus. It's like this. People have expectations. They think and question; if Jesus were to come today, where would He set up His kingdom? We know that He will come for us and return with us to heaven. But some believe that He will come to stay down here and rule the world. If there is a religious governing body, such as the one we saw formed today, the expectations would be that He would settle there. Only it will be the devil pretending to be Jesus. That is a broad stroke picture of what will happen, but I don't exactly know how he will appear and how he will assume control. I don't know because the Bible and Spirit of Prophecy don't spell out in what way he will command the nations. This evening, I heard some people here make an observation that because the President is Catholic and the Pope is the chairman of this religious coalition, he will do as the Pope instructs him to do. That is a guess on their part, but it makes a little sense. The false Jesus, the anti-Christ, will take control and command nations. In the Bible, this new world order is symbolically portrayed as the Beast, the False Prophet, and the Image of the Beast. I think we should at least be able to see that kind of coercive power form and know from that that we are very close…very close indeed. What was on the view screen this evening was at least the beginning of that power. Son, the time is getting shorter."

The lights flickered several times, causing the electronics to shimmer, fade, then come back on again. "I hope we don't lose power," Mike said. "It will end up being a cold night if it goes out. I'm going to raise the temperature on the floor just in case. I'll call you if anything changes, otherwise assume everything is fine. Take care. Stay warm. I love you all."

"We love you, too."

CHAPTER 11

Mike slept on the floor of his office, using a scarf and gloves as a pillow and his overcoat as a blanket. The wind ripped at the edges of the building, threatening to tear off chunks of bricks in an effort to assail the occupants inside. The whistling sound woke him up. The uncomfortable floor transposed its rigidness to Mike's joints, making them stiff. He had to stretch. News reports could be heard emanating from the break-room TV. He stiffly walked toward the sound, bending his back and holding his arms above his head. Shelly and Glenda had slept there, using the cushions of the couch and chairs for beds. They were visibly in a bad mood. Marshall was pouring coffee from a fresh brewed pot and offered a cup to his floor manager. Mike declined.

"Good morning. I'm not going to ask if everyone slept well. I think the answer will be less than inspiring." Mike got a cup of water and gulped it down. It was a morning ritual for him to start the day with water and continue it throughout the day, a hydro-replenishment minus the empty calories that normally would add to the waistline.

Without preamble, the women left for the bathroom. Mike was alone with Marshall.

"They're in a grumpy mood this morning. Just goes to show you that you really don't know a woman until you sleep with her," Marshall observed. It caused Mike to think there might have been some attempt at a liaison during the night. Knowing Marshall by association, he knew who the culprit was.

"Any news of note on the monitor?" he tried to change the topic.

"I wanted to turn it on, but they wouldn't have it. It's like they own this room."

"We can go into my office and watch the news. That'll give the ladies a little privacy."

"Naw, I'm staying here. It's a free country. By the way, I've been meaning to ask you a question. What kind of a Christian are you? Zack tells me you know a lot about the Bible."

"I study the Word regularly. I think all Christians should read the Bible."

"But, what kind of Christian are you?"

"I'm a Seventh-day Adventist Christian."

"Mormon?"

"No, I—"

"Jehovah's Witness?"

"No. Seventh-day Adventists are not Mormons or Jehovah Witnesses. We are a Protestant denomination that believes in the soon coming of Jesus."

"Yeah, I do too. He'll come when we clean this mess up."

"Remember, we have to agree to disagree because we want to remain friends. I have a different view. I believe this mess will get worse and the only cleaning will be when the earth is made new after we return from heaven in the New Jerusalem."

> *Seventh-day Adventists are not Mormons or Jehovah Witnesses. We are a Protestant denomination that believes in the soon coming of Jesus.*

"Where do you get that information?"

"In the Bible, from the book of Revelation."

"Revelation. Isn't that the book with all that whacky symbolism stuff?"

"Revelation has a lot of symbolism, yes, you're right. But it's there for us to understand if we study. Jesus told us that we need to understand. He said, 'When you see the abomination of desolation, let the reader understand.' I take that to mean we should study it."

"What's this abomination of deso ... despot supposed to be?"

"Abomination of desolation. You said 'despot' which is pretty accurate as well. The abomination of desolation is when Satan assumes control of the world by pretending to be Jesus. Because he is who he is, I'm guessing he will be a despot, too."

"Why would anyone want to follow Satan?"

"Good point! But remember he will be impersonating Jesus and many good-hearted people want to follow Jesus. Satan will attempt to sell the public with a false bill of goods about making this world a better place."

"So, you're saying I'm all wrong."

"No, I hear you say you want to make a difference for good. I see that Jesus is your motivation. I just don't want you to get on the wrong side of this controversy between Christ and Satan. It's going to be very deceptive. Jesus is coming and we have to be ready for him."

"You mean the rapture." Glenda spoke from the doorway.

* * * * * *

Snug in their beds, wrapped in thick comforters, the fragmented Larsson family slept late. Alarms had been turned off. Conversely to Mike's experience with the wind waking him, the howling wind was like a humming lullaby. When Rachael finally woke, she felt guilty for sleeping in cozy warmth when she knew her life's partner was in Spartan conditions. She went to the kitchen encased in a thick full-length robe and fluffy slippers. She had plans to make a special breakfast and then start a big pot of chili simmering on the stove for later in the day. With the late hour, she knew that they would only need two meals for the day. Her plans caused her to think about her Bible reading the night before. The Israelites, in the wilderness, were cared for by God Himself. He fed them two meals a day, morning and evening, as they longed for and traveled to their new land of promise. She mused as she mixed pancake batter. *I wonder what He will do for us on the way to heaven?* Her thoughts ranged over a number of collateral subjects. *We won't be eating to stay warm, that's for sure. Our first meal in the heavenly city will be a feast, the Marriage Supper of the Lamb. I wonder what He will prepare for us.* A smile graced her face as she worked lumps out of the batter. She never allowed herself the style of leaving the smaller lumps in pancake batter. It seemed strange to leave them in when she wanted only the best for her family. She worked the batter until it was creamy smooth. *Jesus only wants the best for His children. Any meal He provides for the feast will be the utmost blessing to us all!* Her smile broadened and her chin lifted in anticipation.

"What's for breakfast, Mom? I'm starved!" Jason called as he bounded down the stairs.

"Is there any time when you are not hungry?" she answered back. Jason leaned over her arm to look at the bowl of pancake batter. A finger slipped along the edge, attempting to snag a taste of the uncooked contents. "It always tastes better when it's cooked and after I've added the blueberries, young man."

"Come on, Mom. I'm dying here. I need some fuel for the day ahead. A day full of no surprises, no activities, and house arrest because of this blizzard!"

"You could set the table, pour the juice, and place the fruit in the center. By that time, I should have the first pancakes ready for your desperately empty fuel tank." Jason started to prepare the table with a typical teenage lack of attention to detail. The plates were scattered, not placed, the silverware was in a clump in the middle, and the glasses were stacked inside of each other at the table's edge. He sat down to read the news on his Onyx 4000-TS, forgetting to get the juice out of the refrigerator. He reminded his mother of his father and how he was always trying to be up on the news. As she gazed at her son, it reminded her of the mutual concern she and Mike had about his cavalier attitude toward the transpiring events.

"Jason, you saw the news recap of the New York conference of churches. How do you feel about that?"

"It happened. Not much can be done about it. It's above my pay grade. Incidentally, about my allowance…"

"Jason, it seems to me that you are avoiding talking about deep spiritual things. Are you okay? Your father and I pray for you every day. We're concerned."

"Why, Mom? I'm a believer. I believe in Jesus. That's all that is needed, right?"

"Yes, that is the basic truth. But, no, that's not all that is needed. We have to be completely committed to Him in everything. Believing in Him is not a bargain. It's an emotionally, intellectually, spiritually expensive relationship. We are about to be tested with the greatest test of faith for all time. I'm afraid it will test me beyond my ability to cope. I'm more afraid for you than for me because you are my son. I don't want you to be disqualified, like the Apostle Paul said of himself. He struggled to be qualified—worried that he might fall short."

"Ma, I'm ready. Aren't I?"

Rachael looked down and flipped the first batch of pancakes. She was searching for a way to get through to her son. "What I'm telling you is that we have to be, as you say, 'above your game.' How can I explain the difference? I know. When you make pancakes the instructions tell you to mix the batter but not to worry about the little lumps that may occur. I can't do that. If there is the tiniest lump in the batter I will keep mixing until it is gone. My mother taught me to mix the batter, too. She told me the same thing, 'Don't worry about the little lumps; they'll disappear when you cook them.' I couldn't do that then and I can't do that now. I want perfect pancakes for my children. My children deserve the very best that I can give. Jesus will always get my best. I will not try to slide into His love at the easiest level. He gave me His all. I will give Him my all. The only one who can judge if you are really ready is you. Only you will know if you are giving Him your all."

Jason stared at his mom in what appeared to be deep thought and then he pointed to the frying pan. "Are they ready?" Rachael lifted the pan off the flame. Peeking under the edge of one of them revealed that they were just right, not too dark, not too light.

"Here, for you. I did my best."

* * * * * *

The question about the rapture changed everyone's focus. Glenda was in the doorway and Shelly was just behind her. It was as if Marshall was not in the room. They directed their eyes at Mike and past Marshall. Glenda sat down at the table to listen to Mike's answer while Shelly went to replace the cushions from the floor to the couch and chair.

"The word rapture is not in the Bible."

"It's not? I'm sure it is. We talk about it all the time at church. The rapture is going to take us away from all this. The wicked and evil people will be left here to make a better world if they can. And all the Jews, His chosen people, will see what they missed and then they will believe in Jesus, finally," Glenda explained.

"No, you've got that wrong. The rapture comes after the millennium and before the time of trouble. We have to make our best effort now. We have to bring in the millennium ourselves," Marshall countered.

"I heard that the rapture comes after the seven years of tribulation but before the thousand-year millennium," Shelly interjected.

"I'm a mid-trib believer myself." Leo spoke from the doorway. He and George had heard the discussion and decided to join in. Zack was behind them. Blank faces stared at Leo. "I believe that the rapture will take place three and a half years after the start of the tribulation. The second half of the tribulation will be the worst part, but we'll be gone. 'Two women will be working in the field, one will be taken and the other one left behind.' There'll be driverless cars crashing on the highways because the driver will be taken and the passengers won't know what happened. It will shock everyone who is left behind to get it right with the Lord. That's when the final half of the trib begins and the millennium starts after that."

"So, Jesus comes at the middle of the tribulation?"

"Yes."

"No."

"After the millennium."

"In the middle of the millennium? What?"

"No, He comes in the middle of the tribulation, before the millennium."

"The trib is after the millennium and He comes before the trib."

"The tribulation is what starts the millennium and He comes before the second half."

"Which is it? Does He come before or after the thousand years of peace?"

"Both. He comes before in the rapture, secretly, but then He comes again after the millennium when every eye will see Him. That's when He raises the dead, after the millennium."

"You've got to be kidding! He has two second comings?" Zack asked.

"Mike, you're the only one that's not talking. You know the Bible pretty well. What do you say?" George entered the conversation.

"Yes, what does the Seventh-day Adventist say about this?" Marshall interjected.

"You're SDA? I have an aunt who's an SDA. Nice, but decidedly different. She goes to church on Saturday," Glenda remarked.

"SDAs go to church on Saturday? How's that going to work with the new order of churches forming? That's one of the five points of agreement. Everyone goes to church on the same day, Sunday," Shelly observed.

"Hey, folks, give him a chance. Let Mike answer one of your questions at a time," George tried to help Mike.

Mike was aware that this was a very spirited conversation. His answer now could very well turn people away from his witness. "I want you to know all of you are my friends. I want to keep it that way. If what I say disagrees with what you believe, please don't be offended. Give me a moment to get my Bible out of my desk."

He left and Marshall murmured, "He keeps a Bible in his desk?"

Opening his Bible, he began: "The first question was about the rapture. It is true that the word rapture is not in the Bible. It is a word that describes what many believe will happen. It comes from the words of Jesus in the gospel of Luke. 'One will be taken and the other left.' It can give the impression of a secret sudden rapture where people go to heaven. A lot of people believe that concept." Mike pointed at Glenda when he spoke. "For a point of commonality among us all, we agree that Jesus is definitely coming. Am I right?" They shook their heads in agreement. "How He is coming is a mystery with several clues to help us. The clues are from the Bible. I prefer to use as many references about a subject in the Bible that I can get and then put them together for a logical whole. In Luke, He speaks of 'two women grinding at the same place; one will be taken and the other will be left.' Later in the same book, chapter twenty-one, Jesus speaks of, 'distress of nations…men fainting with fear and foreboding of what is coming in the world; the powers of the heavens will be shaken. And then they will see the Son of Man coming in a cloud with power and great glory.' That is a reference which gives the impression of a visible return, and that return is in a troublesome time.

"Next, we can look at the book of First Thessalonians, chapter five, 'For you know very well that the day of the Lord will come like a thief in the night.' That also gives the impression of a sudden, secret coming. But in the next book of Thessalonians it says, 'Don't let anyone deceive you in any way, for that day will not come until the rebellion occurs and the man of lawlessness is revealed, the man doomed to destruction. He will oppose and will exalt himself over everything that is called God or is worshiped, so that he sets himself up in God's temple, proclaiming himself to be God.' When we see that happen, we'll know that Jesus' second coming hasn't happened yet, but is very near. Then, back in the first book of Thessalonians it says, 'For this we say to you by the word of the Lord, that we who are alive and remain until the coming of the Lord, will not precede those who have fallen asleep. For the Lord Himself will descend from heaven with a shout, with the voice of the archangel and with the trumpet of God, and the dead in Christ will rise first. Then we who are alive and remain will be caught up together with them in the clouds to meet the Lord in the air, and so we shall always be with the Lord…" That gives the strong indication of a huge event with shouting, voices, and the trumpet of God. Then the book of Revelation helps us as well. Chapter one says, 'Behold, He is coming with the clouds, every eye will see Him…' There are many references to Jesus coming back to earth. Each reference gives a hint of what it will be like. In the book of Acts, angels tell the disciples that just like Jesus ascended into the clouds He will come back in the same way. These few texts give you an idea of what's going on when Jesus comes. They also give us an understanding of how all our beliefs, as different as they are, can find a basis in Scripture. Our only hope is to reconcile *all* of the texts into a single logical whole." The group was nodding their heads, some in agreement with Mike's last sentence, while some were nodding their approval of Mike's knowledge of Scripture. It was difficult to tell from their exteriors whether they had altered their thinking. George was impressed. He was about to ask for some clarification, but his phone rang. It provided a chance for individuals to break away from the conversation. Mike took a moment to reflect on the up-tempo of his condition. He wondered if the electrical attacks to his face were enhanced by the lack of sleep. It was wearing on his nerves.

* * * * * *

The house phone rang while the three were cradling their Onyxs in the living room. Rachael noticed that the ID number was from a hospital. A splinter of worry stabbed through her thoughts before she answered. Sheila's voice sounded excited.

"Rachael, I had to call you as soon as I could. I mean, I called you after I called George first, of course. But it is so wonderful. I just had to tell you."

"What happened?"

"I prayed."

"Tell me what happened."

"I have to start from the beginning. I really thought about what you and Mike said about God. I kept thinking and wondering if I prayed, would God answer? Then there was this morning's Rapid Response. I tell you, when we work on a shift during a storm we can expect all kinds of things to happen. I guess it's because of the low atmospheric pressure. Anyway, after two heart attacks I was pretty tired and then Peds called with a heart failure on an infant. We all ran to the Pediatric floor. I guess I'm different when it comes to a small child. I get all emotionally attached.

"It really was intense, more so than regular, if you could call any Rapid Response regular. The parents were in a corner worried sick, crying. I was attending on the right side. Two nurses were performing CPR. Doctors were calling out for meds and monitoring read-outs. There was STAT this and STAT that. One of the biggest problems was trying to get a line in the baby's arm. The original one had failed. I started to put one in. The veins were collapsed or too small to find. I tried the arm, the foot, the leg. Nothing worked. I remembered what Mike said, sometimes his prayer is simply 'help.' My hand with the needle was paused above the skin—above, not touching. I prayed to Him. I said, 'Help!' The nurse in front of me said, 'What?' and I looked at her. She was confused because she looked at the needle and back at me. When I looked down, it was in and working! I could see the tiny speck of blood in the tube. I was so surprised I almost forgot to tape it down. The medicine went in after that and we had a response. Soon, we were able to pause manual CPR to see if the child could continue on its own. It was a breathless moment where we all stared at the monitor. The little tyke survived. I prayed another prayer only this time it was two words, 'Thank you.'"

"I'm so pleased for you. How do you feel?"

"It's a surprise to me. I don't know how I feel. I prayed and He answered. I don't know how He did it."

> *I don't know how I feel.*
> *I prayed and He answered.*
> *I don't know how He did it.*

"Sheila, I have to tell you, you did the right thing. Some people will pray selfishly, asking for cars, houses, and money. You prayed for the baby, not for yourself. God honored you and your unselfish request. You know, we are His hands in this world to help others."

"But, I don't think my hands did it. I think it was Him."

"You were there. You were holding the needle. He worked through you. He only works through willing people, especially when they pray. What are you going to do now?"

"I guess I'm going to pray again, but I really don't know how."

"It's easy. It's just like you are talking to me. Jesus says we should pray to the Father through Jesus and the Holy Spirit translates what we are saying into the right words for the right reasons. You don't have to worry about what you are saying because the Holy Spirit makes what you are saying beautiful and correct. Picture it this way. God is leaning forward, listening to you, because He really wants to know you. Jesus is next to His Father, listening and claiming you as His very own family. The Holy Spirit is standing beside you with His arms around you, explaining the words you are saying in a manner consistent with God's will for this world. How can you go wrong with all that help? And then, near you is your very own personal angel who receives instructions to help you, to protect you if you want his help."

"How do you know all this?"

"The Bible. In the Bible Jesus says, 'He will command His angels concerning you to guard you.' And in another place, 'The Spirit also helps our weakness; for we do not know how to pray as we should, but the Spirit Himself intercedes for us.' There are more texts that explain the relationship you have with Jesus and His Father. You can't lose with a team like that on your side."

"I like the help I got today."

"There's more to come."

"Ummm, Rachael, after my shift today, or maybe after this snowstorm, can I come over to your place and you can show me some more things out of the Bible?"

"Anytime."

"Thanks. I've got to finish my shift. My break is over. I've got to go."

"Do you have enough time to have me say a little prayer?"

"Yes, please."

"Dear Lord, thank you for answering Sheila's prayer today. Help her some more in ways she can see. In Jesus' name, amen."

* * * * * *

"I don't know about you, but I'm hungry. We ate everything we had last night. What are we going to do now? Does the Bible say anything about that?" Marshall asked.

Mike knew Marshall was speaking sarcastically. It was a putdown of himself and the Bible he didn't care to use.

"As a matter of fact it does and there's also another text that talks about seeing the king visibly. It's found in the book of Isaiah, chapter thirty-three, I think. Here it is. I've got it marked. 'He who walks righteously and speaks with sincerity, He who rejects unjust gain and shakes his hands so that they hold no bribe; He who stops his ears from hearing about bloodshed and shuts his eyes from looking upon evil; He will dwell on the heights, His refuge will be the impregnable rock; His bread will be given him, His water will be sure. Your eyes will see the King in His beauty; They will behold a far-distant land...' I believe this is talking about the end of time and the far distant land is heaven."

"That's all very well and good, but we're going to need food," Marshall added.

"Okay then. Let's make that a priority. Maybe we can make a quick foray out to see if there's any building open that can help us. Who's with me?"

"I'll go," George answered.

"Me too," Zack added.

"Take Marshall with you. He's the hungry one," Glenda said while throwing a knowing look at Shelly.

"That's four. That's enough. I suggest we go in two teams of two and we'll go in different directions," Mike planned.

"I have a suggestion. There's a Chinese restaurant on the next block. I know the owner lives above the place. You might try there," Leo added.

"You know there's an all-night convenience store on Eighth Street. Maybe someone got marooned there like us. I've got an extra thick scarf if one of you could use it." Shelly looked directly at Mike.

"Thank you. But I have a scarf," Mike declined.

"I could use it. It would be like a knight in shining armor sallying forth with the fair maiden's token of love," Marshall opined.

"Never mind, I'm feeling a chill coming on." Shelly almost gagged.

The four intrepid scouts went to find food and the remainder of the stranded band organized for the day. The news reports were not encouraging. Weather radar indicated more wind and drifting snow. Precipitation for the next 24 hours was expected to be between eighteen to twenty-four inches of accumulation.

Mike and George fought through huge drifts that carved crescents around the corners of buildings. They were headed toward the Chinese restaurant. George wanted to talk, but was hampered by the wind, which tore the words out of his mouth and threw them a dozen miles away. He gave up.

The restaurant was dark. They peered through the top of a window, lying on a snowbank piled against the glass. As their eyes adjusted, they could see a light in the kitchen. They tapped on the window to attract attention. Eventually a man came to the window. He motioned for them to go around back to the alley. The back door had less snow in front of it because the wind was blowing it away.

The proprietor was more than happy to have the business. They ordered ten servings of eight of the most popular dishes. Mike and George waited in the empty dining room, delighted that it was warm. George took the opportunity to tell Mike about Sheila's answered prayer. George was just as happy as Mike. It was interesting to realize that underneath it all he was pleased that his wife had found an experience with God.

"George, are you going to start praying again?"

"Yes, I think I will."

"That's great. What are you going to pray for first?"

George was surprised by the question. "I haven't thought about it. I guess I'll pray that Sheila will continue having a great experience."

"And for yourself?"

"I suppose I'll pray for a baby. Sheila so desperately wants her own. I'd like God to answer a prayer for her. We've been trying forever."

"That would be nice, wouldn't it?"

"Yes."

"If God chooses to answer your prayer now, that child might be born in heaven."

"You really believe that Jesus is coming soon?"

"Yes, I do."

"I've never met anyone like you. I was impressed with your knowledge of the Bible. I wish I knew as much as you."

"It's not difficult to learn. I study a little every morning and take notes when the pastor's preaching. I'll help get you started."

"Thanks. That discussion up in the office was something. It seems like everyone has a different viewpoint. I remember some of that from my home church. It didn't make sense then and didn't make sense up there until you explained it from your Bible."

"You know, when we get together to study the Bible, let's start on the subject of Jesus' second coming."

"It wouldn't hurt if you did the same thing with all of them up there. I don't know if they would accept it though; they seem to be an independent bunch."

"I'm willing if they're interested. Do you think they are uninterested?"

"They act a bit like my family—willing to say what they believe, but not necessarily interested in listening to what others believe."

"Do you think your family will be happy with Sheila's discovery?"

"I'd rather not tell them. Who knows what things they will say or do to Sheila? They might even tell her she didn't pray right or something. I wouldn't want her to get discouraged."

"I wouldn't want that for her or you for that matter. I'll pray that God continues to lead in your lives."

"Mike, do you have a tooth ache?"

"Why do you ask?"

"Because you look like you're in pain. Your face is a little crooked."

He didn't want to open up to George before he told his own children, so he dodged the question. "I have an appointment with the doctor day after tomorrow to check on things."

The order arrived in four large shopping bags. They would have a difficult time getting it back to the office.

* * * * * *

Rachael was wondering how long this storm would last. She turned on the all-news channel, which usually had updates on the local weather on the half hour. What she found was a White House press conference in the making. The press secretary stood amidst the press corps, casually answering questions in a friendly stance of mutual brotherhood. He was working the press corps like a leadoff act in Las Vegas.

On cue, he slipped to the podium and announced the President.

~ ~ ~ ~ ~ ~

Ladies and gentlemen of the press, the President of the United States of America.

Good afternoon. To begin I would like to quote from Charles Dickens' book, A Tale of Two Cities. Everyone knows his opening lines, but not many remember the phrases that follow: '… it was the epoch of belief, it was the epoch of incredulity, it was the season of Light, it was the season of Darkness, it was the spring of hope, it was the winter of despair…'

These words frame my observation of what is happening in our world today. The central portion of our great country is enduring a massive snowstorm covering the Plains States and the states bordering the Rocky Mountains. My personal prayers are directed toward these citizens, asking that they are warm and have enough food to carry them through. I will also ask for the participants in tomorrow's National Day of Prayer to make of them a special prayer concern. Snow totals for this storm are estimated to be three, almost four feet in some areas. It will require a lot of labor and time for these communities to dig out from under this onslaught of nature. It is truly a winter of despair. They look forward to a spring of hope.

We glimpse ahead to a spring of hope, metaphorically. We are on the cusp of an epoch of hope. Before us lies the greatest time of all history, when we will usher in the golden age of faith. Yesterday we all witnessed a monumental event—the coalescing of the Christian church into a unified whole. Christian leaders of all denominations have come together. The Protestant and the Cath-olic wings of the church have agreed to put their minds, hearts, and resources together to form what I see as the grand epoch of religious hope. I couldn't be more proud as a President, more delighted as an individual citizen, and more elated as a Christian man seeking commonality of belief amongst his fellow worshipers. This is an enormous achievement for everyone in the world and for generations to come. And, a legacy for my presidency of which I will be most proud. My grateful thanks and admiration goes out to the spiritual leaders who brokered this alliance. It remains now for other non-faith groups to recognize the wisdom of this alliance and join hands with them for the dividends it offers.

As in any great achievement, there are also those who, out of ignorance or arrogance, form an opposition to goodness. It represents an epochal incredulity. Some have hijacked several of the shipments of the solidarity bracelets. In one place, it was accompanied with violence. The motive for this act of crime is difficult to fathom. Why would anyone want to subvert a noble cause of helping disaster victims? My counselors tell me there might be some profit in black market sales from the miniature chips, or from the powerful little moti-vator cells. I can only say that this type of robbery will not go unpunished. I have a team putting the finishing touches on a fool-proof method of positively identifying, and managing, all citizens. Crime needs to be terminated. Defeat-ing and ending crime is the next big focus for my presidency. When plans are finalized with my teams, I will be bringing those exciting prospects before the public. We all will see a Season of Light, rather than a Season of Darkness. It will be the best of times rather than the worst of times. Thank you. My press secretary will answer any questions you might have.

~ ~ ~ ~ ~ ~

Janelle and her mother were leaning towards the view screen, as if that would make what they just witnessed more palatable to their lives. Sitting comfortably in a family room, lights shining from table lamps, soft carpet beneath their feet, and music softly playing in the background, seemed surreal compared to the hardships they knew were coming. The presi-dent's announcement portended future calamity. He was throwing down the gauntlet for those not in the alliance of churches, for those consid-ered of no faith. Without investigating, Rachael knew with certainty that the Adventist Church would not participate in such a conference, even if asked. The coalition of faith was considered the in-group by the President and all others as non-Christian. Then his remarks about defeating crime did not bode well for the nonaligned groups. If he zealously fought criminals it was only a sliver away from the oppression of those outside of his definition of faithful citizens. Formerly, at the State of the Union Address, there were baby steps being taken towards the end, now there were full-size strides. Next, there would be giant steps running toward perdition in the name of conviction. Trepidation and elation were twin emotions competing for their attention. Time was short.

Janelle and her mother were gazing at one another; Jason returned to reading a book. The realization shared between them generated a mutual concern for Jason.

"Jason, what do you think about the President's comments?" Rachael asked.

"He's a politician. He's full of himself. He thinks he can single-handedly change the world. Good luck!"

"Jason! Can't you see what's happening?!" Janelle said exasperatedly.

"Yeah, he's happy that the churches are getting it together. Big whoop! Whoops for them and good for us. I know what you're after; you want me to get all excited about this trip down the road to the kingdom. I know all the predictions from the Bible. I had to read them just like you did. I'm not like you. I take it one day at a time. We'll see what happens next."

"You don't understand! This is not a field trip to the museum. This is life or death! If you're not ready you'll be shaken out at crunch time!" Janelle appealed with fervor.

"What your sister is saying is that we need to be concerned about our condition of faith. Satan will attempt to deceive us, make us believe that doing things his way is the best way. It will be more comfortable, less difficult, to accept the popular choices. Our responsibilities include a close walk with Jesus, a strong prayer life, a clear understanding of how events will unfold. The devil will trick us. He will look and act like Jesus in many ways. You have to be on your guard," Rachael appealed.

"I know all that stuff. I don't think one has to get all hyper about it, just play the ball the way it comes to you."

"Jason, this isn't a soccer game!" Janelle almost yelled.

"Can I point out something for you?" Rachael asked.

"Go ahead. You will anyway."

"No, I won't. I'm asking for your permission."

"All right, go ahead."

"A week ago you wanted to play the soccer tournament on the Sabbath. You said you thought God would understand. That sounds like someone who wants to sin for fun, then presume God will forgive afterward. Some call that 'cheap grace.' God is very forgiving, but the individual that has that kind of attitude is a person that really is not sincere about the wrongs, the sins, that they commit. We are facing a time when our inner selves will be tested for the strength of conviction on our need for a Savior. Your family is worried about you and your strength of conviction. I am worried about myself. I want to be strong, but I'm afraid I am weak. I pray every day for strength," she said.

"I'm all right. Don't worry about me."

"You can't tell me to stop worrying about you. I'm your mother. I will worry about you until you are on the way to heaven. That's when I will stop worrying."

CHAPTER 12

Mike was looking at the reflection in his computer monitor. His face was contorted slightly. It was a new wrinkle in his dilemma. The twitching of his cheek muscle seemed to be increasing in frequency. He heard a rap on his door and reacted by rubbing the side of his face, leaving his hand in place.

Glenda sought Mike in his office when the others were otherwise occupied. She peered around the door.

"Mike, I need to talk to you."

"What's on your mind?"

"It looks like we may end up staying another night here before this storm lets up. The weather report is not favorable. I was hoping for some better privacy for Shelly and me. Can we sleep somewhere where…uh… Marshal can't get to us? He kept us up 'til late last night making suggestive comments. We hinted we needed to sleep, but he didn't take the hint. We don't want that for tonight."

"Take my office. I'll sleep somewhere else."

"Thank you. You're so kind. But, I'm not sure that will stop Marshall from coming in here. Could you stay with us so he won't come in? We could make it a threesome." Mike's mind reeled at that suggestive remark. He decided to drive past the deeper meaning to her words.

"That wouldn't look very good. There's a lock on the door. That should keep him out."

"But what if you need something in here? I'd leave the door unlocked for you."

"I'll knock first."

"I've never met a man like you before. You live your faith, don't you?"

"I do."

"Your wife is a lucky woman. Does she share your faith?"

"Absolutely, that's what attracted me to her in the first place."

"She's an SDA like you. What do SDAs believe? I know they go to church on Saturday, but that's all I know."

"Our name sums up a portion of our faith. Our name, in a way, means love—two different kinds of love. We show our love to God when we worship Him. Seventh-day means we worship God on the seventh day of the week. In the Bible, God asks us to worship Him on that day. The word Adventist means we are looking forward with anticipation for Jesus' second advent. We want to please Him by worshipping Him on His chosen day and He wants to please us by sending His Son back to take us to His kingdom. Both aspects are based on love. It's reciprocal love. He loves us, we love Him."

"Why Saturday?"

"Because, it's His day. The Bible tells us that He created the world in six days and rested on the seventh. That's His day. He wants us to do the same— rest and worship Him."

"Sunday is the seventh day. Why do you say it's Saturday? Monday is the first day of the week and that makes Sunday the seventh, right?"

"No, not according to the Bible, or the calendar. Look over there on my wall. Sunday is listed as the first on the left."

"Why is that so important? God accepts our worship on any day."

"God always listens to His children, but He still wants us to honor Him on His day."

"I would ask you to prove it from the Bible, but I think I know how that would turn out. You know the Bible backwards and forwards."

God always listens to His children, but He still wants us to honor Him on His day.

"It never hurts to study His word. There's always a reward when you do."

"How are you going to fit in with this new church resolution to come together as one church? One of the five tenets is a common day of worship."

"I can't go back on my promise to obey His commandments. I would be denying myself the blessing that is contained within its hours. I chose to honor my Lord and collect the blessing He has reserved just for me. He has a blessing reserved for you, too."

"Sounds nice, however a lot my friends are in my church. It meets on Sunday. They would not have it for a minute if I were to switch. Besides, the commandments have been abolished. It's more fun that way."

"I would like to call upon your confidence in me; you say I know the Bible and I do. Please understand that, from my biblical perspective, the commandments have not been abolished and worshipping God on the proper day is very important to Him. You should seriously consider understanding the reasons why I, and millions of SDAs, worship God on the Sabbath."

"Maybe I will, sometime."

"Sooner is better than later. My wife and I would love to study the Bible with you. Just say the word."

* * * * * *

Later that evening, Mike heard a commotion in the outer office. There was yelling and threats. He rushed to see what was happening. He was responsible for the floor and even though this was technically not a working day, with a number of staff missing and getting a free day off, he had to be the leader. Marshall was in George's face, pointing a threatening finger inches from his eye. Everyone else crowded around the two.

"You're not American! If you can't line up with the rest of us and show your support for the President, then you're not American!"

"All I said was there are people who don't want to wear the wrist bands. You're singling me out as one of them."

"Well, aren't you?"

"I—"

"Religion and politics," Mike interjected before George could answer.

"What?" Marshall turned on Mike.

"I said, 'Religion and Politics.' Those are the two subjects that polite company is supposed to avoid. Some believe that one *or* the other will cause harsh feelings to arise in social settings. In this case it is one *and* the other; both are mixed in to the discussion, double indemnity. Marshall, George, we have been cooped up in this office against our wills far too long. We're getting on each other's nerves. We just have to be careful; choose our subjects wisely."

"But, you talk religion all the time," Marshall countered.

"If you look back over all the times we have been together working as a team, you will notice that I don't bring the subject up unless asked. And, you remember me saying that we are friends and I don't want anyone to be offended when I state my beliefs."

"'Agree to disagree' is what Mike also said," Glenda reminded everyone.

Marshall looked around the room and calculated his standing with everyone. He had to sound retreat in the face of greater numbers. "I'm sorry. I was just excited about the news and was sharing it with George. I guess it just got out of hand."

"What news?" Zack asked.

"The Pope. The Pope's coming to New York to meet with the council of ministers. It's unscheduled and all of a sudden. He announced he would also like to meet the President and get a solidarity bracelet, too. He's showing his support and he's not even American." Marshall finished his answer with a quick dart of his eyes toward George.

"We're getting back to a conversation on religion and politics again. I too am very interested in what's happening, but can we keep things objective rather than subjective? We're tired, in the same clothes, and uncomfortable. Can we agree to break things off if we lose our perspective?" Mike looked around the circle of faces. They mostly nodded in agreement; some said hearty 'yeses.'

"That's not all that's happening," Glenda interposed. The group turned, questioning her with their eyes to continue. "The council of ministers has been busy. Since yesterday they have been in dialogue with other leaders, leaders of the Muslim, Buddhist, and Spiritualist groups. The Buddhists answered with a statement and they're sending a representative. They say they have sought for peace with Christians for years and have been ignored. They are happy to be called. No answer from the Muslims. But the president of the National Spiritualist Association of Churches is coming to New York to meet with them and the Pope. The Protestants are leading the way to reconciliation with of all these groups. I'm surprised they would call the Spiritualists, but I think that's a good thing."

"Why don't they call all the tribes and seek their accord? Native Americans are into spiritualist rites. Chief Blackhawk wrote hymns for the spiritualists," Shelly added.

"I don't know. It wasn't mentioned in the newscast," Marshall answered in a sarcastic tone.

"The President must be ecstatic," Leo said.

"He's been involved in the National Day of Prayer. He's been travelling around the country in Air Force One attending as many prayer services as possible. He is definitely one spiritual person," Zack observed.

"Just for interest's sake, I'm curious about whether he will go to New York or the Pope will go to Washington?" Mike said offhandedly.

"The Pope should go to Washington," Leo stated.

"But the Pope is the President's spiritual leader. The President should go to him," Marshall added.

"It's a cleric vs. a head of state. The Pope should recognize the President's position. It's state protocol," Glenda pointed out.

"The Pope now represents more than half the world's population and he's the head of the Vatican State," Marshall pointed out.

"Out of curiosity, why did you ask that question, Mike?" George asked.

"I am looking at a rapidly changing world. I wonder where and to whom the power is going to slant toward. The President is the President. But in a world view, I'm seeing a force of religious proportions developing. Will the national governments follow the Pope or will the Pope and church leaders work beneath the leaders of their respective countries?"

"That's an interesting perspective. Why is that important to you?" Shelly questioned.

"Again, I'm in a situation where I'm being asked to talk religion. To answer this question is to put me into position to talk about religion and politics. I don't want to offend. Is everyone okay with me answering this question?"

"Yes, I am," Glenda answered.

"I am."

"Me too."

"I'd like to hear what you've got to say," Marshall stated. The rest, Zack and Leo, nodded their heads in agreement.

"Okay. You know I believe we are close to the end of time when Jesus is supposed to return. The book of Revelation shows a construction of a politico-religious organization that controls worship and commerce, which means all buying and selling, and makes judicial laws that are oppressive, even issuing death penalties. The passages in Revelation are talking about the end of time. It worries me when religion and politics come together in a coalition." Mike laced his fingers together to demonstrate his point. "Our constitution defines the principle of separation of church and state. This was important to the founding fathers because of the intolerance they suffered from some state sanctioned religions. Our constitution is a wonderful document for the peaceful coexistence of people from diverse backgrounds. The persecution and prejudice back then produced our national position on the freedom of religion. I'm watching and hearing some indications of religious power joining with government. And, I'm witnessing some religious oppression."

"I don't think you have to worry about what's going on now," Marshall said.

"How so?"

"The council is asking for denominations to join, not demanding. It's not a required thing," Marshall responded.

"Okay, I agree. I see them asking. But, when, or if, it starts to gain power and authority we have to watch out. Before it gains power and authority, it has to come together somehow. For hundreds of years the churches have not been able to do that, now they have. Then, and this is where we started this discussion, the new alliance has to get its power from somewhere and the state is that somewhere. That's why I am wondering how protocol will be observed when the Pope and President meet."

"I think you're making negative arguments about a good thing," Marshall said.

"In one way, Marshall, I hope you're right and I'm wrong. It would be easier if we all didn't have to go through the final conflict between Christ and Satan. It will be messy!"

* * * * * *

Mike awoke to the soft sobbing sounds of someone nearby. He was on the floor of the break room amongst the sleeping forms of the other men. They had decided to use the one room for the men and Mike's office for the women. In the darkened room Glenda was at the door, hesitant to come in, not knowing which lump was Mike. She needed his leadership and protection and wasn't sure who was who, stymied by the unintelligible forms on the floor.

He threw aside his coat and slipped to the door.

"Oh, Mike, Marshall groped me! He was trying to have…" she whispered throwing herself against him.

"No! When? How?" Mike immediately turned to look back in the room. Marshall's form was on the floor. "I'm so sorry, how did he get in my office? Was the door unlocked?"

"I was going to the bathroom. I couldn't do anything. I couldn't scream. He had his hand over my mouth. I struggled, and he ripped my dress; and…" She started to sob.

"Glenda, we have to confront him."

"I'm so embarrassed. It's my fault."

"No, no it's not your fault. He has to be held accountable."

"If everyone knows, I won't be able to look anyone in the face again."

"He's the one who shouldn't be able to look anyone in the face."

Glenda continued to cry and Mike needed some help. He stepped away from her and gently led her to his office turning on the light. He hoped Shelly would help him convince her to act against Marshall. His first gut response was to judge Marshall's character based on the fears the women had after last night, but he felt obligated to hear Marshall's version anyway, after getting Glenda the attention she needed. Shelly came out of a deep sleep and immediately sensed what had happened. She soothed and hugged her friend, uttering one epithet after hearing the details, "That creep!"

"Criminal is more like it. I should have set up better protection for you. I'm sorry. We need to get the police involved," Mike said.

"How? Nothing can move out there."

"It needs to be reported. It's sexual assault. I'm going to call the police."

"She needs to get to a psychologist and talk about what happened," Shelly instructed.

"Okay both, we need to do both," Mike answered back.

"What's going on? I heard voices." George spoke from the door.

"Glenda was assaulted by Marshall," Shelly answered.

"Oh, no. That's horrible." George knelt before Glenda. "I'm so sorry. What can I do for you? Can I get you anything?" He looked up at Shelly and Mike, "I know what I can do. I'll do what I should have done before." George got up and immediately went to the door. Mike tried to stop him, but not in time. He went straight to the break room. He flipped on the lights and went straight for Marshall. "You lousy…" Finishing his sentence was less important to him than grabbing Marshall by the throat and pinning him to the floor. He had one knee jammed into his chest. Marshall was fully awake. He started to fight back. George and Marshall exchanged blows, Marshall on his back, George raining down from above. Mike grabbed George, trying to pull him off. He was like a wolverine on cocaine. Leo and Zack were coming out of stupors rolling into the fight on Mike's side, attempting to pull the combatants apart. Finally, Mike and Leo had George up and backed against one wall. Zack was helping Marshall to stand while holding firmly to one arm.

"What's this all about?" Zack demanded.

"Marshall sexually assaulted Glenda," Shelly spat out her explanation standing in the doorway with Glenda behind her.

"I didn't force her—she wanted it! I heard the two of them talking about her wanting sex with Mike. I thought I'd make her dreams come true."

"You're a crazed idiot!" Glenda yelled from the hallway.

"She says you groped her. That you put your hand over her mouth so she couldn't scream. Is that true?" Mike asked.

"I did no such thing. She wanted it."

"I did not!"

"If a woman says no, it means no!" Shelly yelled. George lunged at Marshall and Marshall moved to meet him. Leo hung on to George and Zack still had Marshall firmly by one arm, yanking him back. Mike was in the middle, both arms up, hands in a position to stop the developing clash.

This dialogue was not going anywhere positive. Mike needed to defuse the tension. "Shelly, can you take Glenda back to my office please? Leo, please take George to your cubicle." There was some grumbling, but they complied with his wishes. He was left standing in the room with Zack and Marshall. A few slow deep breaths later, he said, "Tell me what happened."

"George is a meathead."

"Marshall, just tell me what happened so I can be fair about this."

"I was trying to sleep and I saw Glenda look at me from the doorway, smile, and then go toward the hall. I waited and then went to her. We met there in total darkness; she wanted me so we started in. Then we got interrupted. Now I get mauled by George and she's claiming I forced her." He wiped blood away from his mouth with his wrist.

"How did her dress get torn?"

"I don't know. She must have done that afterward to strengthen her accusations towards me."

"She didn't resist, say no, try to get away?"

"Nope, she liked it."

Mike thought his explanation was too simple, but had to remain neutral. While he was thinking about his next obligation, Zack spoke.

"So how was she? Did she really get into it?"

This threw Mike off his neutral equilibrium. He forgot his perspective. "Guys, I don't believe this. You two are married. A conversation about how good it was should not be happening."

The two looked at Mike as if he was a kindergartener. "You're a little old school, don't you think? This was consenting adults. What does marriage have to do with it?" Marshall countered.

"It's wrong."

"Defined by who?"

"The Bible."

"The Bible doesn't say making out is wrong."

"It's the spirit of the Ten Commandments. 'if a man looks with lust upon a woman.'"

"Oh, come on, this is the modern world. The Ten Commandments were archaic rules for ancient dummies who didn't know their right from their left. God had to train them with baby rules. The Ten Commandments have been discarded. We live in the enlightened age. If two adults want to have a little fun, they can without having all that stupid guilt the commandments generated in the past," Marshall lectured.

"God created sex for our pleasure. I was just asking Marshall if it was good. No wrong in that. God wants us to have fun," Zack added to Marshall's take on the subject.

"The Ten Commandments are still a viable charter for moral behavior. They have not been abolished."

"Look at you, bringing religion into the discussion without permission," Zack retorted.

"The church had the authority to abolish them. The Pope did it hundreds of years ago when he changed the day of worship from the Jewish Sabbath to Sunday," Marshall retorted.

"Where did you hear that?" Zack questioned.

"It was on the Catholic channel a couple of weeks ago," he answered.

Mike was now doubly concerned at the turn of events in his own office, physical and spiritual. "We're getting away from the issue at hand. This question of assault has to be resolved. Marshall, do you have anything more to add in your defense?"

"No."

"I need to check on how Glenda is doing. Don't go near George. I don't want to referee round two." Mike closed the door to the break room on his way out, adding one thin layer between the combatants. He prayed for guidance.

"Glenda, how are you doing?"

"The same."

"I had a talk with Marshall and he has a different story to tell. I heard—"

"He would have a different story, duh."

"I heard from you what happened; do you have anything more to add?"

"No."

"He said you stopped and looked into the break room, smiled at him, and then went to the bathroom. He thinks you were enticing him."

"No, no not … Ah, I wasn't looking at him." Her head came up from looking at the floor to stare into Mike's eyes. He knew instantly what she meant. Shelly did, too.

"I am in the middle of a dilemma. I need to call the police and have them sort this out."

"We talked about this while you were with them," Shelly informed. "She's not sure she wants that kind of exposure."

"It's not that as much as it is some of my fault," Glenda confessed.

"How can this be your fault in any way?"

"I thought it was you. It was dark, no lights. When I heard the door open I…I ah, started it."

"Oh."

"But then I knew it wasn't you and I wanted to stop it."

Mike didn't appreciate where this was headed. He questioned where he should go on the problem. He didn't like the idea of his name being brought into the case, but couldn't think of any other solution than the police.

"Mike, Glenda said 'no' to him and that's when he covered her mouth." Shelly brought Mike back to the key issue at hand.

"Glenda, saying 'no' to him makes this wrong no matter how it started. You're allowed that under law. Also, as a member of this organization, I am obligated to report this."

"Okay, I understand."

"I need to call the police and report this. It happened here at work, on my floor of responsibility. I must report it." He went to his office phone and hit the emergency call button. It was next to a view screen suppression button which he did not push. He wanted the technician to see who he was. A very tired voice answered with no return video.

"State the nature of your emergency."

"I'm calling to report a sexual assault. I know it's a snowstorm, but can you send someone out to make a report, maybe investigate?"

"Sir, that's going to be difficult, we'll get someone to you as soon as possible. Is the victim okay? Does she or he need an ambulance?"

"No, she doesn't need medical help. I know this is a bad time to call with the storm. Can you give me an idea of how long it will take?"

"Sir, you look sincere. It's not altogether about the storm. It's the magnitude of calls that are coming in. In this precinct alone there are four murders reported, multiple domestic violence calls, robberies or looting from snowmobiles, and two rape incidents. We're doing everything we can to get to them all. Snowplows have been diverted to assist the police in getting to these calls. You can understand our difficulty. I don't want to seem callous to your situation."

"I understand."

"Sir, I have all your information on my read-out. I assure you, an officer will be there as soon as one is available. I have to answer another call."

"Thank you." Mike spoke to what he thought might be an empty transmission. He faced two concerned women. "They can't come right away."

"We heard. What's going on? Has the world gone mad?!" Shelly exclaimed.

"It seems so." He was in thought about that very theme. He knew Rachael was concerned about him being marooned; now he was concerned about her home alone with the kids. It was the middle of the night—well, early morning. He didn't want to wake her with disturbing news. He prayed instead. "I need to see if George has calmed down." He left his office and went to Leo and George.

"I'm sorry, boss. I can't explain it. Something snapped. I wanted to kill that idiot!"

"Your fight with Marshall will come up in the investigation of what happened; there might be some action against you. George, has there been some bad blood between the two of you? I know he was giving you heat for sympathizing with those who don't want to wear the bracelets, but is there something more?"

"No, why do you ask?" George contemplated Mike's words and wondered why Mike was asking about former issues.

"Because you said, 'I'll do what I should have done before.'"

"Oh, that." Mike and Leo waited. "It goes back to when I was in high school." He paused, hesitant to speak.

"Did you go to the same school as Marshall?"

"No, it wasn't him; it was someone else. My sister got raped and I didn't do anything. I knew the guy. I should have beat the crap out of him, but I didn't. For years now I wish I had rearranged his face. Marshall reminds me of him, a big, dumb Christian. He had her on a date to a church event of all things!" Mike and Leo were quiet when they heard that. Leo excused himself to go to the bathroom.

"George, maybe that's another reason why church isn't attractive to you; you've had some bad experiences."

"Maybe so."

"I believe that church people should demonstrate God's love and sometimes we don't. I'm sorry."

"You don't have to apologize for them. I know you are what a Christian should act like," George complimented.

"Thank you, but I have to confess to a lot of mistakes. I heard a Christian say once that non-Christians should understand we Christians are human. I think that's just an excuse for not apologizing for their behavior. They must think that non-Christians have a better understanding of forgiveness, better than the people of God who know the power of forgiveness, or should know the power of forgiveness."

"I wish my in-laws understood that. They would never apologize for what they did to Sheila. I guess I need to apologize to Marshall though."

"That would be good, whether he accepts it or not. I have to tell you that I reported the assault to the police and eventually they'll get here to investigate."

"Good! He needs to be charged with this. How long will it take them to get here?"

"I don't know. They're backed up with all the incidents that are going on."

"In a snowstorm!? On second thought, my dad was a teacher and he said kids acted up when the weather changed."

"I don't think it's the snowstorm."

"What is it?"

"The end of time. It's only going to get worse from here onward. God's Spirit of control is slowly being withdrawn from the earth."

The Lord is there for anyone who asks. The Holy Spirit is not being withdrawn from those who are His. He will send His angels to stand guard over you.

"Do you think that's why I snapped and went after Marshall? Is it because God is no longer helping me?"

"The Lord is there for anyone who asks. The Holy Spirit is not being withdrawn from those who are His. He will send His angels to stand guard over you."

"Then I better ask Him now before it's too late."

Later that day the wind abated and the emergency snow routes were cleared. A retired police officer was pressed into responding to the assault charge and came to make notes. It was later in the day when Mike was finally able to exit the office and go home. The landscape seemed to be a scene out of an Antarctica documentary.

* * * * * *

All three stared at the images. A pencil in the hand of the neurologist pointed to the amorphous globs located near the brainstem. The tumors were close together, looking like a misshaped, large peanut in the shell. They were wrapped around the core of the brain stem and, as the doctor explained, they were exerting pressure on the brainstem causing the symptoms Mike was experiencing.

"This could be an Epidermoid or a more serious Glioblastoma. If it grows real fast your symptoms will multiply and I would suspect it was a nasty Glioblastoma. That could cause great complications. If it is an Epidermoid then your symptoms would only increase marginally over a period of time. Your eyes and the area around your temples tell me there is a good chance this is a glioblastoma. Before your surgery we would have another MRI and compare the growth rate. That would tell us a lot. But, either way, let me emphasize, this is not going away on its own and the only way it's going to get better is taking that tumor or tumors out of there. Your symptoms will only get worse. Time is of the essence."

Mike and Rachael returned to their chairs opposite the doctor's desk. They were thinking.

"So shall I schedule the operation? We need to get started," the neurologist urged.

"What kind of recovery time would I need? How long will I be in the hospital?"

"Everyone is different. You are in good health, so you wouldn't take as long as some. Recovery moves faster when physical therapy is started as soon as possible and the patient is motivated. Your hospital stay should be about a week and then a transfer to a rehab facility for a stronger regimen of treatment. Oh, maybe … As I said it depends…"

"When, pardon me for interrupting, when would I be able to resume regular activities like walking, running, lifting, maybe?"

"That would take some time. You have to understand that your balance would be compromised for awhile because we would have to push aside the cerebellum. You'd have to start slowly and work up. In two months you would be able to walk, but it would take a year for you to be back to full strength if there are no setbacks. Does that answer your question?" The doctor watched Mike and Rachael stare knowingly at each other. They were silently coming to some form of decision. They turned to look at the doctor.

"We're sorry, we need to think and pray about this. The timing is all wrong," Mike explained.

"What do you mean 'the timing is all wrong?' What could be more important than getting rid of the tumor? We don't even know for sure if it is benign or not. What could be bigger than this?"

"There is one event that is bigger than this—the second coming of Jesus."

The dumbfounded neurologist swiveled in his chair, wondering if he could breach this bulwark of naive thinking. He had never encountered it before. He was speechless. As a scientist he believed in the scientific solution. He practiced it every day. He pondered the kind of thinking that could cause intelligent individuals to turn down a necessary procedure. In disgust he threw his pencil across the room and gave them a card, saying, "Call me as soon as you come to your senses and decide that we can go forward with this very important surgery. If it continues you risk serious consequences, including crippling disabilities."

CHAPTER 13

Church parking was a nightmare—a good nightmare. Gigantic piles of snow occupied the corners of the lot. Normally, there would still be room enough for the regular attendees to find a place. Today, the crowd was enormous. Adventists were meeting friends and showing them in the doors. Excited jabber filled the air. To any experienced eye, one could see that witnessing had been a primary activity for the majority of members. Current events motivated many to tell and others to listen. The Spirit was manifested in the results.

Pastor Taylor spoke on the results and aftermath of the first Pentecost. He said that what happened to the disciples at Pentecost will occur again. He paused and said, "In the last days the Spirit will be poured out in large measure." He was alluding to a quote from The Great Controversy. "I am sure that the second Pentecost has arrived!" he spoke with elation. The congregation replied with "amen." He then went about telling of the great news from the Adventist Church around the world. He had been linked during the week with church leaders who were telling stories by video conferences. It was inspiring to hear the results of the Holy Spirit's action seen working through the efforts of believers. It touched people deeply.

Jeremy and Sandra were sitting with Darin and Janelle, along with another friend from Darin's old high school. George and Sheila were attending with Mike and Rachael. Rachael had hoped that her neighbor would come, but didn't see her. The emphasis that Pastor Taylor put on the good news was centered upon God working through and around believers in Jesus as the Savior of mankind. His coming was near because of this very strong manifestation of His power. Then the pastor started to relate miracles he had heard performed in various parts of the globe. The cumulative effect drew this congregation into world movement, grand and spectacular. Praise resulted naturally, praise for Jesus' soon coming.

The service turned to a sobering tone when Pastor Taylor announced a board meeting. He said the one agenda item the board would consider was when it was no longer safe to meet in this church. Then he explained that there needs to be a warning to members of that problem. He told them he would put the second to last verse of the Bible on the sign out in front of the church, "Amen. Come, Lord Jesus." It would tell any member or believer that it was not safe to worship here anymore. The idea launched everyone into a feeling about the enormity of their situation. History was at an end.

Jason was attending the service this time instead of continuing his usual manner of wandering around the church building, talking with his friends. It may have been the cold outside that kept him from meandering in the parking lot. Mike and Rachael hoped he was listening.

* * * * * *

Mike's vacation started on Monday. He spent his last day, Friday, ironing out a transfer for Marshall so he would not be on the same floor as Glenda, Shelly, and George. It was the simplest solution for all concerned. Marshall was on temporary leave, pending a full investigation. George was given a suspension without pay for two weeks. The CEO complimented Mike for his management of the problem. He had interviewed the marooned office workers and they all complimented him on his leadership.

Mike and Rachael had a serious conversation on their plans for the near future. They believed that was all they had remaining—a *near* future. Everything beyond that was a new beginning. Plans for this "near future" included very few items for living here on earth. They couldn't help comparing what they knew about life now with what they didn't know about life in the next world. Success in this world required personal application of effort, education, and earned trust from supervisors, not altogether trustworthy themselves. They needed to be dependable in hopes of the leadership recognizing their reliable nature for some promotion in the distant future. "Days not years," was the new measuring stick for daily life.

Building their future here on earth was fast becoming a very minor detail, if not completely unnecessary. Life's success would no longer hang on a capricious thread of acceptance from a secular boss.

A discussion between the two about his tumors came down on the side of trusting God that they would be able to make it through before the symptoms got unmanageable. If Mike developed an inability to physically cope with the demands of the moment, the family would retreat to the cabin and wait from there. But until then he would do all in his power to witness and be a spiritual leader and head of a household fleeing to sanctuary in the time of Jacob's trouble. Their faith was being tested at this late juncture in the last struggle between good and evil. They longed for when "all would be made new." Mike would get a new body free of tumors. They were cutting the ties with the world they knew in hopes of a world that "eye had not seen."

There was an uneasy freedom that washed over them—uneasy, because this was scary new. They no longer felt tied to mundane chores. The monthly struggle to balance a budget, pay the bills, make appointments for orthodontia, etc., would not be draped on their shoulders like a horse's harness. Responsibilities of this life were sliding away as they focused heavenward.

The early pioneers crossing the oceans had grand ideas about the new world, yet they brought weapons for defense, because deep down inside they knew they would be prying land away from the original occupants. Leaving the old world meant divesting one's self, emotionally and physically, from the old world. What Mike and Rachael faced was similar, but not altogether the same; they were leaving an old world and traveling to a new one. No weapons were necessary. Mike and Rachael were pioneers getting ready to embark to a new, non-violent world. They were at the point of divesting themselves of the old-world property. They were making their second offering to the Lord. Their first offering was the monthly tithe and offerings they returned to the Lord regularly through the years. The second offering was the remainder they kept. They came to the conclusion that the investment they made in their house, savings, and retirement fund would be needed to finish the work of witnessing to a world. Using their assets for ministry became their top priority. Mike emptied his retirement account, paid the tax penalty, and banked the sum. Everything was completed electronically. They would make purchases with their phones until they could no longer access their accounts. They wanted to sell the house, but felt it might take too long to realize the equity. Houses don't sell as well in the winter. Instead, they took out a home equity loan on the value of the paid balance and appreciation. The plans they had included the purchase of a used car. With two cars and four drivers needing to be in multiple places at once, an extra set of wheels would help, especially in the case of Janelle, who was constantly moving about with Darin in their witnessing. Mike went to the bank personally to empty out the security box and close that account. Besides a few documents in the box, he had a small amount of gold coins. He reasoned that, when they were unable to buy or sell in the conventional manner, a gold Canadian Maple Leaf sovereign could easily be exchanged for food or other essentials.

Rachael readied some daypacks with water, tissues, first-aid kit, and other convenience items for when it was needed. It reminded her of the small case she had ready for the hospital in anticipation of the twins' birth. The Scripture text came to mind: "Alas for women who are pregnant and for those who are nursing infants in those days." *This is like giving birth*, she thought…Not knowing the day or hour, but knowing there was a limit to how long the present condition would last. She smiled at the thought. Her labor then produced two beautiful children; her labor now would end in delightful rebirth to life made new. Her parents would be alive again. Her husband would no longer suffer.

Her major concerns were the salvation of her children, especially Jason. Her next concern was her sister, and then there were her friends and acquaintances. She had talked with all of them, many two and three times. She would not give up. The number of friends seemed to outweigh the time she had to spend quality time with each. Her days were filled with visits and phone conversations. She was disappointed that her neighbor, Kristine, had not come to church as promised. She didn't want to call and make it seem as if she was judging, but she wanted to encourage her. She asked for the interposition of the Holy Spirit to lead the way. She knocked on the door.

"Kristine, I—"

"I can't talk now. Give me a moment—I'll come over to your house." The door closed quickly. Later there was a knock on the side door. Kristine came in with a frantic hug. "I'm sorry I put you off. I don't know what to say. I was getting ready to come to your church and Fred went nuts! I've never seen him this way before. He's never really been a church person and never stopped me from going to my church, but this time was different. It was like he was possessed…screaming, ranting, pushing me away from the door, trying to barricade me in the bedroom. I didn't even go to my church on Sunday! I hid in my house. Wherever he was, I tried to be somewhere else. He's calmer now, thank heaven."

"Oh, Kristine, that's terrible. I feel your pain. I can hear it in your voice. Here, let me give you another hug."

"I wonder what made him change," Kristine asked.

"It's the times we're in, I'm afraid. Mike was in the middle of it this past week. There was an assault and a fight in his office and when he called the police they could not respond because of the huge number of violent incidents. The control of the Spirit upon the world is slowly withdrawing. In Genesis it says, 'My Spirit shall not always strive with man.' Kristine, we're getting close. I don't know what else to say."

"Guess there is nothing to say. We need to pray," Kristine answered.

"Let's do."

"Especially for Fred."

"Especially for Fred." Rachael's ministry to Kristine was multiplied tenfold. The Spirit was working through her with Kristine and then Kristine was sharing with her friends what she was learning from Rachael and then from her friends with other friends and neighbors. The two prayed together in the kitchen. No sooner had Kristine returned to her home than Mike came back from his errands. They were standing in the hallway when the front doorbell rang. Mike went to see who it was.

"Hello, I'm Mr. Froelich. You don't know me or my wife. We live around the corner one block over. We're here because we've heard about you. I hope we have the right place … I'll be embarrassed if we are wrong, but … I heard that you know what's going to happen in the future. Is this true?"

"Come in, please. You shouldn't stay out in the cold. I'm Mike and my wife's Rachael."

"We're Peter and Melissa."

"To answer your question is not easy. I wouldn't want you to think I can see the future—I'm not a prophet. I do study the Bible and that gives me a broad stroke picture of things that are going to happen. My wife is a student of the Bible, too. We'll try to answer your questions. What brought you to ask us for help?"

"We are disturbed by what's happening in the world. It's frightening. The earth is falling apart and people are acting very strange. The neighbors have been talking about you, so we thought we would talk to you directly. What's going to happen next?"

For the next two hours the Larssons showed the Froelichs Bible prophecy. Mike and Rachael asked them to supper and they shared more information with Janelle helping and Jason as a silent partner, listening. The newly initiated believers left with Bibles and books. They were pleased to have found what their hearts were compelling them to find. Arrangements were made for weekly studies in the Froelich's home.

The Larssons could feel the up-tempo of the interest many had for things spiritual and the increase of sin's harsher emotions. The emotional and intellectual world was on the move, going in opposite directions. They were tired. It was a rewarding, validating, confirming tired. Watching the news neither relaxed them nor fulfilled them. They didn't gravitate toward the news; it was not a regimen they wanted at this moment, however, they needed to know what was happening in the world around them, nationally and internationally. Would it be good or bad? They assumed it would be bad. The dreadful would indicate the closeness of great things to come. Almost, reluctantly they turned it on.

There was a recap of the day's events, small snippets reporting what had happened: news, weather, sports. A link at the bottom of the screen allowed for a viewer to watch the full coverage of any one item. Mike clicked on the one about the conclusion of the conference of ministers, the Pope, and the President. He knew the President had gone to see the Pope in New York at the old UN and had cancelled his schedule in favor of a weekend retreat with the clerics. He hadn't heard how it went. He wanted to hear the President's own words. Past protocol dictated that the local head of state had precedence to go first. In this news conference, the President deferred to the Pope, who spoke briefly about unity in the loving arms of Jesus. Then the President spoke.

~ ~ ~ ~ ~ ~

This weekend has been the highest point in my spiritual life. On a personal note, I've always wanted to have an audience with the Holy Father, but, because of my schedule I have not had the opportunity. This weekend, I am privileged to spend not an hour, but days, with him. Equally rewarding has been the time I have had with these gifted leaders of the churches worldwide. The company of these dedicated church men and women could not be surpassed in any other scenario. They have become more than colleagues; to me they are now my close personal friends. We have dined at a feast of spiritual delights. Many topics have been discussed. The five fundamental tenets of common belief have been prominent in our thinking and acting. We unanimously agree on each. As we studied their import on our present situation, we could see how efficacious they would be to our moral condition. I think our Reverend Smithson said it best when he observed, "Sunday keeping will greatly improve the morals of our society." I agree with his assessment and that is the product of what I most desire. While we met here this weekend, I thought of the power this august group represents. They represent churches of many denominations situated in all the countries of the world. Worshipping congregations from this enormous alliance can be found in multiples in every neighborhood of the globe. It represents a bloc of influence affecting society on a grand scale. With every one of these congregations praying for God's blessings on Sunday morning, it means God will answer. Prayer moves the hand of God. Our country and the countries of the world are now headed in the right direction. I am humbled by the responsibility of leadership in this momentous time. I will now be followed by The Very Right Reverend Robert Grayble, the executive vice-president for world religious affairs assisting the Holy Father in his duties with the council. He will follow me with his prepared comments.

~ ~ ~ ~ ~ ~

Commentators made observations to the camera about the various leaders in a semi-circle standing in the background in support of the speakers. They noted the Archbishop of Canterbury reminding the viewing audience of the miracle he had performed in England bringing rain out of a cloudless day. The camera zoomed in for a head shot on Reverend Grayble as he scanned the room in front of him, bowed in respect to the Pope and the President and then began.

~ ~ ~ ~ ~ ~

My fellow believers, when we started this convocation, we had no idea it would have been so immensely successful. Our purpose was simple, the result was grand. We never expected to be hosts to his eminence the Holy Father and the President of the United States of America. God has richly blessed our prayers and granted us our deepest wishes, years before we thought they were possible.

I have had rewarding dialogue with world leaders and I have come away with deep respect for their wisdom and capability. It validates for me once again the adage that many heads are better than one. I would like to relate to you all of the great thoughts and ideas I heard this weekend. However, that would take at least two more days of occupying this podium. My brothers and sisters have heard enough from me already. But I have chosen two experiences to relate that represent thought and action.

England's Archbishop Warwick's story represents action. I wanted to know how he knew to ask for rain. By now, everyone has seen on video replays of what he did. He answered me and said he felt he had to do something. A voice from inside his office said, "Go! He will be with you." He went. That was action. We need to take more bold action. This congress of minds represents bold action. I expect more action to follow.

Secondly, I relate to you a new thought. This thought came from the President of the NSAC, the National Spiritualists Association of Churches. Reverend Ophelia Marcbright and I had a deeply spiritual session together. I learned from her that we can garner significant information from the deceased through mediums. To demonstrate, she took me on a journey of revelation through the instrumentality of her gifts. I was able to talk with one of my deceased relatives, an uncle; it rocked my soul to the deepest level. In my conversation with Uncle David, he told me there was great activity in heaven. The only plausible reason for this activity was that Jesus and His angels were getting ready to return to earth! I was so overwhelmed by this revelation. To talk to my mentor uncle was big; to hear him speak in his oh-so-familiar voice and tell me about events in heaven moved me in the deepest possible way. Then what he had to say about the activity in heaven was colossal! I shared with all of our brethren and it rocked them as well. [Heads were seen nodding in the background, a few "amens" were heard.] *My colleagues and I are adjusting our plans accordingly. We don't know when this will happen—time is different for Jesus. Then Uncle David did something for us that made us all realize that heaven is so very close to earth. He asked me to reach into my pocket and pull out what was there. I found there his pocket Bible, the Bible he had in his hands, in his casket, buried nineteen years ago! He told me to open it to the page marked by a ribbon. A small piece of paper was there in which he had written a note. It read: "We must all come together on the same day to worship. The Lord's Day will save us from false worship." It was a validation for us from the other side and confirmed for us that we are on the right track. I share this experience with you for its spiritual impact to us as humans and to demonstrate how, by combining our thoughts and abilities, we receive a richer experience. I personally welcome Reverend Marcbright and her organization into this family of churches. The talents of her believers and ministers are needed by all.*

~ ~ ~ ~ ~ ~

"You never know what you're going to see on the news!" Mike observed in shock. "I almost didn't turn it on, but I guess we needed to know."

"Honey, this is moving so fast. We're looking at the formation of the Beast of Revelation 14!" Rachael reacted.

"They got set up," Jason observed.

"Set up?" Mike asked.

"Yeah, the medium hooked the Very Wrong Reverend into believing that he was talking to someone in heaven who could give him the scoop on news about Jesus. It's the anti-Christ that's coming, am I right?"

"Right on, baby brother!"

"I'm not your baby brother! We're twins remember?"

"I was born before you. That makes you the baby." Janelle smiled broadly.

"Hey, you two, I was just thinking that in a short time everyone of us is going to be born at the same time. No one will be older or younger than another. We will all receive our new lives and new bodies at the same time," Rachael pointed out.

"What would you call that? Milluplets? Billuplets?" Jason quipped.

"There's that, but I do know we'll be called the 'redeemed.' Changing the subject, it all seems so unreal. Here we are in our living room. We just watched the start of the fulfillment of last-day prophecy. The twins are delightfully kidding each other like before all this happened. In a little while, we'll go to bed and wake up for school in the morning. I'm wondering, when will all this normalcy suddenly disappear and be exchanged for behavior of people running for their lives and looking furtively to the sky for a hint of an angel wing?" Rachael queried.

Mike was in deep thought, thinking about the items on his list. He was brought back to the room with his wife's question. "You're right. We're still living as if nothing is happening."

"We're really witnessing, Mom, Dad. Everyday I'm talking to someone about Jesus and His soon coming," Janelle answered.

"I'm sorry, Janelle, I didn't mean to imply we were doing nothing different spiritually. I just meant we live the same. I'm still washing the dishes, making dinner, cleaning the house. You know what I mean? We're praying more specifically than ever before. We have a different attitude toward our friends. It's an attitude of desperate concern for their salvation. I even feel guilty that I didn't have this attitude a long time before now," Rachael answered for herself and her husband, and in the process, opened her inner concern to her daughter.

"Mom, I feel the same way. It's as if time has run out and I'm cramming for the final exam and I'm kicking myself for not studying earlier. I know God will forgive us for not doing what He asked us to do earlier, but I don't think I deserve His forgiveness for knowing and not doing."

"I'm changing things up a bit more. Tomorrow, I'm going to make preparations for our escape. I'm going to buy supplies for us to live off of in the mountains. We're going to buy that third car and use it exclusively for ministry. We're going to use all of our cars, all our possessions, for ministry..." Mike was reading the list he had made in his mind.

"Dad, why are you buying supplies to live off of? Aren't the angels supposed to feed us?" Janelle asked.

"Yes, they are. It's a promise. What I'm concerned about is timing. What if we leave too early, before we're supposed to? We could be stuck out there because I made a mistake. I just want a fall back plan in case... in case I get overly excited about everything and run us all away from this. Rachael, for example; when will you stop preparing dinner? Or buying groceries for dinner? Or trading recipes with the ladies at church? You don't know. I don't know when we should leave, 'the abomination of desolation standing in the holy place' is our key. I'm thinking that the anti-Christ is the abomination of desolation. Then where and what exactly is the holy place? Rome? Jerusalem? New York?" Mike also opened his inner concern about his decisions to the family.

"Honey, don't worry. We'll work this all out together. You don't have to carry all of this on your own shoulders," Rachael consoled Mike.

"I just want to do the right thing at the right time."

"We will. We'll take it one day at a time."

"Tomorrow my plans are to shop, buy a used car, and we have that business meeting at church."

"In church we heard that it will be about the plans for closing down the church. The kids from school say it is also about closing the academy. That's what I heard anyway," Janelle informed.

"As usual, the kids are always way ahead of us on everything," Mike observed.

"I'd like to have their information channels," Rachael answered.

"Maybe they can tell me which comes first—the mark of the beast or the desolating sacrilege."

At this time they decided to tell the twins about their father's medical issues. It surprised them that he had such a serious condition and he kept acting normal, and, they were concerned that he was doing nothing about it. The sobering truth was that Mike and Rachael were dead serious about their conviction that Jesus was really on His way. Janelle began watching her father's face and having a pang of worry for his condition. Jason remained quiet.

* * * * * *

Before Mike got started on his plans the next morning, another omen surfaced. They had started to leave the news on in the background while they performed daily activities. At the breakfast table, they watched as the news broadcast did a report on the continuing struggle of the island countries. Not only were their homelands being flooded by rising seas, but their fishing waters were being poisoned. It had long been established that factory wastes were raising the acidic content of the oceans worldwide, and now there was a new danger. Large red blooms of plankton were floating nearby. Domoic acid, otherwise known as pseudo-nitzschia, was a part of the developing problem. Shellfish and other small organisms fed off the phytoplankton in the blooms and received the deadly neurotoxin. Marine populations around and near the islands were either dying from the toxin or starving because of the lack of a food supply. Square miles of the red blooms were spreading. Soon it was feared more areas would be affected. Marine biologists were racing to find a cure and rushing to the scene in their state-of-the-art vessels. Mike and Rachael watched as pictures of dead fish floated belly up in clusters, with volcanic islands partially submerged in the background. The red blooms were eerie in their slimy, undulating appearance. It looked vaguely like coagulated blood matted in the water.

"Could that be one of the plagues?" Rachael asked.

"I don't think so. It would be out of order if it is. The first plague was supposed to be sores, then the sea becomes like the blood of a dead man," Mike answered.

"Maybe this is just the beginning. Later the plague develops into a worldwide phenomenon."

"It brings up the question, are the seven last plagues supposed to be in exact order?"

"We should read Revelation 16. I think it says the sores were poured out on the people who worship the beast and its image. Have the beast and the image appeared as yet?" he asked.

"No, but maybe it has started, you know, like in its infancy. The alliance of churches is forming in New York," she answered. The two put the worn Bible on the table, searching for clues about what might happen and when. The only clue from Revelation was the order presented and the fact that the first plague was specifically directed at those who "bore the mark of the beast."

They left an hour later to buy a modest, dependable used car for youth ministry and then to stock up on nonperishable goods to store in a mountain hideaway. Rachael asked "where," knowing full well that Mike loved the cabin sanctuary they inherited from her folks after the car accident. He said it would be best to have a stash nearby, just in case it was needed. Their objective would be to go to the cabin and, if that was not safe, move on to some caves they had explored a half mile further up the mountainside. It was a good plan if they undershot the right moment and had to fend for themselves or if his condition warranted leaving earlier.

It was a good plan if they undershot the right moment and had to fend for themselves or if his condition warranted leaving earlier.

* * * * * *

The business meeting was just as Janelle predicted. The academy principal was in attendance to make an announcement and explanation. Everyone huddled together in groups on their knees, appealing to the Lord for guidance. The school board chairman opened the meeting with a short description of what was to be covered: the closing down of the school and the plan for closing the church.

Principal Chennault began first because he had another church board to attend across town. He made a brief statement.

"Our board has decided to close the school officially in four weeks. All support money from area churches is excused. The funds we have in hand, we'll disperse to teachers and staff to use as they need. Until we close 'officially'…" He used his fingers to make quotation marks in the air. "… we will not take attendance. We recognize that individual families will need to take their children out to execute their own plans for avoiding the oppressions to come. Some will need to travel and others will want to explore other options. Some of you will ask why we don't close the academy now. It's because if we do, it might invite unwarranted attention that our children are not in school, bringing the authorities to our doors, charging parents with truancy. You know what I mean. Any questions?"

"Yes, I have something to say." One parent stood up. "I have sacrificed everything to put my two in school. I have taken on extra work to pay your high prices for tuition and now you just close down on a whim!"

Another joined her, "And, what about me? I just paid next month's tuition. And, that's it? You close down! I've got to go find another school for my children in the middle of the year."

The room was quiet. Many were trying to fathom how, as leaders in the church, they could be unaware of the forthcoming events. Mike and Rachael looked at each other with surprise hidden behind their placid faces.

"She's got a point." A baritone voice spoke up. Bodies turned to see who had uttered the words. "I have been quiet about all the assumptions being made. Oh yeah, it's very nice that the students started the revival and the parents tried to mimic the results. I get it. But, I think everyone's going over the top. Closing the school and the church is premature. We should wait," he concluded. "I have donated thousands of dollars to build the school and then again when we had to have a new church building to be a representation of our love to God—a house where He could be proud to listen to our praises. I was asked to give generously for that project too. Now you are throwing it away," he added. His additional comment dripped with exasperation.

The principal and the pastor exchanged looks. The principal was standing front and center in the line of fire. Pastor Taylor decided to join him. "I know everyone in this room has appreciated your generous contributions to the church and the school. I know I appreciate you personally, and your ministry of giving. We're here tonight to responsively plan out our next few weeks. I think I speak for all of us when I say, if suddenly things started to change back to what they were maybe five or six weeks ago, we would continue with our activities of Sabbath services and midweek programs. I think the school feels the same." Pastor Taylor looked at his friend as he ended. He got a nod in response.

"Yes, most certainly we would. We have about four more weeks to reverse the decision the school board has made. On a side note, I will gladly refund Mrs. Knecht's tuition payments for the year. This is not about money; it is about being ready for the Advent. Apart from filling up my car with bio-gas and buying a few essentials, you can have my paycheck. I sincerely believe I and my wife won't need much to carry us through." Most in the room were in agreement with his comments. Principal Chennault excused himself to go to his next appointment.

The pastor looked around at a stunned room. The exchange in thoughts lingered in his mind. He wanted to continue with his prepared remarks, but the words had to be carefully chosen. Consensus of opinion was still not guaranteed. "I have a responsibility to the church members. Up until a couple of months ago I felt it was my duty to nurture and prepare the members under my care. Then, in these last few weeks, God laid on me the responsibility to lead them through a very perilous time. Part of that means I must tell the members when it is no longer safe to continue the normal practices of life here on earth. Jesus tells us we have to run. Well, He doesn't say it quite like that; He says we should '*flee.*' I don't want to be an alarmist, however, but one of these days I will have no choice. When the time comes, I will call and visit, if necessary, as many of my members as possible and tell them to leave their homes and get away from the tribulation to come. Jesus said it will be so bad that those days will have to be shortened or there won't be any true believers left on the earth. I stand before you tonight concerned that we are very, very close. It's not time to flee tonight or tomorrow, but that day will come. On that day, I will not be concerned about my house. I will not be concerned about my silly stamp collection. I will be concerned about you. I won't make that call to your house prematurely. I hope it will not be too late. It will be my best guess so as not to unnecessarily inconvenience anyone. I have already preprogrammed my phone system with a conference call blast that will send a message to everyone possible. It stands ready to be used.

"Tonight, I want us to all be on the same sheet of music. If the powers in control at the time of the end want to catch true believers easily, they would come here to the church first, during one of our services, and simply round us all up. I know God will protect us if that hap-

> *I stand before you tonight concerned that we are very, very close. It's not time to flee tonight or tomorrow, but that day will come.*

pens, yet I still read the Scripture where Jesus says we're to flee. I would prefer to follow His advice. Tonight, I want the members to guide me in how this should be done."

"Pastor, I think your idea of placing a message on the sign is a good one, and the message phone call will be very effective," Mike stated.

"Okay, does everyone feel the same? It does mean that we will continue as normal if things don't get worse and maybe slide back to what they were," Pastor Taylor said.

"I have another idea. Could you leave the doors unlocked when you send out your message? I would like to come here and spend the time in prayer until they cart me away."

"I can do that. I'll leave the doors open. The church building then will be used to the very end of time. I like it."

"I'm too feeble to be a'fleein'. If they want me, they can come get me. What are they going to do with an old lady anyway? I'll whack'em a couple of times wit' my cane when they get too close!" Mrs. McKessy spoke.

"I was thinking I would come by and take you with us, you and Veronica." Pastor Taylor answered.

"Thank you, Pastor, but I'd just slow you down. Besides, I don't know what to pack! Don't want nothin' that would clash with the décor in heaven. P'raps Veronica will take you up on your kind offer." She acted as if the pastor was giving her a ride to church on Sabbath morning.

Tension seemed to ooze out of the room with her down-to-earth attitude. Other comments on the situation and the plans for the near future occupied the remaining minutes of the meeting. There was no point to planning other church programs; voting wasn't needed to repair this or buy that. The meeting ended with prayer. Groups formed to talk over the latest news of the formation of the beast and surmise about the next things they might be witnessing. Pastor took Heidi McKessy home and the evening was complete.

* * * * * *

Jason had a surprised look on his face when Mike told him he would need him tomorrow. "No school? What about my homework? I've got a test coming up. I've got perfect attendance for the school year; will this be an excused absence?"

"School is almost a thing of the past. In four weeks the school will close its doors and all the students will be home with their parents," Mike answered his son.

"This is sudden, but good," Janelle reacted. "Now we can do some serious witnessing."

"Just when I get going on a straight 'A' average," Jason complained.

"You've got a straight 'A' average? I'm pleased," Mike responded.

"I'm proud of you," Rachael added.

"I know I haven't been the best student in the past, but this year I wanted to surprise you."

Janelle had to speak up, "Listen to us. We're talking about past values. Grades are going to be 'so yesterday' as Jason always says about tech stuff," she observed.

"Yes, you're right. The things of this world are passing away. It's difficult to turn the old off and focus completely on the new. But, I'm still pleased with you, Jason. I accept your hard work as a wonderful gift. You were on a roll with your school and your soccer this year…in heaven you'll excel at anything you choose," Mike complimented.

"I'm pleased, too. You like to surprise us, don't you?" Rachael gave Jason a hug he really didn't accept enthusiastically. At least it wasn't in front of his buddies.

CHAPTER 14

Janelle took the new witnessing van and went to pick up Darin and April on the way to school. Rachael planned on making as many house visits as possible. Father and son loaded up the 4x4 with food supplies and the family camping equipment. They would be gone all day and may have to overnight in the cabin and come back home the next day. It would be a great time for Father and son to talk.

Janelle was a careful driver. Because of that fact she was aware of the driving behaviors of cars around her, and the commute to school seemed more frenzied. Speed limits were being ignored. Stop signs were used as reminders to look both ways instead of to stop. Anxious drivers tailgated the van, angry that they had to follow a car driving the speed limit. Horns blared. Drivers gesticulated with hands and arms. After picking up Darin and April, Janelle was worn with worry. Never had she faced such difficult driving conditions—conditions brought on by people.

At the last busy intersection before making a turn on to a quieter road leading to the academy, she waited for the light to change. In front of her eyes, two cars collided at high speed. A red pickup T-boned the mini-van in the side panel behind the driver, sending the car twirling until it hit another oncoming car from the opposite side of the road. The result was a heap of twisted metal laying on what once was considered the side of the van. The red pickup juddered down the road for several hundred yards before the driver got out and ran away. The third car, a sedan, was smashed up to the windshield, the hood looking like a pelican's beak.

Darin and April instantly left the car to render aid. Janelle put the car in park and opened the door to do the same. Behind her another angry driver honked their horn repeatedly demanding, in not so gentle terms, for her to get her car out of the way. She got back in and pulled up on the curb out of the way. The driver accelerated violently, speeding away in angry car language.

At the scene Darin was helping people out of the sedan first. He used parts of broken seats to lie some of the injured down. Others, he sat on the curb. April was attending to children in the van by squirming through a broken and twisted sun roof. Blood and glass were everywhere. The mother of the children was trapped in the front mashed cab of the van. Her torso was trapped between the seat bent forward by a bent door frame and the steering wheel. Janelle ran to help the mother through the empty windshield opening. Before she got there a scream lanced through the turmoil of voices, "MY BABY, my baby, help my BABY!" Janelle knelt on the pavement in front of the twisted gaping hole and the mother screamed at her, "Not me, save my baby!" Janelle could see April holding a lifeless baby she had retrieved from a crushed child seat and was trying to move outward toward the sunroof which was now a side window. Quickly she met April and took the lifeless form from her hands. April returned to release another child from its child seat. Janelle tried to find a life sign amidst the crumpled and ruined little body. Using the kiss-of-life, she attempted to blow air into the little body. It was akin to blowing air into a stoppered test tube. One look told her life could not be sustained with a chest crushed so flat. The broken legs dangled at odd angles. She wept as she handed the baby to a woman having just arrived to help. The lady convulsed and laid the child on a snow bank with her little coat covering it from stocking cap to matching pink socks. Janelle assisted April with the second crying child, carefully avoiding the jagged glass of the roof window. The kid had been kept safe by the protective child seat on the opposite side from the impact. April followed.

Multiple sirens were heard down the street. Both Janelle and April knelt to talk the mother into relaxing. They asked her to breathe easy because the ambulance would soon be there and the emergency workers would get her out. The mother was frantic. Darin joined the girls looking in the window. "Is my baby okay? Where is she? Is she okay?" Darin stood to look for the baby. Janelle stood too and made him step out of view of the trapped woman. She gazed deep into his eyes and silently shook her head. Darin got the message. April stood, her head on a swivel. She found what she was looking for, the familiar coat, went to it, and picked it up. She swaddled it, using the coat as a blanket. She took a strand of hair away from the crumpled little face and tucked it behind an ear. Then buried her face in the little form and sobbed a prayer.

Darin and Janelle watched. Others watched. The little dead form jumped like it had been tickled by someone blowing raspberries on its belly. It squirmed again. Legs started to kick and an arm wrestled out of the coat and grabbed a fist full of April's hair. It cooed as if nothing had happened. April's face showed complete shock, then glee. Then she looked heavenward. There was a murmur of response from onlookers. Darin looked at Janelle. "You gave me the impression there was no hope."

"There wasn't," Janelle answered.

"She's right. I saw the injuries myself," the lady whispered.

"Is my baby okay? Why won't somebody answer my question? I want to see my baby!"

April hurried to bring the baby to its mother. She knelt in front of the window and unfolded the coat. The baby was moving. The crowd could see the healthy child in clothes soaked in its own blood. The mother relaxed and then tensed. "She's bleeding! Where is she hurt? Where is the blood coming from?" Not a mark or scratch gave a clue as to where the blood had left the baby's body.

Emergency workers arrived and pushed the crowd back. April said she would hold the baby for her until they were done. She stood back and held her first miracle.

* * * * * *

Rachael was on her way to Cheri's house when Rochelle called and asked for her to visit as soon as possible. She needed her help. Reluctantly she turned the car in the other direction. Rochelle wanted Rachael to sign a statement for the court stating, "If you really are my friend you'll help me with this statement against Chris" Rachael couldn't sign such a document because she had never seen Chris do anything abusive and she didn't like being put on the spot having to prove her friendship. Rochelle was deluded. Her obsession clouded her vision. Silent prayer ascended immediately asking God for a way out of this dilemma. Rachael desperately wanted to warn Rochelle of the coming danger. Instead of telling her friend she wouldn't sign, she thought of a different tack. "At this point it wouldn't do any good."

"What? What do you mean it wouldn't do any good?! Chris is a monster that needs to be stopped! Are you on his side now?"

"What I mean is, there is no time left. Your court date is scheduled for when? Three months from now? Other things are going to happen before then, big things."

"You mean Chris is going to do more things to my Loren by then. Over my dead body! He's never going to see her again!"

"Rochelle, this is a matter of life or death. The…"

"You've got that right!"

"No, Rochelle, listen to me! The Lord is coming. He's coming now, not years from now! You and Loren's lives are in danger—you have to get ready now. The Lord is coming in days, not years!"

Rochelle was quiet for a moment. Rachael thought she might have gotten through. She took a breath to tell her more, but Rochelle began, "That's what Chris said when he called. He said 'Jesus is coming. Please get yourself and Loren ready.' I hung up on him before he said anymore."

"Rochelle, can't you see? People are concerned about you. We care about you. There is no time left. The Beast of Revelation is forming. Just like prophecy said it would. You've got to get down on your knees and pray like you have never prayed before. Our sins have to be forgiven. We have to stand before God cleansed from our unrighteousness. The sins of deceit, covetousness, envy, *hatred*, and lust have to be off of our record. There's no time left."

"So you say there's not enough time for me to go to court and keep Chris away from Loren?"

"That's correct. Divorce court, custody issues, getting even with Chris…those are all things of this world, a world that will be gone in a few short weeks, maybe."

"I just paid a huge retainer for my lawyer. That's a lot of money!"

"Money and things money will buy will be gone, too."

"I'm going to need to think about this."

"Not think, pray. You're going to need to pray about this."

* * * * * *

The clean up at the scene took hours. Police needed witnesses. The EMR team wanted information about the injuries to the baby. They checked the little body over completely, examining every millimeter of skin. They couldn't explain the source of blood with no discernible incisions, cuts, or abrasions. April was grilled about what she saw and what she did. Afterward the team accepted the fact that the baby was alright and assumed the blood had to come from somewhere else.

Darin was most preoccupied with what April did. He wanted to know what she said in her prayer, what she felt in her body at the time of the healing. Did she hear God tell her to say or do anything? Did she feel the power of God moving her? He praised her and said, "We are God's team now. We're doing His will and performing works for His glory. You're not on the fringes of what's happening—you're in the middle of it." He was completely into the moment. He wanted to tell everyone what happened when they finally got to school. The result was praise and thanksgiving from those who heard about April's experience. Darin acted like April's agent of explanation.

It was the first most talked about event at school. The second was the decision to close school in four weeks. The teachers didn't teach normal class subjects. Every class was an ad hoc talk and share session on news events and the ways that students could reach friends and neighbors before it was too late.

It was sobering to stare at the first big change in the daily activities of life. All guesses, all opinions, about what was happening existed on the theoretical level. The end of school was tangible, real, and measurable. They could count the days until they would be at home or in the woods looking for signs to know what to do.

A curious thing happened. Text books started to reappear back on their storage shelves. The students had been assigned use of them for various subjects. They were school property and the kids didn't see a need to keep them. They were old and tattered; it was the last year they were to be used. They were scheduled to be replaced with an upgraded system of expensive electronic readers that would have all the latest texts. The shelves were tidy. Each volume neatly aligned with the next. In the upheaval of the second advent they would undoubtedly be rattled to the floor, destroyed, yet there they were, in formation, a testament to the past.

* * * * * *

The car ride to the mountains took many hours. Mike engaged Jason on many subjects, hoping they would result in a deeper conversation about the futurities before them. Jason answered his father with good answers, some of which included references to scripture. There was no denying the fact that Jason knew the facts of the final conflict. It appeared he understood the facts which included details of events to come. The distressing part for Mike was the nonchalant attitude Jason seemed to exhibit. He wanted more out of his son. He wanted fervency. Jason didn't give it to him and Mike didn't want to force it out of him. Their conversation seemed to slide to memories of the times the family had spent at the cabin. It was great to reminisce.

Jason got animated about relating one story and it caused Mike to grieve, wishing Jason would have the same enthusiasm toward his spiritual commitment. He kept with the story and let Jason carry-on about the details. Perhaps this will help get Jason excited about the family's next big "adventure" together. He thought, and at this point he would accept anything.

When they arrived at the cabin they stopped to add a few more things to their load. They stashed sleeping bags into the 4x4, along with some extra odds and ends. They continued up the jeep track in four-wheel drive. The snow made travel difficult. They managed to cut half off their trek, before they had to stop. The rest of the way up to the caves would have to be on foot. Fully loaded down, they hiked to their sanctuary. They cached the supplies in a cleft and returned to the vehicle for another load. It was not easy work. When completing the second delivery, they mounded rocks over the supplies and returned to the SUV. They were exhausted. They returned to the cabin and decided to stay the night next to a warm crackling fire. Before stepping in the front door they stopped for a moment at the grandparents graves.

"It won't be long now. Grandma and Grandpa will be alive again," Mike prompted.

"That'll be nice," Jason answered.

"Amen. It will be good to talk to them again. I've missed them," Mike remarked.

Jason saw another indication of change in his father. It looked like Mike had a lazy eye with a twitch. He didn't know what to say and he didn't feel comfortable unpacking emotions with his dad. He felt sorry for his dad, but didn't know what to do.

* * * * * *

Principal Chennault ran to each classroom asking in an excited tone for everyone to come to the auditorium. The students and staff filed into their seats, wondering what this was all about. A large viewer was at the podium end of the room. Principal Chennault stood in front of the podium.

"I thought you all should see this. I am back recording this and starting it at the beginning. This is strange and revealing at the same time." He clicked the remote and the video began.

~ ~ ~ ~ ~ ~

[It was a broadcast from Brazil where a reporter from Costa Rica had tracked down the snake lady for a follow-on interview. Some had no clue as to what that was all about. Again, the subtitles translated the spoken words this time from Portuguese and Spanish to English.

The reporter recounted his first story about how the lady had chased the snakes out of town and also healed the people that had been bitten. Briefly he recounted how he had tracked down Guadalupe for another interview and happened upon a bigger story. The scene cut to his second interview which occurred in a hospital. He asked why she had moved to Brazil and she indicated that she had been summoned by her mentor. Then he asked her how she knew what to do with the snakes and if she knew it would work. Then Guadalupe, this time without a snake around her neck, said that her inspiration came from a minister of the International Spiritualist Association of Churches, who was her mentor. When the reporter asked who, she pointed to a man clothed in a Chamanto, a reversible wool poncho like those commonly worn in the mountains of Chile or Peru. He was placidly standing in the background until the reporter moved to talk to him. It was then that he suddenly moved into the crowded hospital ward and the reporter had to follow him. The man suddenly seemed busy after having sedately stood in the background of the picture. He touched one man and moved on to the next. A woman he helped out of bed. Another he laid his hand on her stomach. It did not come to the reporter right away what was occurring; he followed in hopes of getting an interview. The cameraman figured it out and panned the camera back upon those that had been touched. They were in the first moments of rejoicing over their good health. The camera swung back to the man in the poncho who took a patient's wheelchair away from his bed and rolled it into a storage area where others were lined up. He turned and asked the man to get out of bed. Without watching to see if the patient had followed his orders he walked out the door into a patio with a damaged fountain overgrown with weeds.

Next to the seedy, waterless fountain invalids were scattered about on mats, in rusted iron garden chairs, or sitting on broken curb stones that bordered the ancient walkways whose cracks were filled with weeds. The healer stood next to the fountain and extended his arm. Palm up, he asked everyone to stand and with an upward sweep of his arm he added emphasis to his command. Most blinked stupidly. The incongruity of asking the lame, the maimed, and the limbless to stand was beyond comprehension. Then the miracle spread around the room. Weeds disappeared into cracks; cracks melded together; tumbled statuary jumped back on pedestals. The cameraman didn't know where to center his focus. He panned from right to left zooming into incredible pictures. He caught a formerly legless man in a wheel chair feeling his new leg to see if it was an illusion. Another was standing with his cane and then dropped it. In the foreground a withered branch sprouted leaves, producing a bud followed by a flower. Sounds of happy surprise erupted accompanied with a gurgling, bubbling fountain splashing water into a crystal-clear pool filled to the brim.

Glimpses of the reporter were seen in the movement of the all-seeing camera lens. He had forgotten his intent to interview the healer; he was celebrating with the restored. One man performed a cartwheel, a woman sang, others walked, sprang, and leapt. One man playfully splashed water into the air. The reporter was back-slapping, hugging, and dancing with a man in front of his wheelchair. Catching the camera on him, he broke away from the dancing man and approached the camera. He addressed the viewing audience exclaiming,] *"Isn't this wonderful?"* [The picture centers on the fountain with the joyous celebration and then fades.

The next scene is a frame of the reporter and the healer sitting together in an office; the reporter is holding the microphone toward the healer.] *"The people call me, Doctor Angel Moreno."* [Immediately the name appeared under the image.]

"Where do you come from?"

"The mountains over the border in Chile," he answered.

"When did you realize you had this amazing power to heal people?"

"I have always known I've possessed the power and the authority. The power has been with me from the beginning."

"Are there any more like you?"

"Yes, of course, I have many assistants. They do as I command. The spirits are very obedient."

"I understand you're a leader in the Spiritualist Association of Churches, is that correct?"

"It is partially correct. I am also a born-again Christian. The Spiritualist and the Christian churches of Brazil are coming together under my leadership. Soon I will travel to England to help establish a union there. There is a great work to be done in bringing this world together spiritually."

[The interview ended abruptly when Doctor Moreno stood, moving away from the camera and from more questions. The next scene was a single shot of the reporter making his final recap. He explained that all the things he had witnessed could not be placed in this short report. He mentioned a few quick events and then said this story was incomplete. The station was sending him on special assignment to attend Doctor Moreno's visit to England and onward to Europe. He ended by saying,] *"I expect to bring to you many more wonders and miracles from this humbly dressed man, like the ones you've seen in this report."*

~ ~ ~ ~ ~ ~

The students were quiet, sitting in chairs trying to understand the import of the video. Coach Weldon and Principal Chennault stood in front. "I need to explain a little, the title 'Doctor,' is really honorary. It is used when people revere someone for leadership. While you were watching this video presentation, Coach Weldon showed me a quote from the Great Controversy. Coach Weldon, would you be so kind as to explain to the students what you explained to me?"

"Instead of explaining let me read it first. 'Satan himself is converted, after the modern order of things. He will appear in the character of an angel of light. Through the agency of spiritualism, miracles will be wrought, the sick will be healed, and many undeniable wonders will be performed.' Later on the same page it says, 'The line of distinction between professed Christians and the ungodly is now hardly distinguishable…Satan determines to unite them into one body and thus strengthen his cause by sweeping all into the ranks of spiritualism.' Students, what we see here today is a good representation of what could be happening. Only time will tell if this is it."

"Coach, how can we tell what a good miracle is and what is a good bad, er, or a bad good miracle? Those people were healed and that was good for them. It's confusing," one girl asked.

"Good question. Satan is not going to make this easy for us. He's going to perform and act like an angel of light. He is also going to come and pretend to be Jesus." He saw a hand raised. "Yes."

"Coach, today I witnessed a miracle before I got to school. April, here, healed a baby that was dead. It was a car crash and she prayed and gave the baby back to its mother. I know April. She's not a spiritualist. Maybe that's how we can tell them apart, by what they believe," Darin added.

"Exactly! We have to sift the information to prove what is the pure will of God. I heard about what happened this morning. It was wonderful beyond comprehension. Maybe April could tell us in her own words for everyone to know." Principal Chennault entered the conversation. April hated public speaking; she could not put two words together if more than three were listening. She didn't stand up; she whispered instead to Darin, "you tell them, please." Darin took the lead for her.

"April's a little shy. So I'll tell you the story…" He related quickly the accident and the severity of the wreck. How the mother was stuck and the baby was crushed. Most had heard the story in fragmented details. This was the first time everything was presented in a logical, sequential whole. It pulled at the hearts of many as he told the story. He concluded, "I know April to be a good hearted, sincere Christian. I've known her for years. She's a shy, humble instrument of God. Everyone will agree with me when I say, we all love her. I believe the true God was the one who worked this miracle through her."

"Thank you, Darin, for relating that story. This is God's way of helping us. He restored the baby to her mother. He validated our faith and showed us an authentic miracle so we can compare it against the false copy. Jesus is helping us get through this very troublous time, giving us the tools to discern the good from the bad."

Everyone understood the seriousness of the dilemma. The future would not be easy. Darin sat down next to April and put a comforting arm around her shoulder. She moved closer and whispered a thank you in his ear.

* * * * * *

Rachael sat a moment in her car, exhausted from her talk with Rochelle. Her plan was to go to a friend named Cheri. Cheri had always been moody and prone to seeing the negative side of everything. It was a burden to visit her under the best of circumstances. She closed her eyes to rest, spooling up her resolve to go to a friend that needed the Lord in more ways than just one. A gentle face appeared before her. She thought she was dreaming, but knew she wasn't. She recognized the face as the same one from her dream. She opened her eyes to see the same face. A kind smile accompanied the words, "Megan needs you now," the soft melodious voice ended and the face faded away. She was astonished by the vision. She wanted more, to ask more, to spend more time with the angel. She knew it was a summons, a call to go to her sister, who possibly was in trouble. She heard herself answer the angel, "I will, thank you for helping me." She obeyed the heavenly directive. Instead of going to Cheri, she drove to Megan as fast as the legal limit and the crazy drivers would allow.

She drove into the driveway and jumped out of the car almost on the run. In her haste she shut the car door a bit too strongly. It made a loud thump. When she locked the car with the remote it made an audible chirp. The two sounds were as helpful as was her presence. When Megan answered the door it was with a look of relief. Before they could talk, Walt demanded Rachael to move her car; it was blocking his from getting out of the garage. His toned communicated anger and frustration. Rachael had not witnessed Walt in such a foul mood before. She didn't want to be his lightning rod for any further temper so she hurried to move her car. Tires squeaked as Walt tore around the corner of the block and out of sight. He was gone, adding his angry driving to the multitude of overstressed operators channeling their unchecked emotions through accelerator pedals.

Megan welcomed her sister for the second time through the front door. She was desperately relieved, but her voice still shook with fear. "I'm so glad you came. I didn't know what to do. I kept praying for help. I've never seen him like this before. We've had our arguments, like any couple. He and I will exchange words and then we'll split up and cool down. This time it was so intense. I was really afraid."

"Oh, Megan, I'm sorry. Normally I would say I shouldn't have come, but I received—"

"No, no. I'm glad you came," Megan interrupted.

"God is protecting you. I know it. He sent me—"

Megan took a deep breath and let it out slowly. A little more relaxed she answered, "Walt *is* a gentle person. He's not like this. It's one of the reasons I was attracted to him. He was the calm one and I was the fiery one. You know me and the fights I had with the folks. Walt was the calming influence I needed. That's why today is so strange. He went berserk, over the baby. I don't understand...well, maybe I do understand." Rachael listened, letting her continue. "It was about me and Tabatha. Tabatha is not his. She's really not mine as well. He has rejected her because I picked a sperm donation from a menu of handsome intelligent men and he's jealous. He claims it's like I had sex with those men. I don't want to have sex with another man, ah, I didn't have sex with another man. I just wanted a baby. Now with all his hatred for the church and his hatred for the baby, I'm beginning to wish I hadn't gotten pregnant. It's as if the baby is not really mine because it's not really his. Does that make sense?"

"Yes and no. Yes, because you are feeling the hatred and rejection from him and no because it is not God's will, or natural, for parents to hate their children. Oh, Megan, my heart goes out to you. You need to hang on to Jesus and He will carry you through this."

"I know. I know I know. I just want it all to stop—even the baby's constant crying." Megan's fists were clinched and on the table. She pounded the table once for emphasis.

"All this is going to stop. We're so close to the end. When Jesus comes our pain will be over."

"I hear you, Rachael. I've been watching the news now all the time because of you. So I see what's going on. Anyway, I tried to explain some of that to him and he exploded even more. I've never heard his voice so loud. He was pounding on the kitchen counter with his fist. He put a hole in the wall in the hallway," Megan explained. "I want him to stop. Anything to get back to what is was before when we didn't have this baby."

"I'm so sorry for you. I'll pray for you." Rachael sympathized.

"Even the news adds to our frustration. It never stops. Everyday there is something: murders, hit and runs, airplane crashes. There was another one on the news this morning. Yesterday was the monster typhoon destroying part of Japan and crashing into eastern Russia. It's distressing; I don't want to hear any more of it," Megan revealed.

"I think our focus should be purely on the Lord. He eases the stress."

"Do you think Walt's behavior might have something to do with all these things happening?" Megan asked.

"Look at how it is affecting you. Your only solution, and Walt's, is to seek the peace God gives. Then—"

"If Walt calms down then I know I can calm down, too. It's my only hope," Megan stated.

"It would be nice if he calmed down, but you have to be settled with the Lord first. With you calm that will take one more burden off of Walt's back. You have to operate out of a cup full of the Spirit of God, not one that is broken or half full."

"I know. I've been kinda praying. I'll get back with God, it's just that… well, you know. I'm a little mad at the people in the church the way they treated us. I want to start attending again, with Walt, but if they are there it makes it awkward."

"Helping Walt has to start with you first. Can we pray together and make a commitment now?" Rachael asked. Megan was silent for a few moments.

"I need to calm down first. I'm still jittery from the argument. I'll pray later."

"I will pray and you can listen. Maybe that will help you calm down. Then we can pray together."

"No, not now. Okay? I have to feel comfortable with God first. Right now I'm angry with God. I don't want to be angry with you, too."

* * * * * *

Janelle left school early. No accounting for absences meant she didn't have to stay to the end of school. She parked the van, stomped into the house, threw her almost empty school bag in the corner and flopped on her bed. Almost instantly the phone rang. She knew who it was, but didn't want to answer. Her foul mood carried her away from the world and everything in it.

* * * * * *

Rachael left Cheri's house. It was another dismal visit. Cheri had launched herself into a depression fueled with alcohol. She was close to total inebriation and was in the middle of another bottle of Jack Daniel's. Rachael debated her ability to reason with a mind that was so befuddled with the effects of a self-delivered sedation. As she drove across town she thought of the visit and wondered if it was efficacious. Her travels today were haphazard. Her original plan was to make a logical circle from one to the other. God's calling to visit Megan interrupted the plan, sending her back and forth over the city streets. If traced on a map, the lines would look like Cheri trying to draw a stick figure in her befuddled state. The drive home gave Rachael a chance to think back upon the visit.

Courtesy directed Rachael to let Cheri talk when what she really wanted to do was instruct and warn Cheri about transpiring events. The topic of current news presented itself and she tried to direct her friend to the need to get ready. Cheri on the other hand was depressed by all the negative reports on the TV. She sympathized with the poor victims and proudly displayed her solidarity bracelet as her contribution to the cause of helping others. The more she talked the more she edged toward a quivering tone in her voice. She wanted to cry. If she was alone she probably would have sobbed for them and for herself. Rachael wanted to direct her focus upon Jesus. For Cheri, Jesus seemed so distant. Nothing she tried helped. Her changing of subjects did not get her off of a negative train of thought. It just exchanged one venue of thought for another in which she could apply more depressing applications. Finally Rachael went to an object lesson.

"Cheri, the end of a caterpillar's life must be so dismal," Rachael began. Her words caught Cheri where she existed. "If you think about it, the little creature has been eating and then it starts making a cocoon, kind of like building its own casket. It has no knowledge of what is ahead. For him it is the end." Rachael stopped to let the futility of the insect's life sink in and possibly have Cheri think about what's happening next. "When he seals up the cocoon it must be dark and hopeless for him. No future. Then…there is a transformation into a beautiful creature with wings to fly. The sky is the limit. Color becomes its decoration and attraction. The change from the former life to the new life is dramatic; from chewing on leaves to sipping on nectar, from stuck on a leaf holding on desperately with all his legs to soaring on the breeze. As Christians we are caterpillars now and butterflies later. Jesus is coming to rescue us from what is now, to what He has prepared for us. Isn't that a wonderful promise?" Rachael tried to reach her miserable friend with hope.

"That'ss nice thought," Cheri slurred.

"It is a very nice thought. Jesus is coming soon to make it happen for each of us. We have to believe in Him."

"That'ss nice…" It was obvious that Cheri's drinking before Rachael's arrival was in the blood stream and affecting more of her speech.

"Cheri, you have to pull yourself out of this funk you are in."

"Wha'ss'ya mean flunk? I'm not in flunk … a frunk … whassever." Rachael was at the point of giving up. She had to confront her.

"Cheri, look around you. You don't turn on the lights. The drapes are all drawn and the shades are pulled down. Today is a sunny day. You don't even know it. It is like a cocoon in here. Jesus is the bright horizon just around the corner. You're going to miss it. You have to come out of it. You have to become a butterfly."

> *Jesus is the bright horizon just around the corner. You're going to miss it. You have to come out of it. You have to become a butterfly.*

"Okaaay, butterfly. I'm slo sleepy…"

The experience did not lift Rachael's spirits as she drove home. Her conclusion was that her best efforts were defeated by the whisky floating around Cheri's bloodstream. She had heard the expression, "You can't reason with a drunk." Today it struck her full force. She wondered how much of her words would be remembered. The thought was in her head as she led her friend to her bed and tucked her in. I was in her head again as she drove through the heavy snarling traffic. Depression, anger, fear, passion, these were emotions clamoring for ascendancy in the human animal as it struggled to cope with life without the Spirit of God assisting. She could see it in the visits she had that day and in previous experiences her family had had recently. An odd thought cruised into her thinking. It was about creation verses evolution. She drew the conclusion that evolution could not have happened in a world without God. Without His abiding presence mankind would destroy mankind before any civilization could occur. Creation was a greater concept by far. It is so sad that Satan had messed it up with his temptation. A comforting thought was that soon the fall from paradise would be reversed.

* * * * * *

Mike and Jason had it easy. A warm fire bathed their faces and no outside world interrupted their solitude. Their retreat in the mountains resurrected old memories. They talked of the times they played table games, put picture puzzles together, ate homemade fudge that Grandma made, and told stories. Jason especially liked the stories Grandpa told of how his daughter, Rachael, would act up and he would have to put her in timeout. He had to make sure there were no dolls in the area or she would stay in timeout playing for hours. Grandpa played hide-n-seek at the cabin starting when they were five years old. Jason knew every place where he had hidden before.

As they talked Mike thought of an amusing quote by Peter de Vries: "Nostalgia isn't what it used to be." He applied the quip to what it will be like to reminisce in heaven. Would fond memories of this time on earth be a subject of discussion? Certainly some memories would be cherished… like the memory of the day one accepted Jesus. However, a vast majority of memories would be easily forgotten…on purpose.

Jason pulled Mike out of his reverie. "Dad, we had no idea that Grandma and Grandpa were going to die until the day it happened, but now we have an idea of approximately when they will live again. Soon we'll see them again. I know I'm too old for this but I would like to play a few more games of hide-n-seek with Grandpa again, ya'know, for old time's sake."

"I think I'll join in, too. I'll bet we can convince your mom to play as well."

"She'll always be it because she's no good at hiding. The first one found is always it and has to find everyone else the next time."

"She just might fool you. Did you know that she purposely didn't hide very well for you two because she didn't want you to get discouraged?"

"Oh."

"It won't be long now before we see them again."

* * * * * *

Rachael saw the van parked in the driveway. It had to mean that Janelle was stopping for something rather than in for the evening. Her visiting and working with Darin were bordering on obsessive. However, it was good to get at least a moment with her daughter before she raced off in another endeavor. For Rachael it meant a rewarding interlude that would confirm to her that someone was being successful in their witnessing.

The house was quiet. Lights were not on. No music played in the background. Janelle must have turned everything off before leaving and then returned to her room for something she had forgotten.

"Janelle?" Rachael called upstairs. No answer. "Janelle? Are you home?" Rachael reached her door and knocked. "Janelle? Are you here?"

"Yes, Mother, I'm here." A muffled voice grumped from the bedspread. Rachael pushed the door open to see her daughter prone on the bed. When she looked at her face she could see she had been crying.

"What's wrong, sweetheart? Are you hurt?"

"Nothing's wrong, I'm fine!" she stated with a bit too much emphasis. "Oh, Mother, I feel awful." Her contradictory words indicating anger and sadness mingled together.

Rachael gathered her daughter in her arms to comfort her. She stroked her head and straightened some strands of tangled hair away from her mouth. "You can tell me what happened if you want to. I'll listen." Her thoughts were that some witnessing effort had not been successful, like her day had been. She was seeing her daughter's trauma in the light of her own. Her mind focused on ministry rather than the domestic concerns of a teen.

"Darin likes April," Janelle sobbed out the words.

Rachael was taken aback. Her daughter seemed so mature the past couple of weeks. It had been a relief to have her so committed and engaged in her commitment to Christ. To hear her daughter speak of a relationship drama brought her back to the now world—a world of disappointments and young love. Every teen has adolescent heart traumas when exploring the world of love. Later the traumas become increasingly powerful as they develop into life changing events. These smaller issues prepare them for the bigger concerns. Rachael had been thinking in terms of universal themes: good versus evil, faith versus doubt. She had neglected the rudimentary problems that any teen girl would experience. She questioned whether there was time for Janelle to learn from experience. Debate bounced around inside her. What she wanted to say was, "There's no time to worry about this now." But, she couldn't be so callous. This ordeal was ripping her child's heart apart.

"Sweetheart, it hurts a lot inside. I can tell."

"Mother, how can guys be so cruel?"

"I don't know. Sometimes they don't know themselves." Rachael reached a tissue and almost held it to her teen's nose as if she was four years old. She stopped short just in time. "And sometimes they don't even know until we tell them. Have you talked to Darin?" As if on cue, like in TV dramas, the phone rang again. Rachael reached for it and almost answered.

"Don't! I don't want to talk to the likes of him."

"Maybe he needs to know what he did. You can tell him. You can tell me."

"It's complicated."

The phone rang again in her hands and Janelle growled, burying her head in a pillow. This time the indication was not from Darin; it was Sheila.

"Sheila, nice of you to call. I was wondering abou—"

"I got laid off. Fired more accurately."

"What? I can't believe it! What happened?" Rachael was instantly sympathetic.

"Can I talk to you?"

"Yes, of course you can. I can come over to your place if—"

"I'm here now. I'm in my car in front of your house. I was hoping you wouldn't mind."

"Of course I wouldn't mind. Please come in. I'm upstairs; I'll come right down." Rachael clicked off and turned to Janelle. "Sheila just lost her job and she's coming in. Can we talk a little later? I don't want you to think I don't care, I just have to help Sheila at this time and we'll have a good talk afterward. Okay?"

"That's fine, mom. I'll be all right. Sheila's the atheist, right?"

"She was an atheist, but now she's a believer. Satan is trying to make life miserable for her so he can get her back."

"I know, Mom. Go to her, help her, she needs you. I'll be fine. It's not the end of the world…wait, I guess it is the end of the world. You know what I mean."

"Thank you, sweetheart, I'll come back as soon as I can."

Sheila had red eyes when she came through the door. Rachael greeted her with a hug. "Here, let me take your coat. If we go into the kitchen I can make you some herb tea. Tell me all about it. I can't understand why they would lay you off."

"It's stupid really. I have seniority over almost everyone except my supervisor. If they are cutting because of the budget they should start with those who have less seniority."

"And you're a good worker, too. Why? Do you even know why?"

"Yes, I do. I found out by asking too many questions. I called to ask about next week's schedule and the nursing manager said I wasn't on the list. When I asked why, she said I had to talk to the sup. When I called her, the old bat, she didn't try to be diplomatic. She laid it out straight. She reminded me that it was a Christian hospital and they wanted to trim the non-Christian workers off the payroll. I was about to explain that I was a believer now, but, you know, it would sound like I was just begging for a job. She then went on to say that everyone noticed that I wasn't wearing the bracelet showing I was a Christian. She said that would distress the patients who come to the hospital because it worked under Christian values. She said the budget was short and the hospital couldn't continue to pay non-Christians to work there anymore."

"Oh, my, that's bad. I can't understand that kind of behavior. It makes me sick inside thinking about it," Rachael empathized. Inside she was thinking this was wrongful termination, but let it go because she knew that this had to be part and parcel to current unfolding events.

"I prayed to God about my job. I need to keep working for awhile before the baby arrives, so we have enough for the baby. I don't know why God allowed this. Why did He allow this?" she implored.

Rachael wanted to help Sheila with the answer, but the other information was interrupting her thoughts. "Sheila, God has a plan and an answer, but … Did you say baby? Are you and George expecting?"

"Yes." Sheila nodded furiously.

"How wonderful! How absolutely wonderful! It's an answer to prayer!"

"Wait. How did you know we were trying? You've been praying for us?"

"Yes, but it's George who has started to pray for a baby. When you prayed for the help from God for the infant in the hospital, you told George, and George told Mike. Mike told me that George said he was going to start praying for a baby because you wanted one so much and you had been trying for so long. This is an answer to George's prayer."

"I can't believe it. Yes, yes! I can believe it. God answered my prayer; why wouldn't He answer George's?! But, why would God let me lose my job? I don't understand. If I pray will God give me my job back?"

"He could, but why would He need to? The end of this earth is so close a job is not going to mean anything anymore."

"You think so? This is all too … too big to grasp. It's only been a few weeks since I have come to believe in a God and now you're telling me God's Son is coming soon. I'm still struggling with what God does for me and why." Sheila was moving her head back and forth in amazement.

"If God answered George's prayer about a baby, don't you think He will take care of it? He'll provide for you, because you are its mother, and will give you everything you need. The baby won't starve or be cold because of a lack of clothes. All you need right now is enough to get to the time where we have to avoid Satan's people who are going to try to stop you from believing. In fact, what happened today is exactly that. Satan had you lose your job. To stop you from seeing what God is doing for you. You're like a baby who needs help—God's help. Satan wants you to stop looking to God. He's trying to destroy your faith."

"Mom? I saw a miracle today. And, I think I saw Satan, too." Janelle spoke from the bottom of the steps.

"Janelle, whatever do you mean?" Rachael was surprised to see her daughter, and both Sheila and Rachael were intrigued by her statement.

"Today there was an accident on the way to school, a bad accident. We saw a baby crushed to death and then April prayed and the baby came back to life. It was so incredible. I couldn't help but cry for joy to see the mother get her baby back. Then at school the news, well, YouTube was played in the auditorium. It was about this healer in Brazil who was going around healing everything, even fountains and statues. He didn't give credit to God. He said he has always had this power and the spirits obey him. His mission is to get all the different churches, even those who don't believe in Jesus, together. It was eerie the way he talked. I think he was trying to make people believe he is God or is a god of some sorts. I think he was Satan pretending to be God or an angel. Get this, his first name is Angel!"

Rachael and Sheila sat in wonder to hear her shortened version of an astonishing day. The miracle was more than enough to stimulate conversation; the counter story of satanic activity was also surprising.

"Did you say April prayed over the baby? Your best friend, April?" Rachael exchanged meaningful looks with Janelle.

"How did you know it was dead?" Sheila asked.

"I took her from April so April could get the other kid out of the crushed van. I could see her smashed chest, the blood, and the broken legs. I felt for a pulse there was nothing. Another lady took her from me. She also knew the baby was dead."

"She prayed and that was it? The baby came back to life? What about the broken legs?" Sheila asked.

"Everything came back to normal, even the legs. The blood was gone from the baby, but the clothes were still soaked in it."

"That's incredible." Sheila was amazed. "This is all so new for me. Where have I been all this time? I could have been seeing His work before now. If people only knew."

"Yes, if people only knew. I have been trying to talk to my friends about His love all day and I didn't meet with very much success. Some just don't want to listen and some want to wait until later. There's not much later left for people to decide." Rachael briefly related her struggle of the day.

Janelle was thoughtful. "Mom, you reminded me of Julia. I need to talk to her." With that she went to the bathroom upstairs, and returned downstairs to kiss her mother on the cheek. "Don't worry about me. I'll be back tonight and we can talk then." She dashed to the door.

"Be careful. The melting snow will freeze over and make the streets icy."

"I know. I'll be careful."

Rachael and Sheila sat at the kitchen table a little amazed at the quick departure. Rachael was deep in reflection wondering if Julia had anything to do with Darin and April.

* * * * * *

The effects of Mike's tumors were becoming more cumbersome. There didn't seem to be a quiet moment where he wasn't aware of their presence. They weighed on his mind. He did what he always did when he didn't have a plan to surmount a problem. He prayed.

"Father in heaven, I come to You knowing You know exactly what I'm going to say. *Help*. That sums it up completely. Help me, Lord. Help me to continue forward doing Your will. You have created me for a purpose and I am trying to do my best to accomplish what I see You leading me to do. The church members need my leadership; the people at work and in the neighborhood need my witness; my family needs my assistance. That is what I see You placing before me. I will continue to work on what You have called me to do. But, the effects of these tumors are making it difficult. As I pray now Paul comes to mind. He had that thorn in his flesh and asked You to remove it, but Your plan was to let him work with that thorn, whatever it was. The only reason I can think of as to why you let him work with that encumbrance was because it increased his dependence on You. Maybe that is why You have allowed this difficulty to come upon me. If that is so, then I shall depend on you for everything. And, I know You will sustain me. I welcome Your plan for my life no matter which way it leads me. In Jesus' Name, amen."

CHAPTER 15

Anarchy ruled the news. It seemed that nothing could bump it off the front page of electronic newspapers or dispel it from monopolizing the majority of the evening video report. Vivid pictures of burning cars and looted storefronts flashed one after another as commentators tried to explain the reasons people were rioting and looting. The Larssons were having a family dinner for a change. It was refreshing to have everyone there at the table. It was distressing to see how fast Mike's face was changing. He couldn't keep his one eye open and he could only smile on one side of his mouth. When asked he would shrug it off by changing the subject. The foursome knew the source of the wild behavior in the inner-cities and ghettos across America and on the international scene. The reporters were putting their spin on the riots, pointing to bare shelves and high prices for what was left. Others were saying that restlessness of the idle workers from empty factories and businesses generated a social clash between the haves and have-nots. World catastrophes were blamed as the reason for unrest and lawlessness in countries where the humanitarian response was not swift enough. The real reason was the slow withdrawal of God's restraining Spirit.

With dinner complete the family was settling in for some quiet time with a Bible reading and prayer. They turned off the news to shut out the turbulent world when the video device popped back on as if it had a life of its own. Janelle and Jason's Onyxes also flipped on and to the family's further amazement, each of their phones came to life. The FCC system which regulated the airwaves had an emergency broadcast alert signal sent through all devices that specifically used wireless com-links. A voice spoke through the system.

~ ~ ~ ~ ~ ~

This is the Emergency Broadcast System. This is not a test. The President has a very important announcement. [A brief pause before the President's face could be seen on the video devices.]

Good evening my fellow Americans,

I come before you tonight very distressed at the state of affairs in our country and in the world. Criminals have taken it upon themselves to bring about their own form of justice. They have ignored the laws of the land and have decided to take prerogatives that are not theirs. Obviously they are being directed by an unseen evil force. The caliber of these individuals is deplorable, their actions unjust, their behavior reprehensible. As a former military flag officer, I cannot condone by my sympathy or by my intellect the conduct they display. I must act. I am your leader. As your leader I must plan, protect, and prosecute those who cannot act as decent citizens. I am not alone in my concerns and action. I have been in consultation with the heads of state around the world. On this day, at the appropriate times for their countries, presidents, prime ministers, kings and queens, will be speaking to their people in the same manner as I am speaking to you. We are acting in concert.

Unprecedented crime is sweeping the globe. Banks are being robbed. Gold repositories are being plundered. Nations are being attacked by rogue bands of thugs. My own beloved United States is turning into a cauldron of evil. This is not what I envisioned for my country. It is not what my fellow world leaders envisioned for theirs. Whenever a noble endeavor of grand spiritual insight is embarked upon, the dark lord of evil strains to work against it. It is a signal to the righteous that they are on the right path. We must therefore persevere. We cannot give up. We must not retreat. We are on the righteous path.

The only way we can control the chaos is to isolate the lawless ones and thus identify them. We can find the immoral by locating the moral. When the evil hide in dark places like cockroaches in dark, wet crawl spaces, the righteous shine forth and illuminate them. God in Heaven, with His mighty wisdom, has given us a weapon to rid the world of those who perform the Devil's bidding. I hold in my hand the weapon that will defeat Satan and his minions. [The President holds up a small vial and then places it on a velvet pad under a black light. The vial has what looks like glitter in it.] *See this simple solution? It is God's way of bringing in the millennium. It looks inno-cent, but it is intelligent. It looks pretty but it is powerful. It looks small, yet it is strong. It is invisible. The only reason you can see it now is because there is an ultraviolet black light shining on it. When the light is turned off these shiny flecks disappear and this looks like a vial of dust.* [The glitter suddenly disappears when the black light is switched off. A moment later the glitter reappears when the light is switched on.]

One might be thinking, "the President is daft! How can this be a weapon that will solve crime?" When I first saw this marvel, I had somewhat the same reaction. When I learned its properties, I became a believer in its awesome capabilities. The shiny dust, glitter if you will, is thousands upon thousands of miniature computer chips. They communicate with each other and with wire-less links to parent nodes. They are identifiers. This is how we will eradicate crime. If the perpetrator is caught every time, soon the world will be rid of the baser elements of society.

Briefly let me explain how this works. Everyone is marked with these indelible chips. They instantly identify who you are to any authority that needs to know. The chips are arranged in a dot matrix of three lines with six figures in each line, each line communicating with the lines and dots in the neighbor-ing line and then displaying almost infinite information to a central computer. These can be read by scanners, by video surveillance, by video phones, and by television monitors and cameras. There is no way a criminal can commit a crime without being seen and identified. When everyone is tagged with these little marvels then it is only a matter of tracking down the individual. His or her crimes are on video record and therefore they are guilty upon capture. The chips will be placed in a visible area of the body, on the forehead or the hand. Don't worry ladies, they are invisible and will not interfere with make-up. They are non-toxic and cannot be easily removed. See, I have mine already on my forehead. A sweep of an infrared light reveals its presence. [The President holds a small flashlight to his head and reveals a pattern of dot clusters in a matrix of eighteen dots in three rows of six.]

It is everyone's duty to help clean society of the scourge of evil. No one is exempt from their responsibilities as citizens. Together we will wipe out crime and when that becomes a reality then spiritual utopia will flourish. The world will broker no compromise. Everyone is a soldier in the battle. Our task for you, my people, is for you to be counted as the righteous. That will not be dif-ficult for the majority of the populace. When you receive this invisible badge of honor you will be solidifying society into one unified whole. All legally responsible citizens will become the tool to expose the profligate, the defiled, and the degenerate. Those who refuse will be immediately exposed as the ones who wish to stay outside the law. Those who receive this tool as a ruse to hide and then commit sins against humanity will be caught by the identifiers in their flesh. We'll have the miscreants whether they do or do not comply with the demands of this government.

Our task for you, my people, is for you to be counted as the righteous. That will not be difficult for the majority of the populace. When you receive this invisible badge of honor you will be solidifying society into one unified whole.

I am declaring martial law. No one is to be on the streets at night except by reason of civil service: police, firemen, emergency medical personnel. I have instructed, through channels, that everyone out at night will be stopped. Individuals wearing the solidarity bracelets will be given a degree of leniency. Starting next Monday and continuing to Friday everyone will report to the nearest station to receive their stamp, no exceptions. Sunday all will start the week with worship and then rest. On that day we will reflect about the condition of our world and the need for strong measures. Every good Christian will be in church this Sunday. Then Monday we'll begin to make things better. Every good Christian will report to be numbered for their country. Every one! Let me repeat, everyone will go to the nearest place for voting. Special equipment will be at the polling places to administer these invisible electronic miracle workers for good. Alternative places to receive these dust chips will be hospitals, clinics, police stations, motor vehicle license offices, and social security bureaus. Electronic reminders and application forms will be sent to everyone through this medium of internet distribution over which I am speaking to you now. There will be no excuse for some to not have this stamp of public approval. I call it the CNS which means Citizen National Stamp. It separates righteous citizens from the baser elements of society who are creating disorder. It also symbolizes the citizen's approval of a morally clean society.

In conclusion, I commend, you, the republic of the United States, for your forbearance in past years of your government stumbling to resolve the issue of spiritual laziness and your leaders grappling unsuccessfully with rising crime. This coming week we'll have turned the corner. From here forward we will not have to fear walking our streets at night, our identities will be free from theft; our property will not be stolen; our bodies will not be assaulted. The perpetrator of evil will be bound by circumstance. He cannot stand against a righteous nation united in its conviction that evil ends here. You, the people, will become the living weapon that defeats the enemy.

Thank you and good night.

~ ~ ~ ~ ~ ~

The video monitors, Onyxes, and phones shut off at the same instant. The family room was quiet. The four faced each other from various angles, each with a knowing, yet disturbed, understanding of the waymark they had passed in their journey to the final destination.

"That's it. That's the mark of the beast. It's mandatory and it has the spiritual components. I expect the spiritual components will become more and more binding as this grows. We need to fasten our seatbelts of faith," Mike predicted.

"Cool! Computers now outnumber *and* outsmart humans," Jason remarked. The others looked at him as if he was an alien.

"How can you be thinking like that? Our very lives are at a cross-roads!" Janelle sounded exasperated.

"Hey, I know what's going on. But, you can't blame a guy for seeing the obvious. Technology is complicating our simple concepts of the mark of the beast and fleeing to the mountains. We are in some deep gumbo. Those mini-computers are going to be everywhere. I saw in the Discovery Channel where they can put that computer dust on roads and give traffic info to traffic lights and stuff. If the government wants to listen in to this conversation in this room, they can. If they want to watch us they can. You saw what happened. Our phones are tracking, listening devices. We'll have no place to hide and no place to run," Jason explained.

"But, you think it's cool. Why?" Janelle challenged.

"It's the hero who meets the unbeatable foe. It's the stuff of epic stories. How are we going to survive the confrontation? God has the answer we don't have. We have to keep reading the story to see how it ends. In this case we can't jump to the end and read the last page. We must see it through to the end. We have to have faith in the writer. God is writing the tale and is making us look like heroes at the same time."

"You think this is a fairy tale?! I can't believe it. Do you even have a serious bone in your body?" Janelle sounded frustrated, almost angry.

"Everyone has a different way of looking at their world. This is a unique view I must admit. But it has its merits. I agree that we don't know how God will bring us through. We have to have faith. Another thing

Jason said makes me think. We need to drop our electronics when the time comes. Fleeing doesn't make sense if we leave a trail of electronic breadcrumbs," Mike defended his son.

"Breadcrumbs? Now you're talking in fairy tales," Rachael quipped with a smile toward her husband. "I see Jason's point. My first reaction was to question his sincerity, but he's right, God is writing our future. We have to trust Him. Tonight, with all that is happening around us and listening to the President command us to get the mark on our foreheads, made my heart pound faster and my legs feel weak. Trusting God is not going to be easy when all around us there will be danger. Jason, we do know what happens on the last page. What worries me is that we don't know exactly what is just before the last page."

"We have to be strong in Him. We have to rely on the Holy Spirit. We need to be fortified in Him. I suggest we have a season of prayer," Mike suggested.

"Amen."

* * * * * *

"Dad, I can't keep ignoring the elephant in the room. I can tell you're in pain. Talk to us about it! Please!" Janelle broke the silence.

"Yes, honey, my heart hurts for you," Rachael added.

"It gets worse when I am tired. I always have a headache and it makes sleeping difficult, which adds to my being tired.

"What can we do? Should we all go to the cabin now where you can rest?"

"I can't. People depend on me. They depend on us."

"Who?"

"Church people, you guys, George and Sheila…people at work. Maybe some will want to know more … our neighbors, the Froelichs. I need to keep witnessing. I can't stop now. *We* can't stop now! Time is short."

"But, your arm is hanging loosely by your side and every now and again you jump like someone is sticking you with a pin. When is too much, too much?" Janelle pleaded.

"Before you answer that, tell me how much pain you are in?" Rachael wanted the truth out in the open.

"Not much."

"Come on, Dad, I don't believe you."

"Neither do I."

"Dad, we all want to know how much it hurts," Jason spoke on the subject for the first time.

"Most of the time it is irritating. When the electrical zap comes it hurts like crazy. The rest is uncomfortable because I can't control my eye or arm, and sometimes my leg. I can't wait until Jesus comes."

"Oh, honey," Rachael embraced her husband.

"I'm so sorry. I can't wait either, but, Dad, maybe I could talk to April. You know, have her come over and pray for you. You could be healed from this," Janelle suggested. Rachael loosened her embrace to look in his eyes.

"It's worth a try, Dad. Nothing ventured, nothing gained," Jason threw in a little too flippantly.

"I ... I feel uncomfortable asking. I've thought about it and it would be nice. I even read some of the healing passages where Jesus healed people, but…"

"But what?"

"God knows if I need to be healed or not. Maybe He has allowed this at this time to remind me that I need to be totally dependent on Him. If I asked selfishly am I forgetting that He knows exactly what is best for me?"

"I don't see it that way. April is only a phone call away. I'm going to call her now." Janelle stood to go get her phone.

"Janelle, please don't. I want this to be between me and God. But thanks for your concern."

Pushing him now was the wrong thing to do. They wanted him to be the vital, strong, spiritual leader he had always been in the past. He wanted to trust Jesus. For him to ask for healing bordered on doubting his Savior's purpose. Their concerns were tied-up and left helpless. What they didn't know was that he felt he was unworthy of a miracle. His unworthiness stemmed from a humble attitude about his role in the big picture of redemption.

* * * * * *

Rachael found Janelle in the corner of the living room staring out the window at a dark street with remnants of snow bordering the sidewalks. "Janelle, we haven't had time to talk. I'm wondering what is happening with you and Darin? He's been calling repeatedly to get in touch with you. It's more than a day now and you're avoiding him. Do you want to talk about it?"

"Oh, Mother it still hurts, but I can't be selfish and ignore the people who are counting on me to teach them about what's happening. I promised myself I would call Julia at 7:30. Kind of a follow-up from yesterday."

"I'm impressed with your grasp of the moment. You are setting your personal disappointments aside for others. I'm proud of you."

"Mom, I'm guessing it's kinda like having a baby. The friends I have will be lost if I don't forget my suffering and continue the process of leading them into a new birth. I'm in pain, but they need me to pay attention to them."

"You're mature beyond your years. I'm proud of you. What happened?"

"I really don't want to think about it. It hurts and maybe I'm jealous, too."

"Jealous?"

"I, ah … well it's hard to explain. I … Oh, Mom. She performed a miracle and Darin was so proud of her and talked about her and bragged about her to the whole school and said everyone loves her and then put his arm around her and she snuggled … aaach. If I say anything it's like I'm against her and the miracle she performed and the sweet little baby didn't deserve to be … and I'm the big horrible person that is throwing sour grapes at them and the miracle and..." Janelle's thoughts tumbled out in a cascade of frustration.

"Have you talked to April? She's your best friend."

"I can't! I can't talk to her and explain how I feel."

"You were ready to call her for your father; why can't you call her about this? She has called several times."

"It's different. For Dad I would. For me I don't want to."

"Darin has tried to talk to you too. Did you know he came over when you were away and I was with Sheila? Don't you want to know what they have to say?"

"I'm mad at him—and April! I don't understand. She was happy for me when Darin and I got together."

"I think you should call them."

"Mom! I can't do that! Haven't you been listening? I can't!"

"Janelle, listen to me. This is more about Satan than it is about you. If he can get you to not forgive your best friends then he has broken up a team. He has driven a wedge between you and them. Your father and I are a team for Jesus. He and I have made a lot of mistakes that have hurt each other. We had to learn and grow. I am so proud of you because you kept going in your witnessing despite your personal disappointment. But, the combination of the three of you is unbeatable, unless you beat your-selves. Talk to them." Without a word Janelle left her mother and went to her room. Fifteen minutes later she could be heard quietly talking on the phone.

* * * * * *

Jason disquieted the house with his shout, "Hey everyone you've got to see this!" Mike and Rachael were talking in their bedroom sitting on their bed. They only had time to turn their heads when their son burst through the partially open door. Janelle was slower and waited at the door leaning on the jamb.

"I found this on YouTube. Baby Sis told me about this guy she saw at school yesterday and I looked him up. There's more."

"Jason, hold up for a moment; it might be better if we watch it from the larger screen downstairs." The family moved down to the family room and situated themselves on the couch. "I have watched more television in the last month than in the last ten years. In this case, I think it's important to know what's going on," Mike remarked. Jason waited for his father to stop talking and then pressed the play arrow.

~ ~ ~ ~ ~ ~

[The reporter from Brazil came on and briefly set the stage. He explained that he had immediately flown to Heathrow Airport after his last report. Doctor Angel Moreno was already there, he didn't know how, and had been performing miracles at the Bournemouth Hospital in Dorset. He went on from there to Salisbury where more healings had occurred. Crowds were gathering wherever he went. Then the reporter met him when he went to Stonehenge. Camera footage started at the scene of the ancient site of Druid worship. Doctor Don Angel Moreno spoke in perfect BBC English as he moved about the circle of stones. The snake lady from Costa Rica was attending his every move.]

This is a place of true worship. The ancients learned from the spirits how to please god. They sacrificed and directed their adoration toward the sun which is god's holy symbol of his blessings to mankind. They knew the right day of worship. In those days many did not believe as the Druids believed. They were savages, unwilling to become enlightened. The Druids were correct when they acted for the better good of all mankind. They turned the unen-

lightened into gifts to god—gifts of honorable and sacred sacrifice. Because of their foresight this country became great. England ruled the world. The British Empire started here, in this place, among these hallowed stones. [Doctor Moreno knelt and silently prayed with his hand held upward resting on one of the stones—the stone made famous with the carving of the Mycenaean sword. The winter foliage turned to spring in less than a minute. Flowers bloomed at the bases of the monoliths. He paused to say more to the cameras.] *Every great empire of the world started with faith, faith in god. Here is a reminder of the Greek empire, placed here league upon leagues away from its cultural source. The Greeks communed with the spirits who were god's appointed assistants. The Greeks called them gods. Later, they invented fanciful stories about their gods and they moved away from true worship. Their empire ceased to flourish. Now all countries, all faiths, must come together and worship god on his day, the day of his son.* [Angel Moreno smiled at his double application of the homophone. He walked through the crowd and touched a man on crutches. The crutches dropped away and the man walked freely, spinning in a circle like a Dervish. He took the sunglasses off of another and lightly tossed them away. The man was cured of his blindness.]

[The video report segued to a scene in London. At the Queen Victoria monument in front of Buckingham palace, crowds massed around the circular drive as lines of invalids were carried or hobbled to Doctor Moreno for healing. He was sitting on the raised wall behind one of the lions. Assistants, including the Costa Rican lady, were guiding invalids up the stairs. In some cases, they needed to be carried. The camera focused on one healed person after another. Wheelchairs were pushed away empty. Crutches were piled in heaps. No one was turned back for lack of faith. All were healed. At one point, Moreno stood up from his place on the monument. He moved down the steps into the crowd. He took a sack from a lady who had purchased her lunch at a deli. She was nibbling on a pork pasty. Moreno reached his hand into the bag and pulled out another to the surprise of the original owner, handing it to a bystander. He took out another and another and then another. People were clamoring for the free food. After twenty some repetitions of the act he handed the small paper bag to a burly man and asked him to continue to give the crowd food. Delighted he reveled in the ongoing miracle and his participation in it. Doctor Moreno moved to a squadron of media cameras and addressed the world. Behind him jubilation continued for the ongoing miracle of food distributed.] *God feeds a willing and faithful world.* [He turned slightly to view the transpiring act.] *Harvests are swept away, famines exist, pesti-*

lences ruin the food supply all because of the unbelieving and those who do not honor the words of his priests and religious scholars. If they had listened and worshipped god on his designated day then all these struggles for food would not exist. [In the background a tumult was developing around the man with the sack.] *If this world does not wake up soon, mankind will perish. It is the fault of the ungodly that these calamities occur. You have not tended the garden of this earth as you were told. The irresponsible and the ungodly must bear the responsibility of the catastrophes we endure. False living must be sacrificed for righteous living. This earth cannot continue as it is. Population growth must be stopped. It was never god's intention for billions of people to exist on this earth. Sexual sin is producing unnecessary births. There is not enough water or food, even fresh air, to sustain the masses of people who walk upon the surface of this globe. If mankind is to survive it must make the difficult choice of deciding who are the true believers and who must be purged. I am only one person. I can only heal so many. I can only feed so many. I pronounce judgment on the worthless consumers, those who defy the will of God and go against the teachings of the true church. God gives me the power to heal, but that power is reserved for the just, who worship god on his holy day of the sun.*

[Moreno turned to look at the crowd behind him, fighting over a small paper bag. The video clip ended and the reporter recapped the report by telling the viewing audience,] *I am sure Doctor Angel Moreno will perform many more wonderful things. His name is so apropos, "Angel." If he is not an angel, then I have to say, the God of Heaven is working powerfully through this man!*

~ ~ ~ ~ ~ ~

"God's miracles are not limited to the righteous only. Jesus healed willingly and lovingly. He can solve the population problem without murder," Mike commented. "This guy is saying God is only willing to help those who are willing to kill

> *God is in a battle with Satan to preserve the truth about His love and fairness.*

off the rest of the world to bring the population down to manageable levels. God is in a battle with Satan to preserve the truth about His love and fairness. Satan is making it sound like population growth is a sexual sin that is ruining the world," he finished his reaction.

"Dad, is this guy Satan? I thought Satan was going to come as Jesus. This guy isn't pretending to be Jesus," Jason asked.

"In the Great Controversy chapter thirty something, I think, it speaks about Satan appearing as an angel of light and performing great miracles. Later, of course, Satan impersonates Jesus. What happens to the angel of light when the anti-Christ appears? I don't have an answer for that. I assume that if this fellow is still on the news when the false Christ appears he will probably be one of Satan's minions. That is my best guess. We should take time to study that some more," Mike tried to help.

"At school yesterday, Coach Weldon was reading about this from the Great Controversy. My copy is up in my room. I'll go get it." Janelle stood to go but was stopped by sounds in the driveway.

"While you go we'll turn in our Bibles to Revelation and Matthew. We'll do some … Who's driving into our driveway? Nobody is supposed to be out at night. The President declared martial law!" Everyone was attempting to look out the window at the same time. Janelle knew. She became visibly nervous and resolutely marched to the front door. The rest of the family moved to the archway leading to the living room and the front entrance. Janelle opened the door and stepped back. Darin came in.

"Janelle, I'm sorry. I don't know what happened. I miss you. I love you," he pleaded. "Will you forgive me?"

"Yes, I'll forgive you." Janelle's voice indicated resignation, her body language spoke of neutrality. Darin spread his arms wide and hesitated, hoping she would allow him a hug. When her arms came up, he hurried to cling to her before she changed her mind. He almost lifted her off the carpet. His words came naturally spoken with conviction.

"You're the one I want to spend the rest of eternity with."

Mike and Rachael moved away from the archway back to the family room. Jason remained where he was. A moment later his mother peeled him away from the wall and pulled him back out of sight.

The hug lasted for many heart beats—too many to count. Then Janelle asked, "All of eternity? Not just the first fifty million years?"

"All of eternity! The first fifty million and all the gazillions after that!" They unlocked to look at each other.

"My grandma said she wanted to grow old with my grandpa. I'm not like my grandma. I don't want to grow old with you…" She hesitated. Darin feared this might lead to something bad. He waited to see what was coming. Then Janelle smiled. "I plan on staying young with you … for eternity."

They moved to the far corner of the living room and talked in hushed tones.

"Do you like April?"

"Only as a friend."

"Then why did you put your arm around her and she snuggled up to you? It hurt me. You hurt me. I thought you were leaving me for her."

"Believe me when I say, 'I didn't mean to hurt you.' April is a good friend. She got us together in the first place. She knew I liked you and she told me you liked me. It was her that got me to sit with you in the cafeteria."

"Then why did you … you know?"

"First, I have to tell you that April and I have been friends for years, not boyfriend-girlfriend, just friends. Until I started attending your church a month ago, we went to the same church from cradle roll on up. When the revival happened at school we were all a part of it. Then April told me she didn't think she had the Spirit like the rest of us. That God wasn't pleased with her. She wasn't successful in her witnessing. And, she doubted herself big time. She thought she wasn't forgiven for something and everything and everybody was passing her by. I told her God had a special plan for her life. I prayed with her and she said she would continue to pray for God's direction. Then the accident happened. It was like a quadruple answer to prayer. God had not passed her by. He was waiting for her gift to be revealed at the right time. Her gift of healing confirmed for her that God was working in her in a mighty way and for the school and for me that I had said the right thing, and for the church…everything. I was so excited for her. I guess I shouldn't have showed so much attention to her. I'm sorry. I was really happy for her getting a gift."

"I guess I misunderstood your behavior. I thought I lost you. I'm sorry I got mad."

"I was wrong. April told me that I shouldn't have put my arm around her and she said she shouldn't have leaned on me. We both feel sorry for sending the wrong message. She feels awful about it. She tried to call you. I felt terrible and didn't want to live without you. I never want to go through this again."

"I was jealous. I need to ask God for forgiveness. Will we get jealous in heaven?"

"I doubt it. God says He's a jealous God, but I think He's talking on human terms."

"Yes, I agree. I think He was talking using our words and emotions down here so we could understand. Now I can see how He feels about us not loving Him like we're supposed to. It must crush His heart like my heart was crushed. I feel so sorry for Him."

"I feel so sorry for you. I'm sorry I hurt you. I love you." They kissed, not passionately, but tenderly.

* * * * * *

The three were searching the scriptures: the gospels, the epistles, and the book of Revelation. They studied the anti-Christ references and Mike got his copy of the Great Controversy out of the den. They were writing notes and trying to establish a sequence of events when Janelle and Darin joined them. It was easier to sit around the table with Bibles opened and holding discussions and asking questions while pointing to references. Sometimes they spoke one at a time to the group; sometimes there were two or three deliberating. The normal evening family worship was usually about a half of an hour, to allow for school work. Tonight, the study went late. None asked Janelle and Darin about their former dissolution of a relationship. Rachael watched the two closely and noted how much they held hands and eyes lingered on each other longer than necessary. After a round robin prayer they talked about what their plans were for the next day.

"We can't be out at night because of martial law. We'll have to limit our witnessing to the daylight hours," Darin observed. "We'll have to skip school."

"That reminds me, Darin, you can't drive home tonight because of the restrictions. You'll have to stay here tonight. You can use our guest room."

"He can bunk in with me. I only use the top bunk," Jason said with a little too much enthusiasm. Janelle was not the least bit happy about that option, knowing her brother's penchant for teasing her about anything she said or did with regards to the opposite sex.

"He's too tall to sleep in that bunk bed. He won't be able to stretch out. I think he would be more comfortable in the guest room bed."

"No, that's okay. I want to get to know Jason. I hardly know him," Darin answered. Janelle had to soften her appeal when he said that. He was so sincere. It reminder her about how much she had missed him in the last day or so.

* * * * * *

Later, Janelle and Darin were in the living room again catching up. Janelle told Darin about her visits and attempts to get acquaintances to become more serious about their commitment. Darin caught her up on his visits.

"I purposely did not go with April this time because I didn't want you to hear about it and add to your frustration about us. I called your mom again because I wanted to go with you, because you and I are such a good team when we work together. Your mom said you were not home. So, I tried my best alone. I'm not as good without you."

"Thank you. I didn't do as well without you, either."

"This morning at school I missed you and I wanted to talk to you. Everyone at school was talking about April again. She put her hand on a kid with flu symptoms and he didn't have them anymore, no fever. Then a church member from Canada called her because she heard about her healing gift. The SDA lady had a child with spinal bifida since birth. She wanted April to pray with her over the phone. She prayed and the lady started yelling. She must have accidently disconnected the phone because the line went dead. April wondered what had happened. Later the lady called her back and thanked her for the miracle. I don't want you to think I'm attracted to April when I tell you these things, but … I kind of feel proud of myself for telling her to believe that God had a special plan for her life. I feel like God was working through me to tell her that. Do you know what I mean?"

"I do. I've prayed for you when you are talking with someone and when I'm listening. I guess I should feel proud that He answered my prayers for you. I need to apologize to April for not returning her calls and for doubting her. Darin, I need your help; rather, our family needs your help."

"Sure thing. What do you want me to do?"

"It's Jason. He doesn't always seem very serious about what's going on. He's … well, cavalier about the mark of the beast and other stuff. When we watched the President explain the mini-computer dust that everyone's supposed to have imprinted on their heads he said it was 'cool.' Then he compared our experience to a novel. I don't think he completely gets it. Maybe you can talk to him."

"I'll try."

CHAPTER 16

"We can't spend all day watching the TV to see what's happening next, but we need to have current information so we can act swiftly. On top of that, if we are going to do the Lord's work we need to be active during the day. We are kind of caught between doing what's right and knowing what's happening. What should we do?" Mike asked. The family, plus Darin, were finished with morning prayer, sitting at the breakfast table.

"I can do it," Jason volunteered.

"Do what?" Janelle asked.

"I can monitor the media while I go to practice with my friends. If anything comes up I can send a message to your phones."

"Let me get this straight, you're going to practice soccer and watch the Onyx at the same time?"

"Yep." Jason looked at Darin and Darin gave him an almost undetectable wink. Rachael, still concerned about the degree of Jason's commitment thought Jason's plan might have some merit. If he watched the news it might give him pause with the gravity of its importance.

"I think that might work, at least for a little while, until we have to throw away the devices to keep people from spying on us. Jason, make sure you explain to us completely what you are sending us. It might be something I would want to show to whoever I might be talking to at the time," Rachael instructed.

"Don't worry, Mom, I'll explain everything. Oh, and just so you know, those people are already spying on us."

"Come on, us? We haven't done anything yet. It's next week when we will have to avoid the stamping procedure. Then maybe ... How would you know anyway?" Janelle asked.

"Oh, I have my ways..." Jason waited for dramatic effect. "I use a counter-spyware program. It detects searches on our systems. The only problem is they know when I know they are trying to know about us, without us knowing...know what I mean?"

"Jason is obviously the man for the job. He will be our eyes and ears. Incidentally, I have to go to work today. They called me in for a special meeting. They said it was important. Sooo, I need to get moving." Mike got up and went for his light jacket. The weather forecast was for a warm sunny day. It hopefully signaled the start of an early spring. The rest divided up to head out for their planned activities.

It wasn't even thirty minutes before their phones chirped with a message from Jason. He had explained that he had linked in with the Adventist News Network (ANN) out of Andrews University and found two interesting items. He said he wouldn't bore them with all the details, but would give them a short summary. He texted a message: students, staff, Helderberg SDA College in South Africa were participating in retreat came upon small native village with outbreak of Ebola virus. Instead of fleeing stayed and prayed. Whole village cured. The next news item was about the Adventist health system in America. Many Adventist hospitals linked with other denominational hospitals under administrative umbrellas for management and coordination of services. Several management organizations and some denominational hospitals are engaging in hostile takeovers of Adventist hospitals. SDA workers being fired.

Ten minutes later, Jason sent another message from ANN explaining: South Korean government has declared Seventh-day Adventist church an anti-government organization, seizing all its properties and assets.

* * * * * *

Mike had to turn off his phone when he entered the CEO's office and presented himself to the receptionist. He was disturbed by the messages he had received, but needed to focus on what the chief had to say. He was guessing it had to do with the investigation of the assault and the fight during the blizzard. After waiting for an hour and fifty minutes he was called in. There were three at the other end of a long conference table: the CEO, the CFO, and the COO.

"Mike, I'll make this quick. You're an excellent worker, have been for years. Your floor has the least amount of personnel problems. Workers are requesting to work under your leadership. Your efficiency reports have been excellent. We liked how you handled the sexual assault situation. You found a way to dialogue with each of the belligerents and create a working situation after the dust settled. Thank you for your leadership. We have a proposal to make.

"We want you on our team. We are shaking up the company. You are a good man and we want you with the executive leadership. We've had to let several, shall we say, un-cooperatives, go. There's room at the top. We have a senior vice-presidential position for personnel management. We want you to take it. It would mean your salary would quadruple and you would have complete use of a company car (new model every year), stock options, and you would be eligible for a year-end bonus large enough to take your family on a vacation to our company villa in Tahiti, if you were so disposed. The perks package is great, especially for you, Mike." He smiled at the other two executives with a knowing smile, something private and still secret. "As I said before, we want you on our team. You have to be a team player. Which brings me to a delicate issue..." The CEO steepled his fingers.

"We know you attend church on Saturday. You would have to stop that activity, it's so ... shall I say, unique. We all here at the top want to be compliant with the wishes of the government and in sync with our changing society. It makes for good business. I know you'll understand. We want you to think about it and then say 'yes.' We need men like you. We know we can trust you."

"I can give you my—" Mike was cut off by the CEO.

"No, Mike, not now. I don't want your answer today. I want you to think long and hard about this and confer with your family. They deserve the good life. Please come back to this office a week from tomorrow, on Friday. Let's say four o'clock. We'll see you then." At that, the CEO rose and walked through the door to his office suite. His vice presidents followed, leaving Mike alone in the large conference room looking out at the scenic mountains in the distance. He stepped to the window and looked out over the vista. It was the first time he had been in this room. After a moment's reflection a song pushed into his thoughts, "I'd rather have Jesus, than..."

He left the conference room and went down to his floor and to his office. He went to the office to find someone else working there. His personal items were gone. Different pictures were hung on the walls. The woman behind the desk was Shelly.

"Mike so good to see you! Congratulations on your promotion! I hear you're going to be the Vice President for Personnel."

"That isn't for sure just yet. They want me to think it over."

"I wouldn't think it over. I'd accept in a micro-second," she responded.

"Mike, how good to see you." Glenda came almost at a run. She hugged him without waiting for permission. "You've got a promotion! We're all so proud of you!"

"Well, as I was saying to Shelly—"

"He's going to think about it," Shelly cut in.

"Yeah, right," Glenda spoke sarcastically. Mike looked around and Shelly knew he was looking for his personal items.

"If you're wondering where your things are, Glenda and I packed them up. We almost sent them up to your new office, but decided to wait for you to come get them. That way we could see you again before you become one of those big wigs without the time to see us little people down here."

"I kept your stuff safe in my cubicle, for a little while anyway," Glenda informed.

"Thank you for thinking of me. Is George around? Maybe I could see him on my way out."

"George is no longer with us. He was fired yesterday, because he fought with Marshall. That's the official word, but like anything else in the company, there's always a possibility of something else," Glenda answered.

Mike thought of his personal items from his office. There were framed photos of his wife and one of his family together, and then some shots of family vacations at the cabin. There was an old photo of his parents kept from his childhood. He longed to be reunited with them after all these years, after their losing

If you can find a use for anything from my office please consider it yours. I won't need them where I am going.

battle with cancer and heart disease. His office Bible would be in the box. Odds and ends made up the rest of the items like a small calculator. In light of the signs of times he knew they were no longer needed. Glenda might go through them. She would see he loved his wife and family. Perhaps she would pick up the Bible he had marked so completely. Maybe she would read it. He spoke to Shelly and Glenda, "If you can find a use for anything from my office please consider it yours. I won't need them where I am going."

* * * * * *

Janelle, Darin, and April made the decision to go to the local high school to continue talk with their friends during breaks and lunch hour. The nighttime restrictions caused them to decide against going to their own school and using the daylight hours for ministry. At the high school they were escorted off the grounds and told if they came back they would be reported to the authorities. They had to find something to do until school was out. They went to the downtown shopping district and walked up and down the street next to department stores and restaurants. A beat cop stopped them and asked why they weren't in school. They said they were performing ministry for their private Christian high school. The cop said they should find another location. They decided to head back to the academy. They were arousing too much suspicion and perhaps it was where the Lord wanted them to be.

Riding back in the van they got another quick message from Jason. "More Moreno. Appeared in Croatia. Some healings. Calls fundamental Islam a wing of international spiritualist church. Calls radical Islam agency of devil. Asks them to lay down weapons and join fundamentalists. Crowds, some for, some against, circle him. Heals children and points to them as new Muslims willing to unite with Spiritualism. Teaches Spiritualism as middle ground to unite all faiths. Many agree, especially mothers of healed children."

The three friends look at each other.

"As Jason would say, 'the plot thickens.'" Darin commented. They jumped out of the van and started into the school. Again, Jason sends an update: "Update on Croatia: rioting erupts after Moreno speech. Cars, buildings, stuff on fire. Christian churches torched by Shiites. Chanting 'We will not unite with Christians!' Moreno rushes into crowd. Flames magically extinguished. Rioters suddenly sick with cramps and throwing up, others die of sudden heart attacks. Peace restored. Some commentators are asking if he could be Jesus."

The three arrived as the school was taking select students to visit senior living centers. They asked if they could go along. Permission was granted. They piled back into the van and went to the first of four facilities on the planned itinerary. Mostly they talked with the residents and shared their faith. The best they could do in most cases was to ask them to maintain their faith. They prayed with everyone. It seemed as if the chaos of the world had mercifully passed by them. No plan had been set up for them to get marked with the computer dust. Some wore bracelets on their arms given to them by family members. Others either forgot or didn't possess them. Intellectual conversations did ensue with seniors deploring the state of the world and praising the President's attempts to bring it under control.

At the second nursing facility they were finishing lunch. Residents were sitting at tables chatting while wait staff bussed dishes away to the kitchen. It was easier for the students to mingle around amongst the tables and have light conversations. They had to stand mostly as geriatric walkers occupied the free spaces between tables. It was abnormally crowded with the students there. Janelle and Darin were at a table engaged in a conversation with a dignified gentleman. He professed to be a Christian. The conversation centered around how close it was to Jesus' second coming. The old man said, "I can't wait to feel strong again."

Janelle answered, "That might happen sooner than you may think. Let's pray about that." After prayer the gentleman tried to stand and grasp his wheeled walker. It slipped out from under him because the brake had not been set. He tumbled to the floor awkwardly after slamming his head on a sharp corner of a dining table. His head was bleeding profusely. Darin was nearby and knelt to see if he was alright. Seeing the blood, he gently took the man into his lap to give him a softer place for his head. Blood poured through Darin's fingers as he tried to staunch the flow. Many of the students were attracted to the scene and stood in a circle. Many prayed. Others handed folded cloth napkins from empty tables to help Darin with the blood. It was apparent that the man was in a feeble condition and needed help fast. A nurse came into the center of the onlookers. "An ambulance is on the way," she said and started to help Darin make the gentleman comfortable. As of one accord, the watching students searched for April and fixed their eyes on her. One whispered, "Can you pray for him?" Without a word April knelt next to the man and placed her hand on his shoulder. The nurse was about to move the hand away when she saw that April was praying. She waited. The man's eyes opened and several of the residents spoke, "John, are you okay?"

"Why of course I'm okay. Why am I down here?"

"Mr. Wilkes, you've had a nasty fall and the ambulance is coming. We'll take care of you."

"Nonsense, I'm fine! Now let me up."

"You shouldn't move. You might be a little dizzy. You've lost a lot of blood."

"Nurse, I think you need to see this," Darin directed. He took the cloth away and lifted the patient away from his blood covered leg. He supported him at the shoulders. The nurse looked at the wound which no longer existed. The head was fine. She directed Darin to help John sit up. She was able to examine the head better. Confused she looked at the head and at Darin's blood-soaked jeans and back to the head. John insisted on standing and, when they hesitated, he got up himself. He reached for his walker and then decided against it. He stomped on the floor three times and said,

"See, healthier than ever. What's all the fuss about? I feel strong again, like I'm eighteen years old!" He looked at Janelle with surprise.

Sirens could be heard coming around the corner and up to the main entrance. Darin persuaded John to take a seat and prove to the EMT's that he was in good health. Stepping back, he felt Janelle's hand slip into his. Then Janelle took April's hand. They smiled at each other broadly. They were a team.

"That was one powerful prayer, little lady." Mr. Wilkes spoke directly to Janelle, who in turn squeezed April's hand.

* * * * * *

"Mike called his wife on the way back from the office. She was at the food court in the mall talking to three of her friends from a monthly book club she belonged to. They were having smoothies and Rachael was telling them how important it was to make their commitment to Jesus. They were Christians of differing persuasions. After telling them that Mike was on the way to join them for lunch, she stressed that the second coming was close and pointed to scripture texts to validate her conclusions. The conversation was positive and she was hoping that her efforts were going to finally see some results.

Mike found them near the Orange Julius® kiosk. He pulled up a chair.

"So, what was the meeting all about?" Rachael asked in front of her friends.

"They offered me the position of Vice President for Personnel," he answered.

"Wow! That's great!" one of Rachael's friends responded.

"You're really moving up in the world!" another commented. Then they saw Rachael was not enthusiastic.

"Is there something wrong?" the third friend asked.

"No, not really. I just know we aren't going to accept the offer," Rachael answered for the both of them.

"Why? That has to be near to a quarter-of-a-million-dollar salary, maybe more. Why would anyone turn that down?"

"Because there is no time left. Jesus will come before Mike would get his first pay check. What's the point of accepting a new position?"

"The point is, Jesus' coming or not, that's one heck of an opportunity! If you turn this down and Jesus doesn't come you'll regret it for the rest of your lives. Besides, no one really knows when Jesus is coming, right?"

"It's not just the salary and the perks and all, it's the condition attached," Mike added. Rachael could guess what was coming. She looked at Mike and then to her friends.

"What's the condition? It can't be that bad, right?"

"I have to renounce my practice of worshipping on the Saturday Sabbath."

"Big deal. Saturday or Sunday, what's the diff? It's the same God we worship either way you look at it."

"It is the same God, I will grant you that. However, the day of worship matters a great deal. Saturday is the day He wants us to worship Him. It is the day He rested on after creation, the day He put into the Ten Commandments, and the one Jesus rested on when He completed His work of salvation on the cross. We worship on His day because that's what He wants. Sunday is the false day of worship," Mike spelled it out as clearly and concisely as possible.

"We trust Him to know what's best for us," Rachael added.

"I can't believe that God would make a day of worship a big issue. I worship Him every day. It's a matter of faith that is more important than which day we go to church."

"Faith is the most important aspect of our relationship with God, faith and trust. It is the same as in the Garden of Eden. Adam and Eve needed to trust God. That is faith. When they were tempted by Satan their faith needed to be exercised. Instead Satan got them to doubt. Doubt is the opposite of faith or trust for that matter," Mike explained.

"I get that, but we are talking about a day of worship, not faith and trust."

"Faith in God, trusting Him, means obeying Him even when it's not the popular or easy thing to do. Mike and I will not accept the job offer because we are trusting God," Rachael assisted her husband in explaining their position.

Faith in God, trusting Him, means obeying Him even when it's not the popular or easy thing to do.

"I think you're mixing apples with oranges. You can have complete faith in God whether you worship Him on Sunday … or Tuesday for that matter. God is not a fair God if He makes a silly law a requirement for salvation."

"Salvation is by faith in our Savior. It's interesting that you use the term, apples and oranges. The fruit of the tree of the knowledge of good and evil was a test of loyalty in the Garden of Eden. Loyalty was a demonstration of faith then. It was a law they needed to obey. Fruit was the test of loyalty; it was testing their faith in God. Today there is another test of loyalty. It is the Sabbath day of worship. Fruit then equals Sabbath day of worship now. Fruit does not save in and of itself, neither does a day today. Connecting faith or trust to both of them changes the importance. Our loyalty to God's holy law is just as important as it was in the day of Adam and Eve. Our faith is the main factor and it is being tested now. All of us need to decide for ourselves if we trust God and his laws," Rachael made her appeal.

"I have never heard of this before. I find it hard to believe that in all the pastors I have worshipped with and have been under their leadership, none have ever mentioned this test of loyalty."

"Keeping the Sabbath is not a popular thing to do. If Jesus was *not* coming soon, we would still reject this job offer," Mike added. "We wouldn't want to go against God's law."

"Well, I don't envy you. You're going against the President's law. You're going to end up with nothing."

* * * * * *

Mike picked his way through heavy traffic. With martial law starting at sundown more people were on the streets during the day. Traffic snarls were on every major road and at every significant intersection. The cacophony of blaring horns and screeching brakes assaulted listening ears and thinking brains. Rachael wanted to know exactly what had happened at work. Mike explained in detail. Hearing him tell of how his old office had been taken over before he had time to "think it over," indicated that it was an accept or be rejected offer. They're biggest concern was George and Sheila. Both were unemployed. They planned to stop by and make a quick visit. Both Sheila and George came to the door.

"We heard what happened. I was at work for a meeting today and dropped by to visit and I was told you had been dismissed. We're sorry and want to offer our help," Mike spoke for the both of them.

"I heard from Mike and just couldn't believe it could happen so sudden. We're here to help in any way we can," Rachael added. She went to Sheila with a sympathetic embrace.

"Come on in. It seems you're the only friends we have now," Sheila said with a defeated tone. They settled into the living room.

"I heard you got promoted to Vice President, congratulations," George said with just a modicum of enthusiasm.

"They just offered the job to me today and asked me to think about it for a week."

"You mean it's not a done deal? They made it seem like you were already hired. They put Shelly in your position already. What kind of game are they playing?" he asked.

"George, it seems they are playing the devil's game. My acceptance of the position is contingent on my giving up my faith in God and keeping His Sabbath day. It's a requirement for me to keep Sunday for me to take the job. Only the devil would be behind such a request."

"I know you; your convictions are strong. You won't take the job if you have to stop observing the Sabbath."

"You're right. I won't."

"So, here we sit, friends, all of us unemployed! What are we going to do?" Sheila questioned.

"We are going to prepare ourselves for the Lord's coming," Rachael said confidently. "Now how much money do you need to get through the next couple of weeks?" she asked.

"We have a little savings and they paid me my final earnings and benefits. We should be good for a little while." George answered.

"Me too. I got my final check yesterday. We're good for now as George said," Sheila added.

"I don't think any of us will need very much, but what you need to do is plan where you are going to go when the very end comes. Like when Jesus said we should flee to the mountains."

"Where should we go?" George asked.

"I have a suggestion. Go to our cabin; we'll meet there. I'll give you directions…" Mike and Rachael's phones pinged, signaling a text message from Jason.

"ANN: General Conference shocked. North American Division President, Kenneth Bostick, arrested for murder. Authorities cite conclusive evidence. Spiritualist medium contacted murdered victim in heaven who positively identified Elder Bostick."

"It seems that many people who believe in God's truth are losing their jobs, and worse," Mike observed.

"What's going on?" Sheila asked.

"Today, the news has been bad for the Adventist church. All our churches in South Korea have been seized. Adventist hospitals in America are being taken over by hostile medical corporations and the Adventist staff members are being fired. Now the news is that a Spiritualist medium was used as a murder witness against a leader in our church. All this is not a coincidence. The devil is behind it." Mike recapped the news Jason was faithfully providing.

George and Sheila knew enough to understand that the closing days of history were upon them. Their employment woes were diminished to almost nothing. Like Mike's mementos in a box in Glenda's cubicle, their careers were not worth clinging to. Detailed plans were made to make a run for it at the appropriate time.

* * * * * *

During primetime all electronic devices pinged indicating a text email from The Whitehouse. For many, getting correspondence direct from the White House was counted as a privilege. For others it signaled doom. It contained an e-form that needed to be filled out and validated before presenting oneself for stamping. The message was a reminder of the President's words about getting stamped and where to go. When the attachment was opened one could read the questions on the form. A brief read revealed the ominous nature of the form. It had to be validated on Sunday, at church, by an ordained minister. It would indicate church attendance and membership, or future membership in that organization. The second shoe had dropped for the completion of the mark of the beast.

There was nothing to say. This was it. The family scattered to various rooms of the house to make phone calls. From the house phone, cell phones, and Onyxes they tried to make contact with friends and relatives.

Many numbers were busy. Wi-fi connections were overloaded. Some got through.

Rachael could not connect or was blocked. She did not know which. She chose to call her friend Molly in England, even though the hour was wrong for her time zone. That connection went through. Molly was up praying. She explained that her country's liberal government was going to impose the same stamping procedure. Their place to report was the local church buildings and cathedrals. Shocking was the fact that an overwhelming majority of the general population had not attended church in years. Birth records, passports, and licenses were required. They compared notes on the similarities and prayed for each other. They didn't know if they would be able to talk again. Rachael disconnected and tried Megan again for the third time. Megan answered and spoke in hushed tones. She didn't want to talk or have Walt hear her conversation. Megan was not positive and more antagonistic towards her sister. The conversation was cut short when Rachael could hear Walt's voice commanding from the other room. "I said bring me a beer, woman! And shut that baby up. I can't hear the TV!" Megan didn't even say goodbye.

Mike called George and Sheila, or rather, they called each other and George's ID came up. Mike closed his call to answer it. He wanted to bolster their confidence in the face of the storm rising before them. He renewed their spirits and prayed with them for strength. Then he called some other friends, their neighbors the Froelichs, and church people. He tried Pastor Taylor's number and could not get through. As an elder in the church he felt disposed to revisit by phone the members who looked to him for leadership. He talked to a few and couldn't get through to many others. He consoled himself that they were as active as he was providing comfort to the weak. Leo from work got through to him. The conversation was, at first, superficial. Leo wanted to congratulate Mike on his promotion. After Mike told him that it wasn't a done deal, Leo opened up his reason for calling. He reminded Mike of the spiritual talks at work and he wanted to tell him that he had hit the nail on the head about the trend of events. Mike gently coaxed him into considering the issues at stake. He said he would help him and his family to get to a safe place when it came to that point in time. He urged him and his family to not get a stamp next week. They needed to be free of the taint of rebellion that was sweeping the world.

Mike then called Alejandro.

"Yes, mi amigo. I kinda thought you'd be calling me."

"So are you seeing what's happening?"

"Yes, but I can't do nothin' about it. I heard what you said before. But this is the only way. A man must take care of his family. I gotta take the mark so's I can buy food for the baby."

"But, Alejandro, this is the end. I told you before how this was going to play out. You—"

"Please don't bother me. I need to feed my family. Maybe later when things get better we can talk. Okay? Adios." Mike heard the sudden click. He felt defeated.

Jason stayed in his room working off his Onyx. Background music kept any sounds he made unintelligible.

Janelle managed to create a chat-room conference call with Darin, April, friends at school, and witnessing contacts over the last few weeks. Jeremy and Sandra were more on the side of persuading rather than the ones who needed to be persuaded. They were an asset to the team. As the conversation progressed several got excited about the news and the end of the world. Others quietly exited the video chat room, their faces disappearing from the monitor.

Later in the evening a chirp from Jason indicated another message about current events. It read: "BBC Sydney Aus. Moreno at it again. Standing in wheat field he destroys the wheat field for as far as eye can see with wave of his hand. He says with Aussie accent, 'The Lord gives and the people by their sin take away. When people worship god through spirits on the right day, then god can restore harvest.' Moreno waves hand again, wheat field comes back. Witnesses say ooh! He says more, 'Chose today whom you will serve.' He waves hand, wheat dies. Moreno walks away."

CHAPTER 17

Mike put the extra bio-fuel in the garage. He figured it might be needed when buying and selling was prohibited. He had three five-gallon containers. He figured that would be more than enough to get the family up to the cabin and a whole lot further if necessary. This simple task took twice as long as it should have because he could only use one arm. He went inside to wash his hands and planned to run back out to the car to make some personal visits to church members, just like Rachel was doing. Physically he didn't feel up to making visits, because it seemed as if he was getting weaker with each movement. He had to push himself to perform the duties of a church leader. Urging himself along, he consoled himself that it was only a matter of time before he would be made anew. It was still morning. He was alone in the house when the front door bell rang. When walking to the door he discovered yet another problem. As he walked he found he was not controlling his direction. He was curving to the left. By studiously steering to the right he went straight to the door, almost walking sideways. With this new wrinkle he quickly dialogued with his Savior, admitting to Him that if he couldn't even walk a straight line he might not be able to carry out his appointed visits. Defeat permeated his emotions. He couldn't dismiss the thought that he might have to be wheeled to the second advent.

Upon opening the door he saw April and Miss Klein, the Academy science teacher. He expected Janelle or his family standing in the background.

They were not there. Immediately he could divine the purpose of his Everlasting Father. He was humbled and thrilled at the same time. The feeling of God's love for him by sending a healer overshadowed the knowledge of God's power to make him whole. He almost fell over in surprise.

"Welcome. Please come in." Mike tried to sound natural. It didn't work. Miss Klein smiled knowingly, seeing the delight in his eyes; April appeared deep in thought.

"We came to have prayer with you. This morning we were both impressed that God wanted us to come to you now," explained Miss Klein.

"I'm glad you came," he answered while propping himself up against the wall. Miss Klein took his arm and led him to an easy chair. Mike tried not to lean on her, but was unsuccessful.

"April and I were chatting and the conversation went to the events that are surrounding us and how we are fitting in. We decided to have prayer and during the prayer we were convicted, more like told, to visit you at home. I thought I heard a voice. April did, too. Isn't that right?" She looked to April for confirmation.

"Yes, I did too. I don't know if it was in my head or out loud," she explained. They were standing and Mike invited them to sit down. Instead, they both kneeled on either side of the chair and put their hands on his arms.

> *We know we have been directed to you by our Lord and so we want to pray for you now without waiting. April and I are both excited for what we know God is going to do for you, one of his faithful servants.*

"We know we have been directed to you by our Lord and so we want to pray for you now without waiting. April and I are both excited for what we know God is going to do for you, one of his faithful servants. We know you have a brain tumor because the messenger told us so. Are you ready for this in your heart?" Mike nodded his head and tried to smile his crooked smile in agreement and then bowed in prayer. April began to pray.

"Gracious Father in Heaven, we would never presume on Your will. However, You have directed us to Mr. Larsson and we know why. So I pray, as Your angel has directed, to apply Your powerful hand..." April moved her hand to the top of Mike's head. "Your will is our will when we follow Your direction. Thank You for allowing us to see Your mighty heal-ing power. In Jesus name we pray, Amen."

It was a simple prayer. It did not command or request. It exhibited confidence in what God intended to do. They knew beforehand what was going to happen.

Mike's first sensation was a total lack of an abiding headache, then a surge of energy that enlivened every fiber of his body. He looked up as if he could see his Savior's loving face. He reached out as if he could hug his Creator. It was then that he noticed that his left arm matched strength with his right. Tears gushed forth as he exclaimed in an emotional voice, "My complete self for Your will. I pledge to You my best." He wanted to jump up and race around the block; instead he surged forward to embrace the two in a mighty hug. He now felt the same ecstatic exuberance that blind Bartimaeus felt rejoicing at the front of the procession of Jesus' tri-umphant entry into Jerusalem. He wanted to thank God in heaven and the two visitors in his living room at the same time. He wanted to physi-cally turn cartwheels but kneeled silently in prayerful gratitude, to shout out loud yet quietly contemplated His goodness.

* * * * * *

Rachael answered the phone on the first ring. She worried about Mike's deteriorating condition and any communication coming from him by phone produced instant anxiety.

"Mike, sweetheart, how are you doing?"

"I'm fine!" his voice coming over strong, happy, and exuberant.

Rachael could guess at the sound of his voice that something wonder-ful had happened. "You're better, aren't you? Something has happened."

"I'm much better. Better than ever before. Mrs. Klein and April came for a visit."

"Oh, honey, it's wonderful. God healed you."

"He did! Praise Him for His goodness."

"I would have called earlier, but I was down on my knees thanking Him for…for making me whole."

"Wait a sec, let's get the kids on the phone so they can share this." There was a pause while two rings competed with each for the attention of their recipients.

"Hello?"

"Wha'sup?"

"Jason, Janelle, you've got to hear what your father has to say," Rachael explained.

Mike told them the story, starting how he prayed for God's help to accomplish His will despite the effect of the tumors. He explained the trouble he was having and then the directives from a voice spoken to April and Mrs. Klein. He ended by telling how great he felt and he couldn't stop thanking God for restoring his strength and vitality.

"That's great, Dad. Now we won't have to carry you to the cabin," Jason answered.

Janelle reacted in a different manner. "Dad, you could have let me call April and you would have been healed sooner."

"Well, yes, maybe. Through all this I've been willing to accept whatever He wants for me and I didn't want to push Him for something He didn't want me to have. This way, the way it happened, I knew immediately His will when I saw April at the front door. Oh my, I feel so great, my headache is gone, my appetite is back, I feel like I could run a hundred miles."

The family rejoiced on the conference call, they had prayer together and Mike promised they would all meet up for supper that evening for a celebration.

After they concluded the call Mike settled into the couch and talked with God about his plans for ministry in the hours and the days ahead. He asked God for success, but neglected to ask Him for help to fight off temptation. He was singularly focused on what he could do now that he was at the top of his game physically.

He took the backpacks that Rachael had packed for each of them for the dash to the cabin and took them out to the garage placing them next to the extra gas on a work bench. He added an extra blanket and a box of granola bars to the pile. He was ready. He went into the house and the doorbell rang, like déjà vu

It was Glenda.

"Hello, this is a surprise." Mike's antenna started to work. He looked at her standing there with a filing box. She was in a trench coat and spike heels. He didn't think it was wise for him to invite her into the house.

"I brought you your things. I know you said we could have anything we wanted out of them, but it didn't feel right to keep your personal stuff," she said demurely.

"Ah, yes, here let me take that from you." Mike took the box and moved it into the living room, setting it on an end table. Turning he said,

"Thank you for bringing…" He came face to face with Glenda who had stepped into the house and closed the door.

"I have some very good news. Can we talk?"

"Sure, what's on your mind?" He did not move from where he was. There was an uncomfortable moment of silence as she waited for him to show some hospitality which was very much a part of his nature.

"Can we sit down, please? Standing in these heels is a little uncomfortable."

"Ah, yes, I suppose."

"Thank you, you're sweet." She slipped passed him and went to the sofa. He was assaulted by a chemical attack of perfume. He sat across from her on the piano bench. She crossed her legs unmindful of the amount of leg revealed by the flap of the coat. "Mike, I need you to take that vice-president job. Please consider it for me."

"I don't plan on taking the job."

"That's the impression most people are getting from you. The CEO called me into his office this morning. He said if I could persuade you to take the job then I would be promoted to be your executive assistant. Please, Mike, consider it. It would mean so much to me if you would. I would be willing to do anything for you, anything." The trench coat slipped a little higher.

"Glenda, my mind is made up. I can't turn my back on what I believe. The job requires that I violate my conscience about what day I worship on. I won't do that. I need to urge you to consider the things I told you about the last days. The world is coming to an end." He stopped talking because she stood up from the couch. He stood too, thinking she was done and heading for the door.

"I could never hope to achieve a position as executive assistant to a vice president. This is my big chance. I don't want to lose it." Glenda untied the belt holding the coat closed and let the coat drop to the floor. She was in a skimpy red evening gown that looked like a satin slip rather than a dress. There was no mistaking the lack of undergarments. She stepped out of her heels and moved toward Mike.

Mike couldn't believe the incongruity of this moment. He was trying to witness, and she was obviously seducing him. A book of thoughts sped through his brain. *No don't! She's beautiful. This isn't right. Maybe…What do I do? Money, sex, or ideology—that's how men are compromised. Satan is using the first two. What am I thinking? Act! Stop this! Don't hurt her feelings. Maybe…Get her out of here!* "Glenda, please don't. I can't take the job because I won't break God's commandment about the Sabbath. Neither will I break any another commandment, like say adultery, for example. If I won't break one, why would I break another?"

"The law of the government is more important than the old ten commandments. They have been obsolete for centuries. We're more enlightened now. We're consenting adults, right? God isn't against a little fun. He created sex for our amusement." Glenda attempted to wrap her arms around his neck. He grabbed her wrists and held them gently for a moment. He could feel their dainty structure and smooth skin. He was hit with a fresh blast of her eau de cologne. His thoughts wavered. Then he stepped away, leaving her hands in the air.

"I'll help you back into your coat." He sidestepped and went to pick up the trench coat. He held it out for her to get back in.

"Oh, how dumb of me. Not here, Rachael might come home. We can go to a cute little motel off 74th street. Yes, that would be much better."

Mike saw a way out of this dilemma. He didn't want to lie. He knew further talk on prophecy would only keep her in the house and perhaps in a further state of undress. If he said nothing she might think there was hope and would leave; he could leave as well. She slid her arms into the coat, cinching the cloth belt tight, stepped into her heels, and followed Mike to the door. He didn't stop to let her out, he bustled straight through and fumbled with the keys in a feigned attitude of distraction and then closed the front door locking it. He chastised himself for walking her to her car. She again attempted to allure him with her legs when she slipped into the driver's seat. "Remember, it's on the corner of 74th and Kipling. See you there." Shamelessly she pulled the coat up revealingly before he had a chance to close the door. She rolled down the window and smiled.

"I need to meet my wife in a couple of minutes. I'm sorry, but I won't be taking the job. Please remember something for me…" He paused. She looked disappointed and marginally hopeful. "Jesus loves you very much and He wants you to be ready for His second coming. All earthly pleasures will need to disappear in favor of allegiance to Him." He didn't see her reaction. He left for his car leaving the side door to the house unlocked. He didn't want to be at the house any longer than necessary in case she came back.

* * * * * *

Rachael was in the middle of helping Cheri vomit. Her imbibing had gotten out of hand. She was suffering from a reaction to the overload of poison, alcoholic poison. Her body was fighting back defensively. Cheri was in no state to think and decide. Warm chamomile tea was the method Rachael chose to help Cheri calm down. If she had known Cheri was in such a state she would have asked Sheila to accompany her. She almost called Sheila when Mike called.

"Honey, I need you."

"What's the problem?"

"Not over the phone. I need to see you in person."

"Okay, we can meet for lunch at the mall, at Butler's Bakery. It's almost lunch time."

"See you there." Mike clicked off.

Cheri was headed for bed to sleep it off. Rachael helped her sip the tea and then arranged the covers around and up to her chin. She was about to tip toe off when Cheri talked. "I want be butterfly slo much, but can't sleem to get started. I don't have strength. I'm ssstuck in my cocoon."

"Cheri, you don't need your own strength. You need His strength. All you have to do is ask. Cling to Him and He will transform you."

"I wish ... easy."

"It's an easy thing to pray. It is more difficult to stay focused on Him. You have to stay focused on Him."

"Tomorrow ... Did I tell you tomorrow? Tomorrow." Cheri rolled over with her back to Rachael and went to sleep with Rachael's hand stroking her shoulder. Rachael was encouraged by the fact that Cheri had remembered her illustration about the butterfly. *Maybe there's hope yet.* She said to herself.

* * * * * *

At lunch Mike told Rachael about Glenda's visit. She had been aware of the attraction because of his telling of the events surrounding the snowbound sexual assault and Glenda's admission back then. So it wasn't a surprise. What was interesting were her words indicating that the CEO had asked her to persuade him and the setting up of an office romance by making her his executive assistant.

"He probably thought her behavior would either be successful now or it would entice you later to accept the position," Rachael surmised.

"I hadn't thought of that. My thoughts were more on the immediate spot I was in and how to get out of it. Rachael, please know I only want you. I'm not going to give into the temptation later."

"I know, honey. I trust you; don't worry. I was thinking about how the CEO's mind might be working. He wants you and he wants to purge his corporation at the same time."

"You know what crossed my mind at the house? I was thinking about what I had learned from a book I read long ago. It was how aggressor countries are able to turn citizens of the opposition countries into spies. The three ways to achieve that were money, sex, or ideology. Satan has used two of them on me for this job. And, Satan chose this time when I am feeling fantastic physically to entice me physically."

"Interesting. In this case he's attacking your ideology with the other two. Honey, would you have taken this job if we weren't so close to the end and the requirement to forget God's Sabbath wasn't included?" Rachael was thinking about how this offer might have affected them at another time and in another less volatile circumstance.

"My knee jerk reaction would be to jump at the chance for a nice salary and all the perks that went with it. But, it does cause one to think in hindsight about how Satan can woo people away from their commitment. Success can go to the head. I would have guarded against that, yet we are seeing now how the leadership works unethically. It would have been a bad environment to try to keep a moral standard. I might have been seduced by wealth." Mike spoke from the heart.

"Looking at the world's behavior in the full light of the soon arrival of our Savior makes us see more clearly how Satan works and the subtle temptations attached to his offers. And, to use your verb, some can be seduced by alcohol, or anger, or religious leaders teaching falsehood," she observed.

"Causes me to think about how important it is to pray no matter what type of career field you are in," he replied.

"Or are considering," she added. "Changing the subject, you look great! It's nice to see you so happy and upbeat. I love it!"

* * * * * *

Church started out to be a disappointment. Cars were entering and then leaving the parking lot. As the Larsson's drove the street leading to church they could see members driving away. Many would flash headlights and make gestures across their throats to indicate the end of something. It was confusing. The Sickles' minivan slowed and Mr. Sickles leaned his head out of the window to give the Larsson's a message.

"They closed the church. The police are turning everyone away telling us that, 'Services have been changed to Sunday. This is the wrong day. Worship validations will be made here tomorrow starting at eight in the morning.' We're meeting out at the Oaks's Ranch. They have room in their barn. Tell everyone that you can," he said softly.

"Thanks, we'll meet you there." Mike rolled up his window and proceeded past the church building. Three officers were meeting cars at the entrance and talking briefly with each before sending them away. The sign out front displayed the message, "Amen, Come Lord Jesus!"

Out at the Oaks's place, cars were parked around and near the barn, on the verges of the front lawn, and behind trees in the orchard. A large banner, slightly weathered, was draped across the wide front porch. It read, "HAPPY BIRTHDAY." Mike and Rachael were directed to the barn and Jason and Janelle were sent to the ranch house for Sabbath School. When they entered the barn several of the men were moving paraphernalia around to make room. The Oaks boys were hitching farm equipment to the tractor and pulling it out of the barn. Others were carrying hay bales and placing them in semi-circles for seating. Mike pitched in.

"Whose birthday is it?" Mike asked, wondering if he knew the answer already.

"I'm surprised you don't know. The Sabbath is the celebration for the birthday of the earth," Mr. Oaks said with a wry smile. "It was the wife's plan to plant an idea in the heads of those wondering why there are so many cars sittin' out front," he added by way of explanation.

"I kind of figured that's why it was up there."

"It's a little old. We've been using it for years. I don't know what we'll use next week."

"Maybe you can leave it up all week, besides maybe we'll have an appointment to be someplace else by then.

Sabbath School began with a song sung from memory, then Judy, the pastor's wife, stood up to make an announcement. She had come in during the song when nobody had a real chance to ask her where her husband might be; they silently greeted her and smiled.

"This week has been a traumatic week for me. But, praise the Lord, this is only temporary. Jerry was arrested yesterday. The police came by to give him the stamp that he was supposed to use to validate Sunday worship. They demanded that he change the church worship services to Sunday and validate the worshippers who came. He said he would not. They repeated their demands and he again refused. They handcuffed him and led him away. They gave him his one call for a lawyer and instead he called me. I spent all day yesterday and late into the night waiting at the police station in case they would let him go. I was sent away with a warning to go to church on Sunday and get my validation in preparation for next week's marking. I was warned not to come back unless I had my CNS stamp. They said I would be able to see him then and only then. They scheduled his court hearing for next week, because the courts are all booked up. I guess the next time I see my husband will be when we are on the way to heaven. Late last night, I mean very early this morning, I put up the message on the sign like Jerry said he would." She ended her announcement to amen after amen. Several ladies jumped up to give sympathetic embraces.

An informal discussion began where people were offering to help her. Then the discussion moved on to talking and asking about what others were experiencing. Mike directed the group to enter into a season of prayer. As an elder and Sabbath School teacher he became the leader of the moment. The Sabbath School time was taken up with people's comments on what they had been hearing and seeing in the media and around them in their slices of the world. Rachael spoke of her talk with Molly in England and that the marking was happening there, just like in the states. Mrs. Oaks had heard that ADRA was asked to leave the scene of many disasters in the Pacific and in West Africa. A deacon spoke up and said that FEMA was no longer allowing ADRA to distribute food and clothing to Hurricane victims. Another member told of how a relative in Soweto, Africa had told her that Adventists were rounded up and forced to be "invisibly tattooed" with the computer dust. The members were further shocked when she said that when some refused, they were supposedly shot. The rumor included that their bodies were tossed into large pits already dug for the occasion. No one could confirm the details. This news alarmed many because it was such an escalation over the news about stamping in England and ADRA being dismissed from disasters. Another member added her story about Jamaica. There the ratio of Adventists per capita is much more significant. The oppression was more secretive. Adventist leaders were disappearing. When trying to find them in jails they were not to be found. Rumor had it that they were in chains slaving on sugar beet and tobacco plantations on neighboring islands. Elder Bostick's arrest was brought up and only a few had not heard of the details.

Mike took notes on his Onyx 4000-B. He wanted to have intercessory prayer for each of these pieces of news. The meeting was a sobering experience. The world was administering body punches to the people of God. It was a spiritual boxing match where the bigger and seeming more powerful aggressor was succeeding in beating down the insignificant yet brave opponent. Underneath the bad news was the foundation of hope that sustained the believers. This, like Judy said, was only temporary. The downtrodden and the prospect of fresh new martyrs were beginning to cry, "how long?"

The youth came into the barn because their Sabbath School session was finished. It was surprising to the adults that time had passed so swiftly. After they settled, Mike proposed a group prayer where people would pray specifically for Pastor Taylor and about each of these stories and the people and the families who were suffering because of it. He said that he would conclude the prayer.

Mike gave a testimony to the church about his healing. He first explained the development of the tumor and the sequela of symptoms that followed. He included the discouragement that started to tear him down mentally and spiritually. Then he told of the visit and the simple prayer April offered. The account spurred the listeners to the wonders and glory of God's greatness. It was just what they needed to hear as they faced the coming events. Hearty "amens" resounded through the barn.

After a short break, church started. The leaders threw together a program with scripture texts and songs. Mike was asked to speak about his study on the events that the Bible and the Spirit of Prophecy foretold. It would be a recap of his family's study earlier that week. The study revealed for some what they could expect and it also opened some questioning on the sequence of events. He threw it open for comment. The appearance of the anti-Christ was debated…when, how, and in what manner. Opinions varied. Some concluded one way and others concluded the other way. Everyone understood that there is latitude in trying to perfectly apply prophecy to fulfillment. Mike said he favored a literal impersonation by the Devil, but recognized that Satan could be very devious, and convincing. He encouraged everyone to study the descriptions of the real return of Jesus so the false return of Satan, in whatever manner, could be easily identified.

Worship in the form of sharing God's promises about protection dominated the end of the discussion. They were assured by mutual confidence in God's holy plan to bring an end of sin and to carry them home. They split up and prayed for each other, asking God to give their prayer partners strength to endure the conflict ahead. When church ended the members put plans together to go to smaller cottage meetings for next Sabbath. They didn't want to unnecessarily expose the Oaks and have them carted off to jail. Cottage meetings would meet at different houses until no longer needed. Mid-week services were cancelled due to martial law. Members slowly left the ranch in deep contemplation about the future.

The morning started out with a church being stolen out from underneath their normal pattern of worship. It was a disappointment. The news from around the world was a further distress. As they prayed and asked God for help and protection, their shared plight bolstered their spirits. The community of believers drew courage from God and from God's children. They were a family preparing for travel—travel of a very different kind. The end of the worship service was upbeat and positive. Brick and mortar create a structure. Faith and love bring a real church into being. People dedicated to serving God without reservation and without questioning His precepts bring about a community of the faithful.

* * * * * *

At home the family changed into more comfortable clothes. They relaxed physically, yet their emotions struggled to subside. The remaining hours of the Sabbath were spent in soul searching and recommitment. Jason and Mike talked in one corner of the house while Rachael and Janelle had the kitchen to themselves. It was time for the four of them to attempt normal conversations. Being focused as they were on cascading difficulties had made them feel abnormal. They wished to be unencumbered with the mounting stresses of spiritual warfare. Mike and Jason talked of the time at the cabin where they hiked and explored the rocks and ridges. Rachael and Janelle reminisced about the grandparents and the evenings they would spend around the fireplace.

"Grandma and Grandpa really loved each other, didn't they?" Janelle said.

"That, they did," Rachael answered.

"I watched them and you could see it. I wanted what they had for a relationship when I grew up. I think Darin is the kind of man I could have a relationship with just like Grandma and Grandpa. He's fun and spiritual. To think I almost lost it, because of my jealousy."

"The important thing is that you learned from that experience," Her mother informed.

"It would have been so awkward going to heav—"

Their revere was interrupted with a pounding on the front door and repeated ringing of the doorbell. It was almost sunset. Mike was the first to reach the door with the others close behind. He opened the door. Walt was there.

"Walt, please come in. It's good—"

"Forget the pleasantries. I came to warn you to stay away from Megan!" he roared. He pointed a finger at Rachael. "You've been filling her head with nonsense and it stops now! Don't ever come to our house again. Don't call her either!"

"Walt, we lov—"

"Shut up! I don't want to hear it!" He turned and left. Over his shoulder he yelled. "Stay out of our lives! Neither of us want to hear your irritating doctrines." He got in his car and slammed the door.

Rachael went to a living room chair and crumpled into it crying for her sister. Janelle put her arms around her mother, Jason sat cross-legged on the floor nearby, and Mike rubbed her back. Their attempt at normalcy was torn from their grasp.

* * * * * *

Sunday the Larssons planned their visiting. The experience at the church told them that the world was closing down around them. They wanted to get around to as many as possible, but didn't want to get into the focus of the authorities attempting to facilitate Sunday compliance. The thought of dashing off to the cabin never entered their minds. They were bent on rescuing as many as possible. Additionally, they wanted to comfort Rachael in her great disappointment over her sister. Walt had always been the gentle introvert, not one to voice a dissenting vote. For him to drive all the way over to their house demonstrated an effort in sustained anger. It spoke of the developing condition of all mankind; without the restraint of God's Spirit characters were changing. Walt was a small example of that fact. On a greater scale was the changing of society's ethics. What nobody thought of doing before because of civil law, they were thinking of committing because of prejudice. It used to be that it was right to live and let live, and wrong to violate another's belief. With the restraining Spirit evaporating from unregenerate lives, minor annoyances because of different opinions became large. Bigotry against race, culture, and especially belief, leaped to the front of men's minds. The prince of darkness fomented dark emotions to where decorum was discarded in favor of setting people straight. Fights erupted on all levels of the spectrum. Homes were filled with domestic brutality. Neighbors squabbled over slights committed years before. On top of these hot coals of emotion, the government was forcing everyone to go to church, to sing songs, and pretend happy friendship. It was a sham in many cases. Without the Spirit of God, services were lifeless rituals. Places of worship were like in-clubs for the elite. The elite in this case were the ones on the correct side of government legality. It needed only a little direction from a powerful leader to turn all this anger toward a single source of frustration. That leader was coming.

The Larssons decided that in spite of the dangers they were still going to go out and serve their Master, to witness, appeal, and teach. Mike wanted Rachael with him; Jason and Janelle took the other vehicles.

Their phones chirped with a message. As a well-lubricated machine they reached for devices to see what the message was. It was different to not have Jason be the sender.

To all Parents and Students,

Twin Feather Lake Adventist Academy is now closed. Because it has been a location for voting in the past, the local authorities are expecting the doors to be open for stamping of foreheads and hands tomorrow. Our principles will not sanction this activity. The school sign, with name, has been taken down. The building will be left open, but no staff member will be present. If they want to use this empty husk of brick and mortar they may use it as they wish. Our prayers go with you. See you very soon.

Philippe Chennault
Former Principle, Twin Feather Lake Adventist Academy

It was another step closer to the culmination of events. The church was empty and the church school was closed. Again, no words needed to be exchanged. Looks were shared and then they went out for another attempt to persuade friends and encourage believers. First on Mike and Rachael's list were church members who were conspicuously absent the day before. Jason split off with the car and Janelle went with the van to link up with Darin and April.

CHAPTER 18

Four o'clock on Friday came sooner than expected. The week had been a whirlwind of activity and a waterfall of news from all points of the globe. The president made his rounds of the country on Air Force One, encouraging by his presence the legacy of his presidency. In his speeches he continued to tell everyone how once this system of marking had been installed crime would drop in dramatic proportions. At each of his stops he had local clergy dressed in clerical garb backing his speech with nods of approval as he made his points. The Larssons adjusted to their new life as Heralds of Christ.

Mike rode the elevator to the top floor, which was the opulent executive suite. He stepped out and reported to the receptionist. She asked him to have a seat and made her way into the chief's office. About five minutes later she came out with a sheet of paper in her hand. Behind her Glenda and the CFO followed. They stopped at the windowed wall to watch. Their facial expressions were akin to that of poker players, completely emotionless.

"Mr. Larsson, the Chief Executive Officer asked me to give you this." She handed him an 8x5 print of a picture. It took him just a second to see that it was a picture of him standing in the elevator with three other riders. The photo was infrared enhanced. A second later Mike could see that his three companions on the way up were clearly stamped in the forehead, and he was not. When he looked up from the picture the receptionist continued, "The CEO has also asked me to inform you that your services are no longer needed. Goodbye, Mr. Larsson."

The photo was infrared enhanced. A second later Mike could see that his three companions on the way up were clearly stamped in the forehead, and he was not.

It was relief and disappointment at the same moment; relief that Mike didn't have to confront the CEO with his reasons for not accepting the job and disappointment that he hadn't had the opportunity to make a fair presentation of his faith. He looked toward the windows to see Glenda hanging on the CFO's arm with a smug look. They turned and attempted a dramatic exit, pretending to be the winners and him the loser.

He took his photo with him to the elevator and pushed the button for the main lobby. There was no need to revisit his old floor and the presence of a security guard was a further deterrent.

However, the elevator was interrupted on its downward flight. It stopped to admit Marshall. His eyes widened when he recognized Mike. Then he mumbled a greeting.

"How are you doing, Marshall?" he asked politely.

"Fine," he answered. Only he was very uncomfortable. Marshall tried to loosen his collar. It was then that Mike's attention was directed to the nasty red rash on the neck ascending up to his hairline. The rash was interrupted with white pustules. A quick look at his wrists revealed more of the same.

"Marshall, are you okay?"

"I said, I'm fine. Now leave me alone!"

More for Marshall than for Mike, it was a relief to have the doors open and Marshall left without a word. Mike was more observant as he went on down to the lobby. The security guard had a small white boil on his arm with an extending red pseudo-pod. Out in the lobby he found one more case of a rash with boils. A woman was headed into the building and her calf had a red weal poking out from a bandage. Two spots underneath the white gauze were suppurating, leaving wet marks soaking through the dressing.

Mike went out to the car where Rachael was waiting for him.

"How did it go?" she asked.

"It was less than expected, I suppose." He handed her the photograph and said, "They gave me this and said my services were no longer needed."

"How do you feel?"

"I feel great. And, I'm happy to be out of there. Do you see what's happening?"

"What?"

"I saw Marshall with a bad case of hives or rash or something. Then I saw two more in addition to him."

"Come to think of it, there was a man who got out of the car next to ours; he had his face all bandaged. Do you think it might be a reaction to the computer dust?" she asked.

"I don't know, maybe. Wouldn't that be something? The dust carries the first plague with it." Mike put the car into forward and looked at Rachael with a knowing smile.

"It's started, hasn't it? These people have the mark of the beast," she commented. She studied the picture in her hands more closely. Looking closely, she could see a small blister on one man's cheek.

In a couple of hours the sun would be down and the Sabbath would begin. Martial law restrictions were being lifted piecemeal. The President had relaxed his regulations by saying that those who had received their stamp no longer had to remain indoors at night. They were supposedly model citizens and no longer under suspicion.

"Are we going home?" she asked.

"Which home, temporary or future?" Mike responded with a smile.

"I was wondering if we needed to pick up anything before the Sabbath begins. And yes, we are headed home...to our future home," she added.

"I thought of something we might need. We can stop and get it at the Quick Stop and top off our tank at the same time."

"What is it you think we need? I did our grocery shopping this morning."

"Several bottles of sunscreen."

* * * * * *

Sabbath worship was observed at Mrs. McKessy's home. Church services were conducted at different locations; Mrs. Mckessy's home was one of many. Several college students were there because the Adventist colleges they attended were now closed. With the smaller group, the worshippers were able to be more interactive in their prayers and concerns.

Members shared more news, some with alarm. The time for Pastor Taylor's hearing was reset for the following Monday. Members wanted to go and listen to the charges. The head elder and a deacon volunteered to go instead of flooding the courtroom with Adventists. Mike was the head elder who volunteered. Several other SDA pastors in the city were arrested at their homes or when they visited their church offices. One member heard from a friend at Walla Walla that a student missionary to Ecuador had been abducted and forced to join the Spiritualist Association of Christian Churches under pain of torture and rape. She refused. She was found beaten and lying on a jungle road by a Good Samaritan who was under conviction to join the SDA movement. Her witness convinced him that no truly righteous church would conduct itself in such a barbarian fashion. He and his family were converted by her testimony. Other isolated stories flooded in from around the close family of the Adventist world, many were tales of close calls with enraged individuals looking to steal whatever was of value in a purse or a wallet. In many instances police arrived just in time to discourage any unwanted attention. It caused many to think that a slow escalation of human rights violations had started and would develop later into a large-scale oppression as small-time prejudicial behavior intensified into sanctioned persecution when the restrictions of buying and selling would be imposed. The last straw would be the death penalty, and many would hasten to pre-impose that punishment, as well. The small party of believers that gathered in Mrs. McKessy's living room was fearful of the coming events, yet took courage from the nameless student missionary who would not submit and, in the final analysis, rescued a family from perdition.

Worship can be generated from different foundations: from celebration and praise of a benevolent God, from thankfulness for His bounty, from gratefulness for His unmerited grace in providing a means of salvation, from His creative power, and many other blessings from His almighty hand. Worship can be generated from future beneficence as well as His past gifts: hope in a new world, a healthy body, a resurrection. Then worship can come from the depths of despair, knowing that there is no other way and the path is certainly dark and fearsome. If sword or noose or flame threatens, there is a God on the side of the believer waiting to pick one up and carry one through. Staring down the barrel of a menacing satanic weapon as it is aimed directly at your head can lead one to flee and another to straighten shoulders and spine to face the explosion. This diverse band of old and young, strong and weak, worshipped with determination to survive. It had a future focus. Trepidation dominated their thoughts. Their prayers emanated from worry, not about assurance from above but from apprehension within. The enormity of the forthcoming ordeal stormed the citadels of their hearts. They picked at the stories and promises of the Bible like doomed prisoners eating their last big meal.

They read from Acts where Paul and Silas were brutally beaten and cast into a dungeon with chains, their ministry on hold and possibly finished. They sang and praised God late into the night. An earthquake broke their restraining bonds. The group tried to take courage from the short account. One pointed out that it is easier to sing and praise God when the beatings were in the past. Another countered with the fact that Paul and Silas' future was uncertain, that they might have been executed. They didn't know then. Another reminded everyone of the quote in the Great Controversy that "the most vivid presentation cannot reach the magnitude of the ordeal" that was upon them. Reminding them of that quote served to discourage them even more. Several spoke of their worries; few were able to give assurance beyond the innocuous phrases of "everything will be all right," and "things will work out." Then Mrs. McKessy spoke.

"I've been through a lot in my eighty-three years. My husband died. Dear sweet man. Three of my children have died, one as a precious baby. Markus was his name, but I've called him Chubby Cheeks. I've been through a lot besides that. I was sexually abused as a girl and almost died from a car accident that left me in hospital for months to recover. For the last thirty years I have only been able to eat a semi-liquid diet. My bones ache every time I move. I don't know why God has preserved me, but I do know that there is nothing that this world can do to me that can't be fixed by Him. He will give me a new body, one without aches and pains. I plan on running naked through eternity, skipping when I ain't running, with flowers in my hair. Satan has control down here for now, but my Savior has control of the future. I trust Him. Whatever they might do to me in the days ahead ain't nothin'! It ain't nothin' that He can't fix in a few week's time from now. If I can't do nothing else, at least I can grit my teeth and spit in Satan's eye. I'm a child of the King, I won't give up, and I refuse to get grumpy like you all are today. Just look at your faces! You should be ashamed of yourselves!"

"Mrs. McKessy? I know why God has kept you alive … He has kept you alive for me. I needed to hear what you just said. You gave me resolve to keep going. Thank you. And, thank you, Lord, for letting me see her determination." Mike looked at Mrs. McKessy who had become the leader of this band of discouraged believers.

"You've inspired all of us with courage," Rachael added to her husband's comment.

"Mrs. McKessy, can we take you and Miss Jones with us to the mountains? We have a comfortable cabin up there. I can't see leaving you here alone with all that's happening. It wouldn't seem right," Mike added.

"No, no. Veronica moved in with me yesterday. We're staying here 'til it's over. Just like Paul said in Philippians, "Christ will be honored in my body either by life or by death." We'd prefer life, but I think God will take care of us here at my earthly home. That's our plan and holy angels will watch over us. We're standing our ground. Ain't that right, Vee?"

"That's right! You and me together to the end. B'sides I want to see Chubby Cheeks."

"Thank you for your kind offer, but our minds are made up," she ended.

* * * * * *

Mike and Mr. Oaks could not make it into the courthouse. As they approached the front entrance they could see that everyone was being scanned for the invisible mark. As an added layer of security, each person was asked to show their solidarity bracelet. Rather than test the system they went to a nearby café to talk. They wanted to show their support for their pastor by being visibly present, but it wasn't possible. They looked around for the pastor's wife and couldn't find her. Because news vans were parked outside the courthouse they figured they could linger around and hear the results. They went inside. The local authorities wanted to make an example of Pastor Taylor and had arranged for news stations to video tape the proceedings. It was only a hearing to determine the charges and to set the date for a trial. In the café a video monitor was turned to the news and they were able to watch the proceedings from across the street.

Pastor Taylor was led into the courtroom dressed in an orange jumpsuit. He had handcuffs with a short chain running from there down to ankle cuffs. He couldn't walk normally. He shuffled, bent over like an old man because the chain connecting his hands and feet was short. He sat down next to a court appointed attorney and tried to place his hands on the table in front of him. The chain was too short and he had to leave his hands in his lap. The overall effect generated a picture of a dangerous criminal in a condition of humiliation.

When the judge entered everyone stood. It was difficult for Pastor Taylor to stand quickly, manacled as he was. His chair almost toppled over backward and he was unable to catch it which was his natural response. His bent frame and distraction with the tittering chair caused him to look disrespectful. It added to the general appearance of a man not in sync with the legal system.

The judge introduced the case and then asked for the district attorneys to detail the charges. They listed several violations, among them: disobeying a lawful order, disturbance of the peace, failure to comply with a police officer's direction in the performance of his duties, and resisting arrest. The DA added the charges related to Federal law which included the newly established law of holding services on the false day of worship, planning insurrection against the local government, and several acts of treason against the United States of America, which they enumerated in detail.

Mr. Oaks turned to Mike with a look of surprise, "All he did was refuse to change worship to Sunday and validate people's forms. He would never resist arrest or make a scene. He's not that kind of a person. These charges are trumped-up," He whispered.

"Satan is never fair, neither is his government. Pastor Taylor disobeyed their demand that he fit into their false system. It is only a matter of time before they will bunch all of us into the same category by association rather than by what they would classify as an act of overt civil disobedience. They won't take the time to schedule a trial; they'll just put us in jail. I think it's almost time to leave our homes."

The judge listened to the listing of offenses and then directed his remarks to the defendant, "Mr. Taylor, how do you plead?"

Pastor Taylor stood and shuffled to the podium between the prosecution and the defense. Shoulders bent he raised his head confidently. "Your Honor, I am Pastor Jerry Taylor of the Seventh-day Adventist Church. I am a Christian man. I believe the Bible and read it every day. It gives me strength and guidance..."

"Mr. Taylor, I asked you how you plead. I don't need your characterization of your daily rituals. Character references are made during the sentencing phase of a trial. This is a hearing to determine the direction of this trial. Please spare me your pontifications on how devote you are. Get to the point," the judge ordered.

"Yes, Your Honor. I have been charged with treason, resisting arrest, and other charges. All of those charges come down to one simple point, one simple demand. I have been asked to violate my conscience about which day to observe in my personal worship. The constitution of the United States of America guarantees me the freedom to live and worship in accordance with my conscience. My conscience tells me to live by the precepts of God's law. In the beginning, the United States based their law on God's law. I am now faced with a dilemma, what God tells me through His word is what I believe and how I act. Just a few weeks ago things have changed. My God-directed conscience is in agreement with the U.S. Constitution, but the rules of law have changed in the minds of many to violate that constitution and my beliefs. The President has taken upon himself to raise a false standard that the general populace has adopted. My dilemma is finding myself in disagreement with public opinion, but not with the Law of God or the law of the land. This court is asking me to plead guilty or innocent of charges not in keeping with established statutes.

"I keep the Biblical Sabbath on Saturday. I will never violate my conscience or go against my Lord and Savior's wishes for me to worship Him on His chosen day. They only reason I am in this court today, the only reason why I am chained like an animal, is because I was asked to go against my conscience and change to a false Sunday worship.

> *I keep the Biblical Sabbath on Saturday. I will never violate my conscience or go against my Lord and Savior's wishes for me to worship Him on His chosen day.*

"Your Honor. You, of all people should know that changing the laws of the land must take due process with a full vote of the government. Above that, you should also know that God's laws never change. I am innocent! I am innocent in the eyes of God and I am also innocent according to the established order of law of the United States of America," Pastor Taylor ended his speech.

"Mr. Taylor, don't lecture me on points of the law. Did you, or did you not, refuse to obey an order that came from the duly elected President of the United States?"

"Your Honor. By asking me that question it makes it seem that you want me to change my plea to guilty against my will."

"Don't get smart with me! I'll hold you in contempt! Now answer my question!"

"Your Honor, I did not want to be disrespectful. We all heard the account of how I refused to change to a false day of worship. In my own words, I said I would not change. If the command from the President was a legally binding law, which it is not, then I would stand guilty, but—"

"Let the record show that the defendant has pled guilty. He is guilty of all charges. He is to be held for sentencing and remanded to the federal court for his acts of treason. Next case!"

"But, what about a jury hearing—"

"Bailiff! Get this criminal out of my courtroom, NOW!"

Mike sat silently staring alternately between the glass of apple juice in front of him and the monitor fixed to the wall. The video monitor displayed his pastor being led out of the courtroom between two hefty deputies. Commentators made their remarks when the scene shifted to the news room. A few minutes later the head elder and the deacon exited the café. They went to their cars, had prayer, wished each other God's blessings in the form of His protection and then parted knowing they would need vigilance and prayer to get them through.

* * * * * *

On the way home, Mike's phone chirped with another text message from Jason. He pulled to the curb to read it. More Moreno. Big meeting of Islam and spiritualist churches. Moreno heads meeting. Moderate Muslims want peace and brotherhood with Christians if Christians will join international spiritualist church. Moreno flies to New York for meeting with Christian Coalition of Churches (CCC). Announcement: All Christian, Muslim, Buddhist, and Hindu faiths have achieved agreement thru the umbrella of the Spiritualist's organization. Radical Islamic factions, Jewish believers, and non-aligned groups are considered antagonistic and should be cast off from society. Second piece of news, massive solar storms recorded and have been on their way toward earth. Will effect electronic signals and create northern lights of massive proportions. May cause dramatic rise in temperatures. Mike read the messages and returned a quick text with a short synopsis of what happened at Pastor Taylor's hearing. He arrived home to be greeted by Rachael; the kids were out with the other two cars. They decided to make visits together and call upon and encourage as many church members as they could. Time was ebbing away.

Jason sent another message. Marine biologists fail. Unable to stop spread of red blooms of plankton. New problem develops ... something besides domoic acid is causing fish to bleed, adding more red to water. Epic catastrophe. Fish are dying everywhere. Pictures sent with this are of dead fish floating belly up. Beaches cluttered with rotting fish and blood-red oceans. Not a Pacific Ocean problem anymore! Moving fast into Indian,

Atlantic, and Arctic oceans, both north and south. This time Jason sent a file with pictures. Mike and Rachael sat in the car outside a member's house viewing the pictures before they went to the door.

"Look at all the red! It does look like blood," Rachael exclaimed.

"The Bible says, 'it will become *like* the blood of a dead man.' Right now it has fish blood with red plankton. Let's hurry up and make our visits."

* * * * * *

Janelle was in distress. Darin had descended into a deep gloom over his father. In extended conversations with his father he could tell that there was no desire to prepare for the final stages. His father had begrudgingly taken the stamp in his right hand to enable him to keep his job and pay his mounting bills. When Darin's father moved out because of the divorce and because his job carried him away out of state, Darin prized every minute he had with him. Now he was desperate. He was losing him forever. Janelle was in his room watching him pack his bags for a hasty trip to the other side of the country. His plan was to catch a flight. If none were available, he would take a bus, or hitchhike. He waffled back and forth in his determination to go or not go. His mother tried to discourage him from going, but stopped short of telling him it was too late. She didn't want to appear as calloused and uncaring about his father's salvation. Accepting the mark was tantamount to turning one's back upon the Lord.

Janelle understood this as well. There has to be a cut off, a final moment where an individual decides for or against. From what Darin was telling her about his father's decision, she could see that it was for material reasons. Darin's dad needed mammon. He had to keep his financial ship afloat. Trusting God was thrust aside in favor of trusting self. His everyday concerns of life overshadowed his perception of the here and now. Now was the time to turn one's back on the world, literally.

Darin's mother was chastising herself for not calling her ex and saying she no longer needed the support money. She felt she was too focused on the monthly check and responsible, in part, for not helping him to understand that money was no longer an issue. Her mind interpreted her lack of action into a sin of greed that caused a fellow Christian to miss the kingdom. She was downstairs in the kitchen thinking she was not qualified to be one of God's redeemed.

The whole house was a miasma of self-doubt and self-reproach. Janelle had hoped to spend the day encouraging their friends, Darin and Janelle's witnessing successes, to stay the course, keep focused on Jesus.

Instead she was in the middle of a whirlpool of spiraling depression, circling downward. Instead her mission focused on Darin.

"Darin, call him. Leaving to be with him may not be any more effective than talking with him on the phone."

"I have to go. He needs me. He'll never make it if I don't talk him through this. I have to make him see what's happening."

Janelle bit her tongue, trying to keep from telling him that his dad had to make his own decision and cannot be coerced into changing his mind. "Darin, please! Your being there won't be any better than talking with him on the video phone. He'll see your sincerity just as clearly, even if you're not there physically."

"Don't stop me. I'm going."

"No, please no. Darin, can't you see you're breaking up a team? Satan is ruining what we've got here. Our friends need us here … together. I need you."

"Don't be selfish. I'm going."

Darin threw his backpack over one shoulder and left the room. Janelle was devastated. She wanted to cling on to him, prevent him from going. He was her rock, her center of gravity. Her spiritual fervor was tied to her teammate. She slowly descended the stairs to the kitchen to find his mom in deep sorrow. She too was in a dilemma of disappointment. She was adding up the difficulties of leading her aging parents and her daughters in this end-time catastrophe. Darin had become her rock, too. Discouragement was leading to depression which was leading further to diminished hope and then, finally to debilitating doubt. Both women sat at the table in a sour mood, criticizing their own parts in the drama. The miasma of the time was sinking positive thoughts

Janelle's phone chirped with her mother's text message. She shut it off and said to herself, *I don't care!*

* * * * * *

Mike felt he needed to put bio-fuel in the car. Before he always filled the tank when it was just above the one quarter mark; now he refilled before it read half empty. He and Rachael went to the neighborhood filling station to top-off. When he attempted to access the pump's computer system, it would not respond. He tried repeatedly to push the start button for ordering the fuel and accessing his bank account. He was about to drive forward to use the next pump in the line when the electronic readout delivered a message, "Display your stamp." A voice from an overhead speaker added another explanation, "Pump number three, the computer can't read your federal validation stamp. If you show it clearly, the system will turn on."

Mike tried not to show his surprise. He got into the car and drove away quickly. He knew that video imaging equipment would record his license plate and somewhere someone would be noting that he was not validated. He explained to Rachael as they drove down the street. "The restrictions are beginning. I wonder if it's universal or just this station." She in-turn texted the twins, Megan, and her friends a short message, "Some restrictions on buying and selling have begun. Just tried to buy fuel, pump needed CNS."

Both their phones chirped with Jason's message. They thought it was a reply.

* * * * * *

The text message Jason had sent was big news. "Surprise! He's Here! Access video." He had included a link to watch. Rachael and Mike decided to pull over to the curb again, to watch with undivided attention.

[The scene was from Vatican Square. A BBC reporter was giving his preliminary report.]

~ ~ ~ ~ ~ ~

Ladies and gentlemen, I am standing in the midst of Vatican Square where the most surprising, the most inspiring event occurred. It was quite unexpected. Emergency personnel were summoned to this location on a report that a gent was about to jump from the top of St. Peter's dome. A small crowd had formed and I, being engaged on another assignment, hastened to see what the sirens were all about. The Swiss Guard was attempting to persuade the individual to grasp something and not remain in such a precarious place. Then the Fire Brigade arrived and made an appeal from the end of a ladder. The individual was dressed in what appeared to be flowing robes draped from his arms. Then he surprised everyone. The video will clarify everything better than I could.

[The picture of a fire truck with an extended ladder first came into view. Then the camera zoomed in upon the end of a ladder with a fireman holding a megaphone attempting to speak to the man standing on the dome. The camera then zoomed further to capture the image of the man in robes with shoulder length hair. It was a precarious position. No visible support seemed to aid the man as he stood on the slanted dome. It appeared he could slip and plunge to his death at any moment. Time passed as the crowd grew and television vans flooded the square. Soon the open area was populated with enough people to qualify as a papal event. The camera cut away to various shots showing the crowds gathering and the ad hoc command post making deliberations as to how to help the man down. The video presentation was edited to shorten the length of time it took before anything happened. Then without preamble, the figure stepped forward and appeared to glide downward to the crowd, past a stunned fireman on the ladder, who received a crossed finger blessing, and straight to the waiting crowd. The flying figure seemed to glow with internal light. The aura intensified into brilliance as he drew near and hovered above the crowd. He spoke.]

Do not be alarmed. I have come, my children, to give you peace. [The crowd went berserk. People were exclaiming, pointing, and then, as if by command, they flattened

> *The flying figure seemed to glow with internal light.*

themselves on the ground. The figure remained suspended about fifty feet in the air, shedding light as if it were a concentric electric waterfall with light flowing away in every direction.] *My kingdom is now of this world. You have heard me say before, I have not come to give you peace, but a sword. This time, I will help you make peace, first with the sword and then with the scepter. We must come together to make peace for the chosen ones.* [Prostrate bodies strained to look up at the same time as they felt they should retain their position of obeisance. Materializing next to the figure were two, then four, then multiples of angels, silently gazing at their leader, faces glowing with reflected splendor. A murmuring arose amongst the worshipping crowd, for the presences of a host of heavenly beings and for another thought that began to dawn on the observing crowd. They were amazed by the fact that their savior spoke in their personal tongue. The truth was that every person understood. Disagreements of astonishment rippled through the square. Some said, "He speaks Italian!" Another claimed, "He speaks French." Others heard differently, each in their own language. Papal legates kneeling on the official balcony heard Latin. It seemed that the BBC video link transmitted English. The miracle seemed to be in the hearing, not the speaking. The Jesus imposter was surmounting the language barrier with the gift of hearing, or so it seemed to the listeners.] *My children, you must understand, the harvest is ready. The wheat and the weeds have been together far too long. It is time to separate the just from the unjust, the sheep from the goats. Then peace will reign from horizon to horizon. You must excuse me, for I must organize the leadership of this world. There is a lot of work to be done. Soon we will walk together in the Garden of Eden.* [The serene face, which resembled the famous painting by Warner Sallman, smiled down upon the crowd. The floating figure blessed the crowd, turned, and progressed, as if by magic, across the square to the stunned staff of the Vatican. He gently glided into the open space, landed, and walked into St. Peter's, disappearing from sight. Some angels followed him into the building and the remainder soared upward and then southwest. Several individuals exclaimed, "The Christ has come! Several others could be heard yelling that they could see, and walk, or had been healed.]

[The BBC correspondent recapped his report with a little too much enthusiasm than a detached, neutral reporter should exhibit. He spoke fast and excitedly after watching his own vid-clip for the 5th time.]

Every time I watch this video I am amazed! I can't see how he remained in mid-air! He just hovered there and moved without wings or any kind of thrust or locomotion. He glowed, like, like a miniature star! He spoke clearly without the assistance of a microphone and without translation. Then the angels … I can't describe it in simple words. It has to be … It has happened. It is hard to fathom, but it must be … Jesus The Christ. He has returned. [The video ended with a BBC logo on the screen. In the background, shouts of "hallelujah" resounded.]

~ ~ ~ ~ ~ ~

Mike stared at Rachael for a thoughtful moment; she, in turn, did the same. They were reading each other's thoughts.

"So Rome is the holy place where the abomination of desolation is supposed to take place. It makes sense from the book of Revelation. I didn't know for sure because I thought it might be a symbolic reference to the seat of religious power where all the religions have come together to form the beast. I didn't know for sure, but now I think Rome must be it," Mike thought out loud with his sweetheart.

"But, if so, why did he leave?"

"I don't kno… Wait, I remember the *Great Controversy* said that he would appear in several places."

"And the Bible said we should not believe anyone who says he's in the desert or secret chambers. Rome is not a desert."

"You're right. Maybe he's going to appear in different places," Mike agreed with his wife.

"Do you think it's time to flee?" Rachael asked.

"Maybe it is. The mark, and the Sunday law, and the antichrist are all here. We were unable to buy fuel this morning, but I haven't heard that there's a complete shutdown of our ability to purchase essentials…time will tell. And then, there is the decree that we should be put to death. I'm not waiting for that to happen. What do you think?"

"We can't leave this minute that's for sure. We have obligations to encourage the members and I have to get to Megan as soon as I can, somehow. Maybe we have a little time; I hope," Rachael wished aloud.

"Then, I think we should make our visits as quick as possible. We need to link up with the twins." Mike drove away from the curb and Rachael started to make calls to prepare the way. Her first was to Janelle, who did not answer. When she tried again she was interrupted with a text from Jason.

"Fake Jesus appeared in Rio de Janeiro. He hovered next to the statue of Jesus the Redeemer on Corcovado Mountain. He and the angels around him made a big scene, lit up the sky. He looked the same size as that big statue. Then they flew down to the city and gave an announcement in Portuguese. Crowds went crazy with celebrations. Miracles were performed.

"More News, this time from NY. Jesus-want-a-be is in old UN building meeting with ministers in a secure room. Reporters trying to get a story on the news about Vatican appearance, discovered that Jesus was there. Rev Ophelia Marcbright acted as Spokesperson making a short statement with an angel on either side of her as she stood at the microphone. She said that Jesus was making plans with all religious leaders for a retreat and planning meeting in Dubai. More to come. Plot thickens!"

Rachael read the text to Mike as they went to the first member's house.

* * * * * *

"This is my fault," Darin's mom said quietly to herself. "I should have told him that the money doesn't matter anymore. I could have told him I didn't need it. Maybe he wouldn't have gotten the stamp. It's over for him. He's lost and it's my fault."

"It's not your fault. He chose for himself." Janelle didn't like what she had said. It sounded so cruel and final.

"Darin senior has always been so conscientious about paying bills; he never missed a support payment. I should have told him. Why didn't I tell him when there was time?" Her self-reproach pushed her downward. "Instead of helping him into the kingdom, I drove him away. I made him worry about money and not about Jesus."

"Everyone has to make up their own minds. You can't be responsible for his decision," Janelle tried to explain.

"But, he's dragging Darin Junior into his decision too. They'll both lose out. It's all my fault."

"You can't believe that Darin would follow his dad and give up his faith in God."

"Yes, I do. Darin loves his dad and hardly ever sees him. He'll do anything to hang on to him."

"You can't believe he would give up heaven, can you?" Janelle asked. Instead of answering a second time, she sobbed and shook her head in agreement. Her transition from faithful strength moved through the dichotomy of vacillating thoughts downward to doubting despair. This negative thinking was compelling Janelle to stay in dark territory. The company she was in was in danger of doubting to the point of a departure from the path of belief. Janelle was sliding down the hill with her. She could feel it and had to resist it. "You have to keep it together. You can't lose sight of the goal. Your girls are depending on you, so are your parents. In this time we need to encourage each other. You have to drive your family away from all this … Wait! Did Darin take your car?"

"I don't know. I don't care. Without Darin, I will never be able to get through this."

Janelle was up and looking out the kitchen window. The car was still in the driveway. Darin had started to walk. Janelle knew he was on the street alone, without the CNS, and without protection. If he was in a car it would at least afford him a degree of anonymity, the car being a shield of sorts to keep outsiders from seeing he was not marked.

"I need to go and get him," Janelle stated. Darin's mom said nothing. "You need to be strong for your girls. You can't give up now. They need you." Without hearing an answer, she went outside to her van and pursued Darin.

* * * * * *

Jason was glued to his Onyx screen because the fast-paced news compelled him to watch the unfolding events. A little red exclamation point inside a triangle flashed on in the lower right corner of his monitor; someone was trying to watch him and his activities. He smiled. He didn't have a high-tech solution to circumvent the spying, but he did have a method for keeping the voyeurs from detecting his lack of validation. He put a small piece of tape over the spot in his screen where he knew the reverse camera would be spying on him. The occlusion would make any viewers think there was something wrong with the system as it accessed his device. Next, he applied his data shredding software to dump all his previous references and correspondence. It would not help his family. He had to get a message out to them without alerting the spies of his knowledge of their activities. He didn't think they had seen his previous correspondence. He texted, "Cold front moved in, definitely hat weather! Pull'em down over your ears!"

* * * * * *

There was a look of consternation when the hat message showed on their phones. Then Rachael figured it out. She took her and Mike's phones and buried them in her scarf and then whispered, "He wants us to cover our foreheads. It means they're spying on us." It wasn't that cold outside and certainly was not cold inside the car, but they fished the winter stocking caps out of door pockets and pulled them down almost to their eyes.

They made several quick visits to members, had prayer with them, and moved to the next. Rachael tried to call Megan, who did not answer. They remembered George and Sheila and called to ask if they could visit because they were in the neighborhood. Their visit with them was very productive and exciting. The couple had been studying hours upon hours every day. They shared their knowledge and planned future moves. Rachael suggested that Sheila accompany her on a visit to Cheri's home. Mike and George went as a team to visit more members.

Cheri did not answer her door, nor did she answer her phone. Her car was parked out front. Rachael was worried. Under normal circumstances she would have called the police to perform a health and welfare check. Today, she could not call attention to herself or Sheila. She did not want to jeopardize their chances of getting away from the persecution to come. They knocked on windows and pounded on the back door. They had to give up. They were in danger of creating a scene.

Mike and George were a great team for encouraging members. George, being a new convert, inspired the longtime members. He made a comment in several homes, "We are a church; we must encourage and protect one another." Mike couldn't help but think of how meaningful that comment was to George, coming from his family of origin.

In the car between visits, Mike's phone indicated a message. He had kept his hat in his coat pocket to avoid wearing it in warm houses and in the car. He slipped his hat on before he answered hoping to foil any voyeurs. Jason was texting again, this time without any deprecating remarks about the false Messiah. "Jesus in Washington, DC. Cameras found him knocking and listening at the front door of the Washington cathedral. News media were already there, because the President was there for evening prayer session. Ministers were surprised to say the least. Secret service agents guarded front door until angels gathered around. They willingly yielded their positions to angels who surrounded the building. Next bit of lesser news: Mississippi and Rio Grande Rivers are running red. Experts believe recent earthquakes have dumped large amounts of red clay soil into watershed basins."

The news was another click in the cog of events. The third plague had started. He and George had an excited conversation about the events to come. George was in wonder on how God would protect and nurture His people when the world's water supply and, later, when the food supply, would run out. Mike made a supposition that perhaps one of the reasons there will be a death penalty leveled at them was because there will be a question in the minds of people as to who should and who should not eat. He also assured George that they would be taken care of by His providence like the Israelites were in the wilderness. The quote, "He shall guide you to springs of living water," came to mind.

Driving about town was like watching a newscast after a catastrophe.

Driving about town was like watching a newscast after a catastrophe. Cars that were in crashes were left abandoned at the side of the road. New accidents cluttered intersections. At one red light they watched as a man walked across the road in front of them. He had boils on his neck and face that had been scratched repeatedly. His hands were bloody. Blood ran down his face, splashing and oozing onto his shirt, soaking it all the way to his belt. It looked like he needed help. George jumped out of the car while Mike moved the car to the side of the road and then followed on foot. George tried to get the man to sit down while he volunteered to call an ambulance. The gentleman yelled at George telling him, in very foul language, to leave him alone. It was strange to want to be of help and yet be considered a guilty person invading another's life. Mike had a bottle of spring water he offered the man and the man slapped it out of his hand. It rolled away in the gutter. Mike and George left.

* * * * * *

Rachael tried to call Janelle. There was no answer. She called Jason to see if he knew why. He tried to reach her, ran a diagnostic, and then clicked back to her call.

"The only thing I can figure is that she turned off her phone," he explained.

"Maybe her battery is dead?"

"No, she charged her battery last week, same time as mine. It should be good for another two weeks."

"So, why did she turn her phone off?"

"I don't know, Ma. Who knows what she'll do next? She's a female and therefore illogical. Can't understand them, can't change them, even with heavy drugs and intensive psychotherapy."

"Just remember who you're talking to."

"Yeah, you're right. I should have thought of that…I'll change that to really intensive psychotherapy!"

CHAPTER 19

The two teams linked up with Jason at home. George and Sheila were invited to dinner and they arrived almost at the same time. They found Jason at home with three guests. They were lounging around the kitchen snacking on dried fruit and juice packs. It surprised Mike and Rachael.

"Mom, Dad, I'd like to introduce you to Greg, Andrew, and Steve—Greg and Andrew Cox and Steve Rojas. Greg and Andrew are brothers from the academy and Steve is one of my soccer buddies."

"Nice to meet you. I'm Mike and this is my wife Rachael, and these are our good friends George and Sheila. What brings you over tonight?"

"Ah, well, Dad, I asked them over because I want to get your permission to invite them to our cabin. They need a place to get away and their folks are not believers."

"Ah, well, we're all in this together. We just have to survive the next weeks, somehow. I'm pleased by your commitment. How did you come to believe if your parents aren't believers, as Jason said?"

"Jason showed us the truth," Andrew answered. Rachael and Mike couldn't stifle a long look of surprise at their son. "He sat down with us during study hall and helped us to see what all the world events are telling us as Christians."

"For me, we sat in the car and talked instead of practicing soccer. He really knows a lot about the Bible," Steve added.

"Andrew, Greg, you go to Twin Feather Lake with Jason?" Rachael asked.

"Yes."

"Do I know your folks?"

"Probably not. They don't attend church or school meetings. The only reason we go there is because our grandparents pay for our tuition. We thought going to the academy was pretty much a waste of time. But, as it turns out, it became the most valuable experience of our lives. Thanks to Jason here. He made the effort to warn us about what's coming, even though we had treated him…ah, poorly," Greg ended quietly.

"The only thing that matters now is that we have to survive. I think you should bring your sleeping bags and some warm clothes." Jason sounded like this was a camping trip.

Mike was starting to put it all together and couldn't help but rejoice silently that his son was not cavalier about his faith. He was different in how he talked and related his views, but deep down he was committed. He was marveling at Jason's success and had to chalk it up to his youthful approach to life and how it spoke to those at his same relational level.

"Fellas, I was wondering, would you want us to talk with your folks about what's happening? Do you think it might help? Perhaps an old guy, like me, talking to the 'Ole Man' so to speak." Mike was thinking that an adult might appeal better to another adult, like Jason's appeal was on his age-appropriate level.

"Sir, that's nice of you to offer. But, I've tried, and Jason tried with us. They're angry and don't want to hear from anyone anymore. They've taken the mark and they want us to take it too. We've been trying to avoid them and put it off. It's getting really difficult to…disagree with them. We stay out all day and late into the night. They're trying to enroll us in another school, but we're gone before they get up in the morning," Andrew explained.

"It's about the same with my folks too. I attend a different school and I'm using every trick I know to avoid getting marked. The marking machine is in the gym. It's only a matter of time before I get caught and dragged into the gym. I'm AWOL from school most days," added Steve.

"Dad, I had an idea. It's only a matter of time before everything comes loose. Why not let them hide out at the cabin now? They could be out of the way and where the police can't find them."

"These boys need to be protected from the system that seeks to take them away from God. There has to come a point when believing children have to separate from non-believing parents. This is opposite from what I had to do in my family. Parents aren't always right," George answered.

"I have a suggestion. George and I can take the boys up to the cabin now and we can watch out for them. I'll be there to make sure they eat right," Sheila suggested.

"We could all join up later and be one happy family of fugitives. Okay, I'll agree to it. We need to get organized and make sure you have everything you need," Mike seconded the plan.

"I think we should go tonight despite the curfew. We'll have to chance it. This is not a safe place down here in the city," George suggested.

"Not until we have supper. Jason, you and your friends need to get some extra chairs pulled up to the table. Mike, you and George can set the table. Sheila and I will make sandwiches." Rachael got things organized.

* * * * * *

They turned the news on after dinner and devotions. All the broadcasts were focused on the one and only subject of the day, the second coming of Jesus. Every angle of the scene at Rome was covered, then his sudden arrival at Rio, then the old UN building, and his appearance at Washington National Cathedral. Added to those appearances was another manifestation in China. Videos were not available due to state approved broadcasts of religious programs, but witnesses described Jesus' sudden dazzling entrance into the precincts of the Temple of Heaven in Beijing, *Ti n Tán, more literally called the Altar of Heaven.* Interviewees detailed how Jesus hovered, with his angels, in front of the three-tiered structure inviting all people to join in prayer to stop the disasters of the world and to bring back the harvests. He reportedly spoke in the dialects of China saying he was the Son of Heaven. Of particular note was the performance of a ritual animal sacrifice to demonstrate solidarity with the ancient Chinese ceremony of appeasement for good harvests.

The scenes captured in video were more compelling in the news cast. The reports returned to the many pictures that showed Christ in Rome, Rio, and DC. Pictures focused on Jesus, his glowing face, his robes, his hands and feet which also glowed like polished brass. Marks could be seen where the nails had been. Every expert was interviewed. The common men and women on the street were asked what they thought about his coming. The stories were nonstop. Commercials were skipped in favor of time to cover every nuance of meaning and celebration. Some interviewees were new believers, stammering out their observations against their former unbelief. Guesses were brought forward as to where the savior would appear next. As if on cue, there was an interruption in the dialogue with a flash announcement.

~ ~ ~ ~ ~ ~

[We are interrupting this broadcast to go to our correspondent in Jerusalem. Jesus is at the Wailing Wall. Herb Hulman is standing by with a report. Herb?]

Yes. Jesus is here. He appeared about fifteen minutes ago and has been walking amongst the crowd, talking with worshippers and Rabbis alike. Angels are everywhere watching Jesus. This is different from what I saw of the videos at his other appearances. Jesus is taking the personal approach, talking with individuals, relating to them as a friend. I listened to some of the conversations and he was telling them how it was when the temple was in its glory. It was like he was a tour guide, explaining the beauty and the workmanship. He was appealing to their national pride. Then, as if by silent command, people started to take off jackets and spread them on the ground for him to walk or stand upon. There was a rush of outsiders flooding the small plaza and they came with fronds torn off of palm trees. It was very much like the once thought fabled but now true historical entry of Jesus into Jerusalem.

Mark, I've noticed, and I'm sure you have as well, Jesus has been circling the globe and appearing at the different time zones. I'm guessing he will be headed west from here. Wait a minute … it appears Jesus is going to speak to the crowd. Let's listen in. [the camera moved off of the reporter and zoomed in on Jesus' face.]

'The last time I came to this world, I came as a man when I was really the son of god. You misunderstood my mission. You had difficulty perceiving that I was god, because I was in every way a man. It is understandable that your ancestors did not perceive my divinity. Today, I come to you as your god. I have appeared suddenly in the temple as you expected. Now it is time for you to accept your messiah. I am here. I've come to save the nation of Israel and all the people of Spiritual Israel. Join with me in bringing in the Kingdom of the son of David.' [He then lifted his hands into the air and the many pieces of prayer-paper stuffed into the crevices of the wall flew out of their resting places and into his arms. He opened the front of his robe and they flew into the opening of his clothes.] *'My children, your prayers have been answered. The petitions for healing in these notes are all fulfilled.'* [A lady in the background screamed in delight; her rash and boils had disappeared.]

~ ~ ~ ~ ~ ~

The recap and the additional appearances around the globe added to the resolve of the faithful gathered around the video screen. They couldn't help but be drawn to the celebration and the enthusiasm of the crowds who actually saw the replica of Jesus. They pitied the masses that were being swept up in the events and the grandeur of the moment. They wished they could stand up and point out the differences between the biblical descriptions of when the real Jesus would come and the behavior of the counterfeit Messiah. Heads were shaking in consternation when Rachael's phone rang. She was hoping it was Janelle answering her many voice messages. It was Rochelle.

> *They pitied the masses that were being swept up in the events and the grandeur of the moment.*

"Rachael, I didn't know anyone else to call. I'm desperate. I need a friend to talk to." Rochelle's voice indicated her frustration. Rachael on the other hand could predict, with certainty, the subject that Rochelle would be on. However, if there was a slim chance that her friend could see the light in the final hours she would endeavor to listen with her heart.

"Rochelle, what's happened? You sound worried."

"It's Loren. Chris is taking her and I can't stop it. What should I do?"

"Chris is taking Loren? How did this happen?"

"He called the Friend of the Court and said he wanted his two weeks visitation to start tomorrow. The FOC is sending out a social worker to make sure his rights are maintained. How can I stop it? I don't know what to do. If I stop it from happening, I will be held in contempt of court. Then they won't listen to my petitions about his treatment of Loren."

Rachael could see the wisdom of Chris through the timing of this visitation. She didn't want to jeopardize what Chris was achieving. Her heart ached for the tug and pull little Loren was experiencing. She knew this little girl would be safe in her daddy's arms when Jesus arrived, but she would go into eternity without a mother. She had to measure her words carefully. "Rochelle, my heart aches for you. I'm a mother; I can feel your pain. You want the best for your baby. What can I say, it must really hurt."

"It does. Should I do something, like hide with her?"

"In this case, I don't think it would be wise to defy the court or the judge. I think the best course would be to pray. God works things out for those who love Him. I would suggest that you take the time while Loren is away to pray for her and for yourself. You never know what the Lord can do for you."

"Maybe you're right. I don't like it though."

"We could pray right now if you want to."

"I'll think about what you said and then maybe I'll pray later. I'm going to sleep with Loren tonight."

"I'll pray for you when I hang up and I'll keep praying for you, okay?"

"Yes, thanks."

* * * * * *

The plans for a trip to the cabin solidified. Jason would go along to show the way. George and Sheila would stop by their home for a few things, while Jason drove the boys by their homes for a quick grab of essentials and then a dash out of town toward the mountains. Mike told Jason to stay at the cabin and not come back. He said he would unless they needed him. They couldn't think of a need that would require his presence back home. They loaded up in two cars and left. Mike and Rachael were watching out the window as they drove away and saw Kristine and her husband walking up their driveway having walked over from the house next door. Mike and Rachael were wondering what it could be. They opened the front door to let them in.

"Kristine, hello. Won't you come in," Rachael greeted her friend and neighbor. Kristine's husband stood out on the sidewalk and watched closely. Kristine didn't come in.

"Our water is fouled up with this red crap. I was wondering if it's the same with yours. If it isn't maybe we could get a couple of gallons from you." She held out several empty glass jugs. "Just until the city can clean this mess up."

"Sure, of course. Here, come with me into the kitchen."

"No! We'll stay out here," Fred's bass voice from behind Kristine commanded. Kristine looked a little ashamed.

"Okay I'll be right back." Rachael took the bottles and went into the kitchen. Mike stayed at the door trying to engage them in conversation. He was unsuccessful. Minutes later, Rachael was back. The jugs were visibly full of clear, clean water.

"Here you go. Don't hesitate to ask for more. I was thinking th—"

"We'll be fine," Fred's gruff voice answered.

"Thank you," Kristine said holding one jug up to the light, looking at the water inside. Then she screamed. The water turned to blood from the top downward. She dropped the one she was looking at as if it was a writhing snake. A quick look at the other enabled everyone to see the transformation a second time. She dropped it too and ran away, with her husband following. He was looking back at a mystery; broken glass and blood littered the front porch. He muttered the words, "Satan's black magic!"

Mike and Rachael were in a daze at what happened. They wanted to run after their neighbors and explain what and why. Fred's demeanor prevented them from that course of action. They also wanted to return to their faucet and see if their water was running red. The plague awed them. There it was on their front porch. After some introspective thought they both turned toward the kitchen. They turned on the tap and watched as clear clean water flowed. Mike was bold enough to fill a glass. He examined it. Then he took a sip. It was sweet. Then he set the glass on the counter and they watched it. Nothing happened.

"God is great!" he said.

"Yes, He is!" she answered.

"I'm not worried for Veronica and Heidi anymore. They will have sweet water to drink until He comes. Bless His holy name." Rachael's response was to take a drink as well. She didn't sip; she drank. It was refreshing.

"I guess we should clean the mess off of the front porch," he said.

They grabbed some paper towels, a waste basket, and a broom and went out to the front. As they started the job they were surprised at the consistency of the fluid; it was blood, thick and gooey. Mike remarked, "The Bible says the sea becomes like the blood of a dead man, but it says the rivers and fountains become blood, not like blood, but blood. Here we are looking at a tangible proof of prophecy fulfilled."

Rachael was carefully picking out the glass pieces when she saw a shadow at the edge of the bushes bordering the front yard. It was Kristine. She rose and went to her. "Kristine can I help you?"

"I came back because I couldn't believe what happened. Satan has some powerful tricks, all right; changing water to blood inside a closed container."

"Kristine, the devil didn't do that. This is one of the last plagues mentioned in Revelation. It happens just before the second coming of Jesus."

"No, no. You had me almost buying that stuff. This is the devil's work. The plagues are what happen in Armageddon. This here is what Satan is trying to do to convince people to reject Jesus. My pastor studies a lot and he says most everything is going to happen in Israel. We're going to be raptured away from all this. Blood is going to flow as high as a horse's bridle. All that is going to be for the Israelites to finally accept Jesus as a Messiah. And they're doing that now. Did you see Jesus at Jerusalem? He's talking to them. They're accepting Him as the Messiah."

"Kristine, listen. Read the Bible for yourself. It will speak to you and tell you what is happening. It will tell you what is real and what is false."

"No, I'm not going to accept your false interpretations anymore. You're leading me away from Jesus. I'm not your friend anymore. Get behind me Satan!" Kristine walked away, leaving Rachael standing on the front lawn. The words spoken were like daggers thrust into her gut. She was defeated, discouraged, and dismayed. Her witness was not accepted, her friend was not coming to heaven with her. She stared at the back of her friend as she walked to her front door. She returned to her house and found Mike pouring water on the front porch to wash the blood off of the cement.

He could tell Rachael was in defeat. The look on her face told the story of what had happened.

He put his arms around her and led her into the living room. There was no consoling her—she was beyond that. There was nothing Mike could say that would make her feel better. His presence was all he could give.

"All my efforts are for nothing. Nothing I said changed their minds. They're lost. It must have been me that didn't prepare, study, or say the right thing. I didn't pray enough. I didn't trust God enough. I didn't let Him work through me. It's my entire fault!" She beat her hand into the sofa pillow. She could not count even one victory for all her efforts. Adding the attempts in her mind produced the equation, years plus many conversations, equals zero.

Then Mike said, "You're not a failure. God used you in a mighty way. Your children are your victories." Saying this reminded her of her need to connect with Janelle. Without a word she went to the study to get a phone number for Darin's mom off the school list of parents. Mike followed. She was desperate to make sure Janelle was all right. She called. She called again. It rang forever. She looked at Mike and called again. She was about to give up when the phone clicked on.

"Yes."

"Hello. Is this Mrs. Patel?"

"Yes."

"This is Janelle's mother. Is she there?"

"No."

"Do you know where she might be?"

"She went after Darin."

"They're not together?"

"No, they're not, well, they might be. Darin left to go to his dad and later Janelle went after him. It's so stupid. It won't work. Darin's dad took the mark and Darin is going to try to save him. It's too late. It's over and my fault. I should've said something when I had the chance. It's my own selfishness that got them all into this. I coulda…"

Rachael listened with a brick in her stomach. She was picking up the morose attitude coming through the line. "Why is Janelle's phone turned off? Do you know?"

"Both of their phones are off. Darin doesn't want to talk to me and Janelle, I don't know why. I tried to reach them, but they're not answering."

"How are they going to reach his dad? Doesn't he live in another state?"

"In Tennessee. Maybe he was going to try to catch a flight or hitch a ride. I don't know; I don't care anymore."

Normally, Rachael would have sought to encourage, be upbeat. She could feel the negativity on the other end. She was two slivers away from the same defeated attitude. Her daughter was racing after a forlorn hope. The dead phone was a testament that her daughter was no longer interested in the updates from Jason, therefore turning her back on the moment of truth, chasing a love interest instead of focusing on God. Her mind quickly spiraled downward. Her efforts to spiritually lead and guide others were thwarted at all levels. She internalized her failure and sought for the broken link that separated her from the promise of God, "Lo, I am with you always." In her mind it had to be an unforgiven sin. She couldn't remember one so, to her, it meant she had a cherished sin. She launched herself into an ocean of unworthiness.

Mike saw her turn off the phone without the courtesy of saying goodbye. The news was bad, he could tell from observing. Rachel cut him off when he attempted to ask for more information, "Don't talk to me! Leave me alone!" He had rarely seen his wife in this kind of a mood. Respecting her wishes he left her alone, despite the fact he wanted more information than what he heard from this end. During the evening he had forgotten his phone and had to search for it. He found it in his coat pocket hanging in the closet in the hallway outside the study. It had been on vibrate only. It vibrated in his hand with a message from Jason. He watched as Rachael turned off her phone and threw it across the desk. He would have to wait for her mood to change. He took his phone to the kitchen table and sat down.

"I'm sitting outside and a block up from the Cox's home. They're getting they're stuff. Saw this on the net. Angel Moreno introduces fake Jesus to crowds at the mosque in Mecca. He points to the east and says, 'Behold the Mhadi! He has come to the mountain. He is your savior to bring in world peace and righteousness. It is the end of the world, the Mhadi is here.' Crowd looks to the east as Jesus appears above the two hills of Al Safa and Al Marwah covered by a protective structure. Hundreds of angels hover next to him. The specter of his luminosity stuns the crowd which flattens upon the ground pressing their heads to their rugs. Jesus descends to the Ka'bah and touches it with his right hand. He turns to address the crowd. 'Long ago Ismael kicked his young feet between these two hills. I answered his desire then for water. I have come to give you everlasting water so you will never thirst again. Join me in making this desert bloom and usher in everlasting peace.' Water immediately gushes out of the old Zamzam well near the two hills and begins to flood the outer precincts of the shrine flowing toward the King Abdul Aziz road and threatens to flood the car tunnel. Jesus joins the crowd as it circles the holy shrine and makes seven trips between the two hills. Several miracles are performed where a blind man is healed and a man on crutches is asked to join Jesus as he walks around the Ka'bah."

Mike tapped his phone, closing the link and thought about his family. The glow of the phone light emanated from it as it sat on the table. He was worried about Janelle and wished she would call. In all the planning and rushing to get Jason on his way, then the neighbors coming over, he hadn't realized the number of voice mail and texts that had been backing up on his phone. The message indicator was blinking. He picked up the phone to access them. Members were trying to reach him. He was the leader of the scattered flock now that the pastor was jailed. They were looking to him. The messages mostly were about the abduction of two sisters from one of the families. He called the family to minister to them but the line didn't connect. Answering Mr. Oaks's message he found out about the abduction and that the news had been reporting a ring of human traffickers grabbing young girls for prostitution purposes. Mr. Oaks believed that the thugs were going after Adventist girls because they were not protected by the mark. Mike had a brief prayer with him and said he had to go. He rushed to the study and almost yelled at Rachael, "We've got to find

Janelle now! Let's go!" His voice was like a thumbtack on a chair. Rachael rose off of her chair as if she had been stabbed. Grabbing their coats they rushed out the kitchen door and into the car.

He rushed to the study and almost yelled at Rachael, "We've got to find Janelle now! Let's go!

Comparing information, they decided to trace the route from Darin's home to the airport. They kept up a constant barrage of calls to Janelle hoping she had turned on her phone. They called Jason again to see if he could access Janelle's phone when it was off. He could not. They knew that they could call the police in an emergency and have them reverse 911 call her, but that was no longer an option because of their status in opposition to the law. They drove to the airport and searched every parking lot for her car. Rachael got out and walked through the terminal at various ticketing booths, common areas, even baggage claim, checking every seating area. There was no sign of Janelle or Darin.

Both Mike and Rachael were becoming distraught. They didn't know where to go or what to do. Their Christian duties were being overshadowed by their personal fears. Their normal urge to minister to others got swallowed in their defeatist attitude. They were defeated by a nameless dread. Over and over they were questioning their teaching and guidance over the years with regards to their children and with the many people they had tried to witness to. It was a short step from doubting themselves about their witness to doubting their connectivity to Jesus. Doubt breeds more doubt. They examined themselves for unresolved sin. The examination turned into recrimination. Silently they drove home in a stupor of stupid self-skepticism, Satan's influence dogging them as they went. They didn't remember that the Great Controversy had warned of this struggle with personal doubt at this time.

At home Rachael retreated to the bedroom and Mike sat in a totally dark living room. It was as if a cloak of evil surrounded them. They didn't encourage each other; they were alone, separated from the bolstering support of a companion of common conviction … like Jesus separated from His Father at Gethsemane.

* * * * * *

Jason drove to the cabin with a full load of refugees. The Holy Spirit got them through without authorities seeing them. It was after midnight when they arrived. The four teens spread their sleeping bags around the fireplace, while George and Sheila moved their small bag of belongings into one of the spare bedrooms. They left the master bedroom for when Mike and Rachael would arrive. Immediately Sheila made some food in the kitchen. The events of the day and the nearness of Jesus' soon coming made it difficult to sleep.

Jason took the opportunity to access the net and garner more information. He typed up a short text to send out to his contacts. He slipped and made a reference to the antichrist in a derogatory manner,

"The Jesus Pretender makes short visit to Senegal, Africa, at the grand mosque in Ouakam. A crowd of sick people are healed and then he returns to meet with world religious leaders in the desert west of Dubai, UAE. No press is allowed into the tents spread out over several square miles. Long range high optical lens are able to capture the arrival of the many dignitaries, Presidents, Pope, and potentates from around the globe. Moreno is there along with Guadalupe, the snake lady. She seems to be on Jesus' right arm."

Soon after he sent the message, he received an echo response telling him that he should show more respect to "His Divine Eminence, Jesus The Christ." Jason immediately shut off his Onyx 4000. It was too late to keep whoever was watching from tracking his location, but he wanted to avoid the attempt at visual referencing. The response didn't sound official: it seemed to be vigilante type hackers attempting to monitor the non-aligned elements of society. It didn't matter if it was official or not—it could still spell trouble if they tried to see him and noticed he had blocked the lens. They might send someone out to inquire. He verbally chastised himself for using the word "pretender," and remembered he had said "fake" earlier. He knew they would be monitoring and tracking him in the future. He now had a reason to travel back down the hill to open his link and establish another location for them to look for him and try to entrap him. That would be his work for the next day: to protect the location of the hideout and get to his folks before they tried to answer him back and give away their locations.

* * * * * *

Sleep arrived late and fitfully. Rachael was face down on the bedspread with her street clothes from the day before still on. She couldn't shake the feeling that all her efforts for naught were because of her sinful condition which she could not pinpoint in her mind. She tossed and turned, beating herself mentally for not preparing her daughter properly and not being the best example to her children. It was a wild swing from being proud of her daughter's commitment to feeling she had let her down in the area of values and priorities. She should have told her that romance is less of a priority than salvation. She mused on the fact that her relationship with Mike had been so spiritually validating that perhaps it had slipped her mind that she needed to prepare Janelle. Her thoughts about Mike soothed her enough for her to fall asleep in emotional as well as physical exhaustion.

Downstairs Mike was spiraling downward spiritually. He felt responsible. His focus went toward the feelings of unforgiven sin. He knew full well that God forgives and buries sin in the deepest sea, but he couldn't shake the emotional feeling of regret that lingered in his mind. He had disappointed Jesus. He searched his inner soul. Rachael's words came back to him about how people are seduced by anger, alcohol, and sex. Suddenly he remembered his encounter with Glenda in the very room he was presently in. He remembered her words and the smell of her perfume and the look of her skimpy dress. It struck him full force that he had been attracted to her. He counted it the same as adultery like what Jesus said in His sermon on the mount. He immediately asked for forgiveness. He knew God would forgive him under normal circumstances, but because of his knowledge of scripture and the inspiration of prophecy, he knew that intercession might have ceased when the plagues started. Wondering if it was too late, Satanic doubt stepped in to ruin his confidence. A forgiving Savior became enshrouded in clouds of doom. Then there was a tug-of-war between the fact of forgiveness and the grief of having disappointed his Lord and Savior. He knew Jesus died for all of his sins, but he felt a failure because he couldn't emotionally forgive himself, especially at a time like this when everything counted. Darkness, darker than a windowless dungeon, pressed him down to the point of giving up. He came to a place where a nightmare of reality blended with a fitful dream of tortured slumber.

CHAPTER 20

It was almost noon when Mike heard Rachael in the hallway. The house felt like it had been transported to the Sahara Desert and left to bake in the sun. He was drenched in sweat. Rachael was still in her clothes from the night before, standing in front of the thermostat.

"Why is it so hot?" she exclaimed. She turned off the furnace which had been set on 68°. It wasn't the reason the temperature in the house was so high. Mike had rustled himself off the couch to look out the window. The sun was so bright it was difficult to see. He needed sunglasses indoors. He knew what it was; they both knew why the sun was so fierce. For a moment they forgot their negativity from the night before. They trooped to the video screen in the family room to get the news. It was more curiosity than anything else. They wanted to know how the media would spin this event. Accessing the web, they called up the news report from a national service and watched.

There wasn't a whiff of a mention about the plagues of Revelation 16. Mankind was trying to explain away, in scientific terms, a phenomenon of almighty fiat. Experts pointed to the dismally thin ozone layer and spoke of a massive solar storm emanating from the sun which must have blazed right through. Graphical representations helped to illustrate the point. Blame was placed on a slow response to eliminate chlorofluorocarbons, dichloromethane methane, and aerial pollution. The broadcasts included pictures of wilting crops and dried up mud cracking into jigsaw puzzle shapes. Spontaneous forest fires broke out in areas where water was already sparse. Almost the entire state of Idaho was ablaze. Pine-beetle-destroyed-forests combusted almost immediately. The intense heat extracted every drop of moisture from all exposed surfaces: animal, mineral, and vegetable. All of the plagues were being explained away as natural disasters. Proud humankind could not accept the truth that the predicted end had arrived. If the media understood the meaning, connected the dots in a logical progression, they would acknowledge the signs of the times. However, recognizing truth requires a guiding Spirit which no longer dwelt with the uncommitted.

The couple could see the catastrophic scourges raining down upon the impertinent petulant public. God's holy presence was still with Mike and Rachael. They knew what was happening and were aware of the future signs now so presently displayed. God had not abandoned them. They had to work out their doubts and shake off their miasma. Angels watched them like mothers watch toddlers struggling to stand up. They knew Mike and Rachael had the truth about a loving, forgiving Savior. The barrier was their own doubt about their worthiness. If they could but peep over the wall they could see Jesus with open arms. The wall separating them was of their own construction. Disappointed in themselves, they looked inward instead of upward. Witnessing the outpouring of the fourth plague caused them to feel the urgency of clearing their record with heaven. All they had to do was drink some sweet tap water from the kitchen to know that they were still in favor with the Heavenly King. He was still watching out for them. All was forgiven; everything was alright.

"Should we turn on the air conditioning?" Mike asked.

"Yes, I guess so. It's still winter, but it's like the Sonoran Desert outside," she answered. She went to the hallway and soon the familiar sound of the air conditioning unit came on. She returned to the family room while keying in a call to Janelle. Still no answer came from her phone. Mike was doing the exact same thing, calling Janelle. Worry began all over again. They couldn't drive anywhere because they didn't know where to go. They hid in their house. They were deeper in their depression than Cheri had been in her alcoholic vapors.

* * * * * *

Pastor Taylor sat in his cell. He was cut-off from his pastorate and separated from the scriptures. Other inmates had access to a small library which had some Bibles, however he was restricted. Across from his cage was an old TV hung on the wall. It blared all day long. He could tell from the reports that the plagues had started. Blazing light and sweltering heat came through the window; added to that was the county jail house had not switched over from winter to summer operation. It was like a sweat lodge. Worry furrowed his sweaty brow as he thought of his family and his church family, *How are they doing?* he asked himself. He wanted to lead them to salvation.

Prayer became the only tool available. He plied it with earnest entreaties. The answer came in a calming thought: "let the one who is righteous, still practice righteousness; and the one who is holy, still keep himself holy." The end had come, his work was finished, and proof of his commitment to God was the fact of his location.

The end had come, his work was finished, and proof of his commitment to God was the fact of his location.

He planned to watch the countdown of the plagues and wait for a big earthquake to spring him from jail. Like Paul he would sing praises at midnight.

* * * * * *

It was also late in the morning when the occupants of the cabin woke-up. The heat definitely had its telling effect on George, Sheila, and the teens, albeit it was modified by the high mountain air and the fast diminishing icy snowpack surrounding their sanctuary. George took the lead in pointing out the fulfillment of the fourth plague. As Sheila made breakfast, he opened a Bible study and discussion of the events that were happening around them. The new converts were enthusiastic about the discoveries they were making. It was tempting to stay with them at the table and explore more of the biblical terrain, but Jason had to protect them and lead a trail of electronic bread crumbs away from the cabin. He explained what he had to do and they had prayer for his safe sojourn back into town. He promised he would get to his folks at the earliest possible moment. He took his device with him, but admonished them to keep their units turned off, the batteries removed, and stowed away. They would go on using only their Bibles as their guide. He left after George pressed the key to his house in his hands,

"Use our house if you need to. Just in case it is no longer safe at your folks' place."

"I will. Thanks."

Getting down the hill was a challenge for the most experienced of drivers. Jason was not that experienced. The road was a quagmire. Melting snow from the burning orb of the sun was turning the hills and valleys into substances akin to superheated chocolate. The only reason he was able to make it to hard surface roads is because he was on a mission from God. Angels were guiding his driving and maneuvering decisions. He was protecting new converts and getting to a place where he could send a message to his family that was directive and protective. If they continued to use their devices it would be only minutes before someone could knock on their door checking to see if they were adherents to the common law of the land.

On the road he encountered another threat more bothersome than the mud and the heat. Self-appointed militia members were visibly setting up operations. In a strip-mall parking lot they could be seen organizing teams for local reconnaissance. Weapons were proudly displayed and passed around to members of the group. They would heft the rifle or automatic pistol and check its workmanship and capacities. The militia had red, black, and blue arm bands with logos. Jason had planned on stopping in that very parking lot to send his first message. He moved on down the road and drove into a residential area. He replaced the battery pack in his Onyx and began sending out his first trail marker. It was innocent enough and very short. Before he began he took the small piece of tape off the screen where any watcher might be watching. He then daubed his forehead with a handkerchief and sent his message. "Wow it's hot! Is this winter or summer?" His forehead was obscured by the dangling cloth. "The fake Jesus can't fix this!" he added. He moved on to his next point of deception.

It took him most of the afternoon to negotiate the crowded streets. Cars were broken down here and there with radiators boiling over and a few engines catching fire. Tow trucks and fire engines were either at the scenes or racing to put fires out. Hoses from fire hydrants were ineffectual; thick red blood clogged the hoses and the normal flow of water diminished down to an ooze. Foam fire extinguishers had to be employed. He went to public places to send his messages making it appear to be an individual on a shopping spree. The streets were also crowded with pedestrians. They were rosy red from sunburn and covered with blotchy boils. It was a scene out of a horror movie where blistered skin, akin to leprosy, covered faces as the afflicted screamed their agony and attempted to look at the sun in an accusative manner. It was difficult to tell if the white blotches were third degree burns or boils from the first plague.

The SUV's air conditioning was on full blast. Fans pushed the frigid air around the interior, creating a sanctuary for Jason. It was a beacon of relief to anyone outside. At one stop Jason was surprised by an intruder attempting to climb into the car. He had had the sense to keep the vehicle locked and the man struggled to open the door. He gave up on the door handle and began to attack the window in an attempt to break it. Blood and puss smeared the glass. Jason eased the gear into drive and tried to pull slowly away. More attempted to stop him, flopping on the hood, impeding his progress. From under nearby trees more desperate people ran to get into the car. These were homeless individuals caught in the elements of heat and hard luck. Juddering the wheel back and forth and moving forward at ever increasing speed he was able to shed the flimsy attachments and race away. He was more wary as to where he stopped the next time.

His last on-the-run message was, "Mom, Dad, Birds of a feather flock together. I need you two feathers to meet me at the lake." It was a veiled message to get his folks out of the house in case his messages were traced to his home. He drove to his old school and parked down the street around a secluded corner with a clear view of the school.

* * * * * *

All of Jason's messages had been read by his folks. It frustrated them that he was sending innocuous statements without any great import. He had been telling them about the heat and the weather. He spoke of the world cup soccer tournament and how he would miss seeing the early rounds on TV. He wrote of a sale at the mall, 30% off. He never once mentioned the cabin and the condition of the occupants. This was not Jason as they knew him for the past weeks. They were curious and frustrated, worried that he had regressed or that someone was mimicking his messages. His communications were of the same nature as his cavalier attitude of before. They questioned if they were losing him, too. This added to their gloominess. They were drawn to, but not interested by, the news. So it played in the background as they moped around the house and picked at their food in the kitchen. Repeatedly they tried to contact Janelle by text and voice. They prayed, but not like before: not together and not with hope. Fear dominated their discourses with heaven. One news cast caught their attention.

Word came out of Dubai that Jesus and the council of world and religious leaders were developing a strategic plan for prosperity and the beginning of an era of peace. The reports came out, not in dribs and drabs, but in torrents as various leaders of countries, also heads of denominations, sects, various world faith groups and ideologies, communicated with their people by vid-phone and email. Their assistants did most of the communication with subordinate leaders around the world. Enthusiastic underlings leaked grand stories to the press. One interesting fact surfaced from several sources. No food had been brought to the site for consumption by the large number of over one thousand people in attendance. Jesus was feeding the multitude himself. One large tent reserved for plenary meetings had been placed directly over a pile of stones. Jesus evidently spoke and the stones became fresh warm bread before their eyes. At another time, platters of food appeared in one tent and the aroma led the attendees to the location. Wine was brought from another tent that had been standing empty. Jesus had instructed the servers to go find it. When they entered the empty tent they thought they had misunderstood which one they were supposed to go to. Then the large stone jars started to appear before them. These reports were circulated like gossip around a world gone drunk with the return of a savior. The end of calamity was at hand. Disasters would cease. Harvests would be restored. Strife between nations and religious groups was about to stop. The only thing left to be accomplished was the purge. These facts were also included with the miracles that Jesus was performing in the desert. Common knowledge was beginning to surface that the only thing that stood in the way of prosperity was the minority of individuals who were preventing change by their fossilized opinions about ancient worship symbolized by the worship on a longgone Saturday Sabbath.

Because Jesus had circled the globe performing miracles, the masses were ready to accept anything, even unfounded rumors coming out of Bedouin tents in the wilderness. There were no direct statements about what Jesus wanted people to do, but the response was the same as if he had commanded them. They were willing to move ahead before he commanded. The people of the world had had enough. They were ready for change. The reporters telling the news were amongst those most elated with the prospects of a new world order. They spoke as if everything was a foregone conclusion.

Mike and Rachael half watched, half grumbled. They wished for things to move back in time to when they could put more effort into their witness, more urgency to their words. They wanted to double their efforts with their children. The progression of current events flashed before them on the vid-screen. The fourth plague baked the garden outside. The heat and the numbing effects of the atmosphere pushed them into retrograde dreams. They were in the world of "woulda, coulda, shoulda," instead of, now is the time that was trying them to the maximum. Jason's inane messages mocked them, neutralizing the reactions. They didn't answer until the second time he sent his message about meeting him at the lake. He added that it was an "emergency."

"Lake? What lake?" Mike asked.

"I don't know of any lake close to the cabin. Is the heat making him crazy?" Rachael responded. "Wait…He spoke of feathers. Is he saying Twin Feather Lake Academy?"

"That makes more sense. He's calling us to the school for some reason and he's hiding information from people who might be watching," Mike answered.

"And we've been sitting here when he needs us? Let's go!" Rachael was on the move as she spoke. She went to the master bedroom.

"What I don't understand is the fact that he's down here rather than up at the cabin. We told him to stay there!" Mike yelled up to the upstairs bedroom as he absentmindedly grabbed his coat on his way to the door. He almost had the coat on when he stepped outside and realized he didn't need it. He tossed it back into the kitchen. It landed on the floor. He pulled the car out of the garage and noted he had a third of a tank of fuel. He would need to put more in later from the tanks he had in the garage. Now he had to hurry and come back for the tanks later. Rachael jumped in as he backed out of the driveway.

"I'm worried something might have happened up at the cabin. Do you think they might be in trouble of some sort?"

"I don't know. I hope not."

The somewhat hasty drive to the academy helped them to gain a little more focus in what was important. When depressed, movement helps to get the mind out of its slump; in addition to that, their hyped-up emotions pumped adrenaline into their systems, increasing brain activity.

They slowed down when they approached the school. They looked at the building and didn't catch the flashing headlights down the street. Both of their heads were turned toward the academy grounds. When passed, they drove a little ways and started to execute a U-turn, Jason beeped the horn. Relief flooded their souls. He seemed all right at a glance. They pulled even and rolled down the windows receiving a wilting blast of heat in the process.

"What's wrong, son?"

"They're watching us. We've got to get rid of our phones and stuff. They'll be able to track us if we don't."

"Why not just tell us instead of coming back down here?"

"Because I got a bounce back last night and they knew where I was. I had to come down here and send a bunch of messages from all over town to lead them away from the cabin. And…I had to tell you in person, 'cause I couldn't send a message that they could read. That would really tip them off."

"Okay, okay, that's good thinking, Jason. Are they all right where they are?"

"I think so. The spooks are watching and listening to me not them, and they aren't using their stuff. I had them take the battery packs out of their devices. They should be all right."

"Good. Let's get back to the house and plan what we have to do."

"No, Dad. That might not be the best place to go. You were the only ones receiving my messages and they must've put two and two together. Especially, since I called you Mom and Dad. Follow me, I know where to go." Jason took off and Mike had to whip around and follow him out of the neighborhood.

"I guess we can stop worrying about Jason. He seems to be on top of everything," Mike encouraged his wife.

"That explains why he sent those crazy messages. Jason has never been interested in 30% off of anything!" Rachael had to chuckle at her own remark. Mike did too. It felt good to have a light moment in the midst of the gloom. Laughter produces positive hormones in the brain. Their determination to help their son also got them off of their negative self-focus.

It felt good to have a light moment in the midst of the gloom. Laughter produces positive hormones in the brain.

"This is different," he commented.

"How do you mean?" she asked.

"Usually, we are using our great wisdom and experience to guide him away from trouble. Look at us. We're meekly following our son who has all the answers, *and* the plan."

* * * * * *

The orb of the sun dipped behind the horizon. Sizzling radiation blurred the landscape into wavy patterns as heat emerged from every surface. Light faded somewhat and night came as a relief from the scorching day. But it was a night like no other night before. The intensity of the sun on the other side of the globe still made its presence known. The twilight ambience of light burned from around the bend of the earth. The sky was glowing akin to the glow of the bottom of a spacecraft upon re-entry. None opened their windows to let in the night air. It remained hotter than the Sahara at full noon.

Both cars parked at George and Sheila's quiet house. The trio entered and went to the kitchen table to talk. The house felt like a blast furnace. Water would help, so they found glasses in the cupboards and drew some from the tap. True to the biblical promise, sweet cool water poured from the tap. The air conditioning was turned on and they began their conversation. Jason explained every detail and their need to stay off the net. It was sobering to realize that common citizens were forming bands of vigilantes to act as police and national guardsmen. It amounted to total anarchy. Anyone, it seemed, was cleared to do what they thought best, or worst, in any situation.

"Perhaps we should leave for the cabin now?" Mike opened.

"No, please no. I want to know where Janelle is and if she's all right. I can't leave her and run to the mountains!"

"I agree with you, but we don't know where she is. How can we find her?"

"We can keep trying to call her."

"No, Mom. They'll find us here and then where would we go? Or, on second thought, we could leave out, go across town, and try to call her. That might work for a little while."

"How about if we go to Darin's house, talk to his mom, and see if they've reported in? We could do that now," Rachael said.

"They may need our help, too," Mike added.

Their phones and Onyx 4000's were stacked on the table in front of them. They were turned off. It was so tempting to pick one up and try to get information on Janelle. They would have to do it the old-fashioned way, on foot and by car. They took what food they could to eat on the way. Jason figured he would use the internet to get Darin's address when they got closer. He feared the watchers would anticipate his next move if he accessed the address too soon before they got there. He knew approximately where he lived. Halfway there the devices popped on with a national bulletin.

~ ~ ~ ~ ~ ~

By Presidential order, all commerce has ended for those individuals who have, by their defiance, neglected to receive the Citizens National Stamp. All individuals without the CNS will now have to report to their local police department to receive the CNS. All other CNS approved sites are closed down. There will be a late fine levied for noncompliance.

All commercial establishments will not sell to any individual without checking for a valid CNS or incur heavy fines if caught.

~ ~ ~ ~ ~ ~

The phones and Onyx 4000's automatically shut off.

"Great! Now they'll know where we are."

"Don't worry, mom. That was a tech blast, an outgoing universal transmission. It went to everyone. Our position would be obscured by the fact that whoever is watching me would have had to listen to the same message. We're good for now."

"Apart from the tracking issue we are trying to avoid, we just got confirmation that the Bible prophecy of not being able to buy and sell has been strongly enforced. Things are close now," Mike pointed out.

"Oh, Janelle, please call us or something!" Rachael called out in desperation. It was almost a prayer.

They got to the approximate neighborhood and Jason turned on his unit for a quick check. He accessed the last name, Patel, and received only two names with addresses and phone numbers. He recognized the one, but didn't highlight it. Instead he scrolled down to another altogether different name and clicked on it. He sent a text to that one saying, be there in a minute. They then went to the Patel house and found it empty. There were no lights, no car in the driveway, no indication of any recent activity. The trek to find Janelle had come to a dead end.

They wondered what to do. Jason suggested prayer. For the adults, this was another confirmation that Jason was definitely out in the lead. They were chagrined. It helped them to realize how short sighted they had been. Their inner grief and self-recrimination were dragging them away from the power source of life. As Jason prayed for Janelle's safety and their protection, Mike and Rachael were silently asking God for forgiveness for their lack of faith. They pleaded with Him to take away their emotional pain of doubt and replace it with confidence in His plan for their lives and for Janelle. They thanked the Lord for their son, who had demonstrated unwavering resolve in the face of overwhelming powers arrayed against them. When they finished praying, Mike and Rachael looked at each other's tear-filled eyes and knew in their hearts what the other had been thinking and praying.

"So where do we go from here?" Jason asked.

"I think we should make some visits," Mike answered. "We need to fortify some of the members. Probation is either closed or closing and encouragement is primary."

"We should try again to reach Megan," Rachael added.

* * * * * *

Janelle and Darin were forced to hear the announcement about not being able to buy or sell. That was hours ago. They were stopped on the highway looking at a distant road block. They were waiting in hopes that it would break up and they could continue on their way. Their flight to Tennessee had been blocked by a multitude of difficulties. Janelle had found Darin hitchhiking his way to the airport. When they got to the airport all the planes were delayed and back-filled with reservations from previously cancelled flights. No seat was available and the stand-by wait list was inordinately long. The two were in a funk about life and how everything they knew was changing. Darin missed his father; Janelle could not live without Darin. She was following him because she desperately wanted to keep the link strong between them. He had always hoped for a resolution between his parents and a reuniting of the family. The fact that his father took the stamp and the last day events unfolding made the resolution impossible. He would never see his dad again. He blamed himself for his parent's divorce. Now he felt even more sinful and unqualified for heaven. The crushing thought bore down on him until he forgot the bigger picture. Satan was using his guilt to capture two candidates.

Janelle's love for Darin monopolized her thoughts when she didn't think upon heavenly things. Up until yesterday, most of her two great preoccupations, faith and love, were united in one adventure with her beau. Her decision to go find Darin and then to travel with him down the road to his father, pulled her slowly away from her faith force. She was losing grip. She needed to come back to her conviction.

Their travel out of town was hampered by roving bands of would-be policemen, ad hoc militia, and opportunists wanting to capture and harass people not in the swing of things. Under self-appointed missions they were hunting the human animal, compelling them to get stamped with the CNS, but having fun at the expense of the ones they nabbed. They had narrowly avoided one group that chased them on motorcycles and only gave up the chase when Janelle pulled into the parking lot of the highway patrol. Darin took the wheel from then on, making wild detours and backtracking to get out of town. They spent the night curled up in each other's arms, hiding off road a hundred yards up an unnamed ranch road leading into some rolling hills. The van was tucked into a tiny space between some cottonwoods and willows. All day they fought to go east. The open highway made them an easy target for these vigilantes and they made little progress and burned fuel on air conditioning for the van. They had just refueled the van, Darin had used cash, and were now watching the next obstacle at a distance.

Darin was at the point of despair. Now they could not purchase any more fuel or a ticket on a train or a bus. He knew he would never see his dad. He decided to give him a video call.

"Dad, I tried to get to you, but I can't make it."

"You were trying to come here, why?"

"'Cause I'll never see you again if I don't."

"Don't be foolish, you'll see me again."

"But, but you took the mark. That means the end."

"Oh, I see, I should have called you. You don't have to worry, son. I love you. When we last talked your concern touched me. Look! I cut it off."

Darin and Janelle stared at the video. A bandaged hand was lifted up to the camera. The gauze was thick and yet there was still some red spots dotting the surface. "You cut it off! By yourself!"

"Yes. It was only the skin on the back of the hand. The pain was worth it to be in heaven with you, it will be like … ah, heaven."

"Dad, dad … I'm so relieved. I don't have to worry about you anymore."

"No son. You don't. Now help your mom and sisters, and your grandparents; they need you. We'll all be united when we get to heaven." It was everything he wanted to hear. Suddenly, his reason for getting down on himself was gone.

A message from the cell phone carriers suddenly filled the screen. All subscribers were asked to validate their CNS, by video, to continue service. They had 24 hours to comply.

* * * * * *

"Jason, I need to ask you a personal question. Do you mind?"

"No, Mom. Go ahead."

"Awhile back it seemed like you were more interested in the soccer tournament than in what was happening spiritually. What made you change your thinking?"

"Pancakes," he said.

"Pancakes?!" Mike responded incredulously.

"Yeah, pancakes. Mom made pancakes."

"I don't understand. Why would pancakes make a differ…" He looked over at Rachael who was nodding in agreement, tears cascading down her cheeks. He could see this was a "ah ha" moment for his wife. Something had happened between the two of them. "Would someone explain to me what just happened." Rachael waved a hand indicating she could not speak and blew into a Kleenex®, his wife was obviously incapacitated with emotion.

"Well, dad. Mom was making pancakes and wouldn't give me ones that weren't completely mixed. She wanted all the lumps out. She said she only wanted to give the best to her kids, just like Jesus only gave His best for us. She made me perfect pancakes, they were even perfectly round like she always does. I couldn't help but think of what I should be giving to Him. Mom was right."

"So, you decided to give Him your all?"

"Yep."

"And then you went out and won your enemies to Jesus, the Cox brothers."

"Yeah, that's about it. The only people my age that weren't Christian were them and my soccer buddies. I wanted a perfect gift to give back to Jesus."

Rachael still could not marshal words to express her gratitude. Validation of her work as a witness for Christ kept choking her with gladness.

"How come you didn't tell us what you were doing? You had us worried for a while there."

"I thought you'd like the surprise."

And then for Rachael's sake Mike couldn't resist saying, "So, your mom's witness to you resulted in your turning to Jesus fully and also saving three of your friends."

"That's about it, yep."

Rachael still could not marshal words to express her gratitude. Validation of her work as a witness for Christ kept choking her with gladness.

* * * * * *

Megan's house glowed with interior lights. Mike debated where to park; he chose to pull up to the curb the next house down. Rachael decided it might be less threatening if she went alone. Hesitatingly, she stepped up to the front porch. She checked the big window and saw Megan sitting on the couch breast-feeding the baby. She wrapped lightly on the window and Megan jumped. She came quickly to the door.

"Please not now. Walt's home," she whispered.

"Megan you've got to see what's happening. Now is the time to flee."

"I don't want to talk to you now, besides he could come out of the kitchen at any moment."

"When can I talk to you?"

"Tomorrow, tomorrow night. He's got a meeting with some friends and then they're going to watch a basketball game together. He'll be gone all evening. We can talk then if you must."

"But—"

Rachael's words of worry were cut off when Megan closed the door. She knew her only chance was to talk to her without interference from Walt, but waiting until tomorrow night meant delaying their flight to the cabin. *Would they be too late?* was the question working on her mind.

Mike listened to Rachael's account of what happened as he drove away toward Mrs. McKessy's house. He worried about the time crunch too. *How much time was left?* crossed his mind. If they stayed another day it would be more time that might give them the answer to where Janelle had gone and if she was all right. Their hopes for quick information were dashed when the message forced itself out of their phones, *All subscribers must validate by video, their CNS, to continue receiving service. This must be completed in the next 24 hours. Service is suspended until validation is complete.* They were cut off from Janelle by electronic means. Their only hope now was answered prayer.

At the McKessy house they were greeted warmly. Heidi and Veronica were comfortable on the warmish side, but surviving well. The two octogenarians had been watching the news, singing spirituals, and commenting on the unfolding events. They shared their concerns about the church members. The news stories had them praying for those whom they knew would be struggling. In their own circumstances they were isolated from a world gone mad. The visiting trio could feel the presence of heavenly beings protecting the two ladies, who seemed like identical twins except for skin color. It was tempting to stay with them. Prayer and praise flowed naturally through the fibers of the house. The elder and his wife had come to visit and encourage; they instead, were filled with hope and promise. The positive atmosphere seeped into the empty cavities of their doubt, dispelling worries and instilling a stronger more solid faith. They should have come over earlier and avoided their slough of despondency. They wanted to stay, but they had to leave…their presences could attract attention from watching eyes. As they walked away, Veronica's words echoed in their consciousness, "We shall overcome."

The trio drove back to George and Sheila's house.

CHAPTER 21

They woke to the blast furnace effects of the sun climbing over the horizon. The air conditioning unit labored to compete against the oppressive heat. It was a losing battle that ended in defeat mid-morning. Soon the inside of the house was hotter than the outside. They were compelled by necessity to go to the car and linger it its luxury. Once again they tried Darin's house, but the Patel's were not home. Getting to the house was a nightmare in avoiding roving bands of vigilantes and road blocks manned by the same. It was almost comical to watch as the vigilantes tried their utmost to stay inside their vehicles until the last moment before stepping out to confront passers-by. Motorcycles were no longer in abundance as the riders would be scorched to a crispy red in minutes. Broad-brim hats and long-sleeved shirts were needed for the brief moment that the militia members spent out under the sun.

Mike wanted to get more fuel for the car, but knew it would only result in a denial and questions as to why he didn't have a stamp. It might even bring in the police if someone reported his attempt. It was time to use his stash in the garage. Secondary roads were his only choice for travel and he had to be careful on them.

Just before he got to the house, the lights went out. It was like the sun had blown a solar fuse. Everything was lamp black. Mike was driving at about thirty miles per hour and suddenly he couldn't see an inch in front of his face. At first he thought he had gone blind. He hit the brakes as a precaution and then the automatic headlights for his SUV turned on. He turned to look at his wife and son.

"That was quick! We're into the fifth plague already, Revelation states, 'her plagues will come in a single day.' That means year in Bible prophecy," Mike said.

"Yeah, that was real quick! I thought the plagues would be longer in duration, ya'know, like the first one," Jason added.

"Perhaps, it means inside of a year's time. The first three have overlapped and still are in effect. But, the sun and darkness are mutually exclusive," he replied.

"I didn't think that the fifth plague would be literal. It says that darkness will be poured out on the throne of the beast," Rachael commented.

"I did too. I guess we have to be flexible in interpreting prophecy. We're not infallible like the Pope."

"Dad, maybe it can still be a spiritual interpretation—darkness is poured out on the heart-thrones of the beast. These people around us are believers in the beast."

"Once again, son, you amaze me."

They drove into their neighborhood and pulled into the driveway. Mike and Jason went to the garage while Rachael went to the house. She immediately found it to be an ice box. The air conditioner had been on since the day before. She grabbed Mike's coat off the floor and draped in on the back of a kitchen chair. She went for some food and water. She filled bottles and lined them up on the counter. Fresh food in the refrigerator was her first priority, thinking that it would spoil. Then she asked herself, *why?* Her habits of thrift, waste not want not, were no longer necessary. She assembled several bags of non-perishables when the guys came in the door.

"All filled up. Well, almost all filled up," Jason announced.

"I'm glad I had those extra fuel containers in the garage; we would not have been able to make it to the cabin if I hadn't. This feels good. Nice and cool. Should we stay here tonight?"

"No, Dad. Like I explained before, whoever it is that is on to me, they know where I live."

"Okay, I understand. I guess we shouldn't tempt fate. Wait, that phrase makes no sense in this circumstance. We're in His hands and it has nothing to do with fate."

"Ah, Dad. I have another question. Since this is Friday and it is like hours before sunset, does this darkness mean that it is Sabbath already?

The sun's not giving its light, but it's still up there. I saw it. It is hard to see, but it is a very dark red."

"Where? I've got to see this."

"Wait, let's carry this food and water out to the car. I'll lock up," Rachael instructed.

They went out to the SUV and deposited the packages and bottles in the back and then they went out on the front lawn to see the sun. It hung ominously above the tree tops. It was eerie in its subdued state. As they walked back to the SUV they could see the destruction of the shrubbery around the house. It was drooping and wasted. The sun had extracted every ounce of moisture from its stems and branches. A good rainstorm might save them, but refreshing replenishing rain was not in the forecast.

* * * * * *

Rachael kept looking at her watch. She had several issues that worried her: her daughter and her sister. The only one where she had any tangible plan was meeting with her sister that evening when Walt was not at home. She didn't want to ignore Walt and his need for salvation, but he was like all the ignorant masses that were going down the road to perdition. Walt was angry and determined to pull his wife along with him. Rachael believed that tonight was the moment of truth for Megan. If there was any commitment left in Megan she would appeal to her to come with them. As soon as she and the baby were in their vehicle they would head for the cabin.

Minutes ticked by as the three sat watching, waiting around the corner. Since it was the cusp of the Sabbath they read scripture, sang songs, and prayed. One of the songs they wanted to sing again was one they had heard Veronica singing, "Swing low, sweet chariot. Comin' for ta carry me home…" They wanted to sing it with the same affection that she had. It was so much more meaningful at this point in their spiritual walk. It brought tears to Rachael's eyes. The words were so much more poignant, so deeply evocative.

They didn't see Walt's car back out of the garage and drive down the street. Their hope was that he had already left. Rachael said, "Now is the time." Mike drove up in front of the house. Rachael went to the door. She felt the cool of the evening and at first thought it might be her nervousness about confronting her sister. It was more than cool; it was cold. The total lack of the sun's power translated back into winter like temperatures. She didn't have a coat on and her fingers and nose were registering the frosty bite. She looked up into the sky. The stars were non-existent. She questioned if there were clouds or if it was still the darkness from the plague. The moisture forcibly extracted from the ground had raised the humidity. Now that moisture was chilling the atmosphere.

Megan had been watching from the window. Before Rachael could knock on the door, Megan opened it to reveal she was holding the baby. Stepping forward Rachael bumped into Megan who was coming out. She had two diaper bags on her shoulders. It gave Rachael the hope that Megan was coming with them and she didn't have to beg.

"Walt didn't go to the meeting and he's staying home to watch the game, so we'll talk out here."

"Oh."

"Take her. She's driving me mad! I haven't a moment to myself. Walt hates her, and so do

Megan had been watching from the window. Before Rachael could knock on the door, Megan opened it.

I!" Megan's words were laced with selfish anger. Rachael was shocked. She heard what was said, but couldn't fathom the incredulity of the act. Megan was throwing away her daughter so she could have peace and quiet. The selfish desires were superseding motherhood. Megan was no longer benefiting from the presence of God in her heart. Her mind had shut out all care and compassion

"Megan, you don't mean…"

"Here, take these." Megan threw the two diaper bags at her. "Now go before Walt sees you. Go!"

"No, Megan, you can't stay. You have to come with us!" Rachael appealed in desperation. Mike saw what was happening and rushed out of the car to help persuade Megan to come.

"No! Get out of here! Leave me! I hate that baby and I hate God for not answering my prayers!" Mike tried to say something, but Megan anticipated him. She held up a hand, took two backward steps, and turned around leaving them on the front lawn. Wet snowflakes, like tears, started to fall. They stood there in shock. To go forward would mean engaging both Walt and Megan in a forlorn discussion. Mercy's door had slammed shut, the sound effects provided by Megan's front door. The light of hope disappeared as the front porch light turned off, a signal that they were not welcome.

Mike and Rachael turned from watching Megan's house. Rachael was weeping for her sister and had her face buried in the soft clothes of the baby she was carrying. Mike held her arm and consoled her as they went to the car to join Jason. He thought of the text which asked the question, *Can a mother forget her sucking child?* but could not bring himself to say it aloud. Big fat, fluffy flakes fell almost vertically from the sky. They reminded Mike of what he thought might resemble manna falling from heaven. It was a spring style snow storm with wet, sloppy roads and white diamonds scattered on bushes. The snow could not cling to the dried grass and shrubbery because of the heat from before. It melted instantly and reflected the only lights left in the world: artificial man-made lights. Jason was at the wheel of the 4x4.

"Dad, I thought you would want to pick up the other car we left at George's house."

"No, we're running out of time. We need to head for the mountains; we really only need the SUV from here on," he answered.

Distraught, Rachael clung to Tabitha. She wanted to believe that Megan hadn't acted senselessly. She wanted to go back and reason with her. Deep in her heart the conviction grew that it was too late. One last act was to search the diaper bags to see if there might be a note.

One bag was filled with diapers and stuff, and the other had breast milk, not recently pumped, still frozen. Megan had cleaned out her freezer discharging all memory of her baby. The other bag had changes of clothing and some formula with a box of baby cereal. No note was found.

Reluctantly Rachael made a request from the back seat, "I need some warmer clothes for the baby and a blanket. Maybe we can stop real quick at the house?"

"I could use a warmer coat in case we may need to walk in this weather. How about you, Jason, do you need anything?"

"No, I'm good."

"Let's be careful, the roads are wet, but they could get slippery. We wouldn't want to have an accident, no matter how minor, and attract the attention of the police," he cautioned.

They made their way through the silent streets. They saw ahead some burning cars and some youths looting the contents of others and then setting fire to them. They took an early turn to avoid contact and drove up a residential street that bordered the main avenue. A tense moment came when they had to drive past two patrol cars where the officers were at the front door of a house shining black-light flashlights on the hands and foreheads of the occupants. The Larssons were curious that the police were not at the scene of the looting less than two blocks back.

When they got to their house, a light was on in the kitchen. They must have left it on by accident. Mike and Jason went to the front door, leaving the 4x4 idling in the driveway nearby; Rachael followed with the baby in her arms. Mike fished the front door key remote out of his pocket and began to unlock the door. Suddenly the door swung open and a man in a sleeveless shirt holding a shotgun greeted them. A blast of beer breath assaulted Mike's face.

"What do you think you're doing?"

"I'm returning home," Mike answered.

"This ain't your home. Not anymore. I'll bet you're coming home after one of your illegal church services. That makes you outlaws and this is my house." He emphasized his words by using the slide action, pumping a shell into the chamber of the shotgun. It was so unexpectedly sudden. Turning away from their everyday earthly lives didn't include in their minds a bold theft of their property. It didn't matter if it was or wasn't their house anymore; they were going to their real home.

"Yes, sir I understand." He muttered in shock. "I was wondering if you would be so kind as to let me get a warmer coat and a few things for the baby." Mike spoke in the gentlest tone possible. The man put his free hand on the entryway wall and leaned against it in thought.

"Nah, I don't think so. But, I'll do you one favor. Give me the electronic keys to the SUV and you won't have to worry about the police taking it away from you." His face registered a determined threat if Mike didn't comply and he pointed the gun at Mike's chest.

"But ... We ..."

"Hand them over now and I won't call the police. It might buy you a little time." His posture changed from a slouch to a wide stance with squared shoulders. The refugees were confronted with the possibility of being rounded up and put in jail and considered kidnappers holding someone else's baby, a baby that would go back to its uncaring, inattentive parents.

"Sir, can we get our things out of the car?"

"Are you kidding me? You must be an idiot! Give me the keys and you won't get into trouble!"

He pushed the shotgun closer to Mike's face.

"I have the baby's things in the car. Please, let me get them, it won't take a minute. Please," Rachael pleaded.

"Get outta my sight!" He turned the shotgun to Rachael's face. Mike stepped in front of Rachael and gave him the key. He started to turn. "Take this. I don't want it." The man took the small plaque off the wall and threw it out on the front lawn. Snowflakes landed on the plaque like dew on Gideon's fleece. It was partially covered, but all three knew what it was and what it said. It was entitled, "Footprints."

> *Snowflakes landed on the plaque like dew on Gideon's fleece.*

Rachael bent to pick it up but Jason was faster, not wanting his mother to slip while carrying the baby. He showed it to his mom and dad. They nodded in silent agreement. Jesus would carry them from this moment on. All three, as if on cue, looked at their foot impressions in the wet grass behind them. Their hearts wanted to see the reality of the conviction that compelled them. Jesus would indeed carry them. They walked slowly down the street thinking that they needed to get to the car parked at George and Sheila's. They passed neighbors who were shut inside silent dark houses. They didn't know what would befall them next. They headed in the general direction of the Froelich's house. A flickering orange glow illuminated the trees in the area of the Froelich's home.

* * * * * *

Janelle and Darin finally made it to his house after driving and hiding through the entire night and through most of the day. The house was empty. He knew immediately that his mom had gone to her folks' place. They renewed their struggle on the streets to get there. It was easier because huge flakes of snow obscured the landscape and decreased visibility.

"I've been thinking. I really lost sight of what was important these last couple of days. Not to say my dad isn't important, but it's just that … I should have thought about you and my sisters, and mom and the grandparents, ya'know? They and you were depending on me and I let them down. I let you down."

"You didn't let me down."

"But, I took you on this wild goose chase to be with my dad."

"I chose to come along, remember? I picked you up because I couldn't bear to be without you. I was throwing away everything for you."

"See! By your coming with me, I became responsible for you turning your back on heaven. I was doing more damage than good by trying to be with my dad one last time," he explained.

"Our choices are our own."

"But, you can't deny I influenced you."

"No I can't, but I chose just the same," she replied.

"My dad's choice to take the stamp dragged me down; his choice to cut it off pushed me back up. Who knows what negative and positive effects we have on people. For all you know, your parents might be giving up because they think they lost you. I noticed you turned your phone off."

Janelle could not deny the logic of his words. She began to worry for her folks. They always seemed so strong in the faith, but the powerful negative forces that worked in her could, in fact, work on them. She chewed her lip just like her mother.

"Will you be all right on the short trip home?"

"I think so. You can't see anything in all this snow. But, I really don't want to be without you."

"I can't explain it. It just seems like you need to be with your folks to help them. Every time I pray I get the feeling that they need you." Janelle thought about that for the rest of the short trip.

They arrived at the grandparents' small bungalow. Drapes were pulled shut and no lights could readily be seen from outside. Darin knew the house and guessed where they might be. A tiny sliver of light came from behind one curtain. Darin stopped the car and handed the key remote to Janelle. They both got out and hugged. Janelle didn't want to leave him. She tried one last time to urge him to let her stay with him.

"Let me stay with you. My parents will be okay."

"Janelle, I feel very strongly about this. You have to join your parents, they'll be worried sick about you. I have to help my mother and sisters, and my grandparents. We both can't be in two places at once," Darin urged.

"I know, I know, but I love you and can't be without you!" she answered.

"I love you too. Think of it this way. The next time we see each other all this fear and hatred will be over." Janelle clung to him and they kissed. She reluctantly released him, as she should, and he started to move away. Her eyes were centered on his back as he walked. He looked back over his shoulder. He stopped. Her emotions soared hoping he had changed his mind. She knew it was selfish to want him with her. His grandparents were feeble. He was the only one who could help them. Her folks were probably beside themselves with worry. "I'll see you in heaven, in a couple of weeks or so," he said. "I'll pray for your safe trip home. I know Jesus will take care of you."

She knew he was right. "I'll look for you with tears in my eyes."

"That's an interesting thought; will there be tears in heaven?" He answered.

* * * * * *

Firemen knocked the fire down at the Froelich's lot; the house was scattered all over the neighborhood. Most of the neighbors that were unaffected by the blast and debris went inside cozy homes because there wasn't anything more to watch. The three were cramped, hiding in the small playhouse, and thankfully the baby didn't fuss while they hid from the rioting mob. They thought it might be a good time to move on to the car. Carefully they worked their way out of the backyard to the front, staying close to shrubbery and shadows from street lamps. Without the street lights there would be very little light to guide their path.

At the first corner Mike spoke. "I didn't heed His advice."

"What do you mean, Dad?" Jason was thinking of the brute in their home.

"Jesus said, 'Let the one who is on the housetop not go down, nor enter his house, to take anything out, and let the one who is in the field not turn back to take his cloak.' I didn't listen."

"I said I needed some stuff for the baby. I didn't listen either. What are we going to do?"

"We walk with the Lord to our other car and see how far it can take us. We shouldn't worry; our angels are protecting us."

They walked toward George and Sheila's house. Flakes clung to hair and clothing. Soon all three looked like animated snowmen. Rachael took her blouse out of her pants and slipped the baby up underneath it to be next to her skin. Mike had on an old button-down shirt with an undershirt. He took his shirt off and put it on her. Then he copied Jason by pulling his arms into the t-shirt and folding them against his chest. Jason had a thin polo shirt that had to perform extra duty as a winter parka.

"As soon as we can get to the other car we can turn on the heat and get warm. I'm not sure the house heating and cooling system will work. When the air conditioner went out it might have fried the electrical and thus, the heating system, too. But the car should work and that will get us the heat we need," Mike tried to encourage them.

"We'll need to find something at their house for the baby to keep her warm and some coats for us," Rachael added.

"So, we're not going to listen to Him the second time?" Jason posed.

"I think under the circumstances we should at least try," Rachael answered.

They took turns carrying the baby and trying to keep it warm. The baby was a burden; however, it was also a little heater that gave its carrier the extra benefit of warmth. Carrying it helped. They jumped up and down to get their circulation going and even tried to jog.

Every major intersection was an exercise in stealth. They kept to the shadows and crossed when traffic was light or non-existent. At one point, they hid behind a dumpster and waited for a parking lot to clear of a group of not-so-quiet peacekeepers. They were gathered around a van listening to a broadcast. All at once the group cheered, pumping their fists in the air. Several were heard yelling, "It's about time!" The hidden trio didn't know what had happened.

Cut off from all information, they did not know what was transpiring in the world. They had been on top of all the way marks in the countdown to the second coming, thanks to Jason's watch-care. Tonight they missed the news. The conference in Dubai finished and the leaders emerged with plans and directives. Heads of States announced the decrees and religious leaders spoke of grand moves to end the strife and usher in peace around the globe. Jesus, flanked by the Pope and the Right Reverend Robert Grayble on the left side and with Angel Moreno on the right, made his announcement. The world would be purged of the contrary element of dissent. Non-aligned individuals were to be executed in favor of a more righteous populace. The few nonconformists will be sacrificed so that the majority will live in bliss. The date had been set. No in-depth explanation was made as to the inhumane nature of the diktat. No reporter commented on the legality of the action. These were stern times and a world in chaos needed swift and decisive moves. Jesus lifted off the ground with some of his angels and flew away to perform wonders. Amazingly, the other three—the Pope, the Reverend, and Angel Moreno—also jumped into the air like frogs, with the help of attending angels, leap-frogging over the media outward bound to points east and west. Then the remainder of the conference attendees moved to more traditional transportation and went to their countries of responsibility. Everything was set in motion.

Swirling flakes of snow attempted to choke the light out of street lights—a shroud for the fugitives. Their fluttering descent mercifully shielded them from prying eyes. But, it didn't comfort them with warmth.

They could only speculate as to the hurrah they saw and heard erupt from the vigilantes in the parking lot. At this point any happiness for the opposition spelled bad times for the escapees. Mike was wondering if the death decree had gone out. He couldn't be absolutely sure, but he had to assume it had. Staying in the city was no longer an option. They had to leave now and hope that Janelle would be all right. They prayed for her to flee to the cabin.

It took another forty-five minutes of chilling movement through the frightening streets. It seemed like a coup d'état had occurred and victorious rebels were rejoicing in the streets, looking for targets of opportunity. The three alternated between walking and hiding, slipping behind and between parked cars. Ears, noses, and cheeks were blushing red. Thankfully the baby slept with the gentle walking movement. Rachael knew it was only a matter of time before she would wake-up and demand to be fed.

At last they reached the house and the car. Jason started the car and remained with it. They couldn't afford to lose it at this point. Mike and Rachael made a quick reconnoiter of the house. They grabbed first warm coats, gloves, and blankets and then went to improvise on baby food. It was more than apparent that George and Sheila had taken as much as possible with them to the cabin. Mike switched on the furnace but it remained unresponsive. Returning to the kitchen he raided the almost empty pantry for food, finding carrots, snack crackers, raisins, water bottles, bananas that were getting too old to eat, and among other things, a small individual size bottle of cranberry/grape juice. A tote bag and several plastic shopping bags were stuffed with necessities. Rachael stuffed another bag with hand and kitchen towels for diapers. They were overburdened with possessions. The incongruity of the moment got to Mike. Soon they would leave this earth with nothing and yet, they needed so much now to get away. Mike's mind went to the meaning of Jesus' words about returning to get one's coat, "let the one who is in the field not turn back to take his cloak." He knew a cloak in biblical times was a versatile garment, but it was also an indication of status. *Was Jesus speaking of wealth and privilege or was he talking of the need and haste?* he wondered. However his mind worked the issue, he still felt compelled to heft as many of the bags that he could and hustle them out to the car. He went back for more and locked the door behind Rachael. Again, the meaninglessness of his actions occupied his thoughts. *We're transitioning to a new life, with different values and yet, I'm locking doors and filling our car with mammon.*

"Dad, we've only got a little over a quarter of a tank of fuel left. We'll never make it to the cabin on this. What are we going to do?"

"We're going to pray. Maybe gas and cooking oil are the same."

"What?"

"Your father is referring to Elisha and the widow's oil. Maybe God will get us there on a quarter of a tank."

"I thought maybe he was going to mix cooking oil with biofuel. It's a different process ya'know. It would really mess-up the engine."

"Well then, we should be on our way. No time to lose," Mike instructed.

* * * * * *

Janelle drove a circuitous route home avoiding main streets and highways. It was a habit she had grown accustomed to in the last couple of days. Relieved, she drove straight into the driveway behind the family SUV. The headlights illuminated a family gathered around the car brushing off snow from the 4X4. The man protecting them had a shotgun in his hands. He pulled it up and pointed it at her windshield. He banged the barrel down on the hood demanding that Janelle roll down the window.

"Who are you?"

"I'm, Janelle," she answered hesitatingly. Then on second thought she forced up her courage. "Where are my parents?"

"Ah, so you're one of them. I ran them off hours and hours ago. Get out of that van. I can use it too. This is going to be a great night. Two cars and house. I'm really climbing the social ladder." He pointed the shotgun in the window straight at Janelle's head. Janelle gasped in fright. She wanted to run away. Just then one of the bystanders called out. "Who is it?"

"It's another one of those idiots who ain't got a clue as to what's up."

Janelle took her opportunity to shift into reverse and step on the accelerator. It startled shotgun toting man and it took him a few seconds to opt for a shot at the

He pointed the shotgun in the window straight at Janelle's head. Janelle gasped in fright.

fleeing subject. Janelle careened out of the driveway, destroying a dried decorative shrubbery on one side. The van swerved out of control sliding into the wet street. Putting the van in forward, she stomped on the accelerator only spinning the wheels. In desperation she leaned forward willing the car onward with her body. It saved her life. The blast of the shotgun at close range sent a small cluster of BB shot through the passenger side window, shattering glass, and sending the widening pattern of shot into the seat behind Janelle's head. Shards of glass and some BBs peppered the interior of the van narrowly missing her head and slicing locks of hair off of the nape of her neck. Traction finally came to her aid and she gathered velocity down the street. At the first corner another blast could be heard from behind at the same instant the back window spider-webbed from the shot hitting the glass. She turned right and then quickly turned left at the next corner. It was then that she felt a warm trickle down her face and hastily checked the rearview mirror. She had small pieces of glass embedded in her scalp and her neck next to her jaw bone. She kept on going, terrified that the man would follow her and shoot again. A hand tried to staunch the flow of blood; it became gooey with the slippery fluid.

* * * * * *

The streets were even more of a spectacle. Houses were on fire. Cars were overturned and burning. Flags were being waved around as groups chanted, "kill them now, kill them now, kill them now!" Some of the flags were Christian flags and the others were the Stars and Stripes. They watched as one house, a block and a half away, was being looted. A woman was pleading with them to stop. She held her bangs back and asked someone, anyone, to shine their black-light on her forehead. Obviously she had been stamped, yet falsely accused. They ignored her, deep into their revelry and thirst for bloody gain.

The three with infant had to back up and retrace their route to get around one riot after another. They were still in town and the fuel gauge dropped to one eighth. The needed highway seemed unreachable. They pulled to the side of the road again for what seemed like the hundredth time when a police cruiser came up behind them, lights flashing. They had no place to go; they were trapped. They hoped beyond hope that the patrol car would go forward to deal with the riot in front of them. Instead, it slowed. The officer in front stared into the sedan and made eye contact with Jason and Mike in the front seats. He looked and then moved slowly forward. From the backseat Rachael gasped, "Follow him!" Both Mike and Jason looked at her in consternation. "That's my angel! I recognize him. He's leading us through!" Jason moved behind the cruiser and down the street, a parade of two. Looters stopped and edged toward the fringes of the strip mall where they had been invading the shops. They were ready to run. Slowly the police car angled around the wreckage of cars and burning donation bins. Display stands were piled along with shipping pallets to create a huge bonfire. Jason kept to the patrol car like a backpack on a student. Another scene followed the first. Here a city bus was tipped on its side and posse members were extracting passengers and checking for CNSs. A produce truck was leaning against a street pole. Crates of vegetables were flying out of the back of the truck, being thrown there by persons inside. Others were scavenging the loot, putting the spoils in the backs of their vehicles. Mike and Jason turned their heads momentarily to see the destruction. Rachael kept watching her angel lead the way. Her fears and concerns of the past days were thrown into perspective. God had sent a messenger to carry them through. She vowed then and there to hug her angel at the earliest possible moment.

Fewer buildings dotted the landscape as they edged out of town. Then the cruiser slowed and pulled to the side of the road. The emergency lights still oscillated in blue and red on top of the roof. Jason pulled up to the side of the vehicle; the angel smiled and reversed the cruiser to return into town. Calmed by the experience, they drove a dark highway slowly gaining altitude. Flying snow created a monotonous kaleidoscope of white upon dark, as flakes angled inward toward the windshield. The trio was in a comfort zone of thought realizing the close proximity of heavenly beings.

Pulling her out of her revelry was a fussing infant clambering for nutrition. This was the moment she dreaded. Would the little one reject the meager offering she would provide? She tried crackers first. There was a box of infant cereal back in the

> *The trio was in a comfort zone of thought realizing the close proximity of heavenly beings.*

SUV they had to leave at their former home. Megan had started her on a little cereal augmented by breast milk. Rachael took out the box of almost empty crackers and crushed them in her hands to make them smaller. She had them almost to dust in a bowl when she discovered she had neglected to take a spoon with her. "I forgot a spoon," she said out loud. "I guess I'll just use a finger."

"Dad, you can make a spoon out of a credit card," Jason instructed. "Here, take my pocket knife."

"I suppose I should cut up my credit cards. Wouldn't want some criminal to get a hold of them," he said with a wry smile.

"Yeah, they might empty your bank account. You wouldn't want that. How would you pay for my college education?" Jason quipped in return.

Mike set to work carving a spoon out of his Visa card. Rachael mixed the dust with water using her index finger. She gave little Tabitha a taste and immediately she sucked on the finger hoping for some milk. Removing the finger to get more caused her to fuss. Mike finished his creation by trimming off the rough edges and handing his work of art over the seat to his wife. Rachael washed it off with water and dipped it in the bowl. It carried a healthier size lump of wet mush. Tabitha took it and squished it out her lips. Obviously, it was a relatively new experience for her and the taste was foreign. Rachael continued the process.

"This is working for now, but I think there's only enough for another feeding. After that, I'll have to improvise. I hope Jesus is coming soon or we get to the cabin," she wistfully said.

Jason turned the headlights off thinking that it would attract less attention out in the countryside if he drove with parking lights only. He didn't want to telegraph their coming or going to anyone watching the road. The smaller lights were enough to weakly illuminate the reflectors along the side of the road. The car was the only source of light. All eyes, even Rachael's in the back seat, were glued on the road ahead. Fed and satisfied, a pacifier soothed the baby. Rachael began to sing, *Guide me, O Thou great Jehovah, pilgrim through this barren land;* The men in front joined in, *I am weak, but Thou art mighty; hold me with Thy powerful hand.* It gave them courage and conviction. It also caused them to focus on how God had sent a familiar angel to get them away from the chaos downtown.

Jason provided an update on their status, "Ya'know, we've been driving on empty for twenty minutes and…" Just then, as he was going up a small hill, the engine started to chug and gulp for fuel. As he came over the rise, it caught again and they drove on.

"What are we going to do if it stops?" she asked. Then as if on cue, it stopped. Jason put it into neutral and let it coast as far as it could.

"Normally it wouldn't be wise to leave a car in the middle of nowhere in a snow storm. And…if we stay in the car to keep warm, someone's bound to pass by and we don't know what kind of a person that will be. We need to stay out of harm's way if we can," Mike voiced the alternatives.

"Fleeing in the winter is a bummer!" Jason exclaimed.

"Can we push the car off the road and hide in it? Then we could stay in the car for awhile and keep warm in the blankets. Maybe the storm will lessen," Rachael suggested.

"Sounds like a plan to me," Jason agreed.

The two men got out and pushed. Rachael was about to help when headlights could be seen in the distance. They were coming fast. Rachael grabbed the baby and the tote bag and Mike grabbed some blankets and water. Jason did the same and closed the doors. They ran to the trees and deep into the woods.

* * * * * *

Janelle got to a nearby park where she could see in almost every direction and be somewhat secluded from view by the playground and bathroom structures. She collapsed on the steering wheel in emotional exhaustion. Not one of her nightmares, in all of her young life, could equal the horror of being shot at. She slowly, mechanically, took a tissue and tried to wipe the blood off of her face and neck. Looking in the vanity mirror she pulled out the pieces of glass stuck in her skin. One was stuck into an elongated gash that was generating the most blood. She dabbed at the wound. "That will definitely leave a scar," she said to herself. Then as an afterthought, "but, not forever." The conversation with herself served to comfort her on the issues at hand. They were temporary trials. Soon they would be over. Her heartbeat slowed and her respirations turned to semi-normal. She prayed. Being alone and frightened was not her first choice. She knew her folks would worry about her every minute. Darin was right in sending her back to her parents and he needed to be with his family. However, neither one of them counted on her home being taken over by a vagrant with a shotgun. It was supposed to be a quick trip to her place and she would be safe. Now she felt that they had both made a wrong decision.

A car drove around the opposite side of the park. She willed it to keep going, hoping it would not see her and stop. She held her breath, waiting to see what it would do. It went onward. Then she realized that she still had her foot on the brake pedal. A red glow from the tail lights bathed the bushes, trees, and swirling snowflakes behind her. Her foot came off the pedal as if it had been about to touch a viper. She had to laugh at herself for not being aware of what she was doing. She knew God was taking care of her, but she also knew that she had to participate in her own survival. It was like salvation; it was free and accomplished at the cross, but she had to want to be forgiven. Jesus told her to flee from the tribulation that had come. She had to perform her part and He would perform His.

She made a compress of a wad of tissue and held it against the wound. Blood was drying and crusting on her neck. She had a decision to make. Should she try to go back to Darin or should she try to find her parents? The second option made her wonder where they could be. They had to be on foot, or maybe not. They could be in the other car. But, why would they be in the other car if the man had tried to take hers also. He was obviously collecting cars for himself. Jason could be in the other car. Where was Jason? Was he helping them? Nothing was for sure.

She had a decision to make. Should she try to go back to Darin or should she try to find her parents?

Darin had said he had a strong feeling that they needed her. He said he felt it was because of his prayer. It comforted her that he was praying for her and her family. On the thought that Darin had a strong feeling, she decided to try and find her folks. Her first thought, after praying, was to go to Aunt Megan's place. It was the only plan that made sense. It wasn't too far and it was in a quiet neighborhood. Driving there she stopped at every road and then zipped across when it seemed safe.

She knew she mustn't unnecessarily alert Uncle Walt that she was there based on the last time she saw him. She had to see if Megan was there or had gone with her folks. She planned on looking around first. Maybe she would be fortunate and they would be making one last appeal to Megan. The house was dark. There was a light on in the back of the house in the family room. The changing scenes of the TV cast an oscillating bluish glow in the room. She pressed her face against the window and tried to see into the room through a tiny crack in the curtain. She could see an empty couch and her uncle's legs sitting in the lounger. No Megan could be seen. She had to get some information; she circled around to the front and quietly tapped on the window of the door. It was cold and the wait was interminable. She tapped again. After several minutes she was about to make a more determined approach and ring the doorbell. Megan came to the door and opened it brusquely.

"Why are you here!?" Her voice was harsh and commanding.

"I'm looking for Mom and Dad. Have they been here?" Megan seemed to weigh the words she was about to say. Her eyes set in a harsh glare.

"They've been here and gone. You need to go." It was not the Aunt Megan Janelle knew. Her personality had changed.

"Were they walking?"

"Why would they be walking, for Pete's sake? They've got a screaming baby with them! I saw them get in their car."

"They have Tabitha! Why?"

"Get away! Leave me alone. GO!" Megan emphasized her words by slamming the door. Janelle was struck with the nastiness Megan was exhibiting. All the good, gentle qualities of her loving and loveable aunt were gone, replaced with the artistry of Satan. She almost tapped again, but a siren was heard coming into the neighborhood. She slipped off the porch and ran to the van. She had to find her folks. She concluded that Megan was so into her own world she was unable to see another person's distress, unable to see Janelle's bloody head and neck wounds.

* * * * * *

They slunk back to the car after the truck went by. This time they succeeded in pushing the car off the road and down into the ditch. Jason went back into the forest to break off pine boughs. He returned to cover the car. Rachael and Tabitha settled in the back seat with a blanket. The fully awake baby wanted to see and experience everything. Going back to sleep was not on her agenda.

Snow was starting to collect on the car. The ground was still too warm to allow the snow to remain in a solid state. Each had their own thoughts about what they should be doing. The cabin was several hours away by car, and many more hours by foot. Walking to their other car several miles away in town was an ordeal under the circumstances. Trekking to the cabin with a baby and all of its needs would be impossible, especially when they hiked away from the ambient lights of the city reflecting off of the clouds. It was tempting to remain in the car out of the snow and cold. Another car jolted them out of their complacency. It raced along the wet highway and seemed to want to go on its way, but the brake lights came on and it slowed as if to stop. Instantly the three were about to run back into the woods. Hands were on door handles and then they relaxed as the red brake lights shut off and the car went on. It caused them to think of their need to be out of sight and moving to a real place of safety. What were they supposed to do? Stay put, or move on? So far they had been somewhat obedient to the divine command to flee. Yet Heidi and Veronica were staying home in their house, too feeble to be running away. God had protected them in the city when they were trying to get past the rioting. Should they sit there and hope for His continued protection? Would it be presumptuous? The baby could be an excuse like old age could be an excuse for the elderly. They debated the alternatives as they kept eyes glued on the dark where the highway lurked behind the black screen of impenetrable night.

Sounds were heard on the forested side of the car. A grizzly bear sniffed at their tracks, following them to the car. It half ran, half walked to the car, anticipating its first meal of protein after waking up from hibernation. He could smell the human meat inside the car. No longer under the controlling spirit of God, he rose up on two legs and placed his paws on the passenger side window. He was crazed by hunger and nature's strange changes of no fresh water, scorching heat, light, snow, and darkness. His keen eyes could see them inside. He pushed at the window attempting to get in. He roared in frustration. Beating the side window caused cracks, but thankfully did not fully cave-in the window. Agitation compelled him to look for another way in. He circled the car, testing windows, beating and clawing on the hood and trunk. Loud sounds of banging and scratching frightened Tabitha. She reacted with flailing arms and feet. She wailed in surprised fear. When the bear climbed on top of the sedan he used all four paws to assault the roof by jumping up and down and clawing at the sun-roof window to break in. The roof bowed inward under his weight depressing almost down to the head rests.

> *A grizzly bear sniffed at their tracks … No longer under the controlling spirit of God, he rose up on two legs and placed his paws on the passenger side window. He was crazed by hunger and nature's strange changes of no fresh water, scorching heat, light, snow, and darkness.*

There wasn't an avenue of escape. They were trapped. Rachael was praying furiously in the back seat, holding the baby to her chest. Mike had his hands on the sunroof window pushing upward in hopes that it would keep from popping out of its rims. Jason had his pocket knife out, pointing at whatever seemed like the most eminent place where the bear could achieve an entrance. A back-seat door window behind the driver's seat shattered under the pressure. Rachael squeezed herself against the opposite door. Jason turned full in his chair to face the forthcoming attack. Mike ripped the lid off of a console between the seats. It was the only weapon he could think off in the moment. It wasn't as much a weapon as a small shield to bat at the bear if he tried to come in. And, the grizzly did find the open window.

He first stuck his nose in the bent window, sniffed, and then reached in with a huge, long arm. Jason attacked, stabbing and poking. Mike bashed it downward with the padded lid. Their efforts were counterproductive—Mike causing Jason to miss more than connect. The bear withdrew his paw in favor of looking in to see where his tasty morsels were. Jason took the opportunity to stab it in the nose. He aimed for the eye, but missed. The assailant became enraged, clawing and roaring into the cavity of the vehicle. Long, dirty, hooked claws swiped the air breathlessly close to Rachael who was cringing against the far side of the back seat. Tabitha screeched with fright. Instead of poking and stabbing, Jason went for slicing at the hairy arm. Countless gashes began to take their toll. Blood drops flew around the interior. The beast went for Jason. The seat became ribbons of fabric and torn leather. The head rest was yanked free and pulled outside. Next the bear came for Jason at a lower vector trying to get at him as he hid behind the seat. The bear found the plastic bags and tote bag of food on the floor and yanked them outside. He tore through them searching, sniffing, and destroying. It provided Mike the moment he needed in which to take the baby into the front and lay her down in the foot space under the glove compartment. He was about to pull Rachael over, as well, but the animal had other ideas. He came at them with both arms ripping and tearing. It stuck its head inside and tried to muscle in further through the partially flattened window. Jason kept low behind the seat, slicing and stabbing from one side while Mike hit and punched from the other. The grizzly dropped back down on all fours and stared at the window. Rachael dove over the seat in the space between the two front seats. Mike pulled her by her clothes to help. At least now she had a barrier between them and the backseat. They waited for the next onslaught. The grizzly approached the side of the car.

* * * * * *

"Think, think! Where could they be?" Janelle told herself. *"No, pray! I need to pray. Where are they Lord? Where should I go?"* Her mind worked over the possibilities. *"I have to find them. They have Tabitha with them and they're walking. The plan was to go to the cabin, but that's too far to walk. Oh, where should I go?"*

To say Janelle was in a quandary was to state the obvious. She felt overwhelmed with worry for her folks and couldn't contact them. Her world was closed down and the modern aids to communication and information were not at her command. She was thrown into one-on-one dependency with God. She knew He was with her. She just had to find out what He wanted her to do. Her next prayer was a stab at dialogue. "Lord, what should I do?" She paused and waited for her thoughts to run free. She was listening. Her mind drifted over several possibilities, but the one that stood out was that she should find them. "Lord, where should I look?" Again, she listened to the random thoughts that floated through her consciousness. She thought they might go to a member's home, maybe even Mrs. McKessy's house. It was the most logical for reasons of distance. But her mind kept nudging her to consider the cabin option. It was illogical to think of them trying to walk all the way to the cabin, in a snow storm, with a baby. She tried to dismiss the thought and go to other possibilities. She forced herself to move on, but the cabin option kept coming back. "They would really be in trouble if they tried to walk there. That can't be where they're going." She had to admit if she was trying to listen to God's answers she was definitely pushing away from a predominating thought. It stopped her and she had to admit she should listen. In the end she decided to go to Mrs. McKessy first and then maybe the highway toward the cabin as a second choice.

She put the car into gear and drove toward Heidi's home. She went two blocks and found a road block of several stalled cars parked haphazardly across the road. She backed up and drove away to another street and found a dead-end sign announcing that the street had no outlet. She took a long detour and ran into a riot rampaging for blocks in the direction she wanted to go. In the dark with the snow whirling around the lights, she was in danger of being lost. She stopped to figure out where she could be and was startled by a sharp rap on the driver's side window and a zombie-like man who demanded a ride. He didn't look human. He looked in dire need of help. She wanted to aid a suffering soul, but not get caught by a lunatic. She hesitated. He banged again on the window and yelled an obscenity. The prints from his hand were on the window, smudges of blood and pus. When he turned his face forward the glow from her headlights illuminated his face. It was a mass of bleeding, bubbly boils. She concluded he was not one of the faithful who had been injured. The telltale sign of oozing sores and his vocabulary spoke of his allegiance to the beast. She drove away only to find him hanging on the luggage rack as she tried to get away. Her inclination was to not hurt him. She didn't have the killer instinct and yet she didn't want to let him in. She slowed down and yelled through the closed window, "Please get off. I don't want to give you a ride!" He persisted, with more highly spiced words, and she tried swerving back and forth to shake him off. She wasn't driving fast enough to faze him. "Help me, Lord." In front of her about a block away a parked car beckoned. Instead of shaking him off she would brush him off. She approached slowly; he got the message. He let go of the handle and tried to run around to the other side of the car where the window was shattered. Janelle saw it and stepped on the gas pedal. She was so close to the parked car that both side view mirrors were ripped off, hers and the parked car. The mirror on her side dangled by a few wires and clattered against the side. It attracted attention as it flapped against the door as she careened down to the corner. He started to throw rocks at her, some of which went through the rear window and clunked against the seats and the floor. She raced around the corner to meet a posse of vigilantes pre-occupied with building a fire with cardboard boxes next to an overturned Cadillac Escalade with fluid dribbling out and down the gutter. Slamming on the brakes alerted them to her and they turned. Their eyes, lit by the flickering flames, created an eerie luster to their glistening orbs. Smoke surrounded them. The combined effect caused them to appear as demons from sulfurous furnaces. Throwing the van in reverse, she started to back away only to find that the man she avoided before was stumbling down the street after her as a creepy rendition of a walking dead man. Beset from in front and behind, she frantically looked for a way out. "O, Lord. What should I do now?"

At that moment the fire caught and jumped onto the Caddy and then whooshed down the gutter following the trail of fuel. Two seconds later the fuel tank exploded sending rolling balls of flame outward. Men ran for their lives, clearing a path for Janelle to motor past.

She raced down the street for a mile and then tentatively looked down another avenue in the direction she was attempting to go. More rioters were blocking her way. She paused to think; *when a door closes it must be a sign.* She knew she had to give up on plan A and change to plan B. The drive toward the highway was mostly through residential neighborhoods, yet she still had to encounter joy-riding teenagers looking to join in on the fun. They were throwing firecrackers at houses and using baseball bats to whack off roadside mailboxes. Out on the highway the night closed in around her. The snow had stopped and no stars dotted the sky.

* * * * * *

The hungry, thirsty, frustrated grizzly shoved at the side of the car repeatedly with both front paws. The car rocked from one side to another. Being pricked with a pocket knife was like being stung by pesky bees while collecting sweet honey. There, the reward was worth the minor annoy-ance. Here, no reward was forthcoming. He was desperate for quick sus-tenance after being rudely awaked by searing, soaring temperatures and a waterless wasteland. Roaring his frustration, he took another swipe at the interior of the car, clawing at air. He ambled off in search of a ready meal, more in the line of fast, docile food.

Tabitha was screaming back at the unknown, unseen beast. Her normally tranquil life had been upended by bashing, banging, and bellowing noises. Stuck down in a foot-well with bodies tightly packed into a small space above didn't help. She couldn't see, only hear, and what she heard was more than her limited experience could tolerate.

Mike and Rachael maneuvered awkwardly to position themselves side by side. He was in the middle still holding his tiny battered shield toward the back, side window. She was attempting to organize the baby into her arms to soothe the troubled soul. The pacifier was lost in the back seat. She stuck a finger in her mouth as a substitute.

Jason was ready to continue the fight even though he felt it was not a fair one. He watched as the hairy backside disappeared in the velvety blackness. Its direction was up and over the road, possibly into the trees opposite. Tension oozed from his body and he took a normal breath for the first time in twenty minutes. "Mom, Dad, I'm guessing I won't be taking this car to college when the time comes. Too bad, 'cause it's a neat, full-size compact car now, more of a low rider really."

Mike and Rachael were breathing so hard that it resembled the exhaustion one would have after finishing a long sprint. They only smiled weakly at Jason's attempt at humor. Their decision to stay put or walk onward was made for them. They had no choice but to stay in the flattened sedan. They couldn't risk tangling with the grizzly out in the open. Mike made efforts to fortify their position against future attack. He reclined the seat fully and then moved in the back. With some struggle he removed the back portion of the back seat and crammed it into the open window. Jason reclined his seat downward, pinning it in place. If the bear came back and tried again it would have to claw at a metal frame with springs covered in leather and padding.

They were in the midst of making a warm nest out of blankets when another vehicle cut the darkness with its beams of light. The snow had stopped and was replaced with a growing ground fog. They held their breath hoping not to be seen. It drew nearer and nearer slowing as it came. In the pitch-black darkness its headlights carved two holes in the night. The vehicle slowed and then came to a stop. A flashlight came out, searched the ground, and played on the squashed car. Multiple doors to a crew van opened and slammed. Voices could be heard.

"It looks like an accident, maybe a rollover."

"Okay, check it out."

Jason pushed his face against the window to see who it might be, possibly someone willing to rescue them.

"Hey, I see someone."

"Take your black light. See if they're one of us. We might have hit the jackpot." Several more doors opened and closed. More flashlights swept the landscape. They came down the hill in clusters. One scanned the ground looking for rollover marks when he stopped.

"Wait! Look at that! Bear tracks. Big ones! Really big ones! Fresh too!" Everyone stopped and the flashlights revolved in strobe patterns in all directions looking for evidence of a nearby bear. One knelt, examining the tracks with a practiced eye and a bare hand. "These are real fresh, not more than a couple of minutes ago. They're still warm." The beams of light whirled around again, only with more intensity and purpose.

"I don't like this."

"Neither do I."

"Let's find someone else and collect their bounty. We're just sittin' ducks out here. The brute could be behind that car for all we know." The self-appointed posse edged back up the hill with flashlights and shotguns pointed like a battleship in every direction. Doors slammed again and the large utility van moved off and down the road.

"'Be thankful in everything,' I never thought I'd be thankful for a bear," Mike breathed.

"There's a bounty on our heads!? Way cool! This is like a western!" Jason exclaimed.

"Jason! I can't count this as an adventure. I'm not sharing your enthusiasm," Mike corrected.

"Me neither!" Rachael shuddered in response. "This is the most danger I've ever been in. I can't just laugh it off."

"Give it a couple of thousand years, then you will. We know the ending, right?"

"You have a weird type of faith, I'll give you that much," Mike tried to be fair.

"It works, doesn't it?"

"Now what are we going to do?!" Rachael went for the most frustrating of issues that faced them. "We're trapped either way. If we stay here, some roving bandits will find us. If we leave this squashed tin can, the bear could get us!"

"We pray," Mike stated.

"I'll pray with my eyes wide open and my bloody knife in my hands. That'll be a first for me," Jason added.

They importuned, hoping for a turn of events that would take them away from their holding cell. It was only minutes until lights again sliced through the fog. They fixed their eyes on the coming vehicle, wanting it to pass by without incident, praying that it would not see them. Jason kicked himself for not jumping out and covering the car with the pine boughs. This is not how they had envisioned escaping to the mountains to meet Jesus. They were cringing at every sound, light, or movement. With dread heavy on their hearts, they watched as the vehicle approached and sped by. Their emotions made a hiccup as they were momentarily relieved that it didn't stop or see them, because in the same instant they felt relief from their fears they also recognized the familiar shape of a van, like their missionary van. Perhaps Janelle had passed them by. Defeat is more intense when it is stabbed with a fleeting instant of rescue and then hope is ripped away once more. The mind can't keep up with the changes in the emotions. If their trepidation was in the basement before, it was in the grave now. They prayed for God to turn the circumstances around. They specifically wanted Janelle to turn around, but then the thought turned to doubt. Was that really their van or was it one that looked like it? It was a popular model.

CHAPTER 22

It didn't matter that the clouds obscured the sky; the fifth plague of darkness enclosed everything in sackcloth. The only ambient light was the reflection of city lights off of the clouds. Fog emanated from the warm ground as it mixed with the cooler air. It made one feel like an actor fruitlessly trying to find the opening to the stage curtain in a darkened theater. Darkness is a perfect medium for the Devil's tantrum—the darker the better. His minions were everywhere, encouraging the baser tendencies of the human animal. Anarchy was the norm. Evil was darker than the plague of darkness. No individual was safe, not even co-perpetrators of crime. Gangs of thugs turned on each other, leaving dead and wounded lying in gutters and draped over garden walls. The clouds were like blankets covering naughty children who thought they could not be seen while they carried out impish behaviors.

> *Darkness is a perfect medium for the Devil's tantrum—the darker the better. His minions were everywhere, encouraging the baser tendencies of the human animal.*

Janelle drove past smoldering shells of burned cars. House fires lit the night sky from a distance. She thought of how this was worse than she imagined it would be. One of the Bible texts her father had read recently came to mind. She tried to, but couldn't, remember the exact words. "The Lord must cut short those days for the elect's sake." She knew it was not correct in the wording she remembered, but the message was very clear to her now. Jesus was saying that this was going to be a terrible time. Her shoulders hunched over the steering wheel as she peered into the fog ahead. The van was cold from the wind blowing in the shattered window. She had the heater on full blast. It only helped a little. Tension eased a smidgen as she drove through forested land. She saw another wreck on the side of the road with its roof smashed down. It was obviously a rollover. It was a relief to be out of the city away from the riots and chaos. Her thoughts jumped from one subject to the other. She wondered how religious people could dismiss the hatred that was being demonstrated in the name of making the world peaceful and righteous. Wouldn't there be at least one person who would say, "this can't be right." Believers with the truth understood, but why couldn't intelligent people put it together? Were their consciences ruined in a flash when the Spirit of God left the world? Feeling anguish for the victims and despair for not being able to find her folks, she was at the point of believing that they had become casualties in the city. Mile after mile passed as she drove the van toward the cabin.

* * * * * *

"She didn't see us. That was our van, right? It had to be Janelle," Jason questioned. His cavalier faith was being pushed to the limit. Mike answered with a, "I don't know for sure."

Rachael was still trying to calm the baby. Tabitha fussed some more. The finger was not as good as a pacifier.

Mike went inside himself to try to figure out a plan and push aside his disappointment. His mouth felt like sandpaper. If he was thirsty, then they had to be thirsty. It was at least something he could do. Rummaging around in the back seat in total darkness he found some water bottles that had not interested the bear. He offered first before he partook. The water cooled his nervous throat and calmed his anxiety just a bit. He wanted to get through to safety and hideout until the Savior came to the rescue. He didn't want his family members to suffer, to be in pain, or be killed. All would turn out right in the end, but avoiding injury would be his first choice. He believed His Redeemer had told him to flee for that very reason. He chastised himself for not leaving earlier. It had to be his fault. A question from Jason jolted him out of momentary remorse.

"I think I should try to cover up the car again with pine boughs; that would help don't you think?"

"Yes, I do," he answered.

"Jason, don't go out there! It's dangerous," Rachael urged.

"Don't worry, mom. I'm not planning on getting to heaven by passing through the digestive tract of a grizzly."

"I'll help him and keep an eye out for the bear. Jason, turn on the headlights so we can see," Mike added.

"If you must go out there, while you're out, can you see what might be salvaged from the food the bear took. It didn't sound like he ate any of it. He took the bags of food and I'm going to need something for the baby. Be careful, please," Rachael asked.

The first thing Jason did was to cover the back of the car so the reflectors in the light panels could not be seen from down the road. The other bough he put on the roof. He wanted more. He cautiously went to the nearest tree to break some off. Mike was busy looking through the trampled mud and grass for anything he could salvage. The tote bag was ripped open. The box of crackers was in shreds, scattered to the four points of the compass. Rachael had taken some small pre-peeled carrots out of the refrigerator and these were thrown everywhere. He collected the ones he could find, brushed them off, and put them in his pocket. They would need to be washed. A hand of bananas was flattened into muddy ooze. He found the bottle of cranberry/grape juice and slid it into his other pocket. The remainder of items were scattered outward as if they had been at the epicenter of an explosion. He collected what he could and brought them back inside the car. He took one long look and saw what looked like a car coming over the hill from the front.

"Jason, quick! A car is coming!" Mike shut off the headlights and ducked into the sedan. Jason jumped in beside them after tossing a bough on the roof. He shut the door. To their consternation, the dome light in the car remained on—a convenience for a driver finding the keys and the seat belt in the dark. Their hide-a-way was glowing nicely at the side of the road. Father and son were trying to turn it off or cover it with their hands.

* * * * * *

Janelle was making good time driving the familiar road to the cabin. No other wreckage blocked her way or decorated the side of the road. The steady hum of the wheels on the pavement acted as a comforting agent as she thought of what she had been through. She almost forgot her primary mission of finding her folks. Then she calculated the distance. They could not have walked this far. She hit the brakes and turned back. With mounting fear in her heart she drove back toward the city of hate. Placing herself in their position she decided that they would not walk directly on the road. She slowed down to a crawl and rolled down the windows. She hoped to see into the woods on both sides of the road. Mounting a hill she saw a tiny glow in the hazy fog. It flickered and then went out. As she neared, she slowed even more. A scary thought crossed her mind: what if it was someone out to get her? She drove into the oncoming lane and then aimed the headlights directly at the car. It looked a mess. With a dab more courage she stuck her head out the window, "Hello? Is anyone in there? Are you all right?"

Almost in unison they yelled out, "Janelle." Jason was out in a flash, waving his arms. Janelle was ecstatic. She had found them. There was a reunion in the fog at the side of the road. Everyone was talking. Rachael was carrying the baby and throwing caution to the wind—she needed to hug her daughter, big bear or not. After quick greetings, questions followed at machine-gun speed. Rachael worried over why Janelle was bleeding; Janelle wanted to know why the car was smashed flat; Mike needed to know why the side window was gone in the van; and Jason was curious about the shotgun blast marks. All the questions came at once.

"Hold on! Hold on. We need to get out of here; the bear may come back," Mike warned. "We need to get away from here."

"Okay, Dad. But, can you drive? I'm exhausted. Wait! Did you say bear?" Janelle quickly scanned the darkness enveloping them on every side.

"I'll tell you when we are on the road and safe. Jason, Janelle, we need to grab everything we can from the car. Honey, get in the van with the baby. There isn't a moment to lose." Mike took charge. Everything they could salvage was tossed into the van, including the pacifier which he found under the seat. Janelle saw the evidence of a bear attempting to crack open the sedan; large claw marks everywhere. Her ordeal seemed smaller by comparison. Soon they were on the road to the cabin.

Mike looked at the fuel tank gauge and found it to be at about a quarter of a tank. Maybe, just maybe, they might make it to their coveted sanctuary. The stories started to unfold. Janelle was ganged-up upon because it was three against one. Her story was told first. Rachael was beside herself with belated worry for her daughter. She crooned over her wounds and dabbed at them with a moistened towel. Jason looked at the destroyed driver's seat and the marks of deflected pellets all over the left side interior.

"It looks like a war zone in here!"

"Yeah, I felt it on the back of the neck, like a whoosh," Janelle explained. Rachael then went to lift up her hair and saw where a sizeable tress had been clipped off. It was indeed very close. She couldn't help but praise God for His providence. She wanted to interrupt and tell of the police cruiser with her angel inside. Her interruption got everyone tumbling over each other again in telling their perceptions of what they had experienced. Janelle reacted with a shudder when she heard more of the grizzly story.

"I thought in the tribulation, that what we would experience would be from the unrighteous trying to destroy the righteous before Jesus could save them. I never thought that the world would go mad and we would have to fear the animals as well!" she said.

"God put the fear of man in the animals. When the spirit was withdrawn from the world, I guess it was withdrawn from the animals too, maybe. I don't know for sure, but it seems like it," Mike guessed.

Additional stories of their ordeals compelled them to thank God for His protection and the way He had protected at the most difficult points in their flight to safety. They even talked about how George, Sheila, and the boys were waiting for them at the cabin.

"What boys?"

"Andrew and Greg Cox, and my soccer buddy Steve Rojas."

"Wait! Did you say the Cox brothers are at our cabin?!" Janelle reacted.

"Yes, we did. Jason spent some quality time with them and led them to Jesus. They knew the message because their grandparents had paid for them to be in the academy, but it took his personal touch to bring them into a heart relationship with Him."

"Hey, you scrawny little Swede, I'm impressed!" Janelle complimented.

"No big deal. The Holy Spirit did most of the work. They were just surprised I'd come to talk with them, mano-a-mano," Jason answered.

At 2:00 a.m. they came to a not-so-sleepy mountain town. They slowed down and Rachael made a request, "Do you think me might be able to get some food for the baby?" They agreed to look. The trip down Main Street revealed that many lights were on. Stores were closed and a log cabin restaurant had a sign out front that read:

BOUNTY HUNTERS WELCOME

FRESH HOMEMADE APPLE PIE

At the other end of town there was a filling station with a 24-hour convenience store. It was open; however, a bar stood next door that was in the midst of late Friday night revelry which spilled out into the parking lot filled with Harleys and pick-up trucks. Mike slipped the van in beside the convenience store opposite and out of sight of the bar. He left the van running and ready to leave in a hurry if need be. He and Jason found baby food, baby cereal, and a bottle. They brought it to the checkout counter which was fortified with thick glass to protect the sales clerk. Obviously, a necessity for the location the store was in. The sleepy clerk started to reach for the items and Mike made his request, "We've had a bit of difficulty and our cards don't work. Could you take some gold coins as payment? The baby is very hungry." Mike slid several gold Canadian Maple leaf coins across the counter—their worth fifty times the cost of the food. The clerk pulled the coins over the counter and picked up one of them, flipped it over and slapped it down on the counter top.

"I'll have to ring up these items." He took all of the items, scanning each one and placing it in a bag on his side of the window. Then he took the coins and put them in his pocket. "Show me your CNS."

"We don't have the stamp. That's why we're needing…" Mike stopped talking because a revolver came out from behind the counter.

"I thought so. Stay where you are or I'll shoot! I'm calling the police." He picked up a cell phone and started moving out of his secure room, unlocking the door. Jason shoved a display stand over and it crashed down in front of the check-out room's door. He next shoved his father toward the door. They ran.

The hasty exit attracted the attention of the parking lot parties; they looked. The clerk exited the store and fired three rounds at the fleeing van. Then he shouted. "They're fugitives without the stamp. Get'em!" He pointed at the van as it sped past another sign advertising a community town hall meeting:

TOWN HALL MEETING

SATURDAY 2 PM

SHERIFF TOM BACKUS

"HOW TO MAKE

A CITIZEN'S ARREST"

Motorcycles were the first to fire up and roar out onto the road. Then trucks and cars were competing to be in the vanguard of the pursuit.

The Larssons were in a losing situation. The van could not out run motorcycles. As the road weaved in and out, and over hills and ridges, they could look back and see the lights looming closer.

"They're going to catch us if we don't find a turn-off fast! And preferably one that's just around the corner or over a hill where they can't see our brake lights," Mike planned out loud. A few minutes later, the lead cycles were a mere hundred yards behind and gaining.

"O, Lord, please help us!" Janelle prayed while swiveling her head back and forth. Her prayer echoed everyone else's inner prayer. Mike drove on, and then they all gasped at the same time. They could see a large pine tree, a massive sentinel of the forest, gradually gaining speed as it dropped for the highway in front of them. This would end their flight right here with a crash and a capture. Defeat was in every fiber of their bodies except Mike's right foot—it was flat to the mat with the accelerator in between. The trunk of the tree came breathlessly close to the roof as branch tips scraped on it, catching the roof rack on the left side of the van, ripping it off. They were safe on the other side as the giant spruce tree shattered branches into kindling and cratered a long trough in the road behind them. The pursuers were momentarily cut off.

Mike raced the van over a small hill and found a turn-off to the right in a dense forest. Unknown to them, angel engineers had created a road into the forest and just as quickly had replanted full-grown trees behind them within seconds. They quickly turned off the engine and lights and held their breath. Three minutes later

> *Unknown to them, angel engineers had created a road into the forest and just as quickly had replanted full-grown trees behind them within seconds.*

motorcycles roared by and ten minutes after that the trucks and cars raced around the bend. When the lights winked out in the distance, it left them in pitch black darkness in the van. It took another fifteen minutes before they began to relax. Tabitha redirected the focus with her fussing in the dark. The pacifier was once again not enough and she wanted something to fill her tummy. Mike offered a handful of carrots from his pocket. He cautioned that they would need to be washed off. In the dark they would have to go by feel.

"Mom, she can't take raw carrots! They have to be cooked," Janelle reacted.

"I know, I know. We have to improvise." A distinctive 'thwrack' with a hollow echo sound came from Rachael's corner. She had taken a bite of a carrot.

"Mom... what are you doing?"

"I'm chumamwing am carmmroute."

"What?"

Rachael paused until she had space in her mouth to talk clearly. She kept chewing while she answered.

"I'm chewing a carrot into tiny pieces and then I'll feed it to her." She kept chewing and chewing.

"Ugh! That's awful!" Janelle exclaimed.

"My grandma's grandma did it for her children during the depression. It's called premastication. Some call it kiss-feeding. We'll see if she takes it. Actually, we'll have to feel if she takes it because I can't see a thing."

"Mom, what if she catches something from you? Her tiny little system is so new, maybe not completely developed yet."

"Well, I guess we'll just have to see if a pediatrician is among the saved."

Janelle had to smile at that thought, but no one could see her reaction. Mother and daughter strived together to give the baby something that would satisfy her hunger, feeling her mouth and chin constantly. Rachael would feed her and Janelle would catch the food she would spit out and then attempted reentry. Tabitha was not interested. They tried water out of a regular bottle with a screw-on cap in what they imagined was tiny little sips. Finally they asked for the interior light to be turned on. They found Tabitha covered in carrot mash. She looked like a raggedy pumpkin, soaked down the front of her onesie. She had to be changed but there was nothing to change her into. They swaddled her in towels to keep her warm. The carrots were marginally working. More sips of water were administered and then the pacifier plugged up the access. They knew it would not last. Thankfully, Tabitha went to sleep. The rest decided to try the same. It was almost four in the morning and they were exhausted. Jason took a spare jacket and shut it into the door frame at the top and tucked it into where the window used to be at the bottom. It cut down on the flow of cool air from outside. They all shared blankets and snuggled together the best they could.

Hours later they all awoke to the hungry cries of Tabitha. No one complained. The only sound uttered was a 'thwack' when Rachael bit into another carrot for the baby. It was tempting to eat one for herself. She was hungry. They all were hungry. Mike looked at his watch. The glow of the illuminated face was like a bright floodlight compared to the darkness outside. It was nine in the morning.

"I guess the plague of darkness is still happening, because it should be day by now. It's nine o'clock," he informed. No answer came from the crew, just the sounds of rustling around to stretch in the cramped space and the sound of Janelle rocking the baby in an attempt to console her. Soon the rocking had no effect. The pacifier no longer served its purpose. Rachael then brought the masticated carrot to the rescue. Rather than finger-feeding she went for the direct approach. Tabitha was on a strike. No matter how hungry she was at the time, food is what she wanted, not this strange tasting stuff. Some of it finally found its way into her belly. More carrot mash was proffered and wasted; the last little baby carrot was gone.

"You know, if this was a normal morning we would be on our way to church. This is Sabbath morning," Mike commented.

"Why don't we have worship right here," Janelle suggested.

"This will be different; we can't see a thing. Who's going to read scripture?" Jason asked sarcastically.

"I was thinking we could try to remember scripture and share it with one another," Mike answered.

"We could do that, and also, I think it would be nice to count our blessings. The Lord has been protecting us in so many wonderful ways," Rachael added.

"Do we have to sing? I hate singing, I'm not very good at it," Jason requested.

"Could this be the last worship service we have in this horrible world?" Janelle remarked. "I don't want to go through any more of this madness."

"This madness proves that Satan's claim is false. He claims that he can rule this world better than God; without God's controlling spirit, he has failed. This madness will only get worse if God allows it to continue," Mike explained.

"We almost died. I was almost killed. The people who rule this world now are stealing everything they can get their hands on. It's law by brute force. The strongest wins. Evil prevails." Janelle let her feelings and fear talk.

"The universe is watching this. Now there is no doubt. God has been vindicated. The story of Job in the Bible has been amplified to include the entire world. He protected Job's life when everything around him was destroyed—God's answer to Satan's argument. His hand has been with us because we are His. We've seen how He has sent His angels to help and protect us. One of those angels was named April. We have narrowly escaped capture, or worse, death. For instance, the bear almost killed us, but it didn't. Then the evidence of the bear saved us from who knows what at the hands of those men. God didn't send the bear to attack us, but because it did, the Lord could turn the experience into scaring the men away. We have seen with our own eyes the Lord's protection, but I believe that there are things He has done for us that we didn't see. I praise Him for His greatness," Mike said.

"I feel His presence. I know He is caring for us. I'm scared, but I'm assured we'll get through this," Rachael added.

The four frightened fugitives from false power shared their love for a God who kept them safe while His opposing argument with Satan was demonstrated. Bible texts came to mind and they repeated them, giving up-to-date applications of the meaning in terms of their immediate experiences. They even sang songs. Jason didn't join in, for obvious reasons, but he did listen to the words in the same way he had contributed when the Bible texts were applied. He even attempted to quietly sing, "We're marching to Zion," because it was so relevant. They didn't want to conclude with prayer because each prayed and then wanted to pray again. They didn't want to end because the Spirit of God joined them and they felt it. What brought their worship service to a close was a baby fussing for food.

"We have to get to the cabin and get something for this baby," Rachael directed. "I can try more water, but it won't help. She's just spitting out the pacifier."

"I think I'll try to head for the cabin," Mike answered. He turned on the engine, checked the fuel gauge, and backed out onto the highway. He drove, calculating in his head how much fuel he might still have in the tank, the relative mileage, and the distance they had to go. It didn't look promising. The turn off was an intermediate goal he set in his head. He wanted to at least get that far. It would mean walking on a dirt road rather than the open highway. It wasn't that he lacked in faith; he was just being practical.

Tabitha's fussing escalated; they had to stop to clean her off using more of the precious water. With a dry towel around her little bottom they continued down the road. In another hour-and-a-quarter she fussed again. It built into a full cry and she cried every mile. The small amount of carrot was not enough. She needed sustenance, demanding it in the only way she knew how.

"Mom, she knows the pacifier is not real food; she spits it out immediately. What are we going to do?" The traditional solution was not available. Rachael had nothing to offer. The van sputtered.

"Dad, if we can get to the top of this hill then we can coast down the other side," Jason counseled.

"The top of this hill is our turn off and the road to the cabin goes up from there. We'll have to stop up there anyway. I don't want this car to give away where we have gone. Those bounty hunters will recognize our car." They held their breath as the van sped forward. Mike tried to gain speed at the same time he gently rocked the van back and forth to get every ounce of fuel out of the tank. He sighed in relief as the van topped the hill and chugged to a stop. The road they needed angled up to the right. Without explanation they obeyed the unspoken requirement. They got out knowing they had to walk it from there.

"Dad, leaving the van here will tell the mob where we went," Jason pointed out.

"I know. I have a plan. When we get everything out that we need we'll push it down the highway."

"So what do you think they'll believe when they see a crashed van with no casualties inside?"

"They'll believe we've been raptured."

"Good one, Dad. I just wish I could see it."

The family took everything they thought might be useful. Jason fashioned a makeshift pack out of one of the jackets. Water was dwindling: only two half-liter bottles were left and one was partially gone. There was also the small bottle of cranberry/grape juice Mike was hanging on to for later…he didn't know why and he felt somewhat guilty for not offering it to the baby. He knew it would only last a little while in the child's stomach, but perhaps it would be needed to keep Tabitha quiet if the vigilantes were nearby and they were hiding. They wanted to hurry because Tabitha was giving away their position. She was attracting any listening ear in the vicinity. Maybe this would be the time to give the baby a little sip of the juice.

Rachael and Janelle walked several yards up the road while Mike and Jason set the car in neutral. Rachael took the baby into her arms and Tabitha reflexively went for her breast. It caused her to think of a way to fool the child into quietude. She pulled up her blouse, loosened her bra in the back, and let Tabitha have something familiar. It was an instant success. She attacked with fervor and the cries were absent in the darkness. Everyone breathed in relief.

"Mom, what did you do? She's quiet," Janelle asked.

"I gave her a better substitute for the pacifier. Maybe that will keep—" Rachael stopped mid-sentence. She felt the let-down response. Tabitha was eager, finally getting what she had been squawking for forever. Smacking noises were the loudest sound in the forest, until the grunts of the two men were heard pushing the van toward the cusp of the hill.

When the van started rolling on its own, father and son closed the doors and let it go. Eerily the dome light in the interior of the van glowed as it faded into the night. Then the light went out and nothing could be seen. The only noise was the sound of tires on pavement. They waited. Then the faint sound of gravel came back to them, then bushes gave up a snapping noise, and finally, there was a horrendous echo of crushing metal and shattering glass. Another smaller impact followed and then breaking and snapping of saplings as the wreck rolled down the hill, ending with a solid thud against a tree.

"Cool! I wonder if anybody survived the accident," Jason said sarcastically.

"We did," Mike answered. They turned and walk toward the women.

Janelle was figuring out what had happened with her mother and the baby. "Mom, I don't believe it! I didn't think that could happen at your age."

"Thanks for highlighting my age. No, this does not happen at my age and at anyone's age unless you have a baby. It is another of His miracles," Rachael spoke in a hushed whisper. She was in awe of the Creator, Who could perform wonders beyond comprehension.

This is evidence that He is with us always.

"Mom, this is evidence that He is with us always. We should have thought of this earlier and saved ourselves from all that fussing and crying. It is another miracle," she said emphatically.

"What miracle? What did I miss?" Jason had caught the last fragment of their conversation.

"Mom's nursing the baby," Janelle said enthusiastically.

"What, you've got milk? All this time you've been holding out on us."

"Jason! For Pete's sake! This is a beautiful miracle of His love for us and for a helpless infant. Can't you be serious for anything?" Janelle remonstrated.

"I can, but humor helps us feel alive and normal. I agree this is a miracle. Jesus is making it easier for us to avoid capture and for Tabitha to get some food. Now, if He could rustle up a hot pizza I would be ecstatic."

Mike came over next to his wife and put his arm over her blanket draped shoulder. He could hear Tabitha under the shirt having a field day. "God is good," he whispered while remembering years before when his best friend on earth nurtured his newborn twins.

The family started their trek up the road. They would pass several ranches on the way. They had the lay of the land memorized because they had traveled that way so often over the years. They walked for about 200 yards when realization hit them. It came to Janelle first.

"Hey, how come we can see? There are no stars, or moon, or light reflected off of clouds. The plague of darkness is still upon us and yet we can see the road as if it was a normal night."

"You're right! Where's the light coming from?" Mike asked.

"Before, when we turned the lights off in the car we couldn't see our own hands. Now we can. This is amazing!" Jason responded. Silence enveloped them as they walked. They were taking in the phenomenon.

"This is wonderful and kind of eerie," Janelle said.

"It's like we have our own night light glowing vaguely in the room somewhere, only I can't see where the somewhere is," Jason added.

"It says, 'You are a chosen people, a royal priesthood, a holy nation, God's special possession...who called you out of darkness into his wonderful light.'" Mike quoted from memory. "He is the source of the light, Jason, unseen, but present with us."

Rachael was burping the baby over one shoulder. Tabitha had on the almost dry orange-colored onesie with towels stuffed inside. Between gentle thumps Rachael commented. "I thought of something else. Here we are walking on a dry road and on either side is un-melted snow. It's like the Israelites going through the Red Sea on dry ground."

The snow attracted Jason's attention. He bent closer to examine it and picked some up in his fingers. "This isn't snow!" His remark attracted the attention of the others. They looked at it, felt it, and even smelled it. Jason was the bravest when he tasted it. "Wow! This is like cake," he said. "Better than pizza!"

"It's sweet and soft," Janelle added.

"Manna," Rachael pronounced.

"Manna," Mike said introspectively. Now he knew why he had the compunction to hold on to the little bottle of juice. "I have an idea. It's

Sabbath; we should have communion." They stopped walking and gathered in a tight circle. Each had a small portion of manna in their hands. Mike pronounced the words, words he knew by heart from administering the sacraments to shut-ins as an elder. With prayer they ate the bread knowing it represented the body of Christ. Then Mike opened the little plastic bottle and gave it to Rachael to taste first, she in turn gave it to Janelle who served her brother. Mike sipped last, offering prayer. They remained motionless. It was a holy moment. Their communion comprised of actual bread from heaven, closer to the real bread from heaven, The Bread of Life—Jesus Christ.

CHAPTER 23

"What about the bear? Or any bear for that matter," Janelle asked.

"We're miles from that bear," Jason quickly responded.

"But if another crazed animal attacks us we're in trouble out here in the open. What are we going to do?"

"We'll do the same thing I'm doing now—pray," Mike answered emphatically. They trudged up the incline and crested a hill. They knew they would be descending into a glen with a couple of mountain homes nestled in the edges of the clearing. Looking ahead they saw some movement come out of the trees. It was thought to be a house cat on the prowl. Then they saw the size of it and stopped short wondering where to hide. The big mountain lion strolled across the road and into the woods on the other side of the road from the glen. It was one of those moments where they wondered if it was coincidence or the hand of God that kept the cat from coming their way. They didn't move as a precaution just the same. Where the puma had exited the road there was not a sound, not a whisper of a leaf moving or of a twig cracking. They watched breathless until a shadow appeared ten yards from where the feline had disappeared. It came at them with head up, sniffing the air as it came, following its nose. It could smell them, but was unable to see them. They stood rooted to the ground like fence poles. Circling them it sniffed, puzzled by the proximity yet drawn by the game it sought. They were sure that he could hear their heartbeats pounding against their chests. It hesitated then circled closer

… wanting but not finding, smelling but not seeing, salivating but not tasting. Abruptly, it went into a crouch, every muscle taut, its tail unmoving, and its attention on the ground to the side where they stood. Suddenly, it pounced, snatching a field mouse out of the grass and sucking it down. Partially satisfied the lion moved into the bushes in search of something more substantial than a snack.

They remained where they were, feeling, not thinking, that they were in a fortress safe from the terror that moves by night. Mike roused them from their stupor. He quoted a fragment from Hebrews, "… who through faith … received promises … stopped the mouths of lions, quenched raging fire, escaped the edge of the sword, won strength out of weakness…"

"Dad, why did you stop? Doesn't that text go on to say that the faithful avoided being a bear's breakfast?"

"No, it doesn't. It continues with, 'became mighty in war, put foreign enemies to flight. Women received their dead by resurrection. Some were tortured, refusing to accept release that they might rise again to a better life. Others suffered mocking and scourging, and even chains and imprisonment. They were stoned, they were sawn in two…'" Mike left off the rest of the quote because he could see the look on his wife's face. "No, son, I'm pretty sure that it doesn't mention getting eaten by bears. Although we have been through a lot, we haven't been through the entire gambit of what Christians have been through in the past. I count myself very blessed in what has happened so far."

"I have had more than enough to frighten a normal person to death. I too, am feeling fortunate that our experience hasn't been worse. I know God has sent His angels to protect us and feed us. I see miracles of His love for me, this baby, and my family. We are going to make it to the end. I know it."

The family moved forward, watching for signs of animals in the woods and vigilantes on the road. They were confident, but not blithely stupid about the fearful time they were in.

* * * * * *

Manna filled their stomachs. At one point a natural spring bubbled out of the ground next to the road. They refilled their empty bottles and drank deeply, renewing their spirits with the cool liquid. It was at the spring where they noticed that the manna they plucked from the stones and grass along the road did not exist before and behind them. It only appeared when they came upon it and melted when they passed beyond.

A moving miracle of sustenance reassured them in a journey they thought would end at a warm cabin.

The darkness changed around them. Instead of a thick impenetrable shroud enveloping the world where none could see without artificial light, the sky became a lighter shade of ominous black resembling a fierce storm of great magnitude. Angry clouds stretched from horizon to horizon. The difference from this stormy condition and that of a super cell of giant tornados was that there was no wind. Silence predominated. The bubble of faint light disappeared. They could see the road in the modified darkness. Knowing what the clouds normally forecasted, the family anticipated howling gales to buffet them at any moment. It compelled them to move faster to arrive at their sanctuary of logs before being drenched or sucked up into a funnel. Mike checked his watch and saw that it was becoming evening. They also took note of the fact that the manna had suddenly disappeared.

An ambush assailed them. Civilian militia had set up a road block and they appeared from every bush and tree. Flash lights were used and were thrust into the faces as well as a myriad of gun muzzles. Shouts commanded them to lie on the ground and not to resist arrest. Mike and Jason presented the most likely to resist so they were beaten to the ground with rifle butts. Knees where planted in the middle of their backs to keep them from getting up. Janelle lay down willingly in the face of the violence she saw happening to her brother and father. Rachael on the other hand had the baby sleeping on her shoulder. She went to her knees and hesitated in going further.

"Get down you whore!" one commanded and threatened to hit her.

"It's the baby. I have to be careful," she answered back.

"Give the baby to me and then put your hands behind your back."

"Please no. I have to protect her. She needs a mother's touch." Tabitha was aroused by the shouting, and started to cry. The ruffian went to yank the baby away, while Rachael swung the baby away from his lunge. "No, please don't take her away. She's my responsibility."

"Why fight with her? Just shoot her, then she'll let the baby go all by itself," another voice directed.

"Yeah, let's shoot'em," a youthful tone added. "We can collect the bounty on their dead bodies day after tomorrow. It don't matter dead or alive. What's I want ter know is if the baby counts as a full bounty."

"Nah, I don't think so. We just sell 'em to whoever wants one."

"Okay, okay so we don't have to tie these up just shoot'em and drag their bodies into the trees." This person spoke while chambering a round in his weapon. The metallic click alerted the others telling them to do the same. Rachael was still kneeling.

"Geet down and put yer face to the ground," the first voice demanded. "One bullet to the head, that should do it." Rachael slowly complied laying on her side clutching Tabitha to her breast.

Mike didn't want to see his wife executed. He was helpless, pinned to the ground with several heavy knees in his back. He turned his face away and prayed. Jason struggled and was beaten. His movement distracted the posse and gave Janelle the chance to scramble away from her captor and cover her mother.

"No, don't kill my mom! She must take this child to heaven. Kill me instead."

"All right. Have it your way." Cold steel pressed against Janelle's temple. Jason wrestled with all his might trying to save his sister. One arm got away and reached for Janelle, falling short of touching her.

"What's going on here?" Loud words broke through everyone's concentration. Men began to stand. The Larsson's could not see what or why.

"It looks like you are committing murder."

"But, the death penalty is on their heads. We can—"

"That day has not arrived. You are ahead of the decree. Stand back away from them and let them up."

None of the family could see who it was that was talking. Mike could see boots and pants. The pants were army combat uniforms. He knew his Spirit of Prophecy. These were their rescuers. As he gained his freedom from the ground he stood up, first looking at Rachael and Janelle. Jason was helping his mom to stand up. A conversation was going on with the new leader and the leader of the militia. The members of the posse were in the middle of a circle of soldiers, all armed and in battle paraphernalia: helmets, weapons, and LBE's (Load Barring Equipment) over bulletproof vests.

"We will take custody of these individuals and bring them to the proper authority. You can go on about your business and return to your homes."

"But what about our bounty money? We caught them first. They're our captives." The commander in charge just looked at him, waiting for the proper response. "Ah, okay. We'll do as you say." He left the discussion. "Come on fella's we've gota' let this go." Grumbling, the posse of militia left and went down the hill out of sight and around the corner.

Rachael looked at the commander and smiled a broad smile. She knew him by sight. "Thank you my longtime friend," she said gratefully.

"You're welcome." The commander looked around at his troops and they, without being told, knew where to go. They left the area silently moving back into the woods following the path of the posse. The Larssons wanted to stay with the commander; they wanted him to walk with them. Rachael articulated what they all felt. "Won't you join us? We are on our way to our cabin. It would be our pleasure to have you as our guest."

"Thank you, but there are others that need our help." He smiled and lifted off the ground, losing his uniform and gear, changing in mid-flight to robes of light. He flew in the direction of the cabin and the mountain rising up behind it. In the stormy light they could make out the familiar line of the mountain ridge that watched over the cabin. Their

Rachael looked at the commander and smiled a broad smile. She knew him by sight. "Thank you my longtime friend," she said gratefully.

journey was almost complete. It was becoming dark, night was coming, but not like the total dark night of before.

The road diminished in size and condition as it passed by summer houses and ranches. More hours passed when they reached the last turn of the road where it branched off from a cabin entrance, their nearest neighbor. The road to their place was in two tracks like two parallel paths in a forest. They knew it was about a mile and a half from there; they had taken this road as a gentle Sabbath afternoon hike many a time. It was not long now and they would be safe. It was getting late, almost midnight. The manna ceased to exist along the roadside. It surprised them again, but this time they connected the dots. The manna was for them, not for those out in the night seeking subjects to terrorize and torture. They stopped, unsure of what to do. Up ahead through the tree tops a fire sent flames up in the air. The cabin was burning. The sanctuary they were hoping to hide within until everything passed was now a huge conflagration. Their minds flew to concern for their friends rather than focus on their own safety. They wanted to run toward, not away, from the fire, knowing in their hearts that the fire was probably a result of evil actions from this earth's merchants of malevolence. They were loitering on dangerous ground. The manna had stopped because the unregenerate were nearby. They hesitated only a second. Instead of following the gentle incline of the road as it wound up the hill, they cut off the road and went straight up hill. Hurrying through the trees they worked the worry beads of their minds, wanting information about their friends' safety.

Breaking out into the open space in front of the cabin they came to a halt next to the grave stones for Rachael's parents. They stopped dead, breathing heavily. Tabitha was the only one not breathing hard because of the hill. She was in Mike's strong arms. Now she started to fuss because the blast of heat from the fire made her uncomfortable. Absent mindedly Rachael took the baby from him and burped her on her shoulder. Her complete focus was on the fire.

All of them were spell bound by the tragedy. This was their earthly sanctuary. It was to be their pivot point between earth and heaven. It was to be where they would wait for Him, their Redeemer. All the efforts were to get here to travel there. The fear of bears, bullets, beatings, maulings, their concern over the possibility of capture, imprisonment, starvation, and the unknown, had compelled them to follow the Divine command to get to the mountain, their mountain, to be safe from what was to come. Now they were looking at their last earthly hope going up, literally, in smoke. Emotions were wrapped around a compelling question, "now where do we go?"

The call to be missionaries in their own milieu also weighed down upon them. They had to win souls for the kingdom. It was their willingly accepted burden. Even if Probation had closed they still felt responsible to nurture them and to guide them as they grew in faith. They watched the possibility of their work burn. They castigated themselves because they should have been here with them. They prayed that the five brands plucked from the burning were not in the blazing inferno. Another question arose in their thoughts, more urgent and frightening than the former question, "Did the beasts who started this fire torture their friends into compliance with the world of hate?"

Their concern for George, Sheila, and the boys was superseded by the arrival of another gang of vigilantes. This one was more organized, being under the direction of an officer of the law. "Cuff them!" were loud words that interrupted their trepidations. Men circled the Larssons dragging them away from the heat. Plastic straps came out and Mike and Jason were secured behind their backs. This time they were allowed to stand. They came to Rachael to cuff her and she raised her hands in front with the baby cradled in between. The man looked at her, debating his options. He decided to let her hold the crying baby, so he secured her hands in front allowing her the ability to hold and bounce Tabitha. Another command broke their suspended concentration. "Not her. We can have some fun with her." The officer pointed at Janelle.

Another voice spoke up from near Jason. "Hey, look what I found. It's a knife with blood on it. They must have used it in a ritual sacrifice or something." The cluster of vigilantes paused to look at Jason's small pocket knife and then their attention went back to the two men manhandling Janelle. Instead of tying Janelle's hands behind her back they roped them and threw the rope over a tree limb. The men hoisted her arms upward to the point where her toes barely touched the ground. She kicked outward and backward trying to keep balance rather than swing. The men took it as resistance.

"Look at this one! She's a fighter."

"No, don't. She's just a girl," Mike pleaded.

"You're beasts! Leave her alone!" Rachael yelled.

"You should have thought about this possibility when you decide to ruin the world with your Satan worship. Obviously you've been worshipping Satan with blood sacrifices. Now you can pay for your sins."

"Mom, Dad, don't worry. We'll be rescued. Just like last time," Janelle instructed. She ended her words of hope with glances around into the dark edges of the clearing. Mike, Rachael, and Jason did the same. Rachael was looking for a familiar face and a soothing voice.

"Look at them. They think they're going to be rescued. Stupid idiots, they had their chance." The commander of the posse moved toward Janelle; he started to unbutton her shirt. She twisted and turned making it difficult for him to loosen her clothing. "Hold her!" he commanded. Another interruption happened.

"Sir, we found the ones that were staying at the cabin. They were up in some caves at the base of the mountain. They had a cache of food and gear with them, and no CNSs."

The leader stopped pawing at Janelle to look at the new group of refugees that had been brought into the open area. Recognition swept across his face, "Greg, Andrew! What are you doing up here?"

"We came here to meet Jesus."

"What? Are you one of them?!" he yelled. "Everybody knows that Jesus is in Idaho protecting the cities from the huge forest fire. He's not coming here."

"Dad, that's not the real Jesus. He's a fake. The real Jesus is coming in the clouds and He will take us to heaven with him, not keep us down here while he runs around the globe pretending."

"Jesus is not a fake. He called fire down out of the sky to stop the forest fire from reaching the cities. That's the real Jesus, not a fake! Sons, come here. I have the stamping equipment with me. We can get you all squared away and you won't have to be arrested. *I* won't have to arrest you," Officer Cox corrected himself. He also left out the part about the forthcoming execution.

"Dad, we have eyes. We can see what you were doing to Janelle. If you were a follower of the true Jesus you would not be doing what you are doing. We won't be joining the wrong side. Leave Janelle alone, Dad!" Andrew commanded.

"Yeah, that goes for me too. Leave her alone!" Greg added.

"Don't talk to your father like that! Now get over here!"

"They won't stand with the wicked! Neither will the rest of us," came the answer, but it came from Jason. Separated by yards and by bonds preventing them from physically demonstrating their solidarity, they nodded in agreement.

"Yes, Father. We won't stand with the wicked, we will wait for Jesus. He is coming and we are His!" Greg's pronouncement steeled the resolve of the righteous. Heads came up and shoulders straightened.

> *We will wait for Jesus. He is coming and we are His!*

Officer Cox wanted to teach his sons a lesson. He wanted to beat them into compliance. His anger was a tsunami of rage. He couldn't control it. He whipped his service revolver out of its holster and fired it into the air, "Kill them! Kill them all!" He yelled. He pointed his weapon at Jason, the leader who had stolen his children. His hand went tighter on the pistol grip, his finger flexed on the trigger. Then a shock ran through his arm as a brass instrument demolished the silence from horizon to horizon. A single trumpet with the magnitude of resonance beyond human experience shattered the air. For the wicked it was frightful; for the redeemed it was salvation. Heads swiveled in panic. No source could be seen or detected. The sound was everywhere and inside. Internal echoes reverberated causing instant headaches. Hands clapped over ears and heads bowed low to avoid arrows of pain that the sound unleashed. Yet the Redeemed look up to see a rainbow of promise painted on the clouds—a vast thick brilliant rainbow of solid light, bolder, broader, a vibrant spectrum of rich color without an insignificant sun to generate its existence.

The clouds were still black edged with light from behind; no angel host could be seen. Angry bellows seemed to shake the earth. Massive thuds were heard in the ground around them. Trees were being smashed by giant balls of ice. Wood splintered into flying shards ricocheting through the forest. A lightning bolt so wide and so colossal flashed across the sky igniting what seemed to be the air itself. Vision was washed out in the brilliance of the flash and then when it returned it became blurred as the ground trembled. Still no being is seen. Pebbles danced on the ground and trees swayed as the earthquake gathered momentum. The sky remained black save for a single break from which emanated intense light. A figure is seen sitting upon a throne, eons of light years in the distance, and a voice caresses the air from within, "They come! Holy, harmless, and undefiled." Now the iniquitous hands are clasped over ears in grief and despair rather than from audible pain. They want to hide. This behavior is in stark contrast to the party of faithful believers who are no longer fugitives. They are veterans coming home from war. Myriads of angels burst forth through the aperture rushing to the earth in echelons of force. The voice speaks again, "It is done."

The earthquake crescendos upward into a massive, mighty rumbling; the mountain behind them crumbles into dust. Gigantic veins in the ground open up, cracking the surface of the earth like cakes of mud on a dried lake bed. The party of believers is distracted by the convolutions beneath them. They miss the resurrection of the dead nearby. Grandma and Grandpa rise off of the earth. They are surprised by all that is around them. They thought they were on a freeway; instead they are at what seems to be a wilderness junkyard.

Jason catches sight of some people in the air. At first he thought it might be angels coming from the earth. Then realization dawns.

"Mom, is that …? Can't be. It kinda looks like Grandma and Grandpa, but … they're so young!" Jason exclaimed.

"It is! It's them…" Rachael chokes with emotion. "It's Mom … and Dad! They …" she stops at what she sees unfolding before her eyes, her fingertips gently touching her upper lip. She doesn't want to interrupt the moment. Janelle asks for clarification.

"Mom, look at the angel, he's bringing grandma someone's baby. Why would he do that?"

"That's not someone's baby; that's my baby sister Annalisa. She gets to grow up in heaven."

"I didn't know you had another sister."

"Yes, Anna only lived two days in an isolette in ICU. Mom never got to hold her in her arms when she was alive. Now she is … Mom gets to hold her little ba … O, Lord. Praise Your Holy Name!" Rachael looks upward to direct her praise to her Lord. She sees Him riding on a white horse flanked by the vast armies of heaven.

The bonds fell to the ground, unnoticed because they are lifting off of the earth. Their attention was momentarily diverted from their Savior because they had to look at the rumbling, folding, crumpling earth as it is torn apart beneath them. It was falling away below. Then they looked again at a Savior who was beckoning with His hands for them to follow Him. Higher still higher they fly, gaining altitude and gliding to the west. All around them parties of the redeemed gathered together in the sky. They were greeting one another as if it was Sabbath and church was about to begin.

On their left, the grandparents flew unaided, but escorted by their angels. It caused Mike to scan the immediate area. He found several angels in tight formation just above his family. One he recognized as Rachael's special guardian. The others he did not know who they belonged to specifically; he desired to know which one was his personal angel, which one had kept by him in times of difficulty.

George and Sheila, with faces radiant and grateful, edged toward Mike and Rachael on their right. Rachael was still clutching Tabitha to her chest. Sheila asked if she could help carry the infant. Rachael smiled and replied, "Sure, you should probably get a little more practice before yours comes along." She started to hand her over. The child was so light—light as a single flower plucked from a vase. She too was flying. She let her go and only held her tiny little hand. Sheila held the other.

Here and there people burst out in spontaneous praise singing naturally and confidently. Different words, tunes, and stanzas were uttered from every direction. It was like they were a choir practicing. It was a growing, building experience. Vocal instruments were warming up for a grand concert soon to be unveiled in a mighty paean of adoration. As the saved gazed at the rising participants gathering for the trek homeward, they could see change happening before their eyes. Old faces became new faces, bent legs became straight, broken bodies healed, all in an instant. Muddy and torn clothes morphed into white gowns flowing and fluttering in the breeze of forward motion. Bifocals dropped to the earth.

Rachael's attention was momentarily diverted by a voice, "Look I'm a butterfly!" Cheri spoke to Rachael in thanksgiving. Rachael cried. She shouldn't have doubted. Her words had meant something; her work had been fruitful.

Jason grouped with his three buddies, cheering with one another with high fives, exceptionally high fives. They were ecstatic in their celebration.

A victory had been won. The opponents had been put down. The goal had been scored, achieved, and counted.

Janelle saw Darin, and asked her folks if she could fly next Him and his family. Her parents nodded in agreement. They watched as she literally flew into his arms, wiping away tears of joy. Mike and Rachael's eyes lingered on their daughter, the pleasure washed over them. Their primary job as parents was to see their children into the kingdom of heaven. They were going to receive a "job well done" from Jesus. They watched with pride and pleasure. Mike saw one of the accompanying angels split off and follow Janelle. Another had followed Jason. He now knew with reasonable certainty which heavenly guardian had been with him through the years. The scene was too much to take in. It was also too much to relate to. He wanted a long talk with his unseen but now very seeable friend. That conversation would have to wait. He wanted to soar through the skies looking for his parents. He wanted to revel in the moment with George and Sheila. He could think of a hundred things he wanted to do. He almost wanted to write it down on an electronic note pad and then remembered he would never forget anything again. Most of all he wanted to hug his best friend and earthly life's companion, and stay with her wherever she might be.

The light was dazzling. Their eyes had to get accustomed to its brilliance. Everything was in radiant clarity. They could see for hundreds of miles in every direction and make out the most intricate detail. Friends and acquaintances, pastors and church members, could be seen. Pastor and Mrs. Taylor were found. They wanted to look everywhere, except downward. At the same time, they wanted to keep their focus on the Redeemer. Songs were sung from every quarter. Everyone had their meaningful favorite. Veronica sang in her alto voice with a two-word alteration to her favorite spiritual, "*He has* overcome." Another favorite that could be heard was, "How great Thou art," specifically focusing on the stanza, "When Christ shall come with shout of acclamation…"

Next to Veronica Jones was Heidi McKessy. Both were in their youthful exuberance. The unusually talkative Heidi repeated one simple word over and over, "Weeeee!" She was joy-swinging through the air holding "Chubby Cheeks" in front of her holding both arms out playfully teaching him to fly.

With arms spread wide and holding hands, groups flew in winged formations like geese on migration heading for a comfortable habitation. Little Tabitha was a short link in a line of six adults with two babies— Grandma and Grandpa had joined the formation. The two babies giggled in glee as if they had been tossed playfully into the sky. Conversations were short bursts of praise because friends were joining friends, and kin were reuniting.

Mike and Rachael were distracted when they saw a teenage girl fly, with speed, in front of them directly for Jason. He met her with equal enthusiasm. They embraced and kissed. It was obvious they had kissed before.

"What in heavens!" Rachael exclaimed.

"I guess that's one more of Jason's surprises," Mike answered.

"Oh, my. I guess we'll have to keep an eye on those two," Rachael sighed. Mike answered her in return.

"Why?"

THE BEGINNING

AUTHOR EPILOGUE

In some instances, it is difficult to nail down exact sequences in unfolding prophecy. Scholars amicably agree to disagree on many events and when they must occur. Please don't take the above composed story as gospel truth or an exact portrayal and sequence of events. I take the counsel from one of our early pioneers, "In exposition of unfulfilled prophecy, where the history is not written, the student should put forth his propositions with not too much positiveness, lest he find himself straying in the field of fancy." J. White, 1877. To counter the behavior of any individual who may hold strictly to the above sequences, I am writing another story, on the same subject, with a slightly different progression of prophetic events and with different characters. The goal of this above work of fiction is proffered to the reader in an attempt to encourage courageous conviction leading to the time when they will have to be Faithful Fugitives.

I can be reached at jarvidellison@gmail.com for comments and suggestions on the next book.

FUTURE NOTE

As of this writing, Mr. Ellison is writing another novel on the same subject covering the same time period of future history. In this story a non-Adventist young man, in his twenties, is searching for answers, both spiritual and actual. The events of the final conflict play out in front of him as he contemplates his role in life and commitment to his Savior.

James A. Ellison has been published before (Under the name, J. Arvid Ellison). He has written two adult level novels, two teen level novels, and four children's books. These are in the public market. Each of them contains either a moral issue or a teaching point for life. They are:

- *If Two Are Dead* (Thriller)
- *Arrows Through the Heart* (Historical Fiction-Western)
- *Dangerous Fishing* (Teen Fiction)
- *Dangerous Blessings* (Sequel to Dangerous Fishing)
- *The Little Lightning Bug Who Couldn't Play Hide-n-seek* (Children's fiction)
- *Two Names* (Children's fiction)
- *The Caterpillar Who Went to A Slumber Party Alone* (Children's fiction)
- *What Happens When You Go to Sleep* (Children's fiction)

TEACH Services, Inc.
P U B L I S H I N G

We invite you to view the complete
selection of titles we publish at:
www.TEACHServices.com

We encourage you to write us
with your thoughts about this,
or any other book we publish at:
info@TEACHServices.com

TEACH Services' titles may be purchased in
bulk quantities for educational, fund-raising,
business, or promotional use.
bulksales@TEACHServices.com

Finally, if you are interested in seeing
your own book in print, please contact us at:
publishing@TEACHServices.com

We are happy to review your manuscript at no charge.